DARK ADEPTUS

ONE HUNDRED YEARS ago, the forge world of Chaeroneia disappeared amidst rumours of corruption and civil war. Now it has returned and the once teeming factory planet is now a silent sentinel floating through space. Is it an empty tomb or a foul nest of Chaos?

That is the question facing Justicar Alaric of the Grey Knights. The elite daemon hunters are charged with a new mission: to investigate Chaeroneia, determine the presence of any daemonic influence and terminate with extreme prejudice. However, nothing can prepare even the Grey Knights for what they find on the planet's surface. One hundred years of isolation has corrupted the engineer-priests of the Adeptus Mechanicus beyond all imaginings, and their monstrous, possessed machines prowl the surface like predators. In order to complete their mission, the Grey Knights must rely on their faith, and trust a ghost lurking in the machine!

A WARHAMMER 40,000 NOVEL

DARK ADEPTUS

Ben Counter

To Helen

A BLACK LIBRARY PUBLICATION

First published in Great Britain in 2006 by
BL Publishing,
Games Workshop Ltd.,
Willow Road, Nottingham,
NG7 2WS, UK.

10 9 8 7 6 5 4 3

Cover illustration by Philip Sibbering.

A CIP record for this book is available from the British Library.

ISBN 13: 978 1 84416 242 0
ISBN 10: 1 84416 242 7

Distributed in the US by Simon & Schuster
1230 Avenue of the Americas, New York, NY 10020, US.

See the Black Library on the Internet at
www.blacklibrary.com

Find out more about Games Workshop
and the world of Warhammer 40,000 at
www.games-workshop.com

IT IS THE 41st millennium. For more than a hundred centuries the Emperor has sat immobile on the Golden Throne of Earth. He is the master of mankind by the will of the gods, and master of a million worlds by the might of his inexhaustible armies. He is a rotting carcass writhing invisibly with power from the Dark Age of Technology. He is the Carrion Lord of the Imperium for whom a thousand souls are sacrificed every day, so that he may never truly die.

YET EVEN IN his deathless state, the Emperor continues his eternal vigilance. Mighty battlefleets cross the daemon-infested miasma of the warp, the only route between distant stars, their way lit by the Astronomican, the psychic manifestation of the Emperor's will. Vast armies give battle in his name on uncounted worlds. Greatest amongst his soldiers are the Adeptus Astartes, the Space Marines, bio-engineered super-warriors. Their comrades in arms are legion: the Imperial Guard and countless planetary defence forces, the ever-vigilant Inquisition and the tech-priests of the Adeptus Mechanicus to name only a few. But for all their multitudes, they are barely enough to hold off the ever-present threat from aliens, heretics, mutants – and worse.

TO BE A man in such times is to be one amongst untold billions. It is to live in the cruellest and most bloody regime imaginable. These are the tales of those times. Forget the power of technology and science, for so much has been forgotten, never to be re-learned. Forget the promise of progress and understanding, for in the grim dark future there is only war. There is no peace amongst the stars, only an eternity of carnage and slaughter, and the laughter of thirsting gods.

CHAPTER ONE

'I long for death, not because I seek peace, but because I seek the war eternal.'

– Cardinal Armandus Helfire,
'Reflections on the Long Death'

THE SKY OF Chaeroneia shuddered with static and changed, displaying a new channel of geometric patterns. Holy hexagons representing the six-fold genius of the Omnissiah merged with the circles representing the totality of knowledge that the tech-priesthood sought. Double helices, fractals born of sacred information-relics, litanies of machine code, all swirled against the sky of the forge world, casting the pale light of knowledge over the valley of datacores. The smokestacks of the titan works were silhouetted against the holy projections, ironwork bridges spanning gigantic factory towers, sky-piercing obelisks where tech-priests watched the heavens, radio masts where they listened for the voice of the Omnissiah in solar radiation. The valley itself, lined with towering cliffs of obsidian datacores, was a long deep slash of shadow.

Projected onto the thick layer of pollutants in the forge world's atmosphere, the sacred arcs and angles were a visual representation of that evening's data-prayers being intoned by thrice-blessed worship-servitors in the Cathedrals of Knowledge. Beneath the titanium plated minarets rows of identical servitors would be standing, their vocal units emitting streams of digital information, singing the praises of the Omnissiah in the binary of pure lingua technis.

Magos Antigonus knew that meant a new solar cycle was starting. The pollutants over Chaeroneia were so thick there was no sun, so it was only the clockwork-regular services of the Cult Mechanicus that gave time any meaning on the forge world. That in turn meant he had been on the run for three Terran standard days. It was a long time to go with no food or sleep.

The datacore valley was a good place to hide out. Visual sensors were often confused by the pure blackness of the datacores themselves and the impenetrable shadows that flooded between them. The information in the cores was so pure that sensoria were dazzled by the intensity, while even augmented eyes could miss a single man in the darkness. But Antigonus knew he was still far from safe.

He turned to the servitor next to him. Like all servitors, this device was built around the frame of a once-living human being, the baser levels of its brain computing its functions and its nervous system relaying commands to its augmetic limbs. It was a basic manservant model, programmed to follow its owner and execute simple commands.

'Epsilon three-twelve,' said Antigonus and the servitor turned its face towards him, large round ocular implants whirring as they focused on the tech-priest. 'Journal additional.'

Epsilon three-twelve's hands clicked as the long articulated fingers reformed, reaching inside its hollowed chest cavity and bringing out a roll of parchment. A dextrous servo-arm reached out of its mouth, holding a quill.

'Third standard day,' said Antigonus. The servo-arm dipped the quill into an inkwell concealed in the servitor's left eye socket and wrote down Antigonus's words in a stilted, artificial hand. 'Investigation halted. The existence of a heretical cell has been confirmed. Primary goal executed.' Antigonus paused. He had thought that finding them would be the worst of it. He had been utterly wrong. Unforgivable.

'The heretics are between ten and thirty in number,' continued Antigonus, 'representing all Adepta of the Mechanicus, including genetors, lexmechanicus, xenobiologis, metallurgus, pecunius, digitalis and others unknown. Also include ranks from menial to archmagos and probably above. No upper limit to penetration of Chaeroneia's ruling caste.'

Antigonus stopped suddenly and flicked his ocular attachment upwards. Its large glass orb surveyed the sky above, still swarming with the sacred imagery. He was sure he had heard something. But he had been on the run for three days and had been unable to risk accepting maintenance on Chaeroneia for some time before that, so perhaps his aural receptors were failing him just as his motive and circulator units were wearing out.

Epsilon three-twelve waited patiently, quill poised over the scroll. Antigonus waited a few moments more, the ocular orb searching up and down the valley. The sheer sides of the chasm were glossy and black, drinking in the pallid light, while the floor was littered with rusting, unrecognisable chunks of machinery. Antigonus was sure he and his servitor were well-hidden behind one such massive slab that looked like the engine from a mass-lifter vehicle. However, he knew better than to think that made them safe – a heretic tech-priest with a powerful auspex scanner set to detect Antigonus's life signs could sniff them out.

'The nature of the heresy itself is not fully understood. Secondary objective incomplete.' Antigonus shook his head. The ways of the Machine-God were often argued over by the tech-priests of the Adeptus Mechanicus, but he still did not understand how any of them could turn to such base heresy as he had witnessed here. 'Sorcery and warpcraft are suspected but not proven beyond doubt. The heretics venerate the Omnissiah, but through an avatar or mouthpiece. The nature of this avatar is not known, but cross-reference previous entries on any pre-Imperial presence on Chaeroneia.'

A hot, dry wind swept down the valley, throwing a few pieces of rusting sheet metal around. A maintenance servitor drifted overhead on thrumming grav-units, its fat belly full of antioxidant foam to spew over any fire or corrosive spill that might threaten the precious datacores. Far above, the data-sermon was coming to an end, the sacred geometry fading. In its place, work rotas and diagrams of emergency procedures flickered by, ensuring that the forge world's menial population was constantly reminded of its duties to the Mechanicus. So many people lived utterly normal lives in the factories and mineshafts, never knowing the monstrous blasphemies festering in the ruling population of tech-priests.

'The origins of the heresy and the individuals responsible for its dissemination are unknown. Tertiary objective incomplete. But see note on pre-Imperial presence above.' That was the most frustrating of all. Antigonus's evidence was compelling but incomplete. He had read the debased datapsalms describing the Omnissiah as a force for destruction instead of knowledge. He had witnessed minor tech-priests, their bodies swollen with forbidden biomechanical augmetics, using base sorcery to escape the tech-guard commanded by Antigonus. He had seen those same tech-guard driven mad by warp magics that any tech-priest would abhor. But he knew so few details. He did not know what the heretics wanted, or who they were. He did not know how all this had started. He did not know how to stop it.

Now it was just him, fleeing through the underbelly of Chaeroneia with his servitor in tow, augmetics failing through lack of maintenance. They were hunting him down. He was sure of it. The heretics were everywhere on the planet, at every level from the menial barracks to the control towers.

'Personal note.' Antigonus heard the sounds of the scratching quill change as the servitor dutifully altered its handwriting to something less precise. 'The cell is not large but it is well organised, highly motivated and thoroughly ingrained into the society of Chaeroneia. Its existence is suspected only by those who are members or are otherwise under the cell's control. There is no upper limit to the seniority of its members. I can only hope it does not extend off-world. My primary objective completed, I believe the best course of action is for me to leave this planet at the first opportunity and recommend a full purge of Chaeroneia by the authority of the archmagos ultima. I also recommend that the Fabricator General be appraised of the situation on Chaeroneia given that the nature of the heresy is such that...'

Antigonus paused again. He was aware of something huge and dark flitting over the valley, blotting out the projections overhead for a moment.

'There is no logic in fear,' he told himself. The servitor wrote the words down automatically, but Antigonus ignored it.

Antigonus rose to his feet, mechadendrites snaking from below his grimy rust-red robes. His augmentations were not designed for combat, but he could still handle himself if it came down to it – each mechadendrite could extrude a monomolecular blade and he had enough redundant organs to keep him alive through terrible injuries.

They were watching him.

Antigonus whirled around as another shadow passed over him. His left hand – the non-bionic one – reached inside his robes and took out a brass-cased autogun. The weapon was a good, solid Mars-pattern gun, but Antigonus had never fired it in anger. He was a seeker of knowledge, a metallurgist in service to the Priesthood of Mars – he had been sent to Chaeroneia because he had a sharp and inquisitive mind, not because he was a warrior able to face down vengeful heretics by himself. When it came down to it, could he survive?

Antigonus sighted down the barrel at the shadows between the wreckage that littered the valley.

'Query,' said the thin, grating voice of Epsilon three-twelve. 'Procedure terminate?'

'Yes, terminate,' said Antigonus, annoyed. The servitor's limbs folded up as it stashed the scroll back in its chest.

The light levels changed, flooding the valley with a pale greenish glow. Antigonus searched for the source, knowing it must be the searchlight of a hunter-servitor or armed grav-platform, come to chase him down like an animal. But there was nothing.

Then Antigonus looked up to the sky.

Magos Antigonus, read hundred metre-long letters projected onto the clouds.

Join us.

The letters hung there for a few moments then disappeared, replaced by a new message.

You are ignorant and blind. You are like a child, like a menial. Blind to the light.

The Avatar of the Omnissiah is among us.

When you see it, you will know it is beautiful and pure.
You can take this understanding back to Mars. You can be
our prophet.

Antigonus shook his head, glancing around, pan-
icking. His finger trembled on the trigger. He held
out his bionic right arm and grabbed the gun with
steel fingers, steadying his aim. 'No!' he shouted. 'I
have seen what you are!'

We are the future.

We are the way.

All else is darkness and death.

Antigonus began to move, jogging through the
hunks of wreckage, trying to find somewhere they
couldn't see him. They must have a grav-platform
watching him from somewhere above, perhaps even
a vehicle in orbit with sensoria that could cut
through the thick pollutant clouds. Epsilon three-
twelve waddled after Antigonus on its ill maintained
legs, its subhuman mind oblivious to the threats all
around them.

You will never have a greater chance than this, Magos
Antigonus. Your life does not have to continue as a statis-
tical irrelevance.

Antigonus sped up. If they could track him through
the valley then he was trapped. At one end of the valley was a massive cogitator housing where the
contents of the datacores were searched and filtered.
It was staffed mostly by tech-priest information spe-
cialists – the heretics would find him there. But the
other end led into a tangle of workshops and factory
floors, many half ruined. It was populated mostly by
menials and roving servitors. Antigonus might be

safe there. He broke into a run, servitor in tow, the servos on his withered legs grinding painfully as they took the strain.

One chance is more than the Adeptus Mechanicus will ever give you. Look upon the face of the Omnissiah, Antigonus, and understand!

Antigonus ran as fast as he could, the servitor somehow keeping up. He was ill-lubricated and low on power but he re-routed all his non-essential systems to keep him moving. His vision greyed out as his ocular implants switched down to minimal and his digestive system shut down temporarily. The multi-layered factory complex loomed up ahead – its warren-like structure and menial population would mask him from observation. It was his only chance.

Then it seems you are as small-minded and inflexible as all your kind. You are a disappointment.

You are obsolete.

WHO COULD ORCHESTRATE the hijacking of the projector units and the kind of surveillance technology needed to follow Antigonus here? The names were few. Scraecos, the archmagos veneratus who masterminded Chaeroneia's extensive data networks and commanded all the planet's formidable reserves of information. Archmagos Ultima Vengaur, responsible for liaising with the Imperial authorities about Chaeroneia's tithes and adherence to Imperial law. Another archmagos veneratus, named Thulharn, whose domain was Chaeroneia's orbital installations and space traffic. There were very few others with the necessary seniority and ability.

But could a small heretic cell really sway such men? Men who had risen so far in the hierarchy of the Adeptus Mechanicus that they could barely be called men at all any more?

Epsilon three-twelve.

Execute.

Antigonus turned just in time to see Epsilon three-twelve fold out its augmetic limbs, this time with the articulated tines bent into wicked claws. It lurched forward crazily and crashed into Antigonus, barrelling him to the floor. Antigonus's head smacked into the grime-slicked rockcrete.

The servitor's mechanical parts made it heavy and its rugged construction made it strong. Antigonus was trapped on his back and had to drop his gun to grab the servitor's wrists and stop it from clawing at him. He was face-to-face with Epsilon three-twelve – the servitor's eye sockets were polished bone, but the nose and mouth beneath them were grey, expressionless dead flesh.

Antigonus lashed out a mechadendrite and the tentacle-like appendage wrapped itself around the stock of his autogun. Antigonus whipped the mechadendrite back and clubbed the servitor in the head with the butt of the gun. Sparks spat off its brass-chased skull but the servitor didn't move its weight off Antiogonus and the tech-priest felt one of his ribs break in a flare of pain. Painkillers pumped out of his bionic heart and the red mist flowed away. Antigonus used the moment of clarity to wrap one mechadendrite around the servitor's throat, forcing its head back, fighting the servo motors in its spine. He reeled back another and thrust it forward, its tip tearing through the servitor's forehead and into the biological brain.

Epsilon three-twelve convulsed. Its hands broke free of Antigonus's grip and flailed madly. Its mouth opened and its vocal unit let out a grating, garbled scream. The mechadendrite in its head was ripped free by the strength of the servitor's spasms, whipping back and forward like a striking snake.

Antigonus forced a knee up under it and rolled over on top of the servitor, scrambling to grab his gun again. The servitor bucked and threw Antigonus onto the ground, pain rushing up at him again as silvered augmetics crunched against the hard ground.

The servitor was quickest to its feet, spraying gore from the massive pulsing wound between its hollow eyes. A mechanical hand clamped around Antigonus's throat and slammed him against the valley side, the black glass of the datacore material splintering into razors that sheared through Antigonus's thick robes into the pallid skin of his back.

The servitor's mouth lolled open and the tiny mechanical arm shot out, stabbing the gold-nibbed quill through Antigonus's bionic eye.

A white star burst in front of Antigonus's vision. White, knife-like pain rifled through his head. His back, his neck, his eye, so much of him was shrieking in pain at once that he couldn't tell where he was, or what he was doing.

He only just remembered that he still had the gun. Roaring through the pain, he stabbed the gun into the servitor's gut and fired. He fired again and again, until its grip went limp. Antigonus slid to the floor and realised he must have blown the servitor's spine out, severing the connection between its upper and lower body. The servitor stumbled a few steps, its arms and head hanging limp, before the dead weight of its upper half dragged it down to the ground.

Everything was suddenly silent. The only movement was the oily smoke sputtering from the servitor's ruined body. Antigonus's vision, already muted, was now somehow skewed, as if shifted sideways. Antigonus only had one eye left – his normal, unaugmented one, which meant he was limited to the visible spectrum and couldn't zoom in any more. He had lost a mechadendrite and his ribs were broken. He was bleeding somewhere inside, but his internal alterations were probably robust enough to cope with that. Already his bionic heart was forcing his pulse down to calm him. He was hurt, though and it would only get worse without maintenance – and no way in the Emperor's great creation would he ever let anyone on this tainted world repair him. He had to get off-world.

Antigonus struggled to his feet and began to run, the shadows of the industrial complex rolling over him. As black iron and red-brown rust closed over him the heretic projections flickered off overhead and were replaced with work rotas for the menials.

They couldn't watch him from overhead now. But they had hijacked the projection units, seduced the highest ranks of the tech-priesthood and sabotaged his personal servitor which had been sent with him from Mars. They didn't need eyes in the sky to watch him. They would find a way.

CHAPTER TWO

'You may say, it is impossible for a man to become like the Machine. And I would reply, that only the smallest mind strives to comprehend its limits.'

– Fabricator General Kane (attr.)

MAGOS ANTIGONUS WASN'T supposed to die like this.

Light was scarce beneath the complex. A single charred bulb cast a dull brownish glow over the abandoned workshop he had found. Old workbenches covered in rusted equipment were piled up against one wall and the low ceiling was hung with corroded cabling. Antigonus sat against the other wall, rivulets of rust-red water running down his back from the sweating metal behind him, trying to fix the failed servo in his motor units. His legs were withered and weak and without the servo-powered braces that encased them he could barely walk. He wasn't designed to fight. He was there because he had a facility with information systems and he could access Chaeroneia's data networks with ease. His purpose on Chaeroneia had been to debunk the apparently spurious rumours about heretical practices among the planet's tech-priests, then take that news back to Mars to satisfy the tech-priests there that their forge world was free from the taint of blasphemy.

'Primary objective failed,' he thought.

Antigonus sat bolt-upright. The voice had come from everywhere at once. He was alone in the workshop and yet there was something else in there with him. He pulled out his autogun again but he knew instinctively that it wouldn't do any good.

'Heretics!' shouted Antigonus, struggling to his feet. 'You can hide from me but the Mechanicus will find you! More will follow me! More from Mars!'

The only answer was Antigonus's own voice, echoing back through the empty workshops.

Antigonus crept through the darkness, wishing his servos were quieter. There was no one else in the workshop, but they must be near. He knew he couldn't put up much of a fight any more, but he wasn't going to go down easily. They would have to work for their kill.

More will follow. More will die. This is the way of our Machine-God.

The voice was too close, little more than a whisper directly into Antigonus's ear. It had to be someone in the room. Either that or someone controlling a machine in the room, like a servitor or machine-spirit, something complex, something that could speak. But Antigonus had secured the area before he stopped to rest. There was nothing like that in here.

Nothing, that is, apart from his own augmentations.

Clever boy.

Antigonus dropped the gun and grabbed the screwdriver he had been using to repair himself. The heretics were doing to him what they had done to Epsilon three-twelve, hijacking his more complex systems and taking control. Either they were controlling one of his augmentations directly or they had infected him with a machine-curse, an insidious self-replicating set of commands that could cause a system to self-destruct.

Which system? Like many tech-priests above the most junior rank, Magos Antigonus had several sophisticated augmentations, including datalinks that would provide a perfect point of infection. At least they hadn't got his bionic heart, otherwise he would be lying dead right now. His bionic eye was destroyed but the control circuits were still there, spiralling around his optic nerve. His mechadendrites? They were plugged directly into his nervous system through an impulse link. His bionic arm? The intelligent filtration systems in his throat and lungs?

Closer, closer. But not close enough. Know you the way of the Omnissiah, fellow traveller. The avatar speaks with us even now and it speaks to us of your death.

Antigonus jabbed the screwdriver under the housing of his bionic eye and levered the unit out of its socket, forcing himself to ignore the unnaturally dull, cold pain that throbbed from the ruined bionic. With a gristly sound the eye came out, taking a chunk of artificial flesh with it and landing on the floor with a blood-wet plop. Antigonus gasped as the shocking cold of the air hit the raw nerves in the wreckage now filling his eye socket.

Closer.

Antigonus scrabbled on the floor, dizzy and sickened by the awful raw throb spreading across his face. His natural hand grabbed the autogun on the floor and he put the barrel against the side of his head.

Don't let them take you, he told himself. They'll make you one of their own.

Even if you are dead, fellow traveller.

'Get out!' yelled Antigonus crazily. 'Out! The Machine-God commands you! By the light of understanding and the rule of Mars I cast this unclean thing from this machine!'

An enginseer sent by the Adeptus Mechanicus to maintain the war machines of the Imperial Guard would know the tech-exorcism rites off by heart. But such things were not often needed on Mars, the heartland of the priesthood where Antigonus had learned his role in the Cult Mechanicus. Antigonus knew he couldn't banish the thing with words alone, but right now they were all he had.

If it had his bionic arm, it would be using it by now to force the gun away from his head. No, it was something inside him, something it couldn't use to kill him straight away.

'I cast you out!' Antigonus put the gun barrel against his left knee and fired.

A thunderbolt of pain, the worst Antigonus had ever suffered, ripped right through him and knocked him unconscious as his left leg was blown clean off at the knee. Paralysing pain reached down and dragged him back to his senses, gripping hard and not letting go. Antigonus screamed, but somewhere inside him he heard the tech-infection scream too, as part of it was ripped away and the rest fled into the mechanisms of his right leg.

It was in the servos that powered his leg bracings, infesting the systems that carried commands from his nerve-impulses to the motors. Maybe it had got in when he had scoured Chaeroneia's information nets for suspicious power spikes early in his investigation, or when he had been forced to have his nerve impulse units repaired a few days ago. Maybe it had been in him since he arrived, waiting to see how much he would uncover before striking.

Either way, now he could kill it.

His heart was working overtime, leaching so much power from the rest of his augmetics that his bionic arm fell limp. It filled him full of enough painkillers to all but kill him and he dragged himself away from the twitching mess of charred flesh and metal that had been his left leg.

Mmmaake you sufferrrr…

'Don't like that, do you?' spat Antigonus, blood running down his face where he had bitten a chunk out of his lip. 'Did you think they would send just anyone? Someone you could defeat with a machine-curse? They teach us well on Mars, heretic tech-pox.'

Nnnot machinnne-cuuuurse… much worssse… much, much worssse…

Ice-cold fingers of information scraped up Antigonus's spine. The tech-priest writhed on the floor, the edges of his vision turning white, a high scream filling his ears. He fought the chill seeping up through him, forcing its way through his augmetics into his flesh, the whispering voice quivering with anger. It wanted revenge. It was supposed to just control him, but now it wanted to kill him instead.

Antigonus choked back the horror that had infected him and forced it, nerve by nerve, back down into the smouldering servo units in his remaining leg. He tried to pull himself upright but only got into a lopsided crawl, dragging the tattered stump of his left leg behind him as he slithered out of the workshop. He had to get out of there – it was a dead end and he was trapped. Perhaps he could find a menial down here that could help him, or a better weapon. Anywhere was better than the workshop, because the infection, or whatever it was, must have been capable of transmitting his location to the heretics.

The resources required to acquire – or, Omnissiah forbid, even create – such a sophisticated machine-curse were massive. There were relatively few even on Mars who could have done it. Antigonus didn't even want to think about what the heretics must have had to do to get hold of it.

The voice was a low stutter now, hissing darkly from the depths of Antigonus's augmetics. Antigonus made his way painfully out into a long, low gallery, like a natural void formed between the strata of collapsed factory floors. The ceiling dripped rust-coloured water and pools of it gathered on the floor. From somewhere far below came the throb of an ancient, powerful machine, probably one of the geothermal heatsinks that provided so much of Chaeroneia's power. Antigonus dragged himself to where the ceiling had fallen in and a faint reddish light bled down from above.

No ussse, tech-priest... they willll find you, they always do... I am not the only one...

Antigonus ignored the voice and dragged himself up the incline of the fallen ceiling. The floor above was more intact, with knots of machinery and hissing steam pipes everywhere. Somewhere he heard men's voices shouting. As he moved the noises got louder – shouting, machinery, humming generators, the lifesigns of a forge world.

The painkillers dispensed by Antigonus's augmetic heart were killing most of the agony from his shattered leg, but they were flooding his body in such amounts that they made the world dull and distant. Every metre he moved drained him as if he had sprinted it and he kept trying to push himself forward with a left leg that wasn't there.

He was a mess. When they got him off this planet he would have to spend months being cleansed of the tech-curse and then getting all his wrecked augmetics replaced. He imagined the hospitals where servitors trundled the corridors keeping everything clean, the polished steel of the operating theatres and the spidery arms of the autosurgeon that flensed away weak flesh and grafted on strong metal. The bionics experts who would take him apart and put him back together again.

He shook the images out of his head. He was exhausted and starting to see things. If he lost his focus and started letting his mind wander the tech-infection would take a hold and rot him away from the inside.

He rounded a corner and saw he had come across a functioning factory floor – dilapidated and dangerous, but still working. Several massive stamping machines thudded on, forming metal components that were carted away by conveyor belts.

Antigonus tried to find a menial or a tech-priest who could help him. A bent-backed servitor stood hunched over a conveyor line leading from a broken stamping machine, its hands working away to perform some routine modification on parts that no longer moved past it. Antigonus ignored the servitor – even if it had been sophisticated enough to interrupt its programmed task and summon help, the machine-curse inside him could have leaped into the servitor and used it to cut Antigonus to ribbons.

Antigonus pulled himself up against the casing of the closest machine and used it to steady himself as he inched forward on his remaining leg. The machine-curse was hissing and spitting, whispering abuse at him. He had hurt it, but he also knew that such things were self-repairing and soon it would be strong enough to take him over again.

Antigonus rounded a corner and saw more servitors, but no menials. The menials were the lowest class on any forge world, men and women who were little more than living machines ordered and directed by the tech-priests. They were there simply because there were many tasks that servitors could not do, but their servitude was self-reinforcing because it was from the ranks of menials that many junior tech-priests were recruited. At the moment Antigonus could trust a menial rather more than he could a fellow tech-priest, which counted as a sort of heresy in itself.

The servitors ignored Antigonus as he forced himself to traverse the factory floor. A battered iron stairway led upwards – Antigonus didn't fancy his chances of getting up them in his current state but it was better than waiting in the deserted factory for the heretics to hunt him down.

Getting desperate? Now you realise. This whole planet is against you. It is only with the rats and dregs that you can hide. What life is that? Not life at all. So much of you wants to join usss, traveller. It is no great hardship for the rest to agree.

'Shut up,' spat Antigonus as he struggled up the spiral stairs. 'You know nothing. You do not even have the blessing of the Omnissiah, you should not even be.'

No Omnissiah dreamed me into being. No, not that god. Another one.

'There is no other.'

Really? What of your Corpse-Emperor?

'Two faces of the same being. The Omnissiah is to the machine as the Emperor is to His servants.'

What was Antigonus saying? Why was he debating with this thing?

So innocent to think such things. So easily led. My god is something else. My god is one of many, the many who serve the One, the End, the Future that is Chaos…

'Out!' Antigonus was yelling now. 'Stop these lies, heretic thing!'

The traveller starts to understand. Not a machine-curse, not a tech-pox. Something older, something stronger.

Daemon...

There was movement up ahead, footsteps and voices through the grinding of the machines. They were too urgent to just be more menials going about their business. Antigonus spotted the beams of powerful torches cutting through the shadows.

Daemon. It was a lie, just another way of rattling him. Antigonus had to concentrate on getting away. He looked around and saw a cargo elevator, rusted and old. Faded lights winked on the control panel and perhaps the machine still worked. Antigonus got across the factory floor to the elevator, trusting the noise of the machines would cover the sounds of his movement.

He let his mechadendrites haul the rusted gate open, keeping hold of his gun with one hand and steadying himself with the other. The socket in his back where Episilon three-twelve had torn out the mechadendrite was just one of a thousand points of dull raw pain forcing their way through the painkiller haze.

With an effort Antigonus shut the gate behind him and jabbed a mechadendrite at the control stud. The cargo elevator shuddered and moved grudgingly upwards. Antigonus heard someone shouting from below – they had guessed he might be escaping on the elevator but the factory complex down this far was a warren of dead ends and it was better to keep moving that to let them close him down.

He didn't even know what he was running from. Maybe they had hunter-servitors with scent-vanes that could track him through the filthiest corners of Chaeroneia's undercity, servo-skulls with auspex scanners that already had his lifesigns logged. But he had to hope. The grand machine of the universe moved according to the Omnissiah's will and he had to keep the faith that the machine would move to keep him safe.

Antigonus leaned against the back wall of the elevator. Crushed strata of factories and workshops marched past, reduced to claustrophobic voids in the mass of twisted metal. Gouts of steam burst from fractured pipes. Rivers of pollutants and fuel forced their way through fissures in the metal, feeding rainbow-slicked underground rivers. Thousands of years of industrial history were crusted on the surface of Chaeroneia – charred ruins, glimpses of faded finery, strange machines that perhaps represented some technology lost to the Mechanicus, hidden places where escaped menials or wild servitors had carved out a short existence, even abandoned chapels of the Cult Mechanicus long since replaced by magnificent cathedrals and temples far above.

And somewhere, something beneath the surface that had created a heresy worse than Antigonus had ever imagined.

The elevator juddered to a halt. The doors chattered open and freezing vapour rolled in. Antigonus crawled out warily, feeling the temperature dropping rapidly around him and letting his newly unaugmented vision adjust to the half-light. Antigonus saw that he was in a stratum that must have lain undisturbed for decades or even centuries. It was relatively clean and intact and lit by hundreds of tiny blue-white lights mounted on control panels and readouts. Data-engines, huge constructions of knotted cables and pipe work like slabs of compacted metal intestines, stood like monoliths in long rows. Heavy ribbed coolant pipes hung from the high ceiling and the deep chill in the air suggested that the coolant systems were still working. This was archaic technology, the kind that Antigonus had only seen on abandoned parts of Mars and which was obsolete on even the most traditionalist forge worlds. These engines had held information in crude digital forms, before the newer datacore technology was rediscovered and disseminated. Antigonus wasn't even sure how such things might work. There must have been thirty such engines, great rearing knots of obsolete technology, silent and untouched. The structure of this floor was intact and Antigonus couldn't even see the trails of vermin or stains of corrosion that touched everywhere else in Chaeroneia's undercity.

'Lord of Knowledge be praised,' whispered Antigonus instinctively, as it was appropriate to offer a prayer to the Omnissiah when confronted with such old and noble technology. But he couldn't stop and offer proper respects to the machine-spirits – there wasn't anyone to help him here and he had to get help or find safety.

He stumbled past a few of the data-engines, mechadendrites steadying him against the frost-cold metal. There didn't seem to be a way out other than the cargo elevator behind him. Such a facility would be well sealed against contaminants and the elevator itself had probably been protected originally, before its shielding was taken by menials and used some-where else. At most he could hope for an access vent, but he wasn't confident about his ability to crawl through a small space with one leg missing and his head fuzzy with painkillers.

The data-engine closest to him shuddered. It coughed out a spray of super cooled air and some old mechanism inside it ticked over as it wound up to operate. Antigonus shrunk from the engine, reluctant even in his current state to disrespect a machine-spirit. More of the machines seemed to stir, lights flickering. The power coming into the room was fluctuating. Something was interfering with the power supply and Antigonus knew it wasn't a coincidence.

A sudden howling of metal tore from the far wall. Antigonus saw sparks showering and the readouts on the data-engines turned an angry red, their machine-spirits objecting to the rudeness of the intrusion. A whirring, screaming sound of tortured metal filled the floor. Antigonus took shelter behind the closest data-engine, wishing his bionic eye still worked so he could banish the shadows and see what was forcing itself into the room after him.

Had he really thought he could escape?

No escape.

'Shut up. You are no daemon.'

Lie to yourself. It makes me stronger.

A huge, dark form lumbered into view between the data-engines, sparks still spitting off the massive breacher drill that formed one of its forearms. It was a servitor, a heavy labour pattern designed for mining. One arm was a drill and the other was an enormous pneumatic ram. Its torso was broad and packed with synthetic muscle, controlled by the tiny shrunken head almost buried by the massive muscles of its shoulders. It was easily twice the height of a man. It blasted through the hole it had ripped in the wall on a track unit that belched greasy black smoke.

There were more figures behind it. Dark, robed. Tech-priests. Further back Antigonus could make out beams of torchlight – the gunlights of tech-guard, the standing armed forces of the Adeptus Mechanicus. No doubt these men and women were used as ignorant foot soldiers by the heretics.

Antigonus shrunk back, hoping to make it to the cargo elevator. His right knee servo locked and he fell backwards, hitting the freezing cold floor hard enough to send a bolt of pain punching through the painkillers. Antigonus yelled. The tech-priests would certainly have heard him.

Got you.

'Get out! Give me my body back! When I die, you die!'

Run, traveller! Run! My kind never dies, just moves on, always moving, always changing…

A deep, sibilant voice spoke a streak of zeroes and ones – pure Lingua Technis machine code. The huge breacher servitor paused, its drill still spinning, compressed air whistling from its ramming arm.

More Lingua Technis. Antigonus could have translated it instantly if his auto senses had been operating, but all auxiliary power was being diverted to his bionic heart to keep him alive. He was naked, ignorant, helpless and trapped by heretics in this holy place.

'Magos Antigonus,' said the voice again, this time in Low Gothic. 'You are a resourceful man. But a man is all you are. It is impressive that you found us at all and while there was never any chance of your doing us meaningful harm there was always the possibility that Mars would send someone more competent when you reported back to them of your failure. So this is the way it has to be.'

Antigonus gave up trying to get away. His body was half-paralysed. 'They will,' he spat, determined to spend his last few moments defiant in the face of heresy as the Omnissiah would demand. 'When I don't return. They'll send a whole Diagnostic Coven. Blockade the planet. Switch the cities off one by one. Hunt you down.'

'Will they really now?' The lead tech-priest walked into view. His robes were deep grey, made of some superfine mesh that flowed around him like water. His hood was thrown back and Antigonus saw that the upper part of his face was pulled so tight that it was barely more than two gleaming silver eyes in a skull. The lower jaw had been removed entirely and replaced with a nest of slender mechadendrites that hung down to the floor, writhing like tentacles. In place of his hands the tech-priest had nests of long, metallic filaments that waved like the fronds of an underwater plant, fine and dextrous. He moved with a strange sinuous grace, more like some living, bone-less thing than a machine, even though the tech-priest was undoubtedly more heavily aug-mented than almost anyone Antigonus had ever seen.

'Scraecos,' breathed Antigonus. The leader of the tech-heretics was the archmagos veneratus who com-manded Chaeroneia's data-reserves. He had probably tracked Antigonus all the way through security pict-stealers and sensor-equipped servitors. He had just been waiting to see how much Antigonus knew and what he would do next before moving in. He had known all along exactly where Antigonus was and what he had been doing. Antigonus had never had a chance, not from the moment he had set foot on Chaeroneia.

'And that,' said Screacos, his synthesized voice thick like syrup, 'is why you have to die. So curious. And often correct. A dangerous combination.'

Antigonus grimaced with effort and closed his natural hand around the stock of his autogun. With strength he didn't think he had he pulled it out from underneath him and fired.

The shot thunked into Screacos's midriff. Screacos barely moved – he just parted his mechadendrites and glanced down at the small smoking hole in his robe. He shook his head slightly, as if with disappointment.

'Azaulathis,' he said.

Master.

'Kill him.'

The world went white and Antigonus's body spasmed with pain, as if there was an electric current running through him. His augmetics glowed white-hot, charring his skin, burning muscle. He couldn't see, couldn't hear, couldn't feel anything but the pain.

Sparks spat as Antigonus's bionic arm was forced out of the flesh of his shoulder, servos winding so tight the metal splintered. His mechadendrites stood on end, his bionic heart thudded arhythmically sending more bolts of pain through him. The remains of his bionic eye unscrewed from his face and shattered on the floor, leaving a fist-sized gap in his skull. The machine-curse was infecting all his augmetics, forcing them to self-destruct and when it got to his bionic heart it would kill him.

Antigonus prayed. Pain was a design weakness of the human body. All he had to do was fix it and he could move. He put every drop of strength into forcing his internal augmetics into obedience, keeping the machine-curse in check for a few split seconds more. He ordered one mechadendrite to work. Linked directly to his central nervous system, he had more precise control over the mechadendrites than any of his other bionics. And he only needed one.

Antigonus screamed and jabbed the tip of one mechadendrite into the closest data-engine, forcing its interface probe to stab into the ancient machine. Then, he let go.

The machine-curse, like electricity, flowed through the points of least resistance. It rippled through Antigonus's body, leaving trails of internal burning as it went, spiralling up into the mechadendrite and on into the data-engine.

Before it could turn back, Antigonus withdrew the mechadendrite. The data-engine shuddered, its lights winking blood-red as the machine-curse thrashed around inside its systems. The curse was trapped in the data-engine. Antigonus had bought himself a few more seconds.

Antigonus had committed a terrible sin by infecting the noble old machinery with such a foul thing. No matter what happened now, the Omnissiah would never forgive the machinery deep inside his soul. But Antigonus hadn't just committed the sin to stay alive – to a tech-priest life itself had no intrinsic value, only service to the Machine-God. Antigonus still had his duty to fulfil. The heretics still had to suffer.

A massive force ripped through him – the servitor's breacher drill, grinding through his body into the floor. Loops of organs were thrown about the room as the drill bored through Antigonus's abdomen. He didn't feel pain – he couldn't feel anything any more. He guessed his nervous system must be on the edge of shutting down. He was cold and numb. Helpless. He was probably physically dead already.

The servitor lifted Antigonus and threw him clean across the room. Antigonus's ruined body smacked into one of the data-engines, scattering bionic fragments and spatters of blood.

He compelled his mechadendrites to act. One last time, in the service of the Omnissiah. Once last chance to repent of all his sins – because he had failed and he was as bad as a sinner could be.

The metallic tentacles reached behind him into the body of the data-engine. He felt old, grim technology, lorded over by a melancholy machine-spirit, indignant at the destruction and angered by the machine-curse that had infected its brother. Antigonus begged the machine-spirit for forgiveness. He never got an answer.

The servitor's ram arm thudded down onto Antigonus's head and chest, crushing him instantly into the machinery of the data-engine, blood and bone driven deep into the machine's core.

Antigonus's mechadendrites dropped limp.

THE CREATURE ANTIGONUS had referred to as Archmagos Veneratus Scraecos drifted back towards the other tech-priests, similarly deformed and augmented figures who were nevertheless clearly subservient to him.

The breacher-servitor stood at rest over the hapless remains of Antigonus, which no longer resembled anything that might have once been human. The tech-guard, in their rust-red environmental suits wielding brass cased lasguns, fanned out into the room. But there was no one else.

Antigonus had been the only one who had known.

He had probably been right. There would be more from Mars, probably many more, an armed mission with the authority of the archmagos ultima, perhaps even of the Fabricator General. But by the time such a mission got through the warp to Chaeroneia it would be too late for anyone, even the Fabricator General, to do anything.

'Good,' said Scraecos. He turned to the tech-priests who had followed him, loyal to the Omnissiah as revealed to them through His avatar. 'Brothers. The loyal. The true. We have seen the face of the Machine-God. Everything he has told us has come to pass. So the time has come for us to begin at last.'

CHAPTER THREE

'…And so fear you the Unknown, for every foe was once but a mystery.'
 – 'A History of the Ultima Segmentum',
Lord Solar Macharius

'EMPEROR'S DOWN.'

'Frag you it is.'

Suruss pointed to the corner of the regicide board, where a single lone templar piece stood. 'The templar has it in check. He's got nowhere to go.'

Argel peered at the board. The young Suruss looked so pleased with himself he might just be right. 'You little groxwiper,' growled Argel. 'It scroffing has and all.' Argel frustratedly knocked his emperor piece on its side, signifying the end of the game and another victory for Suruss.

'Another game?' asked Suruss.

'Sure. Frag all else to do.' Argel was right. They were on Deep Orbit Monitoring Station Trinary Ninety-One, Borosis system, Gaugamela subsector, Ultima Segmentum. It was a corroded metal sphere about five hundred metres across, most of which was engineering and maintenance space and such stations were rarely equipped with entertainment facilities. Suruss and Argel were lucky they even had space to set up the regicide board. Three months into a nine month shift, Argel had come to the conclusion that Suruss was better at the game than he was, but he didn't have much choice but to play on and hope he got better.

The alternatives numbered two. Stare at the walls, or go and talk to Lachryma. Unfortunately Lachryma was an astropath, a tremendously powerful telepath who relayed psychic messages from one end of the Imperium to the other. Astropaths were all creepy, morose creatures who kept their shrivelled, blinded selves to themselves. Lachryma was worse than most. So regicide it was.

Something blared on one of the upper levels, loud and braying.

'Throne of Earth,' said Argel, 'that's the proximity warning.'

'Must be broken,' said Suruss, who was laying out the regicide pieces for another game. 'There's nothing out here.'

'Every time those things go off it's a mountain of bloody paperwork. I'll go and have a look.' Argel stood, careful not to scrape his head on the low ceiling of the station's cramped living compartment. He scratched the bad skin on his neck and shrugged the enviro-suit over his shoulders. They didn't heat the outer maintenance layers of the station and it was cold enough to kill you.

Another alarm went off, closer this time.

'Gravitational alarm,' said Suruss. 'Looks like they're all on the blink.'

'You gonna help?'

Suruss gestured at the regicide board, half set up for the next game. 'Can't you see I'm busy?'

Argel grumbled obscenities as he struggled through the narrow opening into the primary maintenance shaft. The alarms were blaring and there were more of them – meaning radiation or outer hull integrity, other ones he didn't recognise. Suruss was probably right. It was just the station's machine-spirit getting uppity again. Argel would have to delve into the thick book of tech-prayers and minister to the station's inner workings until the spirit was placated. The station needed a tech-priest of its own, but the Adeptus Astra Telepathica didn't think Deep Orbital Station Trinary Ninety-One was important enough so it was up to Argel and Suruss to keep it working.

Argel was about to start the climb up the primary shaft when he saw something moving down the corridor connecting the living space to the astropath's quarters. It was Lachryma, the astropath herself, shambling forward. Her hands were reaching blindly in front of her and the hood of her robes had fallen back, revealing her wrinkled, shaven head and the white band she wore across her eyes.

'Lachryma! It's nothing, Lachryma, just a glitch in the spirit.'

'No! No, I can see them... I can hear them, all around...' The astropath's voice was shrill and piercing, cutting through the sound of the alarms. She stumbled forward and Argel had to catch her. She was shivering and sweaty and smelled of incense.

'I... I sent a message,' she gasped. 'I don't know if they heard. We have to get out, now...'

It wasn't a fault. It was real. Astropaths were always the first to know when anything really, really bad was about to happen, every spacer knew that.

'What is it?'

Lachryma reached up and pulled the bandage down from her eyes. Except there weren't any eyes – just empty bone, the insides of the sockets inscribed with prayer-symbols that burned a faint orange as if a great heat was trying to escape from behind them.

'Chaos,' she said, voice quavering. 'The Castigator.'

The station shook as if something had hit it. The floor tilted as the gravity generator's gyroscope was knocked out of line and half the lights failed.

'We can get you to the saviour pod,' said Argel. 'Just... just stay calm. And put that thing back on.'

Argel dragged Lachryma back into the living quarters, where Suruss was frantically working the sensorium display among the wreckage of the regicide table.

'It's an asteroid hit!' shouted Suruss above the din of the alarms and further impacts. 'Never saw it coming!'

'We're getting out of here,' said Argel.

Suruss shook his head. 'Not yet we're not. The auxiliary power has to be warmed up. Get the generator ticking over and we can launch the saviour pod.'

'Why me?'

'Because you know what you're doing!'

Another hit, the biggest yet, slammed into the station. Gouts of steam shot through the living compartment and part of the ceiling fell in, spilling broken pipe work everywhere. Suruss fell forward and cracked his head against the sensorium console. The knock sparked one pict-screen back into life and it flickered on.

Suruss held his head and tried to sit up. Argel knelt down and pulled the fallen Lachyrma into a seating position – blood was running down her face from a long cut in her scalp. She was muttering darkly and the orange glow was bright enough to seep through the bandage over her eyes. Argel didn't know what they did to astropaths on their long pilgrimage to Terra, but it seriously messed them up.

Argel looked around the destruction in the room. The outer decks would be even more of a mess. It would be murder getting the auxiliary power up, but the saviour pod was their only chance. And Suruss was right – the only person Argel trusted to do it was Argel.

Argel saw the image on the pict-screen next to Suruss. It had finally switched itself on and was showing a view of space outside the station, relayed from pict-stealers in the station's sensorium array.

'What the frag is that?' he asked.

Suruss looked round. The pict-screen was showing a point of red light gathering in space a short distance away from the station. The stars around it seemed to smear as the light from them was bent around the anomaly and it was growing, flaring out a white-hot corona as it forced its way into real space.

Suruss looked at Lachryma. 'Tell me someone knows about this.'

Lachryma nodded weakly. 'Yes. Yes, I sent a message... all the symbols, everything I'd seen... the planet coming out of the warp, the... the cities made of hatred, the cannibal world... all of it... and the Daemon from the Imperial Tarot, the Beast, the Heretic, all the worst signs... the worst of the worst...'

Argel shook Lachryma. 'But who? Who's going to see it?' Astropathic communications were complex and semi-mystical and completely beyond Argel. Astropaths transmitted images from the Imperial Tarot and elsewhere in the hope that adepts in the Telepathica's relay stations would cross-reference them from immense books of augurs and work out what the message said and who it was supposed to go to. An astropathic distress signal would be no good if it took an adept six months to work out what it meant. 'The Telepathica?'

'No, no... there's nothing they can do, not now.'

'Then who?'

'Perhaps... the Adeptus Terra, so it gets back to Earth... or even the Ordos... yes, the portents will have them running... maybe even the Ordo Malleus...'

Argel frowned. 'Who?'

Then the primary power failed completely.

SEVENTY THOUSAND KILOMETRES from Deep Orbit Monitoring Station Trinary Ninety-One, asteroids streamed from a growing, burning hole in the fabric of real space. The hole grew as a truly immense form forced its way out. The asteroids streaked outwards, a few impacting on the disintegrating orbital station, most of them spinning out and looping back towards the emerging object in complex irregular orbits. More and more of them shot out until the breach was surrounded by a dizzying, shifting mass of asteroids, sorcerous fire licking across their surfaces.

Space puckered and tore as the rest of the object's mass forced its way out and the orbital station was finally destroyed in the shockwave that rippled through reality. Astropaths and other psykers for light years around felt it happen. The star of the Borosis system was turned an unhealthy black-streaked crimson by the unholy force spewing from the breach.

And there, outside the furthermost orbit of Borosis's reach, was a new planet where no planet had ever been before.

CHAPTER FOUR

'Many claim they wish to destroy their enemies. If this were true, most would be compelled to destroy themselves.'

– Abbess Helena the Virtuous,
'Discourses on the Faith'.

THE TRIBUNICIA WAS cold as a tomb. Outside it had the brutal lines of a warship but inside everything was dressed in marble and granite, worn smooth by generations of crewmen sworn to serve the Imperium. Many of them had been born on the ship and almost all of them would die on it, so the ship's architecture served as a constant reminder that this ship would literally be their tomb.

Justicar Alaric slipped out of half-sleep. He was sitting cross-legged on the freezing granite floor in the middle of his small cell. A Space Marine didn't have to sleep normally and could retain some awareness while in half-sleep and something had jolted him back into full wakefulness.

The engine pitch had changed. The *Tribunicia* was coming out of the warp.

Alaric stood up, murmuring the Seventeenth Prayer of Alertness as he turned to his power armour, stacked neatly in the corner of the cell along with his storm bolter and Nemesis halberd. For a moment he just looked at the wargear, ornate gunmetal armour plates with his personal heraldry over one shoulder. He had added a single bright yellow star to his heraldry to commemorate the soul of Briseis Ligeia, the bravest person Alaric had ever met, who had saved him and countless others even after a daemon had driven her mad. She was dead now, executed by the same Ordo Malleus that Alaric served.

Alaric knew he would die in that armour. Most people would never touch it if they knew that one fact as surely as he did.

Alaric intoned the Rites of Preparedness as he picked up the left greave of the power armour and began to put it on.

THE BRIDGE OF the *Tribunicia* was a magnificent cathedral deep inside the heavily armoured prow, with a massive vaulted ceiling and soaring columns of white marble. Scores of crewmen and tech-adepts crowded the pews, working communications consoles or sensorium displays. The command throne of Rear Admiral Horstgeld took up the front pew, just before the grand altar itself, a creation of marble and gold crowned with a golden image of the Emperor as

Warmonger. Horstgeld was a religious man and so the ornate pulpit that looked out over the whole bridge was always reserved for the use of the ship's Confessor, who would take to it in times of crisis and bellow devotional texts to steel the souls of the bridge crew.

Horstgeld rose as Justicar Alaric entered. Horstgeld had served with Space Marines before, even if he had probably never quite got used to their presence. The man who sat on the command pew alongside him, however, had no such reservations. He was Inquisitor Nyxos of the Ordo Malleus, a daemonhunter and the man who had requisitioned Horstgeld's ship into the service of the Inquisition.

'Justicar,' grinned Hortsgeld. 'Well met!' Horstgeld strode down the bridge's nave and shook Alaric's hand. He was a huge and bearded man whose heavily brocaded uniform looked like it had been altered significantly to fit him. 'I must admit, I am accustomed to being the biggest man on my bridge. It will take some getting used to you.'

'Rear admiral. I've read of your victory over the *Killfrenzy* at the Battle of Subiaco Diablo. This is a tough ship with a tough captain, I hear.'

'Pshaw, there are plenty of brave men at the Eye of Terror. I was just fortunate enough to have the charge.'

'You would rather be there now?'

Horstgeld shrugged. 'In all honesty, justicar, yes I would. That's where all the Navy wants to be fighting, we're the only ones holding them back. But I don't run my ship according to what I happen to want and when the Inquisition comes calling one does well to answer.'

'Well said,' added Inquisitor Nyxos. He was an ancient, sepulchral man who wore long dark robes over a spindly exoskeleton that kept his withered body standing. Alaric knew that in spite of his immensely frail appearance, he was an exceptionally tough man thanks to the scores of internal augmentations and redundant organs the Inquisition had supplied him with. An encounter with the rogue Inquisitor Valinov would have killed almost anyone, but Nyxos had survived.

It had been Nyxos who had given the order to execute Ligeia. Alaric didn't resent the man for it, it was what had to be done. And now Nyxos was the Ordo Malleus inquisitor with whom Alaric worked most closely. Such were the mysterious ways of the Emperor.

'The reports from this area of space were alarming indeed,' continued Nyxos. 'While we must send everything we can to the Eye of Terror, the consequences will be grave if we take our eyes off the rest of the Imperium. It will do no good to throw the Despoiler back into the warp if the rest of the Emperor's work is undone behind our backs.'

'True, inquisitor, true,' said Horstgeld. 'But do we even know what we are dealing with here? Or if there is anything here at all? All the records the ship has on the Borosis system suggest it is a veritable backwater.'

Nyxos looked at the rear admiral. His large, filmy grey eyes seemed to look straight through him. 'Call it educated guesswork, captain.'

The engines changed pitch again and the whole ship shuddered. Warning klaxons sounded briefly somewhere on the bridge before someone shut them off.

'Entering real space!' came a call from one of the officers in engineering. 'Warp engines offline!'

'Geller field disengaging!' came another cry. The noise on the bridge rose as well-practiced commands were relayed and acknowledged. Down in the bowels of the *Tribunicia* a couple of thousand crewmen would all be labouring to ensure a safe end to the ship's warp jump – engine-gangs redirecting the plasma reactors to power the main engines, weapon crews manning the ready posts for their broadside guns and torpedo tubes, the ship's small complement of tech-adepts calculating the huge numbers involved in making the ship plunge from one reality into another.

The altar in front of Nyxos, Horstgeld and Alaric rose from the floor and Alaric saw that the sculptures of the altar actually crowned the ship's massive main pict-screen. The screen rose up from the floor until it dominated the whole bridge. It was flooded with grainy static until one of the communications officers powered up the ship's main sensorium and the image swam into view.

'Hmmm,' said Nyxos. 'It's bad, then.'

The pict-screen showed a view of the Borosis system from deep orbit, where the *Tribunicia* had emerged into real space. The star Borosis itself was a swollen, livid red, streaked with angry black sunspots, its corona bleeding off into a halo of sickly red light. Borosis should have been a healthy mid-cycle star, similar in type to Terra's own sun.

'Close in on the planets,' said Nyxos. Horstgeld quickly relayed the order to his comms crew and the pict-screen cycled through closer views of the planets that orbited the sickened star.

The light and heat coming from the sun had dropped massively. That meant Borosis Prime, the closest planet in the system to the star, was even bleaker than the burning globe of rock it had been before – it was dying. Borosis Secundus's atmosphere was gone entirely – once covered by a thick blanket of superheated gases, the planet was now naked, the sudden temperature change having thrown its atmosphere into such turmoil that its layers bled off the planet entirely.

There was a long gap to Borosis Cerulean, the most inhabited world, home to seven major colonies with a total population of about one and a half billion. It was cold and dark. The planet's cities were advanced enough to provide shelter from the eternal winter that had now fallen over the world, but their power and supplies would not last forever. Perhaps the world could be evacuated, perhaps not. That wasn't the Ordo Malleus's problem.

The lifeless world of Borosis Minor, almost completely covered in ice, was an inhospitable as ever, as was the gas giant Borosis Quintus where a few thousand workers were probably deciding how they were going to survive on their gas mining platforms when the solar collectors failed. The change in the star had barely affected the outermost planet, Borosis Ultima, a ball of frozen ammonia almost too small to qualify as a planet at all.

The viewscreen cycled to show the last object in the system.

'I cannot claim to be an expert,' said Alaric carefully, 'But I gather that is the reason we are here.'

There was no seventh planet in the Borosis system. There never had been. But there it was.

It was deep charcoal grey streaked with black and studded with thousands of tiny lights. Around the world were thousands upon thousands of asteroids, tiny speckles of light from this distance, like a swarm of insects protecting the planet.

All Grey Knights were psychic to a degree. They had to be for their minds to be so effectively shielded against corruption. Alaric's psychic powers were all internalised, focused around the wards that kept his mind safe – but he was still psychically sensitive and he could still feel the wrongness pulsating from the new world. It was like the echo of a scream, a smell of old death, a slick and unhealthy feeling against his skin.

'We've had astropaths going mad for light years around,' said Nyxos matter-of-factly. 'That would be the reason.'

'Guilliman's rump,' swore Horstgeld. 'I've been in space all my life and I've seen some things, but never a whole world where there shouldn't be.'

'Try not to get too overwhelmed, captain,' said Nyxos. 'I need a full data sermon on that planet, everything you've got. I'll send Interrogator Hawkespur to coordinate. Atmosphere, lifesigns, dimensions, everything the sensoria can find. And what is the arrival time of the rest of the fleet?'

'Within the day,' replied Horstgeld. 'If you could call it a fleet.'

'We'll need it. That's an inhabited world and if they've got ships of their own we might have to go through them to get down there. And we are going down there.'

'Of course, inquisitor.' Horstgeld turned to his crew and started barking orders, sending communications officers and messenger ratings scurrying.

'What do you think?' Nyxos asked Alaric quietly, as the bridge went about its noisy, barely controlled business.

'Me? I think they were right to send us.'

'I agree. What would you do?'

'I would defer to the wisdom of the Inquisition.'

'Come now, Alaric. You know why I had you accompany me, out of all the Grey Knights.'

'Because they are all at the Eye of Terror.'

'Wrong. You showed an unusual level of independence and creative leadership on the Trail of Saint Evisser. The Chapter made you relinquish your acting rank of brother-captain but they all know your qualities. Space Marines are all very well but even Grey Knights are just soldiers. Ligeia thought you could be something more and I am coming round to her point of view. So, think like one of us, just this once. What should we do?'

'Land an army,' said Alaric, without hesitation. 'Take all the Guard we have and send them down. Right away.'

'Risky.'

'Nothing is riskier than indecision, inquisitor.'

'Quite. And as it happens I agree with you. Is your squad ready?'

'Always.' Alaric's squad was under-strength following the costly defeat of the daemon Ghargatuloth on the Trail of Saint Evisser, but it still represented a concentration of firepower and fighting prowess that no Guard being transported by the fleet could hope to match.

'Good. I want you at the data sermon. You'll probably end up the leader on the ground, one way or another.'

'Understood. I shall pray with my men, inquisitor.'

Alaric left the bridge, knowing instinctively that they would find more on the seventh planet than any amount of prayer could really prepare them for.

'THE EQUATORIAL CIRCUMFERENCE of Borosis Septiam is just under thirty-eight thousand kilometres,' began Interrogator Hawkespur, indicating the pict-grab projected onto the screen behind her. 'Rather less than Earth standard. The mass, however, is the same, suggesting super-dense mineral deposits. As you can see, the thick atmosphere and surrounding asteroid field prevents us from probing the surface but we do suspect the planet is without polar caps, perhaps due to deliberate depletion. The atmosphere shows strong indicators of being breathable, but with severe levels of pollutants.'

The ship's auditorium was normally used for tactical sermons, or public dissections of interesting alien specimens and unusual mutations by the sick bay crew. Now it had been set up for Hawkespur's data sermon and the command crew, along with Nyxos and Alaric's squad, sat in rows around the central stage where Hawkespur was speaking. The pict-grab showed the ugly, weeping sore of a world, provisionally named Borosis Septiam, that had so completely mystified everyone on the bridge. Hawkespur's voice was clipped and professional – she was Naval Academy material from the finest aristocratic stock, a brilliant young woman employed by Nyxos who felt certain she would one day take up the mantle of inquisitor herself.

'The asteroids are in unusually low and stable orbits,' continued Hawkespur. 'It is unlikely that anything larger than a single light cruiser could navigate through them and multiple smaller ships would be out of the question. This precludes a large-scale landing.'

Alaric heard Horstgeld swear quietly. Thousands of Imperial Guard were being transported with the fleet – the initial plan to send them down to the planet had failed before it had even begun.

Hawkespur ignored the captain. 'The temperature readings are particularly anomalous. A planet at such a distant orbit from the sun, especially given the current state of the star Borosis, should be extremely cold. Borosis Septiam's climate suggests temperate conditions over almost the entire surface. This can result only from a massive thermal radiation source or climate control on a planetary scale. The indications we have of extremely high power outputs suggest the latter. Finally, there appear to be a great many orbital installations, apparently man-made. The interference from the asteroids means we cannot get a good look at them but they represent a major presence suitable for an orbital dockyard.'

'What are your conclusions, Hawkespur?' asked Nyxos, sitting in the front row of the auditorium.

'Highly industrialised, with a large and long-standing population. All the data we have has been sent to the Adeptus Mechanicus sector librarium to see if any planet matches it.'

'Any idea how it got there?'

'None.'

'Ship's astropaths have done no better,' said Horstgeld. 'They say it's like a blind spot.'

Nyxos looked round to where Alaric and his Marines were sitting. 'Justicar? Any thoughts?'

Alaric thought for a moment. The Imperium had lost planets through administrative error before – all it took was for one scholar to forget to mark down a world's tithes and that world could eventually disappear off the stellar maps, especially in an out of the way system like Borosis. But this world was suspicious enough to warrant Inquisitorial scrutiny, if only to be sure. There was something so wrong with the world that it would be a lapse of duty to leave it be.

'Since no major landing is possible, we should send a small well-equipped mission down to the surface. An investigative team.'

Nyxos smiled. 'Excellent. Hawkespur? How's your trigger finger?'

'Commendation Crimson in pistol marksmanship, sir. Third round winner at the Hydraphur nationals.'

'Then you'll take the team down. I'll co-ordinate from the *Tribunicia*. Alaric, your squad will support on the ground along with as many Imperial Guard special forces as we can get onto an armed insertion craft.'

'Commendation Crimson?' said Horstgeld approvingly. 'Good Throne, girl, is there anything you can't do?'

'I haven't found anything yet, sir,' replied Hawkespur, completely without humour.

* * *

THE IMPERIAL NAVY was the only thing holding back the Thirteenth Black Crusade and all the Imperial authorities knew it. Abaddon the Despoiler had shattered the attempt to pen his Chaos-worshipping forces up in the warp storm known as the Eye of Terror and it was only Imperial command of space that had kept his ground forces from taking planet after planet all the way into the Segmentum Solar. Every Imperial warship was on notice that it could be ordered into the Eye at any moment and thousands upon thousands of them had been, from mighty Emperor class battleships to squadrons of escorts and wings of fighter craft.

Rear Admiral Horstgeld, for all his experience and commendations, couldn't tear a handful of good ships away from the Eye for the mission to Borosis, even with the authority of Inquisitor Nyxos and the Ordo Malleus. His own ship, the veteran cruiser *Tribunicia*, was the only ship in the small investigative fleet that he considered ready for a battle. The escort squadron *Ptolemy*, under Captain Vanu, was brand new from the orbital docks of Hydraphur and consisted of three Python class ships of a completely untested configuration.

Nyxos had requisitioned an Imperial Guard regiment, the tough deathworld veterans of the Mortressan Highlanders, along with the transport *Calydon* to carry them. The *Calydon* was a corpulent and inefficient ship with barely enough guns to defend itself and Hortsgeld knew it would do nothing in a battle apart from get in the way.

Along with a handful of supply ships and shuttles, these craft comprised the fleet that exited the warp over the course of a few hours just outside the orbit of

Borosis Septiam. Shortly afterwards another craft was detected in the warp which broke through into real space a short distance away, all its weapons powered down in a display of alliance. It was a large ship, easily the size of a cruiser, but of an ugly, blocky design painted a drab rust-red, covered in ornate cog-toothed battlements and training long flexible sensor-spines like the stingers of a sea creature.

The ship immediately hailed the *Tribunicia*. It identified itself as the Adeptus Mechanicus armed explorator ship *Exemplar* under the command of Archmagos Saphentis, who demanded complete jurisdiction over the entire Borosis system.

'I DON'T LIKE it,' said Alaric, looking at the landing craft. 'It's too fragile. This couldn't take half the punishment a Thunderhawk gunship could.'

The ship was being bombed-up and refuelled in the loading bay of the *Tribunicia*, a grimy, functional deck where the vaulted ceiling was stained black with oily fumes. The landing craft was bulbous and simple, with twin flaring engines and a thick black carapace over its nose to protect it from re-entry. It could probably seat thirty passengers plus crew.

'It's the best we have,' replied Hawkespur. She wore a heavy black spacer's voidsuit, ready for take off – she looked very different without her starched naval uniform. A marksman's autopistol was holstered at her waist. 'We're fortunate the *Tribunicia* has an armoured lander at all.'

'Then we have no choice,' said Alaric. He turned to the Marines of his squad. 'We take off in half an hour. Check your wargear and pray.'

A Grey Knights squad ideally consisted of between eight and ten Marines. Squad Alaric consisted of six Marines, having never recovered the losses it suffered during the battle against Ghargatuloth on Volcanis Ultor over a year before. Brother Dvorn was by far the biggest Marine, packed with muscle. He carried a rare mark of Nemesis weapon, a hammer, which was all but unheard of now among the Chapter artificers but which was brutal and unsubtle enough to suit Dvorn perfectly. No one doubted that Dvorn would soon be trained in the use of Tactical Dreadnought Armour and join the ranks of the Grey Knights Terminator squads, the heaviest shock troops in the Chapter.

Brother Haulvarn and Brother Lykkos were the other two survivors of Volcanis Ultor. Lykkos carried the squad's psycannon, which fired ensorcelled bolter shells to tear through the bodies of daemonic or psychically active targets.

Brother Archis and Brother Cardios, who carried the squad's two Incinerators, had both heard the story of how Alaric, as acting brother-captain, had led the mission to the Trail of St Evisser to locate the daemon Ghargatuloth and help Imperial forces destroy it on Volcanis Ultor. But they had not been there. They had not seen it.

'Justicar,' said Dvorn as the other Grey Knights checked the storm bolters and armour seals according to the ancient Rites of Preparedness. 'Do we have any more news on what is down there?'

'I wish we did, Dvorn,' he said. 'But the squad knows as much as anyone in the fleet.'

'But they need us, don't they? Whatever is down there, it's corrupt. Can you feel it?'

'Yes, Dvorn, I can feel it. Anyone sensitive could. And they will need us down there, of that I am certain.'

Dvorn looked at the lander craft. There was a look of disdain on his battered face – Dvorn was not a gnarled old veteran but he was well on the way to looking the part. 'I wouldn't trust that thing to dust crops, let alone land thirty men on a hostile world.'

'I know, but it's the best the fleet has.'

'The main armament is twin lascannon. I could carry more firepower than that and still have a hand free.'

'You probably could, Dvorn, but the Emperor does not make us strong by making our duties easy. We will make do.'

'Justicar,' came Nyxos's voice over Alaric's vox-unit. 'Problem.'

'The stormtroopers?'

'Worse.'

A warning klaxon sounded and the docking doors of the adjacent landing bay slid open. Alaric could see a slice of the dirty purple disk of Borosis Septiam beyond it and space scattered with stars. The rest of the landing deck was protected from the void by a force field so Alaric couldn't hear the engines of the shuttle that slid into the *Tribunicia*. It was clad in heavy, ugly slabs of armaplas and its prow was a massive flat disk ringed with turbolasers. The cog-toothed symbol of the Adeptus Mechanicus was emblazoned on its side. The deck crew had evidently had no notice of its arrival but it didn't need the help of any deck hands or docking servitors as it settled onto the deck. The bay doors slid shut and the void-seal field boomed off.

A deck-officer strode towards the interloper craft, hand on his dress sword. 'You!' He yelled up at the ship. 'I don't see this damn thing on the docking manifests! Explain yourself!'

A dozen turbo-lasers trained themselves on the officer's head. He stopped in mid-flow and took a step backwards.

'I think this is our problem,' said Alaric. 'Follow me.'

As Alaric and his Marines walked towards the shuttle a ramp unfolded from its side. Thick, purplish incense billowed out, followed by a detail of twenty tech-guard, their faces hidden behind the reflective visors of their helmets. Alaric recognised the tech-guard uniforms and distinctive pattern lasguns – they were the standing army of the Adeptus Mechanicus, their regiments raised to defend the Mechanicus's forge worlds. Two tech-priests followed behind the soldiers – they were holding the censer-poles which were the source of the incense. The tech-priests seemed mostly human, suggesting they were lower-ranked members of the clergy. The priest behind them was clearly something totally different.

The delegation was led by a creature that could only be called human with a great deal of charity. He moved as if he wasn't walking at all but gliding, as if his long Mechnicus robes hid some strange motive attachment instead of legs. He had four arms, two with what looked like silvered and intricately engraved bionic hands and two ending in bunches of dataspines and interface units. His head was the most bizarre of all – he had large multi-faceted insectoid eyes and his mouth was hidden by a heavy metal collar with a series of slits cut into it through which he presumably spoke. There was not one scrap of biological flesh visible on him.

The tech-guard fanned out into a semicircle to let their master through. The lead tech-priest looked around for a moment and his inhuman eyes settled quickly on Alaric and his squad.

'Excellent,' said a clearly artificial voice. 'You are a representative of Inquisitor Nyxos?'

'I represent the Adeptus Astartes Chapter of the Grey Knights.'

'I see. By your heraldry I surmise you possess the rank of justicar.' The voice was programmed with a slightly aristocratic, supercilious accent. 'It is unlikely you are in command of Imperial forces here. Please direct me to someone who is.'

'I should like to know who you are, first.'

'Forgive my manners, I was unable to bring my protocol-servitor with me. I am Archmagos Saphentis of the Adeptus Mechanicus, commander of the *Exemplar* and senior tech-priest of the Librarium Primaris on Rhyza, appointed by the office of the Fabricator General to lead this reclamation mission.'

'Reclamation?' said Interrogator Hawkespur, looking almost ridiculously small next to the fully-armoured Alaric. She didn't seem in the least bit fazed by Saphentis's bizarre appearance. 'This is an Ordo Malleus investigation. The Holy Orders of The Emperor's Inquisition have authority over this planet and everything pertaining to it.'

'You misunderstand me.' Saphentis held out one of his more humanoid hands and an attendant tech-priest handed him a dataslate. The slate's screen glowed purplish with an image of Borosis Septiam. 'You are Interrogator Hawkespur, I believe. You yourself sent the specifications of this planet to the sector librarium requesting identification. That request has been fulfilled. The world you have inaccurately named Borosis Septiam is a forge world, a possession of the Adeptus Mechanicus according to the Treaty of Mars. I am therefore here to lead the mission reclaiming it according to the orders of the Fabricator General.'

'The Inquisitorial Mandate supersedes all other authority, including the Treaty of Mars,' said Hawkespur crossly.

'You may well be correct. While you debate the legalities, my men will be conducting an examination of the planet.'

'Forgetting the rules,' interrupted Alaric, 'anyone who goes down there may not come back. We're looking at a moral threat on that planet. The Mechanicus can't deal with something like that on its own.'

'Your concern is appreciated,' said Saphentis. 'But there is little a fully armed Explorator mission cannot cope with. Now, if you will excuse me, I had hoped to extend Inquisitor Nyxos the courtesy of explaining the authority under which I operate, but if that courtesy is not going to be reciprocated then I shall return to my ship.'

Hawkespur glared at the deck officer, who was still being tracked by all the craft's turbo-lasers.

'Not... not without deck clearance, sir,' he said. 'And I'm afraid I can't give it to you. So you'll have to explain yourself to the captain.'

'This craft and this planet belongs to the Adeptus Mechanicus,' said Saphentis sharply. 'If you cannot comprehend this then I certainly hope your captain will be less obtuse. You will take me to him and hope that he extends me the respect for my authority that is due.'

'This is ridiculous,' said Hawkespur as Saphentis drifted away escorted by his tech-guard retinue. 'Men have been executed for questioning Inquisitorial authority. We should launch as soon as the stormtroopers arrive.'

'It would be better to wait, interrogator,' said Alaric.

'Why? There is no point in being tangled up in a debate while we could be learning what is on that planet.'

'I know.' Alaric pointed at the Mechanicus shuttle. 'But if we're going down there, I'd far rather do it in a ship like this.'

THE COMMS CENTRE of the escort ship *Ptolemy Gamma* was, like the rest of the ship, brand new. It was well known within the Imperial Navy that the old ships were the best – construction techniques were lost faster than they were rediscovered, so newer ships were often thought of as flimsy copies of far superior veterans. The communications of the escort squadron had been characteristically petulant, the frequencies fluctuating, the machine-spirits of the comms cogitators sulking and bickering like children. Many libations of machine-oil and tech-rituals of adjustment were needed just to get the *Ptolemy Gamma* talking to the *Alpha* and *Beta*, the other two ships in the squadron. But there were no full tech-priests stationed with the squadron and the tech-rituals did not always work.

'Anything?' asked Communications Officer Tsallen. The comms centre was cramped and stifling, crammed into the heart of the ship between the gun-decks and engineering where it was supposed to be safest. Tsallen had been trying to get the *Gamma* speaking to Squadron Captain Vanu for three hours now and her heavy starched Naval uniform was not endearing her to the heat down here.

'Cogitator three isn't responding,' replied the rating in front of her. Stripped to the waist, he had levered the panel off the front of the massive cogitator and was trying to make sense of the half-clockwork machinery inside.

'There must be something,' said Tsallen. 'The squadron is supposed to be in tight formation protecting the *Tribunicia* and right now we can't even tell her where we are.'

'If it's broke it's broke,' said the rating.

Tsallen sighed. She was supposed to command her own ship one day and this wasn't the way to go moving up the ladder. 'You!' she said, pointing at another rating. 'Are we receiving yet?'

The second rating was a skinny man sweating heavily as he sat at a large receiver station shaped like a church organ. He was listening intently to the static streaming through his headset. 'Maybe.'

'Maybe?'

'It's not letting me isolate frequencies. I keep getting snatches of things.'

'Let me.' Tsallen pushed the rating away from the receiver station and bent over the hundreds of blinking lights and readouts. Most of them hadn't even been labelled yet. She pushed a couple of buttons and pulled a few levers experimentally.

The station shuddered. Its cogitator stacks, shaped like organ pipes, thrummed as they went into over-drive. A bewildering shimmer of indicator lights flowed over the console.

'Did it work?' she asked.

'Looks like it's cycling through all the frequencies, ma'am. Depends on whether it finds anything.'

Tsallen heard a horrible grinding sound and smoke spurted from beneath the console. At least if she'd broken the damn thing it wouldn't be her fault, she thought. That was what the ratings were for.

The rating screamed. His head was jerking, neck spasming and his eyes were rolled back and white. He was clawing at the headset – Tsallen grabbed it and tried to pry it off his head but it was red-hot, burning itself into the man's skull.

'Oh frag! Oh frag, we've lost the whole bloody lot!' shouted someone, probably the rating working on cogitator three. The rest of the comms crew, about thirty men and women crammed into the hot, dark space, started shouting for attention as the whole comms centre started overloading itself.

Tsallen pushed away the rating, who had by now stopped screaming and was exhaling stinking, oily smoke instead. 'Stay calm!' she yelled, drawing her laspistol. 'What is it?'

'Some signal's coming in,' shouted someone in reply. 'Something strong! It's overloading every-thing!'

'Where's it coming from?'

There was a moment of frantic commotion. Sparks flew as one of the cogitators blew, spraying shattered components everywhere.

'Point of origin is Borosis Septiam!'

'Isolate us from the rest of the ship,' ordered Tsallen.

'Primary controls are offline!'

'Then grab a bloody fire axe and cut the cables!'

There was an ear-splitting scream as all the cogitator circuits blew at once. All the lights went out.

Silence drowned the comms centre.

'Anyone hurt?' asked Tsallen carefully.

The sound that came from the main receiver console might have been described as a voice, but it spoke a language so horrible to hear that Tsallen froze. It was painful to listen to, so many dark, guttural sounds overlaid that it sounded like a million onlookers spitting curses at her.

'Moral threat…' said Tsallen weakly, hoping her own vox to the bridge still worked. 'We have a moral threat in comms. Isolate us and get a message to Horstgeld…'

A dark purple glow rippled up from the console, stippling the walls with deep swirling colour. The voice continued. And though Tsallen could not understand the language it spoke the meaning was impossibly clear – malice, anger, hatred, dripping from every syllable. Tsallen forced herself to look at the console readouts – the signal was massively powerful, streaming from somewhere on the surface of the mystery planet below, using a frequency that could barely be received but strong enough to tear through the filtration circuits and bleed, pure and evil, into the *Ptolemy Gamma*.

After a few more moments the physical structure failed and the whole comms centre imploded.

'I PROPOSE A compromise,' said Inquisitor Nyxos. Rear Admiral Horstgeld's personal quarters took up several rooms of cold, dressed stone, piously furnished with solid hardwood and adorned with icons of the Imperial Creed. Nyxos had called the meeting in Horstgeld's private chapel, well away from any of the crew. He had Hawkespur by his side, along with Hortsgeld and Alaric. Archmagos Saphentis and Tech-Priest Thalassa, a relatively unaugmented female tech-priest who attended him, represented the Adeptus Mechanicus.

If Nyxos was unnerved by seeing his hundredfold reflection in Saphentis's insectoid eyes, he did not show it. 'Arguing will get us nowhere.'

'Unusual words for an inquisitor,' said Saphentis. 'And in the circumstances probably the wisest.'

'I am glad we got off to a good start, then,' said Nyxos. 'But first, I need to know what you found at the sector librarium.'

'Am I to understand you are asking as an inquisitor and not as a curious individual?'

'You are.'

'Very well.' Saphentis, Alaric guessed, was well aware that refusing to answer an Inquisitorial interrogation could be met with whatever punishment the inquisitor could devise. 'The planet in question is named Chaeroneia. It disappeared a little over a century ago following an investigation into the potential of tech-heresy among the lower ranks of its tech-priests.'

'You are certain?'

'We are. Chaeroneia is a forge world according to
the principles of the Treaty of Mars and is owned in
its entirety by the Adeptus Mechanicus, hence our
insistence that we are to conduct any investigations.'

'The Treaty of Mars is nowhere accepted as super-
seding Inquisitorial authority,' snapped Hawkespur.

'Perhaps this is true,' replied Saphentis, whose
voice seemed programmed to sound condescending.
'But the time taken to ascertain this for certain is time
none of us have.'

'Hence my proposal,' said Nyxos. 'A joint mission.'

'Under my command, of course,' said Saphentis.

'Unacceptable. Interrogator Hawkespur will represent me on the ground. Justicar Alaric will be in
operational command.'

'The mission shall be attended by myself, Tech-
priest Thalassa and a detachment of tech-guard
troops.'

'Agreed.'

'And the *Exemplar* will be under my command as
part of the fleet,' interjected Horstgeld.

'Very well. My flag-captain, Magos Korveylan, will
accommodate you.' Saphentis's voice was as calm as
ever but Alaric guessed that Saphentis realised he was
getting about as good a result as he could have hoped
– Nyxos was probably being generous letting such a
high-ranking tech-priest accompany the mission at
all.

In some ways, Alaric was glad the Mechanicus
would be coming along. If Borosis Septiam really
was the forge world Chaeroneia, someone knowl-
edgeable in the Cult Mechanicus would be a real

asset on the ground. He didn't like the idea of wrangling for control, though, and Saphentis seemed the kind of man who would refuse to budge once he had decided he was going to be in charge.

The doors to the chapel opened and a nervous-looking bridge officer entered, the pips on his dark blue uniform denoting him as a member of the comms crew. He hurried up to Captain Horstgeld, unable to help glancing at the bizarre form of Archmagos Saphentis and the no less otherworldly appearance of Alaric himself.

'Moral threat on the *Ptolemy Gamma*, sir.'

'Moral threat? What's the source?'

'A broadcast from the planet.'

'Hell and damnation,' said Horstgeld. 'Quarantine the *Gamma*, physical comms only. Have the fleet purge all communications. And have Fleet Commissar Leung informed.'

'Can the *Exemplar* set up a completely secure receiver?' Nyxos asked Saphentis.

'Indeed we can.'

'Good. Have Korveylan do so and start studying that broadcast and work out where it's coming from.' Saphentis didn't move. 'If you please.'

Saphentis nodded to Thalassa, who hurried off to relay the necessary orders to the *Exemplar*.

'It looks like our hand is being forced,' said Alaric.

'Quite right,' replied Nyxos. 'That is the annoying thing about the Enemy, he never gives us time to think. Are you ready to move, Alaric?'

'My men have observed their wargear rites and can deploy immediately.'

'That's what I like to hear. Saphentis?'

'The tech-guard accompanying me represent our most efficient combat unit. They are ready to go, as is our ship.'

'Excellent. Gentlemen, you carry the authority of the Emperor's Holy Orders of the Inquisition with you. Whatever you find down there, it falls under the aegis of the Emperor and must be claimed in His name or made pure according to His laws. His Will be with you.'

Alaric and Saphentis left the chapel for the launch deck. Alaric knew that once down on the planet, the balance of power would shifty dramatically without Nyxos to back up Hawkespur and Alaric – Alaric only hoped that whatever he found on Chaeroneia, he would only have one enemy to fight.

CHAPTER FIVE

'The words of the faithful are the mountains. But the deeds of the faithful are the world.'

– Final words of Ecclesiarch Deacis VII

ASTEROIDS SHOT BY the viewport, streaming trails of dust and gases. The upper layers of Chaeroneia's atmosphere were dirty wisps of pollution, lit by the feeble glow shining from the star Borosis and reflected off the planet's surface. Alaric's first close-up image of Chaeroneia was one of pollution, the filth that wrapped the planet bleeding off into space, infecting everything around it.

'Heat exchanger activated,' came an artificial voice voxed from the cockpit, probably a pre-recorded sample broadcast by a pilot-servitor. It meant the friction of the atmosphere was heating up the ship's hull.

The inside of the ship was cramped and functional. Everything was painted in the dark red of the Adeptus Mechanicus. The cog-and-skull symbol was raised in steel and brass on the low ceiling. Grav-couches lining the passenger compartment held the twenty-strong tech-guard unit, Alaric and his five Grey Knights, Interrogator Hawkespur, Tech-priest Thalassa and Archmagos Saphentis.

'Our readings from the *Exemplar* suggest the asteroids may not be entirely natural,' said Tech-priest Thalassa to Hawkespur. Thalassa's age was difficult to guess owing to the silvered circuitry embedded in her skin, describing complex patterns across her face, but she was evidently of a low rank since her simple dark red habit had few signs of status. 'The guns can keep the path clear but there may be resistance.'

'Resistance?' Hawkespur looked unimpressed. 'Orbital weaponry?'

'We don't know. But this craft is designed for atmospheric intrusion so we can take a lot of fire.'

Alaric looked across the passenger compartment to the tech-guard. They wore full-face helmets with polished brass visors and heavy rebreather units and they were armed with what looked like more complex versions of the standard Guard lasgun. Alaric couldn't see their faces – they seemed more like servitors than soldiers.

The craft shuddered as the turbulence of the upper atmosphere threw it around. Alaric could see the blackness of space overlaid by a gauze of pollution through the viewport, the ugly lumpen asteroids glowing orange where they plunged in and out of the atmosphere. The pallid light of Borosis shone through the crescent of atmosphere that Alaric could see clinging to the side of Chaeroneia's disc, making it glow a sickly purple-grey.

Alaric could feel the world beneath him, reflecting off the psychic core that kept his soul safe from corruption. He could feel it churning, pulsing – the heartbeat of a world. Dull, ancient pain throbbed far below, like the agony of something old and captive. The world was tortured.

'The heresy that Mars investigated here a hundred years ago,' said Alaric, looking at Saphentis. 'Were there any details?'

Saphentis shook his insectoid head. 'Very little. Rumours of improper practices. Unauthorised creation of techniques. Attempted instigation of machine-spirits. The investigation was not intended to prosecute any named individuals, just collate data on potential heresies against the Cult Mechanicus.'

'Do we know if they found anything?'

'No reports were received.'

'That's not the same thing, though, is it? If you know anything about what is down there, archmagos, we need to know it.'

'I have extensive details on the workings of the forge world prior to its disappearance.'

'And now?'

'If much has changed, then we shall learn of it as we must.'

Something slammed hard into the underside of the ship, sending it bucking like an animal as the directional thrusters forced it back into line.

'Impact,' came the annoyingly calm voice from the cockpit servitors.

The ship began to swing, slaloming its way between the asteroids. Alaric saw through the viewport that they were spearing thicker through the atmosphere, congregating on the craft as it plunged towards the surface. Flames rippled across the asteroids' surfaces as they ripped into the next thicker layer of atmosphere, forcing their way down through the air resistance to meet the ship.

'Grav-dampeners to maximum,' ordered Saphentis as the ship bucked again, several small impacts thudding against the underside like bullets.

'I am the Hammer,' said Brother Dvorn. 'I am the point of His sword. I am the tip of His spear.'

'I am the gauntlet about His fist,' said the other Grey Knights, intoning the prayer that had been heard by the Emperor when they had entered the Tomb of St Evisser to face Ghargatuloth.

A red glare crept up the edge of the viewport, the force of re-entry superheating the hull. Flames licked off the edges of the hull just visible outside the ship.

'I am His sword just as He is my armour, I am His wrath just as He is my zeal…' Alaric couldn't hear his own voice as the impacts rang louder and the howl of the atmosphere outside vibrated through the hull, the whole ship shaking.

The tech-guard were calm and unmoving no matter how they were shaken around. Saphentis had all four arms splayed against the wall behind him, holding him firm. Thalassa look less comfortable, thrown about in her grav-restraint. Hawkespur was pulling on the hood of her black voidsuit, always ready for the worst.

Alaric knew the low thudding sound from the prow was the noise of the forward guns, tracking and blasting apart asteroids that were thrown in the way of the ship. The fragments spattered on the hull like gunfire, streaking past the viewport as tiny burning sparks.

The view of space was gone, replaced by a purple-black sky streaked with filthy clouds. Strange geometric shapes were flashing in the sky, projected onto the clouds from far below. The lander was heading for the probable origin of the signal – the analyses on the *Exemplar* had located the transmission source to within seventy kilometres. It was a big margin of error, but it was the best information the Imperial fleet had about where to start looking for answers on the planet's surface.

With a horrible sound like a metallic thunderclap something huge struck the ship head-on. The pressure vessel that kept the passenger compartment at Earth-standard pressure was breached and wind howled through the compartment, flinging debris around. The door to the cockpit banged open and Alaric saw only the ground beyond it, a distant dark mass speckled with lights, framed by the remains of the cockpit. The broken metallic limbs straggling in the air were presumably the remains of the servitor-pilot.

'Autosystems engage!' came Saphentis's voice, amplified above the din. 'Landing pattern beta! Drag compensation maximum!'

Another impact sheared deep into the side of the vessel, stripping away hull plates. The viewport cracked. Alaric could see gouts of burning exhaust jets streaking down from the craft, trying to slow its descent. It was heading straight down, the massive damage done to its prow destroying any chance of even the ship's machine-spirit controlling it properly as it fell.

There was a city below them, like a huge dark spider straddling the scorched black landscape. It was the size of a hive city and the uppermost spires knifed up towards the craft as it fell.

Another impact flipped the craft over and it was tumbling now, completely out of control, the engines spurting to correct its trajectory.

'I am the Hammer! He is my Shield!'

The craft smashed into the first spires of the city and even a Space Marine's resilience couldn't keep Alaric conscious as the impact split the ship apart.

HORSTGELD WAS RAPIDLY losing his patience. Magos Korveylan was supposed to be under his command, but the Mechanicus captain had spun a web of red tape and protocols to prevent Horstgeld from sending any of his officers onto the *Exemplar* – not even Fleet Commissar Leung.

Horstgeld was therefore still on the bridge of the *Tribunicia*, waiting for Korveylan to contact him at the tech-priest's leisure.

The obvious moral threat on the planet below – now called Chaeroneia, apparently – was such that the ship's Confessor Talas was on permanent duty warding the souls of everyone on the bridge. Talas, a hellfire preacher with a scrawny build but undeniable presence, was on the pulpit at that moment uttering an uninterrupted stream of religious fervour.

The Emperor's wrath featured strongly, as did the many places in the various hells of the Imperial Cult that sinners could find themselves in if they gave in to the whims of the Enemy. Horstgeld had employed a Confessor on the bridge for many years and to him the constant admonitions were just the music of the spheres – the rest of the bridge crew had to live with it.

'Transmission from the *Exemplar*,' said one of the comms officers.

'About gakking time,' said Horstgeld as the face of Magos Korveylan appeared on the viewscreen. If it could be called a face at all – half of Korveylan's skull was covered in a featureless cowl of gleaming silver and the other was covered in dead grey flesh.

'Rear Admiral,' said Korveylan. Rather disconcertingly, the voice that came from Korveylan's vocal synthesiser was female. 'Is there any news of our mission?'

'We lost vox-contact with them in the upper atmosphere,' replied Horstgeld. 'What about you? Have you found anything?'

'We have.'

There was a long pause. 'And?' asked Horstgeld tetchily.

'The transmission's source is the surface of Chaeroneia. It is extremely powerful, well beyond the capabilities of any one spacecraft or standard comms device the Imperium has. The navigational beacons within the Sol system are of comparable intensity.'

'Very good, captain. What does it actually say?'

'The signal cannot yet be deciphered.'

'You mean you don't know.'

'The signal cannot be yet deciphered.'

'Hmph. Anything else?'

'It is clear the information encoded into the signal has not been created using logic engine techniques known to the Adeptus Mechanicus. It includes patterns and energy types of a clearly non Terrestial origin.'

Horstgeld leaned forward on the command pew. 'Sorcery?'

'That is a crude but accurate summation, yes.'

'And do we know who the target is?'

'Aside from the fact that the signal is being broadcast towards the galactic north-west, no.'

'Since this is clearly a supernatural threat, I want Fleet Commissar Leung on the *Exemplar*. I don't want any of your men losing their minds over this.'

'Unnecessary. The Magi Psychologis can maintain mental wellbeing among the research crew.'

'Take Leung on board. That's an order. Your ship is a part of my fleet and you command it with my authority. Don't make me use it against you.'

Korveylan held up a hand – her hand, Horstgeld supposed – as if appealing for calm. 'The Adeptus Mechanicus maintains strict protocols regarding…'

'Frag your protocols,' said Horstgeld. 'Do as you're bloody well told or I'll haul you over here for a court martial. And I am not known for my lenience. Prepare to receive Leung's shuttle, Horstgeld out.'

Horstgeld snapped the viewscreen off and it reverted to an image of the Borosis system, the hateful purple-black stain of Chaeroneia in the foreground. He sat for a moment listening to Talas sermonising.

'...for is not the Emperor both your light and your fire? The light that guides you and the fire that waits below to burn the unbelievers? I say, yes! Yes He is! For if you believe, O faithful citizens, then you are His tool, a tool to break down the edifice of heresy and build His temples in its place...'

It comforted Horstgeld to know that one inspired by the Emperor was always there, tingeing everything on the bridge with the Emperor's own authority. And he needed that, because the hell-planet below him, screaming out a signal that only daemonancers and sorcerers could hear, wasn't very comforting at all.

THE TECH-GUARD was dead. He was lying on his back, the length of his spine opened up wet and red, fresh blood glossy in the faint but hard-edged light.

Another was hanging, impaled on one of the shards of metal that ringed the huge wound in the side of the lander craft. His lasgun was still gripped tightly to his chest, his hands constricted in death, refusing to let go of the weapon with which he defended the Adeptus Mechanicus.

Alaric was alive. He tried to move and found he could. Rapidly he worked through the Rite of Wounding, testing each of his muscle groups, searching for tears or broken bones – he was knocked about but there were no injuries he couldn't ignore. He turned his head and saw the rest of the wrecked ship's interior. A couple more tech-guard were clearly dead, one totally decapitated, still sitting strapped into his grav-couch. Other tech-guard were stirring.

Hawkespur was unconscious but breathing – through the faceplate of her voidsuit's hood he could see there was blood on her face, but it looked superficial.

Dvorn, the Grey Knight strapped in next to Alaric, was moving.

'Dvorn?'

'Justicar. We made it?'

'This would make for a strange afterlife, so yes, I'd say we had.'

The Grey Knights squad was alive and its injuries seemed superficial. Dvorn was first out, hammer in hand as always, helping Alaric out of the crushed grav-restraint. Brother Haulvarn checked Hawkespur for injuries then unstrapped her and carried her out through the tear in the hull.

The air was heavy and thick, like strange-tasting smoke. Warning runes on Alaric's retinal display flickered on and the implants in his throat began filtering out the pollutants. Alaric clambered out of the wreckage, his enhanced eyes automatically adjusting to the twilight outside.

The lander had crashed in a valley with sides of twisted metal, layers of crushed buildings lying in hundreds of strata. Far above, the layers became thicker and less compressed until Alaric could just glimpse, at the very top, soaring spires studded with tiny lights, stabbing thin and sharp as syringe needles into the sky. The sky itself was ugly and bruise-coloured, the many layers of pollution tinting the pallid light from Borosis a strange cocktail of splotchy purples and greys. Shapes flickered, some geometric, some strange-shaped symbols like letters in an alien language, presumably projected from somewhere on the surface onto the underside of the cloud layer. The valley was a chasm cutting down through layers and layers of the forge world's buildings, the strata showing how the city had constantly been built on top of itself for the thousands of years the forge world had been in existence.

The valley was choked with wreckage that had fallen down from the top of the chasm – wrecked machinery, burned-out engines, spindly fragments of wrecked servitors. On top of a charred lump of what looked like an engine housing was Archmagos Saphentis, climbing nimbly with the help of his additional arms.

The surviving tech-guard were emerging from the lander's wreckage, along with Tech-Priest Thalassa. There were about a dozen of them still alive. One of them flipped up the visor of his helmet – his face was lined with age and experience beneath shaven dark brown hair and one of his eyes was a large but solid bionic.

'Pollutants fifteen percent air volume!' he said to his men. 'Rebreathers at all times! Colsk, take the dead mens' names and collect their power packs.'

Alaric recalled the tech-guard captain's name was Tharkk. He hadn't spoken to him before – the mission had been assembled and launched in a hurry. They wouldn't have the luxury of returning to the *Tribunicia* with the same kind of haste, that much was obvious.

Alaric clambered onto the engine housing where Saphentis had now stopped to survey his surroundings. The valley floor ahead of them sloped upwards until it met what looked like a plateau a couple of kilometres away.

'Archmagos!' called Alaric. 'Hawkespur looks unhurt, as does my squad. Many of your tech-guard are dead. Perhaps you should see to them.'

'They are unmoved by death,' replied Saphentis. 'They need no help.'

Alaric had dealt with members of the Adeptus Mechanicus on a few occasions – many were tied to the Ordo Malleus by ancient debts and served to maintain the Inquisitorial fleet anchored on Saturn's moon, Iapetus, or attended inquisitors directly as lexmechanic archivists or augmetic chirurgeons. In Alaric's experience the more senior the tech-priest, the less human they were. Saphentis, with his rank of archmagos, wasn't doing anything to buck the trend.

'We will move to the head of the valley,' said Saphentis. 'We will get a better view of the city.'

'Do you have enough details on Chaeroneia to know where we are?'

'I have full topographic and urban maps of Chaeroneia. However, after a century they are unlikely to be accurate. Information is our first priority.'

'I agree, archmagos and as commander on the ground it is my decision. You are under Inquisitorial authority here, don't forget that.'

Saphentis turned his faceted eyes towards Alaric. 'Of course.'

'Squad, we're moving out,' voxed Alaric to his squad. 'Lykkos, get the psycannon up front. Cardios, keep the Incinerator in the centre in case of ambush. Haulvarn, is Hawkespur conscious?'

'Semi-conscious, justicar.'

'Keep her safe. I would like to get her back to Nyxos intact. Let's move out before something comes to investigate the wreck.'

Saphentis issued a stream of clicking sounds which Alaric guessed was binary machine code, filtered by the vox-receivers on the tech-guard and turned into recognisable language. Alaric would insist everyone on the mission use the same vox-channel once they were safe.

Alaric could hear distant machinery pumping away as the mission moved up the valley. Long and high-sided, the chasm cut out all but a sliver of sky as it wound through the darkness. It headed gradually upwards and Alaric hoped that it would reach a point where they could get a better look at their surroundings. There was something other than just the sounds and the darkness, too – the same psychic resonance he had felt in orbit, a sinister presence that seemed to be coming from everywhere at once, diffuse and all-pervading. It flashed through him as the images on the clouds above changed – complex occult wards and sigils, like the symbols cultists painted on their temple walls or etched out on the floor for their rituals. Occasionally shapes would flit across the clouds. Alaric hoped they were aircraft.

'Advanced machining,' Saphentis was saying as they moved past the burned-out heaps of wreckage. 'They have not regressed. They have progressed. Chaeroneia was a Gamma-level macro economy, but it now seems to be approaching Beta-level sophistication.'

'Is that normal?' asked Alaric.

'Not in a century,' said Saphentis.

Tech-priest Thalassa had recovered her wits and was quickly alongside Saphentis. She was mostly human so she stumbled as she fought her way across the uneven wreckage – Saphentis could help himself along with his extra arms. 'We should find somewhere we can interface with the planet's data repositories, archmagos,' she said. Alaric guessed from her circuitry-covered skin that she was Saphentis's data expert. 'I could extrapolate our location from Chaeroneia's last surveys.'

'Could you find out what has been happening for the last hundred years?' interrupted Alaric.

'Maybe,' said Thalassa, looking nervously at Alaric. Alaric remembered how people tended to react to Space Marines – with fear and awe. 'If the data vaults are similar to Mechanicus standard.'

'Contact!' came a shout from one of the tech-guard, barking out of Saphentis's vox-receiver. Alaric span around, Brother Lykkos beside him training the psycannon barrel over the dark valley floor. The tech-guard had hit cover, lying or crouched, squinting along the barrels of the lasguns to cover all the approaches.

'Tharkk?' voxed Saphentis quietly.

'Colsk reported movement,' came the reply.

'And yourself?'

'Can't see anything yet – wait!'

Alaric saw a slim, pallid shape stumble out of the gloom. It looked humanoid. Its pale body was naked except for tattered strips of parchment nailed to its torso and its bare feet shambled across the debris with only enough coordination to keep it upright. Its shaven head was a wreck – the lower jaw was gone and the one remaining eye was a rusting, weeping mechanical optic. It only had one hand, its other arm ending at the elbow in a fitting where the mechanical forearm had been removed.

Alaric overheard one of the tech-guard voxing. 'It's a servitor, sir. Scavenger.'

'Deactivate it,' was Tharkk's reply. One of the tech-guard drew a laspistol sidearm and put a las-bolt through the servitor's head. It shuddered, stiffened and fell to the ground. The tech-guard smashed its skull with the butt of his lasgun.

'Scavengers are dangerous,' said Saphentis. 'Others may be combat-capable. Stay on your guard and do not allow us to be caught out again.'

'Anything else I should be warned about?' asked Alaric as the troops got moving again.

'A forge world is not unlike any Imperial world in that respect,' replied Saphentis. 'It has its criminals and malcontents along with dispossessed menial scavengers and rogue servitors. But they are far less numerous than in a hive city or area of comparable population density.'

They were coming to the end of the valley, where the ground sloped up to meet what looked like a plateau level, spreading away from them. Alaric's retinal readouts were telling him that without his throat implants and superior ability to filter and absorb poisons, toxins from the polluted air would be building up in his body at an alarming rate. Thalassa was breathing heavily, but Saphentis wasn't showing the slightest discomfort.

'We need to be on the same vox-net,' said Alaric. 'If I can't co-ordinate the whole force at once then…'

They had reached the top of the valley slope, level with the small circular plateau that looked out on the cityscape beyond. And Alaric saw one of Chaeroneia's cities properly for the first time.

CHAPTER SIX

It is good that we have seen such terrible things, for now death will be no great sorrow.

— Commissar Yarrick
(attr., at the walls of Hades Hive)

THE CITY WAS an unholy fusion of black iron machinery and a pulsing biological mass, as if something vast and alive was reaching up from the bowels of the planet to strangle the steel city. Below them huge rounded masses of grey muscle bulged up from the city's black depths, ripped through with ribbed cabling and punctured by vents spewing evil-smelling steam. Deep shafts lipped with wet fleshy mouths belched black smoke. Strips of flickering lights suggested there were corridors and rooms hollowed out of the masses, that they were inhabited by whatever had done this to Chaeroneia. In some places slabs of muscle jutted out above the blackness, balconies or walkways, even launching pads for shuttle craft were painted in stained black and purples. Sensor-spines stuck out like poisoned barbs. Massive vertebrae reared up, weeping dark-coloured pus where they broke the skin, bent tortuously as if some massive creature had been chained and shackled under the city.

The forge world's towers soared out of the chasms below, masses of flesh like tentacles wrapped around them as if holding them upright. The towers were in the half-gothic, half-industrial style of the Adeptus Mechanicus but all similarity to an Imperial city ended there. The black steel spires were fused with the city's biological mass, so that some were like massive teeth sticking out from rancid gums or huge steel leg bones, skinned and wrapped in greyish muscle. Bulbous growths fused obscenely with sheer-sided skyscrapers. Sensorium domes trailed waving fronds of tendrils. Pulsing veins snaked in and out between the girders of skeletal buildings, seemingly picked clean of their meat. Foul-coloured fluids leaked from wounds hundreds of metres long or sprayed from the mouths of iron gargoyles, gathering into waterfalls of ichor tumbling far down into the city's depths. Bridges of sticky tendrils, like spiders' webs, connected one spire to the next. In places the flesh was rotten and scabbed, covered in weeping sores the size of bomb craters and sagging under its own dying weight.

This had once been a forge world. The signs were there – massive cogs churning in the biological masses below, the thrum of generators over the reedy, stinking wind, the thousands of lights that burned in the spires. Here and there a balcony was edged with the cog-toothed pattern common to the Adeptus Mechanicus, or even a half-skull symbol almost buried in parasitic growths. Huge pistons pumped through the sides of a massive blocky building, but they looked more like the gills of an enormous sea creature than the workings of an engine. The machinery that had driven a world now resembled the organs of single creature, huge and monstrous, turned inside out and draped around a city of sweating black steel.

The tech-priests and Grey Knights had emerged from the valley onto a large circular platform, perhaps originally a landing pad, which jutted from a huge slab of city-layers that looked like it had been forced up from the prehistoric depths, like a tectonic plate driven up to form a mountain range.

'Throne of Earth,' breathed Brother Lykkos. 'Protect us from this corruption.'

'Pray that He does, brothers,' said Alaric. He turned to Saphentis. 'The truth, archmagos. Have you ever seen anything like this?'

'Never.' Saphentis was as inscrutable as before but Thalassa was looking at the sight in open horror, her hand over her mouth and her eyes wide.

'Did you know what we would find?'

'We knew there was something wrong.' Saphentis's voice was passionless. 'But not like this.'

Alaric looked up. As he had suspected, occult symbols were projected onto the clouds, graven images and writing in forbidden tongues spanning the sky on a truly vast scale. Tiny shapes – grav-platforms maybe, carrying cargo or passengers or patrolling the skies – skimmed just below the cloud layer. The sky was the final heresy, swirled with the colours of festering wounds, purples and greys as diseased as the city itself. This world was so steeped in corruption that even the sky was infected.

The tech-guard were joining the tech-priests and Grey Knights. They were showing little reaction to the horrible sight, just spreading out for the scattering of cover by the opening into the valley cleft. Hawkespur was on her feet by now and she saw the city too. Through the faceplate of her voidsuit's cowl Alaric saw even her eyes widen in shock.

'We're in the open here,' said Alaric. 'We have to get into cover. If they can see us here then they can trap us.'

'Tharkk,' voxed Saphentis. 'We require shelter. Fan your men out to find–'

Something large and wet slammed into the platform with a fleshy thud. A massive stain burst across the surface of the platform, dark and bubbling. 'Down!' yelled Alaric before the surface erupted into scores of spiny limbs, shooting up and out with a sound like thousands of breaking bones.

One of the tech-guard was speared by a spike-tipped tentacle, lifted off his feet and slammed against the jagged metal wall behind him. Las-blasts fired in return, severing thorny tentacles, impacting in bursts of foul greasy steam.

A tentacle snaked around Brother Haulvarn's leg but he hacked it off with his Nemesis sword. The other Grey Knights fell back, along with Saphentis and Thalassa. The tech-guard moved to surround Thalassa but Saphentis could evidently look after himself. Circular saw blades snapped into position on two of his limbs and he slashed around him with little apparent effort, sending twitching fragments of tentacle raining down around him.

'Cardios! Flame it!' ordered Alaric. Brother Cardios stepped past him and blasted a gout of blessed flame into the growing monstrosity, scorching wads of ichor off the metallic surface.

The tech-guard were falling back – one of them had seen there was a way into the neighbouring building, a monolith of sweating black iron that looked chewed and tunnelled as if by giant worms. The Grey Knights followed, cutting around them as the tentacles swarmed to surround them.

A dark, roughly circular shape buzzed into view, held aloft by a trio of flaring grav-engines on its underside. A jagged bone crown sat on top of the platform and Alaric just glimpsed a figure in the centre of it, held in place by dozens of thick ribbed tentacles. Half-machine, half-biological weapons crowded the platform's edge – Alaric guessed that one, a wide-mouthed mortar-like weapon squatting near the centre, had fired the bio-weapon at them. The other weapons opened up, stuttering down a rain of fire. Alaric returned fire, feeling the air around him split apart by the shells flitting past him, trusting in his power armour to keep him alive until he hit cover.

Brother Lykkos's psycannon put two fat holes through the base of the platform and black ichor sprayed out, the platform bucking as if in pain. The figure in the centre fought to keep it under control, working the vehicle's apparently biological brain like an organist at the keyboard. The break in fire let the Grey Knights hurry out of the range of the tentacles and into the rust-pitted hole that led into the neighbouring spire.

It was dark inside. Alaric's augmented vision could easily follow Tharkk's tech-guard as they spread out in the wide tunnel, wary of what they might find but intent on getting away from the attack outside. The place was dark and dank, the curved walls and floor slick with cold blackish liquid.

The gun-platform outside steadied and sent heavy chains of gunfire stammering around the tunnel entrance. Lykkos and Brother Archis returned fire for a few moments before heavy shots began slamming into the metal, hard shells of writhing parasites that burrowed quickly through the iron where they hit the wall.

'Get back!' shouted Alaric as he followed the tech-guard into the tunnel. 'Keep together, we don't know what's in here.' He quickly found Captain Tharkk in the darkness. The tech-guard officer's face was still covered in the opaque rebreather helm, lit a hard-edged green by the screen of the auspex scanner he was consulting.

'Up or down?' asked Tharkk.

Whoever now controlled Chaeroneia now knew where Alaric and the force were. If they went up they would run out of levels quickly – even though the upper levels were probably less likely to be inhabited they would be easier for the enemy to cut off, trapping the force inside. There was no telling what might be in the spire's depths where the black iron met the heaving biological masses below, but there would certainly be more places to hide.

'Down,' said Alaric. 'Grey Knights, to the fore,' he voxed. All Space Marines were trained – created, even – to fight up close and brutal and they excelled in enclosed spaces where their superior strength and weight of firepower counted for the most. If they were to forge their way to safety, the Grey Knights would be the ones to get them there.

There was more noise from outside. The grav-platform had stopped firing but Alaric could hear more, heavier lifters with deeper engines. Full of reinforcements, maybe. And there was something else – something huge and heavy, travelling up the outside of the building with a sucking, scratching sound that reverberated through the narrow tunnel.

Alaric shouldered his way past the surviving tech-guard and led the way. The tunnels spilt and looped up and down, but the Larraman's ear implant meant Alaric had an excellent sense of balance and direction, picking the course that would take them into the centre of the spire and downwards. Faintly luminescent colonies of fungi clogged some tunnels, others were half-flooded with viscous grey gore. The sound of pumping pistons echoed from down below, the sound of the creaking, shifting iron from all around.

The tunnel opened up ahead. Alaric stopped and waved forward Cardios and Dvorn, who crouched down by the opening where the tunnel led into a much larger cavity in the iron. There was barely any light – while the Grey Knights could see perfectly

well, presumably along with Saphentis, he didn't
know if the tech-guard would be able to fight in the
darkness.

There were too many things he did not know.

The tiny pilot flame on Cardios's Incinerator flickered as a warm, damp wind flooded down the
tunnels. Dvorn's hammer was hefted as if he
expected an enemy to be standing just past the corner, waiting to be beheaded.

'Large space,' voxed Dvorn. 'We're in an elevated
position. Wait – movement.'

Alaric moved forward to crouch behind Dvorn. The
tunnel led onto a balcony formed from the biological curves of the chamber beyond, a large cavity that
looked like it had been eaten out of the iron. Scores
of sub-tunnels led off in every direction and from
one of these the figures Dvorn had spotted was
emerging.

Menials. Alaric knew that the Adeptus Mechanicus
included a massive underclass of menials, men and
women bonded to perform the thankless tasks the
Mechanicus required – labouring in the forges and
mines, serving the needs of the tech-priests, crewing
the Mechanicus's ships, even defending the forge
worlds. It was from the ranks of the menials that the
tech-guard were drawn and many tech-priests had
been recruited from the most able.

But the menials he saw for the first time on
Chaeroneia were different. Menials might be
effectively controlled by the Adeptus Mechanicus but
they were still ultimately free. Everything about these
creatures told Alaric they were slaves. Bent postures,
pallid skin covered in weeping sores, uniform

jumpsuits so filthy Alaric couldn't tell what colour they were. Heavy dark blue tattoos disfigured their faces, broad barcode designs that wiped out any semblance of individual personalities. They had glass vials of strange-coloured liquids carried in harnesses around their waists or shoulders, with tubes leading off to the veins in their throats and wrists. A few were armed with battered autoguns and lasguns but if they were supposed to fight at all, most looked like they did it with bare hands and teeth.

There must have been thirty menials driven out of the tunnel into the gallery. Behind them was a figure standing a clear head taller than any of them, wearing long robes stained black. Its head was a nightmare, with a long, grinning equine skull wrapped round with tendrils of dark meat. One of its arms ended in long segmented whips instead of fingers, soldered directly into the blue-grey skin of its hand. As it lashed the menials forward in front of it, it chattered out a stuttering noise of dots and dashes.

'Machine-code,' said Archmagos Saphentis, who was crouching just behind Alaric.

In response to the code, two massive lumbering shapes followed the tech-priest into the gallery. The torso were those of bloated muscle-bound humanoids, the legs huge pneumatic pistons. One of the beasts had twin heavy bolters in place of its arms, while the other had a circular saw blade and a pair of massive shears. They belched hot vapour and sprays of oil as if they were steam-powered – Alaric guessed they were combat-servitors. That would mean they were physically powerful but extremely limited in their responses. In an open conflict they were at a severe disadvantage, unable to improvise like a good soldier had to, but in the close confines of the tunnels they would make for extremely efficient killing devices.

'They're hunting us,' said Dvorn.

The horse-skulled creature, who seemed to be in control, directed its menials to spread out while the two servitors stomped forwards to flank it. It beckoned one menial towards it with its whip hand – the menial in question had knee joints that bent the wrong way so it could move on all fours like a dog and its nose and mouth were gone, replaced by a bunch of knife-like sensor-spines.

The dog-menial listened to a burst of machine-code speak and darted forward, head jerking as it tasted the air, crawling up the walls as it rushed around trying to pick up a scent.

Before Alaric could have his men withdraw the dog-menial stopped, head arrowed right towards where Alaric crouched overlooking the balcony.

'Fall back,' hissed Alaric. 'Everyone back!'

The leader screamed a stream of machine-code, high and piercing. Heavy bolter fire streaked up from the gun-servitor and the menials bayed like animals at the sudden din. Alaric could hear sound from all around as the spire's inhabitants were alerted to the intruders in their midst – scrabbling, crawling, slithering, bestial howling and more bursts of machine-code.

Alaric found Saphentis as the force moved back through the tunnels. 'Are they Mechanicus?'

'Not any more,' said Saphentis simply.

Gunfire flared up ahead. In the flashes of the las-blasts Alaric could see tech-guard swapping fire with pallid, scrabbling menials. Brother Haulvarn returned fire and storm bolter shells tore down the tunnel, blasting a menial against the wall as Lykkos blew another one apart with a psycannon shot. But there wasn't enough space for the rest of the Grey Knights to get to grips with the enemy.

A hideous grinding sound tore up from below Alaric's feet. He dived to one side as the floor of the tunnel erupted in a storm of flying iron shards and something immense chewed its way through – a circular head like the mouth of a voracious metallic worm, ringed with grinders that ripped out lumps of metal and forced them into the bladed steel spiral of its throat. It roared as Alaric just swung his trailing leg away from its maw and Alaric felt his psychic wards flaming beneath his armour, describing a white-hot spiral around his skin.

The more powerful ward, the one woven around his mind, filled his head with a red scream as something very powerful and very angry expressed its psychic rage.

Witchcraft. The reason they were here.

The worm reared and Alaric realised it was mechanical, steam belching from its segmented body, whirling guts of clockwork deep inside its churning form. Alaric fired a spray of storm bolter fire down its throat and the worm spasmed in pain, vomiting acidic gore and broken cogs.

'Move!' yelled Alaric as he fired again but the monster surged forwards. Alaric paused only to grab Tech-Priest Thalassa and haul her clear as he dived into a side tunnel. The worm roared past and Alaric saw how thick greying muscles wrapped around its body until its tail was a long lash of biological sinew, whipping behind it.

'Witchcraft,' said Alaric. 'That thing was made with sorcery.' He flicked on the vox-channel. 'Grey Knights! Fall back!'

Alaric darted out of the side tunnel and lunged with his Nemesis halberd, hacking off a good length of the worm's tail. Gore sprayed from the wound as it lashed in pain and the thing's scream was truly terrible, vibrating through the iron like an earthquake. The worm's body contorted and its pain spasms forced it off course, chewing its way up through the ceiling of the tunnel.

'We've got hostiles up ahead!' came Brother Archis's voice, crackling over the vox. 'Heavy resistance! They're bottling us in!'

'Then fight!' replied Alaric, hauling Thalassa after him as he headed towards the sound of gunfire. Thalassa's eyes were wide in horror and her breathing was shallow – she was in shock. Data expert or no, Saphentis should never have brought her.

Alaric saw, up ahead, the Grey Knights and tech-guard fighting against the menials trying to force their way in through the side tunnels. Saphentis was in the thick of the fighting, his more normal bionic hands dragging enemies out of the throng while his blade-tipped arms cut them apart. One menial dived out onto a tech-guard and the vials at his waist emptied themselves into his veins. The menial's muscles swelled massively, bone cracking where the muscles on his arms and back pulled his spine apart. The menial roared and ripped off the tech-guard's arm, then pistoned a fist into his face with enough force to leave a dent in the tunnel floor.

Interrogator Hawkespur took aim and snapped an autopistol shot through the menial's head. It didn't drop and she loosed off several more, the shots slicing its head apart until it toppled onto the dying body of the tech-guard.

The Grey Knights were holding the front of the tunnel, storm bolters and Nemesis weapons keeping the way forward choked with bodies. A chain of heavy fire strobed down the tunnel and the Grey Knights took cover, using the menial bodies as a barricade. A couple of shots thudded off Alaric's power armour.

Alaric could hear noise from all around. Heavy battle-servitors stomped towards them. Something cackled a stream of zeroes and ones. They were completely surrounded.

Justicar Tancred and his Terminator squad could have pooled their psychic power and called up the cleansing fire the Chapter's Chaplains called the Holocaust. They could have forced their way through with their massive terminator armour and Tancred's own sheer strength. But Tancred and his squad were dead, annihilated so completely Alaric hadn't even been able to recover their bodies from Volcanis Ultor. Alaric's squad was on its own here, surrounded and exposed.

The wall near Alaric was being chewed away by breacher drills, screeching and showering sparks into the tunnel. A battle-servitor the size of a tank was lumbering into view at the far end of the tunnel, storm bolter fire ricocheting off it as it blasted at the Grey Knights. They had nowhere to go and a dozen ways to die.

'To me!' yelled Alaric. His squad broke cover and headed for Alaric, leaving the tech-guard to deal with the rampaging servitors. They ducked the chains of fire and reached Alaric just as the wall gave way, chunks of crumbling iron collapsing in a drift of metal.

Menials, crudely combat-fitted with drills and saws, clambered through the gap. Alaric met the first with the butt of his halberd, shattering its ribs even as he blocked a huge circular saw with the halberd's blade. The first menial reared up again, its ribcage collapsed and oozing gore. Nothing human could have gone on fighting. A breacher drill bored up into the collar of his armour, forcing him back as the tip ground through the ceramite in a shower of sparks, aiming for his throat.

'Perdition!' yelled Brother Dvorn as he smacked the drill-armed menial across the tunnel with his Nemesis hammer. 'Blasphemy!'

They were blasphemous, too. Muscles and nerve bundles slid over the menials' metallic parts in a way that Alaric had never seen in Mechanicus bionics, as if there was something else inside the menials, something independent and alive. That was blasphemy if ever he had seen it. Alaric reached up and grabbed the armature on which the second menial's saw was mounted, pulling and twisting. Tendrils of flesh wrapped around his wrist but the arm came away, the menial screaming bestially. Warm, foul-smelling blood spattered over Alaric. He hacked down into its body with his halberd and it died.

Brother Haulvarn spitted two menials at once on his sword and Dvorn struck again, his hammer's head smashing right through one menial and embedding itself in the nearest wall. Dvorn didn't miss a beat, filling another menial with storm bolter fire as he ripped the hammer head out again. Alaric looked around to see where Thalassa had got to – she was on the floor curled up, with her hands over her head. It was surprising she was still alive.

'Archis!' yelled Alaric but he needn't have bothered – Brother Archis was already ramming the nozzle of his Incinerator through the hole, pulling the firing lever and drenching the space beyond with burning promethium.

Alaric glanced through the hole. The menials had fallen back in confusion – Alaric guessed they were so corrupt they could understand a simple order to kill anything beyond the wall and now they had done so they needed someone to direct them to do anything more. The space beyond looked like a heavy engineering plant, with enormous pistons pumping into an oil-belching engine block.

'Fall back to me!' yelled Alaric over the din of gunfire. 'Saphentis! Tharkk! Back to me!'

The tech-guard broke from their own firefights and hurried towards the Grey Knights, who covered them with a spray of rapid storm bolter fire. Alaric led the way through onto the factory floor. The air was heavy and hot with steam and the machinery that surrounded them was on a huge scale, with massive hinged sections clanking as the masses of engineering reconfigured themselves.

There didn't seem an obvious way out. As the tech-guard got through the hole and reorganised themselves to cover it, Alaric waved over Interrogator Hawkespur.

'It's a dead end,' he said. 'We won't have time to find another way out.'

'What do you suggest?'

'Fight here. Hope they run out of troops.'

'Agreed. If they're only menials we can take on several waves of them. More battle-servitors and our chances will not be high, though.'

Las-fire from somewhere above interrupted them, spattering against the filthy metal floor. The tech-guard scattered, Tharkk yelling at them to take cover and return fire. The Grey Knights fired back instinctively, spraying shots up into the darkness overhead, then followed the tech-guard. Several slabs of machinery rose to shoulder height, like the teeth of a tank trap and behind them was an imposing bank of machinery that belched hot, choking fumes.

'Save it!' shouted Alaric and the Grey Knights stopped firing, getting into cover and peering into the darkness. Their ocular augmentations would help them see the threat before anyone else. Archmagos Saphentis drifted serenely back towards them, too, seemingly unconcerned about getting shot. Alaric had not imagined Saphentis would be a fighting man but now he was covered in blood and his blade-tipped arms were clogged with gore.

A shape drifted down overhead. It was like the gun-platform that had ambushed them outside but this one was more ornate and large enough to carry three figures, two of them far larger and flanking the third. A glistening corona surrounded the platform. Alaric guessed it was an energy field, which meant that most bullets would probably bounce off it. Lykkos's psycannon would be their best bet but it would have to be a damn good shot. The field was probably being generated by the pulsing, brain-like mass on the platform's underside. The platform extruded several biological looking guns, which trained themselves on the chunks of machinery that hid the Grey Knights and tech-guard.

The two larger figures were battle-servitors, bristling with guns. The third was the horse-skulled creature Alaric had seen earlier, now connected to both the platform and the servitors by a web of vein-like filaments running from his back. More smaller platforms were drifting down beside it. Some were simple gun platforms, others held parties of menials or what looked like more regular troops, hooded and crouched, with guns hardwired into their forearms. Maybe a hundred troops and those were only the ones Alaric could see.

The leader raised its arms, palms up, elongated face pointed upwards. It brayed a long, atonal sound and the guns on the platforms dipped slightly.

'It's a tech-priest,' whispered Brother Haulvarn, crouching down at Alaric's side. 'It's one of them.'

If it was a tech-priest, it was corrupted down to the core. It emitted a stream of dots and dashes, more machine-code, apparently directed at the tech-guard.

Archmagos Saphentis peered out of cover and replied, reeling off his own stream of machine-code.

The two exchanged machine-code a couple more times. Then the enemy tech-priest brayed and the guns were again trained on Alaric's force. The platforms began to descend, the menials and troops making ready to jump down onto the factory floor and attack.

'Whatever you said,' growled Alaric at Saphentis, 'it didn't work.'

The first shots fell, glowing black bolts of energy as powerful as lascannon shots shearing through the metal. One tech-guard was blown clean in half and the others hit the floor, the cover disintegrating around them.

With a massive grinding sound, the bank of machinery behind them began to open up. Hinged plates of corroded iron the size of tanks were reconfiguring to reveal a black and forbidding space beyond.

'Hawkespur!' shouted Alaric. 'We can't take them!'

'We don't know where it leads!' she replied, taking aim at the lowest platform. She loosed off a shot and a menial fell, knocked off the platform by a perfect hit. More fire was falling against them, tearing deep gouges in the floor, sending superheated shrapnel through the air.

'Move or die!' replied Alaric. 'Grey Knights! Tharkk! Covering volley, then retreat!'

The lowest platform was already disgorging its troops. Crimson and black bolts of energy were raining down now, scoring molten red scars everywhere. Another tech-guard fell, blown open by chattering automatic fire as his fellow soldiers withdrew through the storm of fire.

Alaric ran through the opening, turning to make sure Hawkespur made it. Brother Dvorn grabbed Tech-priest Thalassa as he ran, carrying her with one hand while he fired all but blind over his shoulder with the other. The inside of the machinery was tight and infernally hot, lit by a ruddy glow from furnaces deep within the machine. The machinery ground around them and the opening shrunk, fire thudding around the entrance. Saphentis was the last in, his robes flapping around him as gunfire punched through the fabric.

'Where now?' asked Hawkespur.

'Anywhere,' said Alaric.

The floor was sinking below and slabs of machinery closing over them. Alaric imagined them being crushed as the machinery closed, the ceramite fracturing, his bones splintering, dying in the furnace at the heart of the black iron spire.

'Close in!' barked Captain Tharkk. 'Form up around the archmagos! Fix bayonets!'

Something rumbled far ahead, massive and closing fast. The ceiling opened up above them again, this time in a spiral that bored rapidly straight upwards and the sound got louder. The floor began to open too, and the dull red glow subsided leaving only blackness.

Alaric could just see the troops around him clinging to anything they could find as the space became a sheer shaft, heading straight down into the lower levels of the spire.

The glimmer he saw above was a rush of foaming fluid pouring down towards them. Alaric hadn't seen much of Chaeroneia but it was enough to tell him it probably wasn't just water.

The flood hit and Alaric held on, the weight of industrial waste dragging him down. He gritted his teeth and held on but the metal beneath his gauntlet was giving way. With a yell of defiance he fell, sluiced downwards. He was battered against the sides of the shaft and the armoured bodies of his fellow Grey Knights. He had no control any more and whether he lived or died now was down to where the flow went and whether he could break the surface before he drowned. Everything was noise and motion, deafening, blinding, one hand gripping the haft of his Nemesis halberd and the other reaching out for a handhold.

He found none. The blackness rushed up around him and he willed himself to survive as everything, outside and inside him, went black.

CHAPTER SEVEN

He that counselleth as does the Enemy, so shall he becometh that enemy, no matter that a friend he claimeth to be.

– 'On Heresy', Chapter MMIV,
Lord Inquisitor Karamazov

'Show me again.'

Horstgeld had not been in the tactical chancel for some time, ever since the *Tribunicia* had last been at war. Most of the intervening time the ship had run patrols or formed blockades and there had been no need for the complex holographic displays that could be projected into the centre of the circular room. The chancel was decorated with tasteful marble busts of past captains and Naval heroes and could hold several officers, but now it held just Rear Admiral Horstgeld and Chief Navigation Officer Stelkhanov.

Stelkanov pressed a sequence of control studs at the base of the central holomat and the grainy holo image appeared again – the equipment was old and should have been replaced decades ago.

'I grant it's not an excellent quality image,' said Stelkhanov, 'but it was enough to work with.' Stelkhanov's voice was slightly stilted thanks to the fact that he had been sleep-taught Imperial Gothic late in life, having been recruited from the engine-rooms where the press-ganged scum could barely speak Low Gothic at all.

Horstgeld watched the image roll by again. It was from a deep-space scan, picked up by the ship's sensoria in the ultra-orbital space beyond Chaeroneia. The swathe of space rippled, bulging and contracting in a dozen places, before flares of hazy energy indicated that something had broken through. Then, just as fleetingly, the images were gone.

'When was this picked up?' asked Horstgeld.

Stelkhanov consulted the dataslate he carried. The greenish glow of the holo picked out his refined, aquiline face – it was hard to believe the man had once been dragged out of the short-lived engine gangs. 'Seventy-nine minutes ago,' he said.

'And what do you think it is?'

'A fleet, captain. Newly arrived from the warp.'

'Quite an audacious conclusion, Stelkhanov. We haven't got any fellow hunters in this subsector, let alone this close into system space.'

'Then it is not Imperial.'

'Hmm.' Horstgeld stood back, running a hand unconsciously down his beard. 'Anything else?'

'It is substantial. And what little data we have suggests it is moving quite slowly, as would befit a large fleet remaining in formation. It is tempting, sir, to connect this with the anomalous signal detected by the *Ptolemy Gamma*.'

'I need more information before I decide, Stelkhanov. Have Navigation and the sensorium crew make this your second priority. First is still contacting Hawkespur and Alaric on the surface. We don't even know if they're alive.'

'Yes, sir. What preparations should the fleet make in case this is a hostile force?'

Horstgeld hadn't anticipated fighting a space battle here at all. Inquisitor Nyxos had been unable to acquire a fleet that was up to a major battle in any case. 'Reinforcements. Locate everything Imperial in space that's bigger than an orbital yacht and that can get to us within ninety-six hours. Prepare to send a fleet service order if we have to. If we're going to have a stand-off, then I want the numbers to do it. Understood?'

'Understood, sir. And Magos Korveylan?'

'She doesn't need to know just yet.'

'She?'

'Until I learn better, yes, 'she'. And make sure Commissar Leung knows, too, in case the *Exemplar* has seen the fleet already. I don't trust those freaks not to up and run at the first sign of getting their paintwork scratched.'

'Of course, sir.' Stelkhanov turned smartly and left the room.

Hortsgeld ran the image through again. Maybe ships, maybe some stellar phenomenon, maybe a shoal of rogue kraken or just yet another sensorium glitch. But if it was another fleet, it was definitely something he didn't need.

THE RAIN WAS toxic. It fell in thick, viscous globules, smacking down against the colossal wreckage and forming corrosive rivers of slime that wound through valleys formed by fallen spires. It stripped away dead flesh, so the enormous biological masses were reduced to forests of bleached ribs or banks of ragged gristle.

The rain probably wasn't rain at all but industrial and biological waste from above, maybe even the same flood that had poured down through the body of the black iron spire a couple of hours before. It fell down into a vast chasm, a wreckage-choked gap between the foundations of two spires, lit by sickly bioluminescence from algae colonies that clung to the pitted metal several storeys up. This was a place far, far below the city of spires, an undercity where anything that survived the fall did not live for very long. It was picked clean of life by time and corrosion, cold and dank and everywhere there was the chemical smell of death. The biomechanical masses that powered the city groaned and shifted far above and below there was the deep, sonorous sound of the rock beneath the city gradually giving way as it was compacted beneath the great weight of the iron spires.

Beneath a huge width of discarded engine cowling, there was shelter from the acid rain. The rain wouldn't have done anything more than strip some of the paint off the Grey Knights' armour, but Alaric knew that to the surviving tech-guard, Tech-priest Thalassa and Interrogator Hawkespur, it could have been lethal. So they had taken shelter here.

Somehow, they were still alive. The flood of waste had thrown them down through successive layers of the spire. The lower levels were industrial and Alaric had been sure, from the glimpses he caught of the massive machinery surrounding them, that they would be crushed or boiled at any moment. But sluice gates and purge valves had opened in front of them and they had kept going, finally being spat out into a large pool of festering waste a short distance away.

Chaeroneia hadn't wanted them dead, not yet, not like that. It wanted to make them suffer, first.

'Haulvarn, Archis, take watch,' said Alaric. The two Grey Knights saluted and went to take the first watch. The force couldn't stay there for long, but they needed a while to regroup and form a plan. They couldn't just blunder about hoping they would find something, otherwise they would be spotted and hunted down, and next time the planet wouldn't give them a stay of execution.

Hawkespur and the remaining tech-guard had started a small fire to keep themselves warm. There were only four of them left – Captain Tharkk and three tech-guard regulars. Their armour was battered and their fatigues were black with filth. As Alaric watched one of the tech-guard took his helmet off. His head was shaved and there were large, deep surgical scars in the back of his skull, where it looked like plate-sized sections had been removed and replaced. There was a barcode on the back of the man's neck.

Alaric walked over to where Archmagos Saphentis was sitting on a chunk of fallen wreckage, discussing something with Tech-priest Thalassa.

'Your tech-guard,' said Alaric. 'Emotional repressive surgery.'

Saphentis looked up at him. Alaric saw his face reflected a hundred times in the multi-faceted eyes. 'Quite right. I require it of the men performing retinue duties.'

'It would have been useful to know. Just like it would have been useful to know that your augmentations made you so combat-capable. And I would know what you said to that tech-priest.'

'He did not appreciate our presence,' replied Saphentis simply. 'I suggested he surrender to us and he did not accept it.'

Saphentis's artificial voice made it impossible for Alaric to tell if he was telling the truth or being sarcastic. 'I am in command here, archmagos,' said Alaric. 'Were you a Grey Knight you would do long months of penance for your reluctance to be led.'

'But I am not, justicar. And perhaps it would be better to discuss where we are and what we might do, rather than argue the point.'

'Do you know where we are?'

Tech-priest Thalassa, who had been viewing this exchange with some trepidation, showed Alaric the screen of her dataslate. 'The Mechanicus had detailed information on Chaeroneia before it was lost. The planet has changed much but from what little information we have it is most likely that we are here.' The screen of the dataslate showed a complex blueprint of a massive city, as dense as a hive on a heavily populated world, set among the blasted desert wastes that had covered much of Chaeroneia. The blueprint was labelled 'Primus Manufactorium Noctis'.

'Noctis was one of the largest forge cities on the planet,' continued Thalassa. Alaric noticed that her voice was wavering slightly, her eyes were ringed with red and her breathing was slightly ragged. It was easy to forget how frail normal humans were compared to a Space Marine like Alaric – she had ingested and inhaled enough pollutants to kill her given time. 'It was mostly dedicated to heavy manufacturing but it had some research and data facilities. Like this.'

The blueprint swung around and zoomed in on one structure, a large, smooth tower like a stack of massive cylinders, rising from the industrial tangle. 'The manufactorium's datafortress,' explained Thalassa. 'For the secure containment of information.'

'If it is still there,' said Saphentis, 'it could tell us what we need to know about where Chaeroneia has been and what has happened to it.'

'And you suggest we should go there?'

'No other course of action readily presents itself.'

'How far?'

'Not very far,' said Thalassa. 'Perhaps three days' march if there are no major obstacles. That is, if the datafortress is there at all and I am correct about our current location.'

'Could you make it?' asked Alaric.

Thalassa looked at the floor. 'I don't know.'

'Tech-priest Thalassa would be useful at the datafortress but not essential,' said Saphentis. 'I can perform similar functions.'

'I don't like it. There is too much about what lies ahead of us that we do not know. Nothing has killed more men on the battlefield than ignorance about what they are facing.'

'I do not see any other choice, justicar.'

'Neither do I. But I would be more prepared if I knew everything about the enemy here that you do. There is a reason you came down to this planet yourself. There are a great many tech-preists who are more capable in battle than you.'

'Thalassa,' said Saphentis, 'Tell Captain Tharkk we will move out shortly.' Thalassa nodded and hurried over to the fire where Tharkk and his men were tending their wounds. For the moment, Alaric and Saphentis were out of their earshot.

'Go on,' said Alaric.

'They were Mechanicus,' began Saphentis. 'After a fashion. They have changed. Some tech-heresy has taken root. The fusion of the biological and the mechanical is permitted by the Cult Mechanicus only so that weak flesh may be replaced or improved, or that the otherwise useless might be made useful in the sight of the Omnissiah, such as is the case with servitors. The large-scale biomechanics we see here are forbidden, for they do not place machine and flesh at the command of tech-priests but create new forms of life entirely and such is not permitted by the tenets of the Priesthood of Mars. Successive Fabricators General have pronounced on this countless times.'

'So the enemy are tech-heretics?' asked Alaric. 'The same that were investigated here a hundred years ago?'

'Without doubt. And the heresy must reach to every level of Chaeroneia's priesthood. More importantly, what we have seen on Chaeroneia represents a pace of innovation considered heretical. The Cult Mechanicus forbids designs and techniques not of the most ancient provenance. Many centuries must pass before quarantined knowledge is allowed beyond our research stations. But here there is innovation and creation. All around us! This world could never be created by the existing tenets of the Mechanicus. The pace of invention here must be astonishing.'

'You sound as if you admire them, archmagos.'

'That is not true, Justicar. Heresy is heresy, as you yourself must know well. I would thank you not to make such suggestions again.'

'An ally who agrees with the enemy becomes that enemy, archmagos. I will be watching you.'

Brother Haulvarn stomped over hurriedly. 'Archis can see gun-platforms, justicar. They're moving like they're looking for us.'

Alaric looked round at him. The strike force was still in poor cover and vulnerable and they didn't need a fight right now. 'How far?'

'Two kilometres. Five plus platforms, at least two troop carriers. Sweep formation. They're about five hundred metres up, too.'

'Then they'll be on us soon. We need to move out.'

'We would be better hidden if we kept to derelict sections of the city,' said Saphentis. 'This planet will have fewer eyes on us.'

'That at least I agree on,' said Alaric. 'I'll work out a route with Thalassa. Get your tech-guard ready to move in five minutes. And in case there is any confusion left, you are under my command. As long as we are on this planet, you follow my orders.'

'Understood, justicar.'

'You don't have to understand. You just have to do it.'

The tech-guard were soon up and armed, their emotional repressive surgery meaning that they would not be affected by the trauma of the fight they had just gone through. Hawkespur was looking closer to exhaustion than she would ever admit and Thalassa was still half-numb with shock, moving like a woman in a dream. But they weren't the ones Alaric was worried about. The Grey Knights had taught him a great deal and the Chapter believed that one day they could call him a leader – but one lesson he had not learned was how to deal with an enemy that was supposed to be under your own command.

Alaric glanced at the shadows stretching above and saw tiny points of light darting about, the grav-platforms Archis's keen eyes had spotted. Chaeroneia had a lot of ways to kill intruders and Alaric knew they would discover a few more before they reached Thalassa's datafortress. But they had to go there because the datafortress meant information and once Alaric understood what he was up against on this world then he could finally turn around and fight it.

ONCE, WHEN THE Imperium was young and the Emperor was still a living being walking among His subjects, there had been hope. But that had been a long time ago indeed.

That hope had existed in the form of the Emperor's own creations – the primarchs, perfect humans each representing a facet of the strength mankind would need to fulfil its manifest destiny of possessing the galaxy. They had been such astonishing beings that even on the eve of their creation, their genetic material was being used to create a generation of superhuman warriors – the Space Marines of the First Founding, twenty immense Legions of them, made in the image of the primarch on which they had been modelled.

The primarchs were scattered across the galaxy. In the Age of Imperium no one knew how or why this had happened – whether agents of Chaos had snatched them away from holy Terra, or whether the Emperor had sent them forth as infants to be strewn around the galaxy and there learn the qualities they could never acquire living in the Emperor's shadow.

The Emperor, at the head of the Space Marine Legions, conquered the galaxy, gradually retrieving the scattered primarchs, who had grown into mighty leaders on their adopted worlds. In the Great Crusade the primarchs were reunited with their Legions and led them in the greatest military campaign mankind had ever seen, conquering the segmenta of space that would eventually form the backbone of Imperial territory, from the Segmentum Solar to the outlying Halo Zone and Veiled Region.

And the greatest of these primarchs was Horus.

Horus was the primarch of the Luna Wolves, the Legion that represented the most complete military machine in the Imperium. Resolute, valiant and commanded by Horus with a brilliance that rivalled the Emperor Himself, the Legion was such a finely-honed force that it was said that Horus wielded it with the precision of a master swordsman. There was nothing they could not do. When the Emperor acknowledged Horus as the Imperium's greatest war-master the Luna Wolves became the Sons of Horus, their new designation reflecting the masterful command of their primarch.

But Horus was too brilliant. His star shone too brightly. As the Crusade reeled in more and more of the galaxy he came to see the arrogance and tyranny of the Emperor. The Emperor did not do what He did for mankind – He did it for Himself, to know that the human race lived and died under His dominion. Ultimate power had corrupted Him and no one, not even Horus the Magnificent, the Warmaster himself, could sway His belief that He was the master of mankind.

This was where the seeds of the Heresy were born. Horus, the greatest man who ever lived, came to surpass the Emperor and to understand as the Emperor never could that the true destiny of mankind lay beyond the stars, in the untamed, pure realm of the warp, where the only entities deserving of worship resided. They were the Chaos Gods, the beings who wished to see mankind elevated from corruptible, heavy flesh to pure, enlightened spirits. But the Emperor was filled with hate that Horus should pay fealty to anyone greater than the Emperor Himself. So Horus was forced to entreat the powers of the warp for aid and so became the first and greatest Champion of Chaos.

The Horus Heresy divided the galaxy. In a mere seven years of war Horus led a rebellion that reached Holy Terra and the walls of the Imperial Palace, marching with fully half of the Space Marine Legions whose primarchs he had convinced of the justice of their cause. The rest sided with the Emperor, cowed into obedience by their fear of the knowledge Horus promised to teach the galaxy.

Among the greatest of the Sons of Horus was Abaddon, Horus's right hand in battle, a force of destruction who blazed his way across the galaxy at the behest of his primarch, submitting his own life to the wishes of the Warmaster. Abaddon witnessed the final tragedy of the Heresy, when the Emperor and the Primarch Sanguinius ambushed Horus on his flagship. Horus slew them both but not before he was dealt a terrible wound by the Emperor's sword and with his last breath, entreated Abaddon to keep the Sons of Horus alive and not sacrifice them needlessly on the walls of Terra.

So Abaddon took the Legion and withdrew, masterfully evading the vengeful Legions of the Emperor and taking refuge among the daemon worlds of the Eye of Terror. With Horus dead, the surviving primarchs still loyal to the Emperor conspired to cheat the people of the Imperium into believing the Emperor was still alive, now a living god inhabiting his corpse.

The Sons of Horus renamed themselves the Black Legion in eternal mourning for the greatest man who had ever lived, the man who should have inherited the Imperium and led mankind to an era of enlightenment in the warp. Meanwhile, the Imperium sank beyond redemption, corrupt and worthless, its people slaving to uphold the worship of a traitor long dead, its institutions dedicated only to eradicating truth from the galaxy. There could be no redemption for it now.

Abaddon probed the defences of the Imperium. In twelve Black Crusades he found the gaps in the Imperium's armour through which the Black Legion and its allies could finally deliver the Imperium's deathblow. When the board was set and the pieces in place, Abaddon selected the finest of the Black Legion's heroes to lead their own armies in a grand, all-conquering campaign that would see the inheritors of the Imperium streaming from the Eye of Terror. The campaign would culminate in the destruction of Terra and the end of ten thousand years of resistance to Chaos.

Those chosen were the best of the best, leaders and warriors without peer, whose names would soon strike fear into anyone who had ever sworn fealty to the Corpse-Emperor. Among their number was Urkrathos, Chosen of Abaddon, Master of the *Hellforger*.

URKRATHOS STAMPED ONTO the bridge that led to the ritual chamber of the Grand Cruiser *Hellforger*. Above him was the chamber's ceiling like a distant black metal sky, hidden by clouds of sulphurous incense that rained a thin drizzle of black blood. Ghosts ran through the billowing clouds, spirits trapped by the sheer malice and power of the *Hellforger* and condemned to writhe around the ship's decks. Below was a churning sea of gore, swirling like a whirlpool, through which naked figures fought to reach the surface and were always dragged back down, punished for their insolence or failure with a permanent state of agony, always on the verge of drowning, never reaching the release of death. Their thin, pathetic screams wove together into a dark howling wind that blew across the bridge.

Suspended over the sea of sinners was a huge circular platform, with raised edges like the seats of an amphitheatre. This was the ritual ground, a place infused with unholy energy by the torment of those being punished below. It was covered in blood-stained sand into which complex designs had been drawn in dried blood and lengths of offal, the ritual carcasses discarded in a pile to one side. The sacrifices had been specially bred on a daemon world deep within the Eye of Terror, each one worth a lifetime's fealty to the Dark Gods. More incense billowed from burners made from the skulls of the *Hellforger's* less useful crewmen and more heads hung from spiked chains from the distant ceiling, weeping black rain onto the sacred ground.

'Feogrym!' called Urkrathos, reaching the ritual floor. Feogrym was a wizened, hunched figure sitting in the middle of the arena. He looked up as Urkrathos approached and slunk forward, crawling towards the *Hellforger's* captain. 'I need to know now. We have entered real space and it will not be long before we reach the world. Is it genuine?'

Feogrym scampered forwards on his hands, dragging his legs behind him until he was almost prostrate at Urkrathos's feet. 'Feogrym knows!' he spluttered. The sorcerer's face could have been mistaken for that of an extremely wrinkled, wizened old man from a distance. Up close it was clear it was actually a mass of tiny writhing tentacles that only formed human-like features out of a force of habit. 'Master, the Fell Gods speak, they speak... yes, they talk to Feogrym, tell him the truth, yes they do and old Feogrym can tell the truth from the lies...'

Urkrathos kicked Feogrym away from him, the boot of his power armour crunching through ribs Feogrym could heal easily enough. 'Don't try that nonsense with me, sorcerer,' he said impatiently. 'Abaddon warned me about you. You're no holy moron, you'd stab us all in the back the second you saw the chance. Take it from me you won't get that chance. Now, once again, sorcerer, is the signal real? I will not have this fleet wasting its time chasing echoes around the warp.'

Feogrym clambered to his feet and dusted the blood-caked sand off his tattered brown robes. 'Yes, the signs have been conclusive,' he said, rather more sanely. He looked nervously up at Urkrathos, who was twice the height of a normal man in his full terminator armour. 'Lord Tzeentch speaks with me.'

'His daemons speak with you, old man and for every truth a daemon tells nine lies. You had better be right.'

'Of course. Have I not witnesses?' Feogrym pointed to the far side of the room and Urkrathos saw, through the billowing incense, the hundreds of desiccated corpses sitting in ranks around the amphitheatre like an audience. Urkrathos wondered for a moment where Feogrym had got them all and then realised he couldn't have cared less as long as the sorcerer discharged his duties to the Warmaster as he had agreed.

'So. What do you know?

'Listen.'

Feogrym spoke a few words, dark sounds that didn't belong to any register a human was supposed to hear. Urkrathos scowled as he recognised the dark tongue used by worshippers of Tzeentch, the Change God. Feogrym was one of those degenerates who worshipped one Chaos god over all the others, not realising that they were all part of the same many-faceted force that men called Chaos.

The blood rose in flakes off the floor, the flakes liquefying and running together like floating pools of quicksilver. The pools quivered and hundreds of crude, shifting faces were hanging in the air, their mouths working dumbly.

'Bridge,' commanded Urkrathos through the ship's vox-net. The vox-net whispered back at him as it transmitted his voice to the bridge crew. 'Play back the signal.'

The signal burst in a barrage of sound from the sky, bellowing through the ship's vox-casters. The blood faces began gibbering wildly, flowing into one another in agitation.

'Focus!' snapped Feogrym. 'Truth from the lies! The Changer of Ways commands you!'

The volume of the signal dropped and Urkrathos could make out the individual sounds, dots and dashes like some primitive code, wrought into a complex rhythm which he could tell had old, old magic pulsing at its centre.

The faces murmured a low babble of sounds, until words began forming in their speech, the words that formed the true message hidden so deep in the signal that only Feogrym's black magic could get to it.

'By the Fell Gods and the destiny of warp,' they began, 'By the death of the False Emperor and the dying of the stars, we bring to you, Warmaster Abaddon, Beloved of Chaos, Despised of Man, this tribute. For now these last days are the final fires burning, the black flames that consume a galaxy, the storms of the warp that drown out life, the End Times and the dawn of a galaxy of Chaos. We swear fealty to the Gods of Chaos and their herald, Abaddon the Despoiler, with this tribute that it might strike fear into the followers of the Corpse-Emperor and that through it they may see the true face of death…'

'Enough,' said Urkrathos. Feogrym waved a hand and the voices screamed silently as they dissolved into gobbets of blood that flowed up into the incense clouds. 'This is genuine?'

'Daemon-wrought,' said Feogrym. 'Most ancient. Yes, it is real.'

'Abaddon suspected rightly, then. It is an offer of tribute. Does it tell us what they are offering?'

Feogrym spread his hands. His tentacles writhed and for a moment Urkrathos saw the pulpy, grey mass that made up the sorcerer's real face. 'Would that I knew, Lord Urkrathos. Perhaps the exact tribute is so great they wish for you to know of it for the first time through your own eyes, magnificent as you are.'

'I warned you, Feogrym. I am less easily flattered than your acolytes.'

'Of course. Nevertheless, if they are new to our cause they may wish to impress us with their offering by not revealing it until we are there.'

'I have been around for ten thousand years. It will take a great deal to impress me.'

'And is it your intention, Lord Urkrathos, to give them the chance?'

Urkrathos glared at the sorcerer. The ways of Tzeentch, Changer of Ways, were by definition impossible to divine. Warp only knew what went on in the creature's head. Urkrathos didn't care. As long as he could serve Abaddon and the greater reign of Chaos then he would accept whatever the gods threw in his way.

He would still kill Feogrym, though, when the time came. A chosen of Abaddon was not to be mocked with impunity.

'I will keep my own counsel on that matter, sorcerer,' he said.

'So you will, then?'

Urkrathos scowled. Even without the enhanced strength of his terminator armour he could have pulled the sorcerer apart like a bored child might pull apart a fly. But he also knew that Feogrym was the type of creature that would not die just because you killed him. He would have to find some other way of destroying the man when he had outlived his usefulness.

Urkrathos turned and stomped off the ritual floor, leaving the madman to his divinations. Perhaps he would strip the soul from the sorcerer's body and cast it down into the pool of torments below them, so he would serve to fuel the spells of whatever sorcerer was sent by Abaddon as a replacement. The gods would be pleased by that.

But for now, Urkrathos had what he had come for. The Black Legion's fleet at the Eye of Terror had picked up the signal and Urkrathos had confirmed it was real. Now all that remained was to reach the planet and collect whatever was due to the Warmaster and perhaps bring the signal's author into the war effort. The Imperium was resisting with the tenacity of a hive of insects and the Black Crusade needed all the bodies it could throw into the fire. Urkrathos would be greatly rewarded if he could bring new allies in on the side of the Fell Gods.

Urkrathos reached the far end of the bridge and the deck elevator at the end, a shuddering, stained cage of steel that reeled up and down the throat-like shaft to give Urkrathos access to all levels of his ship. For now he was heading to the command deck, where he would give orders for the last stage of the journey to Chaeroneia.

CHAPTER EIGHT

'Beware in all things, lest the path forwards be the same path leading to hell.'

    – Primarch Roboute Guilliman, Codex Astartes

ALARIC LED THE way with Archis at his side, the pilot light on the Grey Knight's Incinerator always lit, ready to douse anything they encountered with flame.

They were leading the strikeforce up a narrow, treacherous path formed from a huge serpentine skeleton. The skeleton was wrapped around a thin, endlessly tall spire of smooth black glass, its ribs forming the precarious steps of a spiral staircase.

Alaric glanced down. He couldn't see the floor of the city's underhive now, only a layer of pollutants trapped between the cold air below and the warmth pulsing off some mass of flesh living in the tower opposite. The snake's body was getting narrower towards the skull and Hawkespur and Thalassa were both roped to members of Alaric's squad. The Grey Knights might have been far larger and heavier but, paradoxically, their augmentations and training also made them far more dextrous.

'Entrance up above,' said Archis. 'See it?' The nozzle of his Incinerator was pointed at an opening just ahead, a large hole smashed in the black glass. The edges still looked sharp.

'We're going in,' said Alaric. 'Haulvarn, watch the rear. Everyone else follow us.'

They had been travelling along the hive floor for some time, always keeping in cover as best they could. Several times Alaric had been sure there were grav-platform patrols homing in on them, but each time the Mechanicus had lost the strikeforce in the wreckage and gloom. Apart from a few rogue menials and stray servitors they hadn't seen anything else alive down there, not even vermin – just bones and waste fallen down from above. But they couldn't stay down there forever since the datafortress itself, assuming it was still there, was several layers above the hive floor. They had to head up and hope there were enough connections between the spires to take them there. The black glass spire was the first one they had found that looked like it provided a reliable way upwards.

Inside, the spire was quiet and cold, evidently riddled with irregular tunnels, like flaws in its crystalline structure. The tech-guard and Grey Knights clambered in, the tech-guard having to take great care not to cut themselves through their fatigues on the edges of broken glass. Saphentis glided through the gap, climbing effortlessly with his additional bionic limbs, hauling Thalassa behind him with a spare hand.

'Tech-priest, are you alright?' asked Alaric.

'I am fully functional,' replied Saphentis.

'I meant you,' said Alaric, looking at Thalassa.

'I'll be fine,' she said, though she looked far from it. 'I just don't like heights.'

'A fall from more than six metres is potentially fatal,' said Saphentis. 'Assigning any higher risk to greater heights is irrational.'

'Do you know where we are now?' continued Alaric, ignoring Saphentis.

Thalassa consulted her dataslate. 'We've been going steadily for a day. We're about half of the way there horizontally, but we still need to get much higher.'

Brother Haulvarn was last in. Haulvarn had been with Alaric for a long time, since before the capture of renegade Inquisitor Valinov that had started Alaric on the road to confronting Ghargatuloth, and he was the most level-headed of Alaric's men. Just the kind of man you wanted watching your back. 'The way's clear,' he said, making a final sweep of the outside with his storm bolter raised.

'Good. Archis, stay up front. We don't know what's in here.'

Saphentis ran a bionic hand over the faceted black surface of a wall. 'This looks like data medium,'

'You mean there's information in it?' asked Alaric. The Adeptus Mechanicus often used crystalline substances to store large amounts of data but they never let on just how they achieved such an advanced trick.

'Perhaps. Corrupted and incomplete, of course. Thalassa?'

Thalassa put a hand against the smooth surface. Small, drill-tipped probes emerged from her palm and bored a little way into the crystal. Pulses of light ran across the circuitry embedded in her skin, outlining her face and hands in the gloom.

'We don't really have time for this,' said Hawkespur quietly. She had taken off the hood of her voidsuit and Alaric saw there was a smudge of pollution around her nose and mouth.

'I know. But this mission is all about information. The more we have the better our chances.'

Thalassa gasped. She pulled her hand sharply away and breathed quickly for a few moments. 'There's hardly anything left,' she said. 'The damage is extensive. I could only find a few basics before the local data net collapsed.'

'Nothing that can help us?' asked Hawkespur.

'Well... there's the date.'

'And?'

'It doesn't make any sense. The corruption must be even worse than it looks. Even the datelines on the data are off. As far as this planet is concerned we're somewhere at the end of the forty-second millennium, that's more than nine hundred years out.'

'Let us hope the datafortress is more intact,' said Saphentis.

'And let's keep moving,' added Hawkespur.

The strikeforce moved upwards, through the flaws that spiralled up through the black glass. Here and there they found great silver probes drilled deep into the glass, like massive versions of Thalassa's own dataprobes. In other places crude faces had been hacked out of the crystal, faces with one eye or two mouths, or bestial features that blended with the fractured structure of the glass.

They clambered upwards for more than an hour, Thalassa always lagging behind, until eventually the flaw opened up into a massive glass-walled chamber, its walls sculpted into sweeping curves like crashing waves.

Alaric was first out with Archis. The chamber was the size of an aircraft hangar and pale blueish light shone from the walls, glinting off every curved edge so the room seemed like an arching skeleton of light.

Rows and rows of spindly machinery filled the floor, ancient and deactivated, their joints and moving parts sealed shut by a chalky patina of corrosion.

'Grey Knights, get up here and sweep. There's nothing moving but there are plenty of places to hide.'

Saphentis followed the Grey Knights out. He took in the sight with his faceted eyes, pausing to drink it in – the machines were spindly and elegant, a world away from the massive machinery more typical of the Adeptus Mechanicus. He knelt down by the closest machine. His insectoid eyes changed colour, thin lines of red light playing across the workings as Saphentis scanned their every detail.

'Fascinating,' he said to himself.

'Really?' said Alaric as he directed his Grey Knights to check the floor for hostiles. 'Enlighten us.'

'This appears to be an autosurgeon. Very sophisticated. But its function is unlike any I have seen before. It seems designed to only dissect, not to knit back together again.'

'Throne of Earth,' whispered Alaric, 'what were they doing here?'

Saphentis moved over to another machine, one with a large cylindrical tank of clouded glass and several armatures poised to reach into it. 'Here… here the parts were placed.' A probe extended from one bionic finger and emitted several rapid flashes of light. 'Yes. Yes, traces of biological matter. Here they were placed and broken down.' The next machine in line had a long conveyor belt that ran maybe a third the length of the room, passing through dozens of rings on which were mounted hundreds of tiny articulated arms. 'And then, the rendered substance was taken along here and woven together… into long strands… muscles, yes, that's it, ropes of muscle.' Saphentis straightened up and looked right at Alaric. 'Do you see? They took their unwanted menials and fed them in and they were rendered down and their proteins woven back into raw muscle. The living things they fuse with their machinery, this is where they began making them.'

'Just another tech-heresy,' said Alaric bitterly. 'It doesn't sound like anything to get excited about.'

'I forget, justicar, you are not one of us. To a tech-priest, this alone is a revelation. Do you not see? This world is self-sufficient! It makes perfect sense to me now. This is just one sign. How could a world live a century alone and yet build so much? How could they create what they have here, without raw materials from any other world? Chaeroneia had great mineral wealth but there is not one forge world in the Imperium that could survive in isolation – raw materials, manpower, food, it all had to be imported by the shipful. But not here. Here they took the one resource they had in abundance and made their whole city out of it.

'Their menials, justicar! Humans! It is so perfect. Humans breed, they grow, all of their own accord. They bred a surplus and took those they did not need, fed them in here and created the living things they fuse with their machines. There are magi pecuniae who have spent generations seeking a way to make a world entirely self-sufficient. Here, they solved that problem in a mere century. Amazing.'

Alaric rounded on Saphentis. 'Archmagos, you seem to admire this world more than you hate it. That is a very, very dangerous thing to suggest to me.'

Saphentis held out his arms, presumably in an attempt to look apologetic. 'This is pure heresy, justicar. Of course I realise that and I should not have to point it out to you. But the fact remains that their ways have suggested solutions to problems that have plagued the Mechanicus for thousands of years. The Omnissiah despises the man who has knowledge placed before him and yet refuses to understand it.'

'Well, the god I worship hates a man who lets himself be seduced by the ways of the Enemy. In any other situation I would have you arrested as a heretic, archmagos, and you could explain your admiration of this world to the Inquisition. And when we get off this world I will do just that. But if you do anything more to suggest you find Chaeroneia worthy of any kind of respect, I will have Hawkespur officiate at your execution here and now.'

A few strange colours flickered over the facets of Saphentis's eyes, too quick for Alaric to follow. 'Of course, justicar,' he said after a pause. 'My apologies. I forget how zealous a servant of the Emperor you really are. I will submit to the will of the Inquisition, as must we all.'

'Floor's clear,' voxed Brother Haulvarn.

Justicar glared at Saphentis, willing the archmagos to show some flicker of emotion. But Saphentis was completely inscrutable. 'Good,' he voxed. 'Let the tech-guard have a few minutes' rest. Then we're getting out of here.'

'Understood.'

Saphentis stalked away to continue examining the machinery. Alaric watched as Captain Tharkk's tech-guard sat down in a perfect circle on the floor, their heads bowed, letting a few minutes of rest chase away some of the fatigue. Their emotional repression surgery meant they wouldn't complain or despair, but they were still susceptible to exhaustion like any unaugmented human.

'You don't trust him,' said Hawkespur. She had sat down on the rusted-up conveyor belt next to Alaric.

'Do you?'

'An interrogator of the Ordo Malleus doesn't trust anybody, justicar.'

'I don't think Saphentis was sent down here just to find out what happened to this world,' continued Alaric. 'This is a forge world. There must be plenty of things here the Mechanicus would dearly want to get back. He's looking for something down here, something important enough to risk an archmagos for. Maybe it's even something to do with the tech-heresy that's taken hold here, he certainly seems interested enough in that.'

'Perhaps,' said Hawkespur, 'but Saphentis could still be useful. He could get us the information we're looking for, he knows the datasystems on this planet better than you or I. And your squad is the best chance he has of surviving down here. He's a tech-priest, justicar and they are logical people. He knows full well he can't cross you.'

Alaric peered across the room, to where Saphentis was calling Thalassa over to help him examine a complex piece of machinery. 'I could need Nyxos's authority to back me up if it comes to that. Down here that authority resides in you.'

'Of course. Saphentis will have to listen to reason in the end.' Hawkespur hacked out a rasping cough and held her throat again.

'You're ill,' said Alaric.

'Tumors,' replied Hawkespur. 'The air here is poison. Nyxos's medical staff will deal with it once we're off-planet. I'm more concerned about our immediate situation. Such as the date.'

'The date? Thalassa said that was just corrupt information.'

'Chaeroneia's systems seem to think the date is nine hundred years hence, correct? Well, that might not be an error. Time flows differently in the warp, justicar, and I think we both know where this planet must have been for the past century. But while it was a century from our point of view, in the warp a thousand years could have passed.'

'A thousand? Terra preserve us.'

'It would explain the comprehensive rebuilding that seems to have occurred. The corruption of the menial workforce. The pervasive nature of the tech-heresy.'

Alaric shook his head. 'A thousand years in the warp. No wonder this planet is sick. But it also begs the question, doesn't it? If the planet really is self-sufficient enough to survive for a thousand years completely cut off in the warp, then why return to real space now? Why return at all?'

'That's question number one,' said Hawkespur. 'Number two is, what pulled it into the warp in the first place?'

THE FORCE LEAVING the old flesh weaving spire was small. It made sense – only a tiny craft could have slipped past the asteroid field. The force consisted of six humans, one heavily augmented human (evidently a tech-priest, one of the unenlightened) and a squad of six Space Marines of the Adeptus Astartes. The livery on the Marines was unusual, with simple gunmetal grey as the Chapter colour and the twin symbols of a book pierced by a sword and the stylised 'I' of the Inquisition. There were no records of the Chapter in the historical files that remained from Chaeroneia's past as an outpost of the Imperium, but then many Chapters could come and go in a thousand years.

The cogitator-beasts that lived in the command spire of Manufactorium Noctis had lost the intruders soon after they arrived. The beasts, their brains massively swollen globes of pulsing fluid shimmering with cogitator circuits and calculator valves, had padded impatiently around their cells, scratching with metal claws at the walls in frustration. Then the intruders had been spotted again by one of the many flying biomechanical creatures that circled the city's upper spires. They roared in excitement, bounding around their cells in the pitch-black, bile-streaked menagerie floors of the command spire. Their brains, half-grown and half-built in the newer fleshweaving complexes elsewhere in the city, filtered the information into individual useful facts and assembled them into conclusions that they relayed in machine-code up to the very top of the command spire.

The cogitator-beasts had concluded the intruders were from the Adeptus Mechanicus with Astartes support, probably come to investigate Chaeroneia's re-entry into the physical universe. That meant the Imperium still existed, along with the old Adeptus Mechanicus whose beliefs would soon be replaced with the true revelations of the Omnissiah. For this information the cogitator-beasts were rewarded with gobbets of thick nutrient paste rendered from non-essential menials and piped into their cells where it was hungrily lapped from the filth-stained floor.

Far above in the isolated priests' chambers of the command spire, Archmagos Veneratus Scraecos reviewed this information. His thought processes had long ceased to resemble anything human and the cognitive functions of any human were insufficient to comprehend the revelations of the Omnissiah as revealed to Chaeroneia's tech-clergy a thousand years before. Streams of machine-code flowed through his mind, the images of the intruding enemies, their location relative to the other structures of Manufactorium Noctis, the many tech-priests, menial forces and combat-able servitors stationed nearby.

'We have regained contact with the intruders,' said the being called Scraecos, his words turned into packets of machine-code pulsed through the nerve endings that spun a data-network all over the command spire.

'Good,' came the reply, summarised from the thought impulses of the hundreds of tech-priests who resided in the spire. 'You, Scraecos, are responsible for the resolution of this event and are granted permission by the holy revelations of the Machine-God to assume individuality of consciousness for the duration of your task.'

'Praise be to the Omnissiah, I become one at His request,' replied Scraecos.

Suddenly the nerve endings around him were numbed into inaction by the will of the resident tech-priests and Scraecos was an individual creature again. His senses no longer comprehended the whole command spire, only the small womb-like cell where he lay, bathed in amniotic fluid in a large fleshy sac wound round with neuro-circuitry. The film of skin over his bionic eyes lifted and his vision swam back, showing him a world well beyond the visible spectrum. He felt his body now, too and it was heavy and crude around his mind. He flexed his mechadendrites and eased himself out of the fluid onto the slick, spongy floor.

He was no longer connected. He had to communicate with the other tech-priests by more mundane means. 'I have assumed individuality,' he said out loud, the nerve-endings in the walls absorbing the sound waves and turning them into data. His vox-unit was uncomfortable and unfamiliar. Memories – if they could be likened to something as human as memories – were coming back to him, the centuries in service to the Imperium, the dawn of his enlightenment when the Omnissiah's avatar had first been uncovered and the years of rebuilding in the warp as Chaeroneia was transformed into the Omnissiah's perfect vision.

'It is good,' came the reply. 'You possess the experience required to do the Machine-God's will. State your immediate intentions.'

'The standing declarations of the Omnissiah are clear,' said Scraecos. 'As given to me personally by the Castigator, there is one course of action compatible with the holiness of the planet's ground and the principles of the Adeptus.'

'State this course.'

'Kill them all.'

Scraecos let the weight of his physical form fall back onto him completely. He had been formidable in physical combat a long time ago and his body was still in efficient and uncorroded condition, which meant he was still a capable killer. He remembered the feeling of blood spattering on his few remaining areas of biological flesh, its warmth, its smell and felt a flicker of human emotions like bloodlust and exultation. Eventually, such crudeness would be gone from Scraecos and he would be a perfect being of logic in the sight of the Omnissiah.

Yes, Scraecos could kill. But there were far more effective murderers on Chaeroneia. Scraecos's first task, then, would be to summon those killers from the furthest corners of Chaeroneia's dataconstructs and give them the scent of their prey.

CHAPTER NINE

'Know the enemy not and the battle cannot be won. Know the enemy too much and the battle will be doubly lost.'

– Lord Admiral Ravensburg,
'Naval Maxims Vol. IX'

'ORDNANCE READY,' SAID the chief ordnance officer as Rear Admiral Horstgeld strode onto the bridge. 'We can fire at fifteen minutes' notice.'

'Excellent,' said Horstgeld. The bridge was buzzing. The *Tribunicia* had not fired a shot in anger for some time and Horstgeld had almost forgotten how it felt when danger was near. Now only the Emperor's guns and the Emperor's torpedoes stood between the good of the Imperium and the depredations of the Enemy.

It was a good feeling. It was why Horstgeld had been put in this galaxy.

'Preacher!' shouted Horstgeld heartily. 'What does the Emperor demand of us?'

'Obedience and zeal!' came the response from the raw throat of the confessor up on the pulpit. 'Defiance unto death!'

If the command crew disliked Horstgeld's habit of having the Confessor spouting prayers, they didn't show it. Navigation were assembling the rag-tag fleet into a battle line. Communications was relaying orders back and forth between the other ships under Horstgeld's command. Engineering was keeping the plasma reactors at full close orbit manoeuvring capacity and Ordnance was shepherding the ship's stock of torpedoes into the firing bays. The *Tribunicia* was old but she was tough, she had seen battle before and she was relishing it again.

But then, most of the crew hadn't seen what Horstgeld had seen – the full size of the approaching fleet.

Horstgeld paused briefly to kneel before the image of the Emperor that crowned the viewscreen. The screen was now showing a map of Chaeroneia's orbit, with the positions of the Imperial fleet and the complex maze of asteroids below. The Emperor's golden mask glowered down over the bridge as if admonishing the crew to work harder in His name – which of course He was, watching over them from the Golden Throne on Terra.

'Grant us the strength to forsake our weaknesses,' said Horstgeld. 'Our Emperor, preserve us.'

'Captain?' Stelkhanov stood over Horstgeld's shoulder. 'Ship's archive may have found a match.'

'So soon? I thought we'd have to ask Segmentum Command at Kar Duniash.'

'The archives found something in Ravensburg's histories of the Gothic War. The largest ship in the approaching fleet matches various energy signatures logged by the *Ius Bellum* at the Battle of Gethsemane.' Stelkhanov handed Horstgeld a sheet of complicated sensorium readings. 'The chances of a false match are very low.'

'Throne deliver us,' said Horstgeld. 'It's the *Hellforger*.'

'Sir?'

'Comms! Get me Fleet Commissar Leung. And put our reinforcements on screen.'

The viewscreen shifted to show the details and schematics of the ships that had answered Horstgeld's call to join the fleet at Chaeroneia.

'What in the hells is this?' he demanded, rounding on the Communications section. Several officers occupied the pews of the section, relaying streams of vox-commands and scanning ship-to-ship channels. 'I asked for warships! Subsector Command was supposed to send us everything they had!'

'These are all that were available,' replied Chief Communications Officer Kelmawr, a squat and powerful woman who had earned her stripes in boarding actions during the Rhanna crisis.

Horstgeld turned back to the screen. 'The *Pieta*... that's... that's a pilgrim ship for the love of Earth. It's barely even armed. And the *Epicurus* is a bloody yacht!'

'It's refitted,' said Kelmawr. 'The Administratum confiscated it and turned it into an armed merchantman...'

'Contact Kar Duniash. Tell them we have a crisis here. If Segmentum Command there can't help us then we're on our own.'

Horstgeld sat down on his command pew, shaking his head. It wasn't enough. They might have been able to hold off a grand cruiser, since that's what the *Hellforger* was. But not a whole fleet. Especially since the *Hellforger* had last been seen during the Gothic War in the service of the Chaos lord, Abaddon.

Chaos. The Enemy. Horstgeld couldn't tell the crew but the very soul of corruption was represented by ships like the *Hellforger*. Chaeroneia itself wasn't the only moral threat any more.

'Not good news then, Rear Admiral?'

In all the hubbub, Horstgeld hadn't even noticed Inquisitor Nyxos sitting quietly on the pew, almost hidden under the hood of his robes.

'The fleet is in the service of Chaos,' said Horstgeld. 'The flagship is the *Hellforger*. At Gethsemane it launched a boarding raid that killed…'

'I have read my Ravensburg, Horstgeld. They teach us rather more history in the Inquisition than I suspect they do in the Navy.'

'And we do not have enough ships to hold them off.'

'You are ready to abandon Chaeroneia?'

Horstgeld looked into the old man's eyes. He didn't like what he saw. He didn't believe the most outlandish stories they told of inquisitors – burning good Imperial servants at the stake, destroying whole planets – but he did know that an inquisitor's authority stood above all others and they did not take kindly to those who gave up in the face of the Emperor's enemies. 'Of course not,' he said. 'But there is little we can do.'

'You may not have to do all that much. Have you regained communications with Alaric and Hawkespur?'

Horstgeld shook his head. 'Comms are working on it but there is too much interference. At the best of times the pollution in the atmosphere is so thick it would be difficult to get any signal down. With the asteroid field it's all but impossible.'

'What about the *Exemplar*?'

'Magos Korveylan hasn't had any luck.'

'Hasn't she? I thought the Adeptus Mechanicus didn't believe in luck. I understand Commissar Leung is on the *Exemplar*?'

'He is.'

'Good. I am sure the combined efforts of Leung and myself will convince Korveylan to place contacting Alaric rather higher on their list of priorities. Can you live without me for a few hours?'

'Yes. But I might need your authority getting further reinforcements from Segmentum Command.'

'I will see what I can do on that account, but you must understand that my priority here is discovering what became of Chaeroneia. If we can get that information then you may not have to make a stand here at all.'

Horstgeld smiled bitterly. 'That won't happen, inquisitor. There's something on Chaeroneia the Enemy needs and they're going to go through us to get it. You're not going to just let them walk onto that planet.'

Nyxos stood up and smoothed down his robes. 'Quite right, of course. But I have my priorities. I shall require a fast shuttle and a couple of armsmen in case Korveylan proves recalcitrant.'

'Of course. And inquisitor... we can slow the enemy down. Perhaps force them out of formation and delay a landing, but not much more than that. I believe you represent the will of the Emperor and I will sacrifice this fleet if you feel it is necessary, but there is a limit to how much time we can buy for those men on the surface.'

'Unless I tell you otherwise, the Emperor requires you to reach that limit. There is nothing I will not do to seek out the foes of the Emperor and I will accept nothing less than the same from those under my authority. Now, if you please, my shuttle.'

Horstgeld stood and saluted – if this was the last time he would speak with Nyxos face-to-face, he wanted it to look formal. 'It will be ready by the time you get to the flight deck. Wish us all luck, inquisitor.'

'The Inquisition doesn't believe in luck either, Horstgeld. The Emperor protects.'

With that Nyxos swept off, looking imperious now rather than the hunched old man he normally appeared. Horstgeld knew then that Magos Korveylan would be on the same side as the rest of the fleet, whether she wanted it or not. That, at least, meant the Enemy would have to work a little harder to break through the fleet and reach Chaeroneia.

THERE WERE HUGE gliding things, like hollow-boned manta rays the size of fighter craft, that floated on industrial thermals in the lower reaches of the pollutant layer. Metallic snakes like animated cables, slithering through rainbow-sheened pools of caustic oil. Plumes of fungus made of living rust. Tiny bright insects made of metal, like intricate clockwork toys, scuttling like cockroaches looking for nuggets of iron to eat. Chaeroneia had once been typical of a forge world, with barely any indigenous flora or fauna able to survive the constant pollution – but the planet's thousand-year corruption had given rise to a unique biomechanical ecosystem where half-machine creatures flourished like living vermin.

Thalassa steered the strike force around the most obviously populated areas of the city. A dozen cities had been built on top of the original manufactorium and each one had seen areas fall into dereliction while others had prospered. The force moved through caverns formed from the fossilised remains of biomechanical factory-creatures, through twisting caves formed from their skulls and waist-deep seas of rancid coolant fluid that drizzled from some power plant far overhead. Aside from feral menials and wandering servitors they avoided the city's population successfully, though Alaric could feel a hundred artificial eyes on him and he knew that someone in the city knew exactly where they were. Gun platform patrols had been everywhere and Alaric had let his Marine's training take over his every movement, seeking out the best cover at every turn. His instinct had begun to rub off on the other troops, with even Archmagos Saphentis starting to move like a soldier.

And they had seen such things. Spires of glass. A slumbering monster with shiny grey skin that sweated a river of black blood. A creature like a corpulent tank-sized spider that writhed its way between the towers, exuding a stream of thick sticky strands which solidified into hardened bridges. Chaeroneia was becoming an exhausting parade of dark wonders, every turn bringing something new and terrible.

The journey had been arduous. Tharkk had called for more regular rest breaks to keep his tech-guard from collapsing from exhaustion and Tech-priest Thalassa had to be carried across the rougher ground. Something in Interrogator Hawkespur's metabolism had reacted badly to the pollutants, and tumours were breaking out in her throat and lungs so her breathing got more and more laboured and she had to stop to cough up lungfuls of foam. The Grey Knights were competent at battlefield first aid and Saphentis could have been an able surgeon, but Hawkespur was beyond help. Without a fully-functional medical suite, she would die within a week. Hawekspur herself hadn't commented on this at all – she was the finest naval stock, brilliant and brave enough to serve as interrogator to an inquisitor of the Ordo Malleus, and she didn't let anything as trivial as her own death get in the way of her duty.

'We should nearly be there,' said Hawkespur at the end of the third day. They were walking on the floor of a chasm between two multi-storey factory complexes, rearing up like tarnished steel skeletons. 'We should rest. The fortress will probably be guarded and we don't want the tech-guard going in exhausted.'

'You're not doing so well yourself,' said Alaric. Though the hood of Hawkespur's voidsuit was up he could see her reddened eyes through the visor.

'I could do with a rest, too,' she said grudgingly.

'You're no good to us dead, interrogator. I heard you were the best shot on Hydraphur.'

'Just a third-round winner, justicar.'

'Good enough.' Alaric looked around their immediate surroundings – the lower floors of the closer factory complex looked deserted and they would cover them from observers overhead. It was a good place to hole up before making the final slog down the datacore valley that led to the fortress. 'My Marines just need an hour of half-sleep. We'll take the watch, tell Tharkk to have his tech-guard rest. Thalassa, too.'

Hawkespur looked around. 'Where is Thalassa?'

Alaric followed her gaze. He could see the Marines of his squad, spread out through the formation with Lykkos taking up the rear. Tharkk and his remaining tech-guard were in the middle with Archmagos Saphentis. But not Thalassa.

The chasm floor was littered with debris and trash. There was plenty of room for Thalassa to be hidden if she had fallen. 'Damnation,' said Justicar. 'We need her.' He switched to the vox. 'Grey Knights, I need a visual on Tech-Priest Thalassa.'

The acknowledgement runes flickered back negative. 'I helped her over the broken ground two kilometres back,' replied Brother Cardios. 'I haven't seen her since.'

'Captain Tharkk!' called Alaric.

The tech-guard officer jogged up to Alaric. 'Justicar?'

'Was Thalassa with you?'

'No, justicar. No orders were given to assist her.'

'We can't spend time looking for her,' said Hawke-spur.

'I know,' said Alaric. 'Tharkk, get your men into the cover of the factory. Hawkespur, go with them. Get some rest. Grey Knights, search by sections, half a kilometre range, then pull back and take the watch. I'll stay here.' He turned to where Archmagos Saphentis was sitting unruffled on a fallen slab of rusting machinery. 'Archmagos, you were responsible for Thalassa.'

'She was subordinate to me. I was not required to watch her. There was a difference.'

'Was? You sound like she's already dead.'

'And you believe she isn't?'

Alaric turned away from the archmagos and stomped into the shadow of the factory complex. Saphentis was probably right, that was the worst of it. Since the moment they had crash-landed he had known Chaeroneia would have ways of killing them without them even knowing, But they couldn't afford to lose Thalassa – Saphentis could perform some of the same functions but he wasn't a data-specialist like her.

Saphentis had been responsible for Thalassa and that was what worried Alaric the most. Thalassa had been horrified at Chaeroneia, as any right-thinking human would be, but Saphentis had not shown such revulsion. He seemed to be impressed by the way the planet had reinvented the Mechanicus creed. If Thalassa had suspected Saphentis wasn't on the planet for the benefit of the Imperium, but to fulfil some other agenda, would Saphentis have had any compunction about killing her? Probably not. The higher the rank, the less human the tech-priest and Saphentis was both high-ranking and soulless.

Alaric watched Saphentis idly pick up a chunk of rusted wreckage and incinerate it in a crucible formed from the palm of one bionic hand, watching the smouldering nugget giving way to a wisp of black smoke. The strikeforce now needed Saphentis more than ever, so Alaric couldn't just storm in accusing Saphentis of being a murderer and a traitor – Saphentis would just flee into the black heart of the city and the Grey Knights probably wouldn't be able to find him. Alaric wasn't even sure if he could take Saphentis in straight combat if it came to that, since Saphentis's combat augmentations were formidable and Alaric didn't know the full extent of what he could do.

And Saphentis knew it all, too. He knew full well Alaric couldn't do without him. If Alaric's worst suspicions were correct then Saphentis was just using the Grey Knights and tech-guard as a bodyguard while he searched for some tainted prize on Chaeroneia, and the wrench of it was that Alaric couldn't do anything but go along with Saphentis and hope he had the wits to know when Saphentis was about to betray them. This was what Alaric hated more than anything else – the politicking, the petty betrayals that seemed to seethe through everything the Inquisition ever did. There was a time when he had thought organisations like the Mechanicus and the Inquisition stood together in the service of the Emperor, but every day that went by seemed to show him some new way for humanity to fight itself instead of focusing on the Enemy.

At least the Grey Knights themselves stood apart. They were one, devoted, pure of purpose. That was the quality that would see them through this, traitors in their midst be damned.

'Haulvarn here,' came a vox from the squad. 'Nothing here. I'll bring the squad in on a final sweep.'

'Understood. I'll take first watch, make sure each of you gets some half-sleep. We're now a body short and the next stage will be harder.'

In Chaeroneia's gritty twilight, Alaric watched the bulky armoured silhouettes of his Marines as they moved back along the chasm floor. The Grey Knights were some of the best warriors and yet they were at the mercy of this planet, isolated, ignorant and alone. It gave Alaric a glimmer of solace that they had been in just the same position fighting Ghargatuloth and yet they had never once taken a backward step in doing their duty. Even if Chaeroneia killed them, it would have to work hard before they fell.

But the end was surely coming, even if the Grey Knights could hold it off a little while. Thalassa was dead, there was little doubt. She had fallen down one of the many sheer drops or been carried off by some swift predator. And if it was the Enemy's greatest weapon to sow confusion and violence in the Emperor's own ranks, then the Enemy was succeeding.

IMMERSED IN THE quicksilver slime of the datapool, the creature that had once been Archmagos Veneratus Scraecos felt again the pathetic weakness of his remaining fleshy parts. It was cold and painful in there, the liquid metal crushing against him, the weaving filaments cutting into the patches of skin that remained between his augmentations and attachments. Scraecos had long, long ago left behind useless human fears like claustrophobia or the terror of drowning, so the datapool held no dread for him. But it was still shocking to be shown how far he had to go before he was completely at one with the Machine-God.

It was only the deeper, more human part of him that felt shock, of course. That part was gradually being buried by the rest of Scraecos – the haughty, pure logic that knew the Omnissiah's plan made no allowances for concerns like fear or suffering.

The mechadendrites extending from Scraecos's face reached out into the medium of the datapool, gathering bunches of the floating filaments. Dataprobes extended from the heads of the mechadendrites and the information contained in the pool flowed into him. Scraecos saw the structure of Manufactorium Noctis blooming in the logic architecture of his mind, spires and foundations riddled with chambers and tunnels, webs of walkways stretching between the towers. Warm, enormous biomechanoids clinging to the underside of the city, flooding the city with their bioelectric energy and the products harvested from their bodies. He saw the works where menials were bred and birthed and where they were brought back again into the city to form the raw materials for more biomechanical architecture.

Part of Scraecos glowed in admiration at what they had wrought over the last millennium. But that, of course, was only a tiny and insignificant emotion in the sea of logic. The rest of Scraecos simply absorbed it, discarded what he did not need to know and zoomed in on the rest.

The hunter-programs despatched by Scraecos had been exacting. They had demanded even more of the surplus menial stock than normal. Now there would be thousands more biological assets herded into the hunters' hidden places and given over to the hunters' strange ways. Self-aware data constructs, the hunters were relentless and voracious, surpassing even the immediate needs of logic in their pursuit of prey. But they had, of course, a weakness – though Chaeroneia was riddled with data media like the glassy black crystalline medium or the liquid metal of the datapool, there were still plenty of areas in Chaeroneia that were far away from any containment medium. That meant the hunter-programs could not go everywhere, only the places where a medium existed to hold them.

Scraecos illuminated Chaeroneia's data media in his mind. Whole towers of crystal glowed strongly, including the old menial reclamation spire the intruders had left only a short time before. Dataslates held by tech-priests overseeing work in the towers also glowed, tiny specks of moving light. A hunter-program could travel in such a medium if it had to. Many tech-priests themselves were lit up, as large data storage organs were a common augmentation among the overseers of Manufactorium Noctis.

On the horizon, between the city and the command spire complex, was a massive shining area where there were plenty of spaces for hunter-programs to hide. But that was an area the tech-priests of Chaeroneia wanted to keep the intruders away from. So that was no good.

Scraecos concentrated on the places in the city where the programs could hunt. Then he synchronised all the data feeds from tech-priests, sensorium-equipped servitors and all the semi-natural biomechanical creatures in Manufactorium Noctis. A single stream of perception coursed through the datapool, wrapping thousands of filaments into a long pulsing rope, writhing like a serpent.

Scraecos wrapped his mechadendrites around the filament rope as if they were the tentacles of a deep-sea predator, worming dataprobes into its length. The perception burst into him and he had to open up all his capacity to accept it, the datafeeds of millions of perceiving creatures and machines in one tangled burst.

Few tech-priests on Chaeroneia could have done it. Fewer still had the respect of the hunter-programs. That was why the tech-priests, Scraecos among them, had chosen him.

Because something, somewhere, knew where the intruders were.

Millions of images of Chaeroneia flickered through Scraecos's mind. He overclocked his augmented brain until they slowed down enough for him to sort them properly. Hordes of menials slaving over massive steaming engine-blocks. Sacred symbols projected onto the clouds, the endless holy litany of the Machine-God's revelations. Tech-priests gibbering the praises of the Omnissiah from spire-top temples, their machine-code prayers exalting the Great Comprehender who had given the priests of Chaeroneia His revelation through the avatar that had appeared to them long ago.

All magnificent, but not what Scraecos was looking for.

Scraecos concentrated on the wastelands between the spires, where intruders might think they could hide from the city's infinite eyes. Ruined and abandoned places, deep and forgotten. Layers of discarded history, wreckage and decay, swallowed up by the corrosion so daemonised by the literature of the old, ignorant Adeptus Mechanicus. But the God of Machines was also the God of Rust – Scraecos knew that now, and so did Chaeroneia and so these places were as a sacred to the Omnissiah as the most carefully anointed temple. Scraecos searched the alleyways and undercity sumps, the rotting graveyards of titanic biomechanical creatures and the windblown eyries of the flying animals that scoured the spire tops for prey.

There. One of them had seen something. Armoured humans in an unfamiliar gunmetal-grey, the unknown livery of the Space Marines who had infiltrated Manufactorium Noctis. The viewpoint was high and distant but there was no mistaking them. They were moving, spread out in formation, with unarmoured humans and what looked like a priest of the old Mechanicus in the centre.

Good. They were still moving like soldiers, still thinking their military minds could outwit the grand intelligence of Chaeroneia's priestly caste. Scraecos cross-referenced their location and direction.

It was clear where they were headed. And on Scraecos's mental map it was a place almost blinding with the level of data media it contained, a place where the hunters could grow strong and brutal, move like lightning and bear down on anything that would sate their hunger. And they would find prey now, that was for sure.

Somewhere deep, deep down beneath the desolate layers of his personality, Scraecos smiled. The rest of him, the logical majority, simply bade the hunter-programs to depart their logic-cages in the command spire's own data network and go hunting in Manu-factorium Noctis.

CHAPTER TEN

'The daemon can exist in an infinity of forms, but all are identical in one respect. Every daemon is a lie given flesh, for only a creature made of deceit can take form in the truth of the universe.'

– Lord Inquisitor Coteaz at
the Conclave of Deliae

'THIS IS IT,' said Alaric as they reached the head of the valley.

'I don't like this,' said Haulvarn, who was taking point with Alaric. 'Anyone up there could cover us all the way in.'

He was right. The valley was a sheer-sided slash in the architecture of the city, dozens of storeys deep and walled with sheer black crystal like the substance in the crystal spire. Slabs of fallen crystal, like giant shards of obsidian, littered the valley floor. And if there was anything up on the crystal clifftops, they would have their pick of targets as the Grey Knights and tech-guard made their way towards the powerful, cylindrical shape of the datafortress itself at the far end of the valley.

'Then we'll have to be quick,' said Alaric. 'Lykkos, keep watching the clifftops, you're the only one with the range. Everyone else, stay close and keep moving. They'll see us coming.'

A thin, sharp wind whistled down the valley, cold and hard like the smooth glassy sides. The trash underfoot, Alaric realised with a jolt, was composed of ancient servitor parts – rusting craniums, metallic armatures, strands of tarnished steel that once wound round human limbs. Alaric had no doubt that the human parts of the servitors, probably harvested from the less-able menials, had in turn been removed and used to create the biomechanical monstrosities that powered much of the city. The mechanical remains, the servos and the exoskeletons, had ended up here.

The Imperium as a whole did not place great value on an individual human life, but at least humans were ultimately sacred to the Emperor and their deaths, no matter how numerous, were all unavoidable sacrifices. On Chaeroneia, human lives were no more than fuel.

'I am picking up contradictory readings,' said Saphentis, who was looking at the auspex mounted on one of his arms. 'There are unusual energy sources nearby.'

Alaric felt something prickling against his psychic core, the shield of faith that kept his mind safe from the predations of the Enemy. The feeling grew as the force moved down the valley. Something probing his defences, homing in on the beacon of his mind and scraping psychic nails against its surface.

The hexagrammic and pentagrammic wards woven into the ceramite of his armour were heating up. He heard something whispering, a low hissing sound that seemed to form his name, over and over again, just below the range of his hearing.

'Anyone else hear that?' he asked.

'Hear what?' said Hawkespur.

Something moved inside the black crystal of the cliff face, like a creature swimming under black ice. That was all the warning Alaric had.

His wards flared white-hot and he was thrown from his feet as something massive and yet somehow incorporeal ripped past him, hurling him against the opposite face. Crystal shattered and bit into the skin of Alaric's body, scraping deep gouges in his armour. He hit the ground hard, willing himself to keep a grip on his halberd. The screaming sound was so loud it was like a wall of white noise, shrieking right through him, filling his mind.

Gunfire stuttered. Bright crimson las-blasts streaked in every direction.

An ice-cold spectral hand reached out of the crystal Alaric had just slammed into, snaking around his throat and lifting him up. It was not physical, not flesh and blood or even metal. Alaric saw a glimpse of a face that was not a face beneath the crystal, formed of a jumble of geometric shapes that coalesced into snarling fangs and burning purple slashes for eyes.

'Domine, salve nos!' hissed Alaric and the psychic wall around his soul flared outwards, burning the creature's talons with the fire of his faith. The monster screamed and reeled back into the wall, dropping Alaric.

'Tharkk! Get your men in close! Grey Knights, surround them!'

Half-real creatures were leaping across the valley, streaking from one crystal wall to the other. One tech-guard was lifted off his feet as he went and the creature began to devour him. The tech-guard's emotional repression wasn't enough to cut out the pain as he was twisted around in the air, the maddening haze of shapes that made up the creature's body whirling about him. Piece by piece he was sliced apart, geometric scraps of skin flayed off, neat cores of bone bored out of him. The process took a handful of seconds before the creature reached the opposite wall but time seemed to slow down, as if Chaeroneia wanted the man to suffer as much as possible before it was done with him.

Tharkk hauled the remaining two tech-guard into the middle of the valley, Saphentis alongside him. The Grey Knights formed up around them, storm bolter fire chattering up as they tried to hit the creature streaking past them. They were lightning-quick and serpentine, clawed limbs extruding from their bodies at strange angles, their faces horrid slashes of deep burning light like broad strokes painted over reality. They were made of swirling shapes like some corrupt mathematics made real and the crystal of the valley walls seemed to conduct them, so that they arced across the valley like electricity.

Alaric's wards were absorbing the foul magic pulsing off them. The Grey Knights all had the same defences and the creatures hated it. They bent around the Grey Knights like refracting light, the force of the Marines' faith enough to warp the sub-reality they moved through.

The creatures screamed and contorted in torment, strange ugly colours rippling through them as they approached the Grey Knights. But it wouldn't be enough. Moment by moment they were getting closer, becoming quicker and more aggressive as if their first attack had been a mere warm-up.

'We can't stay!' shouted Hawkespur. She had her sidearm out and was sniping at the creatures, her bullets leaving rippling trails through them.

Alaric thought rapidly. She was right. They could hold out here but not forever – a few moments and the creatures could start injuring Grey Knights and carrying them away, getting among the tech-guard and finishing them off.

They had to move. To reach the datafortress.

'Brother Archis,' said Alaric levelly, his voice raised above the otherworldy screaming. 'I think our tech-guard companions could do with some inspiring words.'

'Justicar?' Archis paused between firing gouts of flame at the creatures to glance at Alaric.

'Tell them the Parable of Grand Master Ganelon. I hear you tell it well.'

Archis took aim again and bathed another creature in flame, the fire rippling purple-black where it flowed through the substance of the creature's body. 'There was once a man named Ganelon,' began

Archis uncertainly. 'A Grand Master of our Chapter. He...'

'As related in the Index Beati of High Chaplain Greacris, Brother Archis. I taught it to you myself.'

'Of course.' Archis paused for a second, as if composing himself. '"... and so reflect, novice, on the works of Ganelon, who attained the rank of Grand Master two hundred and fifty-one years after taking on the mantle of the Knight. For the legions of the Lust God had done much evil through the Garon Nebula and the Holy Orders of the Emperor's Inquisition entreated the Grey Knights to make war upon the benighted peoples therein..."'

Archis had learned the parable by heart. Alaric had led the squad in prayers countless times and even the recent additions to the squad, Archis included, took equal responsibilities for their spiritual health. The parable was one Alaric had ensured Archis knew by heart so he could lead the squad in reflecting on its message, immortalised by High Chaplain Greacris eight centuries before.

Alaric waved the squad forward as Archis spoke, the Marine's voice getting stronger as the familiar parable unfolded. The Grey Knights and the techguard moved gradually down the valley, the creatures shrieking past them.

The strength of the Grey Knights was not in their wargear or their training, in their augmentations or in the patronage of the Ordo Malleus. Their strength was faith. That was how they would survive here. That was the one weapon the Enemy could never counter.

'And Ganelon saw the evils done by the Lust God,' continued Archis, raising his voice above the howling. 'But the minions of the Lust God were fell and many and Ganelon was surrounded by sorcerers and heretics and all who knew of it said he would surely die.'

The serpentine creatures flared red as the words of the parable burned them. They still reached out to test the Grey Knights' psychic defences, but their mental claws were burned and they squirmed away through the air, keening angrily. As they reeled the other Grey Knights could fire at them, storm bolter shells shredding the half-physical stuff of their bodies. Wounded creatures writhed behind the surface of the crystal cliffs, bleeding raw mathematics from the tears in their bodies.

'The datafortress is just ahead,' said Alaric. 'We're almost there.'

'If these things move through data media,' said Hawkespur as she stumbled through the underfoot wreckage to keep up with the tech-guard, 'then they'll be stronger there.'

'Let me worry about that. Just stay alive.'

'...And the Lord Sorcerer of the Lust God spake unto Ganelon,' said Archis, 'and offered him great things. The Lust God would give Ganelon anything he desired, no matter how base or beautiful, savage or tender, a lifetime of wonders in return for service. And the sorcerer's magic showed Ganelon all the things the Lust God could bring and they were wondrous indeed...'

Alaric glanced up and saw grav-platforms coming in to land over the datafortress. There would be resistance, then, but he knew there would be. Now he was ready. The Grey Knights were coming into their own – this was the kind of battle they were made for.

'But Ganelon spoke to the Lord Sorcerer. He spoke of the weight of duty he carried and the opportunity given to him by the grace of the Emperor to discharge that duty. And he said to the Lord Sorcerer, what else is there in this universe, or any other, that can compare to a warrior's duty done? What other gift can I receive, for the like of which I would give up what the Emperor has given unto me? And the Lord Sorcerer could find no answer and so were his deceitful words revealed as lies and his magic broken, and Ganelon struck off his head with one blow and won back the Garon Nebula into the Emperor's light…'

Archis was nearly finished. The squad had reached the datafortress, the first step of a flight of steps leading up to a huge black rectangle of the entrance. The datafortress was a single massive cylinder standing on end, its obsidian surface swirling with the magnitude of information it contained. Alaric could feel the weight of all that knowledge, billions of words' worth of information pressing against his consciousness. Information, the foundation stone of the Adeptus Mechanicus and presumably the lifeblood of whatever tech-heresy had taken hold of Chaeroneia.

The creatures were wary, hiding beneath the surface of the crystal or dissolving into barely-glimpsed shapes of shadow that slunk around in the distance. Archis's parable had worked, focusing the faith of the Grey Knights until it burned their enemies.

'What in the hells are they?' asked Hawkespur as they made their way warily up towards the entrance.

'Self-actuating programs,' replied Saphentis. 'Data constructs with limited decision-networks. Evidently the Mechanicus here has endowed them with some capacity to manipulate gravity or matter. Greatly heretical creations, or course.'

'Creations? No, archmagos. The tech-priests didn't make them.'

'Explain, justicar?'

'I know daemons when I see them. This planet was stuck in the warp for a thousand years. I think those daemons infested the data media and the tech-priests are using them.' Alaric glanced at Saphentis. 'They've fallen further than you think. Sorcery, Throne knows what else.'

'Then we are in grave danger here.'

'Wrong again. At first everything on this world was new to me. The Mechanicus, the tech-heresies, it's something our training never anticipated. But daemons are different. Daemons I know. The tech-priests probably think their daemons are the best weapon they have, but we've trained our whole lives to take them on. This fight just shifted in our favour.'

The Grey Knights led the way through the forbidding entrance into the datafortress itself and the weight of information settled on Alaric as his eyes snapped his pupils open to drink in the feeble light inside. The inside of the datafortress was a riot of shapes. The stern exterior had served to contain rampant growths of datacrystal, forming spikes and blades that jutted insanely from every angle. It was disorienting in the extreme – the angles didn't add up right, distances didn't match up properly, everything seemed tilted in a dozen different ways. Strange colours pulsed through the crystal growths as the data-daemons plunged into the architecture of the fortress itself.

'They're regrouping,' said Alaric. 'Saphentis! Get us information! Concentrate on historical data, the last thousand years.'

'Thousand? But it has only been a century…'

'Do it! Haulvarn, Archis, don't leave his side. The rest, close perimeter. Don't let them surround us.'

Alaric tried to gauge how far the navigable space inside the fortress went. It was impossible to guess how far in anyone could get. There was something so fundamentally wrong with the inside of the fortress that Alaric guessed his men could still get lost no matter how big it actually was. It was as if the magnitude of information in the fortress was so great that its weight had borne down on the fabric of reality, making it buckle and bend.

The daemons were there. He could feel them through the wards in his armour, through his skin and down to the core of his soul. Hanging back, watching, waiting. Waiting for something.

And there were tech-priests on the way with grav-platforms full of reinforcements. Saphentis would have to be quick and they would have to get back out through the valley under fire. Alaric knew it wouldn't be easy but the odds were lengthening with every second.

'Saphentis? What have you got?'

Saphentis had his two probe-tipped arms stabbed deep into the crystal, the servos twitching as torrents of information seethed up them. 'Interesting,' he said. 'There is much information. I lack the data filtration matrices that Thalassa possessed. I will need several minutes.'

It was so obvious they didn't have several minutes that Alaric didn't bother saying it.

The crystal was pulsing with strange colours that matched nothing on the visible spectrum. Alaric's wards flared hotter. He glanced at the other members of his squad – Lykkos was touching a hand to the miniature copy of the Liber Daemonicum contained in its compartment on the front of his breastplate. Alaric did the same, mouthing a quick prayer that beseeched the Emperor for clarity of mind and firmness of decision amid the confusion of war.

'To my front!' called Brother Cardios. 'They're coming!'

There was a burst of storm bolter fire and Alaric turned in time to see something lift Cardios up and slam him hard against the crystal roof, shards of obsidian raining down. A giant spectral hand dropped the Marine and more fire streaked up at it, the muzzle flashes illuminating a huge, hulking creature, bullets rending its half-real flesh. Its massive doglike head bled purple-black fire that dripped upwards and the scores of eyes studding its skull were burning black pits. Its body seethed with corrupt mathematics, angles and shapes twisting in on one another so maddeningly it was impossible to focus on it properly, only comprehend that it was massive, powerful and terrible.

A daemon. The data-daemons had combined, subsuming their individual prowess into one creature that did not fear the prayers of the Grey Knights.

Dvorn yelled and sprinted into the space where Cardios had stood, swinging his nemesis hammer so hard it connected with the unreal substance of the daemon's torso and ripped out a chunk of raw logic. The daemon bellowed and swung out a clawed hand, smashing Dvorn against the crystal. Sparks of power bled from the wound in the crystal as Dvorn hit the ground and rolled just as a cloven foot extruded itself from the daemon's mass and stamped down like an industrial piston.

Everyone that could was firing at the daemon now as it lumbered towards them, backing towards Saphentis in a tight formation. Captain Tharkk and the two tech-guard needed their combined strength to drag Brother Cardios back and Dvorn bought them all precious seconds, rolling onto his back and firing into the daemon's underside before jamming his hammer into its belly and pushing up, trying to force it from over him.

The daemon reeled but did not stop, listing to the side and passing through the crystal. As it did so the livid, open wounds sealed up and new angry colours pulsed through its body.

The daemons living in the data medium were projecting this daemon out from there, just as they had projected the bodies of the hunter-daemons in the valley. They were stronger there, but they were also vulnerable, concentrating on fighting their way through the Grey Knights to reach Saphentis, the one who was invading their realm.

Alaric reversed his grip on his Nemesis halberd and dropped to his knees, driving the blade deep into the crystal of the floor.

'I am the Hammer!' he yelled. 'I am the point of His spear! I am the mail about His fist!'

He felt the daemons recoil from him, their hot anger conducted through the blade and up the halberd's haft. They hated it. He knew how to hurt them.

The daemon stopped, head back and screaming, spatters of pure information fountaining from its gaping mouth like blood. Lykkos stepped forward, dropped to one knee and put three rapid psycannon shots through its throat, the blessed bolter shells punching up through its head and spattering spectral brains all over the ceiling. The monster stumbled and the Grey Knights all added their fire, Archis taking aim with his Incinerator and pouring a gout of flame around its feet.

'Behold the fate of the Unguided one!' yelled Alaric, switching to a new prayer as he felt the daemons all around him trying to find a way around the force of his faith. 'For every soul is drawn towards the beacon of the Master of Mankind! Behold the fate of the faithless, for every soul is born to believe!'

Raw pain shot up into Alaric, burning his fingers and the muscles of his arms as he held on. He was in a battle of wills with the data-daemons and he would not give in because there was nothing in this galaxy or any other with the willpower to match a Grey Knight.

Brother Haulvarn saw the daemon reeling and ran forward, leaping up and driving the blade of his sword down into its gaping mouth. Dvorn rolled onto his knees and swung his Nemesis hammer into the daemon's side, knocking it onto one knee.

Haulvarn was on top of it, stabbing down, smouldering multi-coloured gore spattering all over him.

The data-daemons were torn between fending off Alaric's spiritual assault and keeping their creation on its feet. They couldn't do both and the daemon was driven back under Dvorn and Haulvarn's assault, battered further by combined fire from the rest of the squad. With a horrendous sound Alaric hoped he would never have to hear again, the daemon came apart. Unable to retain its foothold in real space, its daemonic flesh unravelled in a swirling mass of colour and light, streaming back into the crystal as it shape was erased from reality.

Alaric fell onto his back, the images of thousands of screaming data-daemons glowing on his retinas.

'It's down,' said Hawkespur.

'We don't have long,' said Alaric . He pulled himself back onto his feet – his ceramite gauntlets were glowing a dull red and the blade of his Nemesis halberd was charred black. He looked at Saphentis. 'Archmagos?'

'I believe I have found all that I can. It is incomplete and corrupt, but not devoid of interesting content.'

'Wonderful. Tharrk, stay close to the archmagos and Hawkespur.'

Captain Tharkk saluted briskly. He only had two tech-guard left, but Alaric knew the mental surgery and conditioning of the Adeptus Mechanicus meant he would be a soldier to the end.

Haulvarn picked himself up and pulled Dvorn to his feet. The two of them were liberally spattered with rainbow-sheened gore, like rancid machine oil.

'Injuries?' asked Alaric.

'Nothing,' replied Halvarn.

'None here,' added Dvorn.

'Cardios?'

'I'm beaten up, but not badly,' replied Brother Cardios, who was sitting propped up against the crystal. His breastplate was badly dented and his backpack was all but shattered.

'I can hear contacts,' said Lykkos. 'Close and approaching.'

'Throne of Earth,' said Alaric resignedly. 'Fall back, we'll have to take the valley.'

'They could pin us down from the cliffs,' said Captain Tharkk. 'And the daemons are there.'

'Exactly. We know what's waiting for us. Now move out.'

Gunfire chattered. Crystal smashed. Lykkos rolled to the side as heavy weapons fire stitched a path straight past him.

'Cover!' yelled Alaric but he didn't have to. The Grey Knights and the tech-guard hit the floor as heavy weapons fire thudded in from every direction. Above it Alaric could hear the machine-code orders gibbered by one of the tech-priests.

The crystal was reforming. With a tortured sound like breaking glass walls were bleeding across open spaces and new pathways were opening. Marines and tech-guard hunkered down behind outcrops of black crystal or in inclines on the floor, shielding themselves as best they could from the fire. Alaric followed suit and glimpsed battle-servitors, their tiny heads fronted with targeter devices and their burly torsos supporting twin-linked heavy stubbers or autocannon, stuttering suppressive fire in all directions.

The fire thinned out as the attacking force got into position. The return fire was desultory – the surviving tech-guard snapped off lasgun shots but most of the Grey Knights saved their ammunition rather than spray fire at targets they couldn't see, without knowing how many there even were. Alaric could see pallid menial bodies and hulking battle-servitors skulking through the shadows between crystal outcrops, probably getting into position for an all-out assault.

'Saphentis!' hissed Alaric. 'Did you happen to download a map of this place?'

'There is no map,' replied the archmagos. 'The structure of the datafortress is largely at the whim of the tech-priest in command.'

'Then how do we get out?'

'Were we to possess the command protocols we could simply reform the structure and create an exit in any direction we wished.'

'And can we get them?'

'No.'

Alaric sensed something moving behind him. He turned to see the wall reforming, a tunnel opening up like a mouth. The shape of a battle-servitor lumbered towards him – one arm was an autocannon and the other ended in a fearsome set of mechanical shears.

'Come with me,' it said through the vox-caster set into its shrunken skull-like face.

Alaric brought his storm bolter up level with the servitor's face. It made no sense – the servitor was in a perfect position to rake Alaric's squad with auto-cannon fire.

'Why?' he asked.

'Because I can help you,' replied the servitor.

'Lies.'

'Then kill me.'

Alaric put a burst of storm bolter fire through the servitor's head. Its brain, through which its motor functions were routed, was destroyed and it shut down instantly, slumping against the wall of the tunnel.

Something else moved, this time far smaller – a tiny scuttling creature like a large flat beetle. It had glinting mechanical mandibles and dozens of intricate jointed legs. It scrabbled up the crystal outcrop that Alaric was crouched behind.

'Kill us all,' it said, in a tinny voice barely loud enough for Alaric to hear. 'But we can help you.'

'How?' Alaric tried to work out what the creature was – it was probably either an example of Chaeroneia's biomechanical fauna, or some artificial thing that cleaned or maintained the fortress. Either way, it shouldn't have been talking to him.

'As I did once before. In the factory spire. Did you believe it was the grace of the Emperor that saved you?'

Alaric thought wildly. It could be a trick, perhaps by the commanding tech-priest, perhaps by the data-daemons. But even if it was, it was unlikely in the extreme that the Grey Knights could fend off another Mechanicus attack, especially after the mauling by the data-daemons. In situations like this leadership consisted of the capacity to make quick decisions and carry them through and in that moment Alaric decided it was better to walk into a trap than let the Mechanicus kill them where they hid.

'What should I do?' he asked.

'Keep them busy.'

Alaric turned to where Saphentis was ducking down in cover, flanked by the tech-guard. 'Say something, Saphentis.'

The archmagos turned his segmented eyes on Alaric, managing to look unimpressed even with such an abnormal face. 'What should I say, justicar?'

'Offer him a deal.'

'You are, as you say, in command.' Saphentis tilted his head back and transmitted a jarring, ugly chorus of machine-code. There was a pause while the sporadic gunfire died down and then a reply came, the staccato zeroes and ones echoing from somewhere far through the crystal labyrinth.

'What did you say?' asked Alaric.

'I told them we would come quietly if they accepted us into their tech-priesthood and introduced us to their own version of the Cult Mechanicus.'

'What was the reply?'

'They mocked us.'

The battle-servitors stomped forwards, the crushing sound of their footsteps synchronised. Alaric risked a glance around out of cover and saw there were at least five of them, massive heavy weapons variants, with a mass of menials following behind them, ready to swamp the Grey Knights as they were driven out of cover. The crystal had reformed into a long, low gallery with plenty of space for the servitors and menials to draw up lines of fire.

In the gloom at the back of the cavern was the tech-priest in command. His upper body was covered in slabs of black crystal data medium, like plates in a suit of armour or scales on an obsidian reptile. His lower half was a mass of writhing mechanical tendrils. There was a faint shimmering aura around him – an energy field, which meant that even if the Grey Knights or tech-guard could get a shot at him it would probably bounce off.

'Grey Knights, each take a servitor,' said Alaric quietly over the vox. 'Left to right, Haulvarn, Dvorn, Archis, Lykkos, then me. Cardios, hang back and flame the menials. Understood?'

Acknowledgement runes flickered. It wasn't much of a plan, but it would buy them the seconds Alaric had promised.

The nearest servitor's arm-mounted missile launcher levelled at Alaric. It would shatter the crystal, leave him exposed and probably cause massive wounds.

The servitor turned suddenly and fired, the missile streaking into the menials behind it.

The explosion sent out clouds of razor-sharp spinning crystal shards and shredded the bodies of the gaggle of menials following the servitor. Another servitor followed suit, spraying autocannon fire at the back of the cavern, stitching bloody ruin through half-glimpsed menial bodies. The tech-priest screamed machine code and fire was streaking back and forth between the Mechanicus force, las-bolts from the menials and heavy weapons from the servitors.

'Stay down!' shouted Alaric as the din of gunfire echoed and re-echoed through the cavern. An explosion threw the massive form of a servitor into the Grey Knights' position, its armoured torso charred and battered, smoke spurting from its track units.

It turned a scorched head towards Alaric. 'Follow,' it said. The crystal floor below it descended, the substance of the datafortress altering around it, forming a bowl-shaped depression with a tunnel leading from one side.

'Move!' voxed Alaric and followed the servitor down. Some of the menials managed to redirect their fire through the confusion and las-fire smacked into Alaric's shoulder pad. The other Grey Knights scrambled down beside him – one of the tech-guard screamed, the first hint of emotion he had shown for most of his life, as a las-bolt punched through his gut and he pitched face-first into the floor. Hawkespur and Saphentis followed, Tharkk and the one remaining tech-guard covering the archmagos.

The servitor, belching smoke, dragged itself into the tunnel and Alaric followed. The tunnel was being created as the servitor went, corkscrewing down into the foundations of the datafortress. The Grey Knights were on his heels and Brother Archis dragged Saphentis behind him as the fire fell more heavily.

Tharkk was the last man into the tunnel, sniping at the menials who were firing from the back of the cavern. Alaric glanced round in time to see the datafortress's tech-priest descend behind him, a grav-unit evidently hidden by the coils of mechadendrites that made up his lower half. The tech-priest spat a machine-code curse and held out his arms. Plates of crystal medium lifted from his limbs, revealing black, putrescent skin beneath. The plates span around the tech-priest in a wider orbit, deflecting the las-blasts from Tharkk's gun as he sprayed fire at the Enemy.

The armour plates surrounded Tharkk and cut him into scores of horizontal slices.

The tunnel entrance closed before the sorry chunks of Tharkk's body hit the floor. The sound of gunfire was suddenly distant, the machine-code howls of rage from the tech-priest dim.

The servitor continued down. The datacrystal walls were dull and greyish, as if the crystal was drained or dead. Alaric looked to see who had made it out – his squad, Saphentis, Hawkespur and the one surviving tech-guard. He hurried up to the servitor, which was trundling down the tunnel apparently uninterested in Tharkk's death.

'What are you?' asked Alaric.

'All in time,' replied the servitor, its voice garbled as its vox unit failed.

Hawkespur caught up with Alaric. Her gun was in her hand. 'Justicar, what happened up there?'

'I think we have an ally,' replied Alaric.

'Who? A servitor?'

'I don't believe it's that simple. But we'll find out soon.'

Alaric led the force further down into the guts of Chaeroneia and as they went the tunnel knitted itself closed behind them. Step by step the planet was swallowing them, and either there would be safety beneath Manufactorium Noctis or Alaric was leading his squad into a far worse trap than the one they had just escaped.

CHAPTER ELEVEN

'When Grand Master Ganelon heard the words of the daemon, there was no need to listen. For the words of the Enemy are lies; even those that are true are spoken only in ultimate deceit.'

– 'The Parable of Ganelon'
as related by Chaplain Greacris
in the *Index Beati*.

'OLD FRIENDS,' SAID Urkrathos, walking onto the command deck of the *Hellforger*.

The daemons who controlled the *Hellforger* looked at him with hatred so pure it dripped from their eyes, black burning droplets of loathing. There were forty-eight daemons welded into the command architecture of Grand Cruiser *Hellforger*, every one slaved into a different aspect of the ship and bound

183

by rites older than mankind to obey Urkrathos's every whim.

The command deck was long, low and infernally hot and it stank like a torture chamber. The walls and floor were pitted, rotting iron that sweated blood and the feeble light came from the tactical holo-display that Urkrathos used in place of a bridge viewscreen. Tangles of obscure machinery and electronics welled from the walls, floor and ceiling like mechanical tumours, hissing steam and spitting sparks as ancient clockwork cogitators maintained the malevolent, spiteful machine-spirit of the *Hellforger*. The daemons melded with the various command helms were massively muscular but helpless, their fangs and talons useless as long as Urkrathos held fealty over them. Some had massive shearing crab-like pincers, others had dozens of arachnid legs tipped with tiny gnashing mouths, or nests of writhing entrails that could strangle like tentacles, or stranger and deadlier things besides. But not one of them could attack Urkrathos or disobey his orders, as much as every single one of them longed to do so.

Urkrathos strode down the command deck. The holo-display projected the image of Chaeroneia into the middle, about a metre above the floor and several metres across. It was a fine planet, dark and sickly, so stained with the warp he could tell how corrupt it had become just by looking at it. The asteroids around the world danced according to a complex but identifiable pattern, with a spell wrought into their movements to prevent any cogitator from guessing where they would turn next. The asteroid field meant that the interloper ships now clustered in medium orbit around Chaeroneia could not hope to land a meaningful force on the planet, which in turn meant that whatever the Imperial ships did, the tribute would remain on Chaeroneia for Urkrathos to collect.

And what a magnificent tribute it was.

'Show me our positions,' ordered Urkrathos. The daemon projecting the holo-display, a foul squat thing with dozens of eyes, gibbered as it wove the image into the air. Urkrathos's fleet appeared on the holo some distance from the world. Urkrathos commanded the *Hellforger* itself, the cruiser *Desikratis* which bristled with guns, the fighter platform *Cadaver* which was the base of the Vulture Flight attack craft, and the three Idolator-class escorts that formed Scapula Wing.

The *Desikratis* was commanded by a titanic daemon who functioned as the ship's sole crew member, its nerve-tipped tentacles reaching into every corner of the bloated, gun-heavy ship. The *Desikratis* in turn commanded the three Idolators of Scapula Wing, towards which it seemed to have a rather paternal attitude. The fighter platform *Cadaver* was commanded by Kreathak the Thrice-Maimed, one of the finest fighter craft pilots of the last two centuries, who also led the elite Vulture Wing.

It was more than enough ships to collect the tribute and escort it back to Lord Abaddon at the Eye of Terror. But Warmaster Abaddon himself had commanded Urkrathos to make certain that the tribute was delivered intact and so Urkrathos had taken everything he could muster to Chaeroneia to make good his duty to the Despoiler.

'Contact the *Cadaver*,' said Urkrathos. 'Tell Commander Kreathak to get all craft ready to scramble. I'll leave him to break up those escorts.' Urkrathos looked closer at the composition of the Imperial fleet. It was pathetic – one cruiser protected by the escorts, another ship of uncertain designation that was a little smaller than a cruiser and a handful of troop ships and assorted transports. 'Leave the enemy flagship to me.'

The daemon charged with communications was a whale-sized monster half-melted into the rusting ceiling, its bloated body mostly taken up with the brain matter that processed Urkrathos's words into encrypted ship-to-ship comms. Like all the forty-eight daemons, it had been conquered by Urkrathos in personal combat during the Black Legions' battles to carve out an empire for themselves in the Eye of Terror, or given to him in recognition for some great victory in the eyes of the gods. By the decree of the Chaos powers, the daemons so defeated or possessed by Urkrathos were owned by him in a state of slavery, forbidden by the will of the gods to disobey him in anything. He had made them the crew of his ship, because it pleased him to have such powerful creatures in such obvious fortitude, held where he could witness their suffering and see the hatred they had for him in their eyes.

It was the only thing worth fighting for, the only thing worth anything – the sensation of owning another intelligent thing completely. The knowledge that he could compel it to obey any and every thought he directed at it. It was what the Despoiler promised – a universe enslaved, where the ignorant were crushed by the feet of those blessed by Chaos. And if any of the Imperial scum orbiting Chaeroneia survived, Urkrathos would make slaves of them, too – because he could.

Once, a long time ago, Urkrathos had fought for the good of mankind and the will of the Emperor. He had been a slave to the Emperor. Horus had taught them that they were slaves of no one and now Abaddon was the one who would prove that to the rest of the galaxy.

'Weapons!' shouted Urkrathos. A lean, muscular creature crucified against one wall snarled back at him. 'I want ordnance ready for firing. Full spread, long fuses.'

'So it shall be,' growled the creature. Its burning red eyes rolled back in their sockets as he willed the command into the minds of the ordnance crew deep within the ship – soon the *Hellforger* would be ready to pump scores of torpedoes into the Imperial flagship and reduce it to a cloud of burning debris.

'It's almost a pity,' thought Urkrathos aloud. 'I was hoping I would have to board them. Maybe I still will, if they survive that long. Make ready the boarding parties.'

The communications-daemon convulsed as it relayed the order to the boarding troops barracked throughout the *Hellforger*. They were the scum of the galaxy, the worst of the worst, deformed and degenerate creatures that had once been men but had over the generations been bred into brutal killing machines. Urkrathos had no Black Legion squads, Space Marine units that had been elite ship-to-ship combatants even before the Heresy and the flight to the Eye of Terror, but nonetheless he seriously doubted if there was anything in the Imperial fleet that could stand up to a boarding assault from the *Hellforger*.

Yes, he would have preferred a proper battle. It was in the fires of conflict that Chaos was praised the highest. But it was enough that the Despoiler would receive his tribute and the Black Crusade fighting from the Eye would be strengthened beyond measure by Urkrathos's victory.

He left the daemons to brood as he walked off the deck and down towards the ship's lower decks where the complement of slaves were kept in the crowded pens. Easy or not, the coming victory had to be sealed with the blessing of the Chaos Gods and to ensure that happened Urkrathos had a great many innocents to sacrifice before battle was joined.

INQUISITOR NYXOS SHUFFLED down the shuttle's boarding ramp like the old man he purported to be. He even walked with a cane and looked ancient and frail compared to the strapping Naval armsmen who accompanied him.

Fleet Commissar Leung was there to meet the inquisitor. Leung was a fine product of the Schola Progenium, an orphan of some interminable conflict who had been brought up in starched Commissariat uniforms and instilled with the sense that only the thin line of cowardice separated any one man from irredeemable corruption. He saluted sharply at the inquisitor's approach, small hard eyes glinting beneath the peak of his officer's cap, black greatcoat around his shoulders in spite of the stifling heat on the docking deck of the *Exemplar*.

There was no one else with Leung. Even a petty officer travelling between ships might expect a complement of armsmen to welcome him onboard, an extension of the protocols one captain was expected to extend to another.

'Greetings, commissar,' said Nyxos. 'I see our hosts do not stand on ceremony.'

Leung removed his cap and tucked it neatly under one arm, parade ground sharp. 'The magos does not recognise the authority of the Imperial Navy or its officer core. She accepts my presence only grudgingly.' Leung's voice was as taut as the rest of him, fast and clipped.

'Well, they do revel in their independence, the Mechanicus,' said Nyxos, pausing to nod his thanks to the armsman who helped him down the step at the end of the boarding ramp. 'Are they prepared to accept me?'

'I believe so,' replied Leung. 'Although I had to arrange quarters for you myself.'

'Good man. Lead me there, if you please.'

'Of course.'

The interior of the *Exemplar* was fundamentally different from the *Tribunicia*. It was as if the two craft had been built by two different species, or in two different eras of history. The brutally elegant gothic lines of the *Tribunicia* were replaced by the blocky functionality preferred by the Adeptus Mechanicus. Cog-toothed designs trimmed everything, even the massive blocks that made up the walls and floor of the docking deck. Several other craft and highly advanced shuttles were also docked, being serviced by heavy servitors and the occasional hooded Mechanicus crewman. The stifling, cloying smell of scented machine-oil was heavy in the air and most unusually, there was little noise from the crew. Nyxos knew places like docking decks for the clamour of crewmen yelling at one another, often in rapid crew-cant that an outsider couldn't understand. The Mechanicus did its business in grim silence, human voices replaced by the hissing of hydraulics and the dim clanging of pistons beneath the deck.

'What are your impressions of the magos?' asked Nyxos as he walked.

'Few,' replied Leung. 'She has little respect for Imperial authorities save the senior ranks of the Mechanicus. Even my own office seems to mean little to her.'

'Let us hope she does not show the same attitude towards the Inquisition,' said Nyxos. 'Does it seem she will obey the orders of the Rear Admiral?'

'Probably,' said Leung. Nyxos noticed he didn't so much walk as march alongside him. 'But she considers herself to be acting independently. Her orders evidently concern Chaeroneia itself, not the fleet sent to investigate it.'

'Do you know which tech-priests she answers to?' asked Nyxos. 'Archmagos Saphentis is out of communication – is she acting of her own accord?'

'It is doubtful. She has frequent high-level encrypted communications. I believe they are with the subsector Adeptus Mechanicus command but she has not been forthcoming about the Mechanicus command structure here.'

'Well, I'll just have to convince her to be more open.'

Leung, Nyxos and the armsmen following them reached a cargo-sized elevator and Leung keyed a sequence into the keypad that controlled it. The elevator's platform ground upwards, rising through a deep square shaft as it passed many intermediate decks. Nyxos saw glimpses of the other decks as they passed – some looked like research labs, with endless benches of baffling equipment and robed tech-priests poring over crucibles or microscopes. Others housed massive banks of cogitators, cooled by freezing mist that clung to the floor like standing water. Tech-guard drilled on internal parade grounds of beaten bronze, ranks of servitors hung motionless on recharging racks, enormous tangles of complex machinery relayed the plasma generators' energy throughout the ship. Rust-red and brass were the dominant colours, a distant mechanical din the prominent sound, with the odd passage of rhythmic chanting filtering up from tech-ritual chambers and servitor-choirs.

The *Exemplar* was evidently a fine ship, the product of an immense amount of resources and fading technological knowledge. Whether she was as good a warship as she was a research centre was another matter, but it did occur to Nyxos that the Mechanicus was risking a very valuable ship and crew to investigate Chaeroneia.

The elevator reached the command deck level, where the walls were studded with niches containing elaborate shrines to the Omnissiah and the half-metal skull symbol of the Adeptus Mechanicus stared down from every column. The air was heavy with scented smoke from the braziers, where libations of machine-oil smouldered. The elevator stopped at the level of a wide corridor, carpeted in deep rust red with complex geometric patterns inscribed on the walls and ceiling, where several tech-priests walked followed by gaggles of menials, servitors and lower-ranked adepts. Several curious eyes, bionic and otherwise, turned to look at the interlopers as if Nyxos had no right to stray onto sacred Mechanicus ground.

Nyxos's thoughts were interrupted by a sudden blaring klaxon. Layered below it was a staccato blast of sound, an emergency broadcast in pure machine code.

'What is it?' shouted Nyxos over the din. Tech-priests and menials were already hurrying around.

'Battle stations, maybe,' said Leung. 'Or a proximity warning.'

'Damn it.' Nyxos flicked on his personal vox-unit. He was loath to use it except in an emergency, but he thought this counted. A very rare and antique unit contained in a lacquered red box Nyxos wore around his neck under his robes, it could tap into any local vox-frequency and let Nyxos hijack nearby communications. 'This is Inquisitor Nyxos of the Ordo Malleus,' he barked into the ship's command frequency. 'I demand to know what this emergency is.'

'State your business,' came a reply in the flat, female voice Nyxos recognised as belonging to Magos Korveylan.

'The Emperor's work, magos,' said Nyxos, 'and do not make me justify my actions further.'

There was a pause, slightly too long for comfort. 'Very well,' replied Korveylan. 'Our sensoria have detected torpedoes locked on to the *Exemplar*. Brace for impact.'

BELOW MANUFACTORIUM NOCTIS lay the remains of the old Chaeroneia, the last vestiges of a forge world loyal to Mars and the Emperor. The old architecture of the Adeptus Mechanicus survived, its industrial scale fused with the columns and vaults of religion and the powerful symbolism of the cog and skull. It lay in isolated pockets where the biomechanical mass of the tainted tech-priests had never reached, chapels and factoria, ritual chambers and sacred libraria.

Two hours after the heretic ambush, Alaric and his small strikeforce arrived in one such chamber. The air was old and stale, but free of the biomechanical stink – decaying flesh and rancid machine-oil – that had accompanied the heretic tech-priests and their menials. Alaric stepped out into the cavernous space, storm bolter ready, still not knowing if he had found an ally on Chaeroneia or was just walking into another trap.

'Spread out,' he ordered. His squad fanned out around him, moving with speed and stealth that normal men would find impossible given the bulky power armour they wore. He glanced back at the sole surviving tech-guard. 'Stay here,' he said. 'Protect the interrogator.'

Interrogator Hawkespur didn't object to being assigned a bodyguard and crouched down by the tunnel entrance. Saphentis loitered there, too.

As he walked out into the space Alaric saw it was a cathedral-sized chapel to the Omnissiah. In the centre of its high domed ceiling had once been a circular hole looking up into Chaeroneia's sky but it was clogged with tons of rubble and wreckage, the weight of the city above warping the dome into a painful, biological shape. Trickles of foul water pattered down from cracks in the ceiling, which was covered in elaborate murals of tech-rituals now discoloured with age and damp. Columns stood around the edge of the circular space, each one carved into a statue of a tech-priest, presumably from Chaeroneia's distant Imperial past. The floor was covered in concentric circles or inscribed equations, long sequences of numbers and symbols that no doubt had massive significance for the intricate rituals of the Cult Mechanicus. Now the floor's bronze surface was pitted and green with corrosion. At one end of the room stood a massive altar, a single block of a greyish metallic substance Alaric guessed was pure carbon, with the remains of libation-bowls and hexagonal candelabra still corroding around it.

'Clear this side,' voxed Brother Dvorn.

'Clear here,' confirmed Haulvarn.

'There are no lifesigns on the auspex,' said Saphentis, who was consulting a dataslate that had unfolded from one of his blade-tipped arms.

Alaric walked, still wary, into the centre of the cathedral. It was silent, with not even the dull industrial background noise of the city above reaching this far down. The air was heavy with the meaning of the rituals that had been performed here before Chaeroneia fell, with generations of tech-priests exploring the deepest mysteries of the Omnissiah through ceremony and contemplation.

'Space Marines,' said a voice from the shadows on the far side of the room. 'No wonder they mobilised so quickly.'

Alaric ducked behind the closest column and aimed his storm bolter in the direction of the voice, finger on the firing stud. He heard the clatter of ceramite on stone as the rest of the squad did the same.

'Please, do not shoot. We are the ones who saved you.' A skinny, awkward figure emerged from the darkness behind the carbon altar, hands raised. It looked like a tech-adept, his body composed mostly of bionics. The metal of his artificial hands and face was deep orange-brown with rust and his robes were tattered and filthy. 'My apologies,' he said sheepishly. 'I have too little flesh to show up on your auspexes, I imagine. I did not intend to catch you by surprise.'

Alaric straightened up, still keeping his aim on the tech-priest. 'Who are you?' he demanded.

The tech-priest walked forward a little, still with his scrawny mechanical arms in the air. More shapes were emerging slowly from behind him. 'Iuscus Gallen,' he replied, 'Adept Minoris. These are my comrades.' He indicated the gaggle of tech-priests following him into the temple. They were in as poor repair as Gallen himself and hardly any of them had any flesh showing between the malfunctioning bionics.

'Did you lead us down from the datafortress?'

'Us? Omnissiah forgive me, no, not us. We never could. That was the magos to whom we answer.'

Saphentis stepped forward, not bothering to stay in any cover. 'As an archmagos appointed by the office of the Fabricator General, I require the presence of this magos.'

Gallen looked at Saphentis with surprise in his one remaining human eye. 'An archmagos! Then have the true Mechanicus returned to Chaeroneia? And brought the Adeptus Astartes with them to cleanse this world at last?'

'No, they have not,' replied a new voice, deep and booming. There was a grinding sound from behind the altar and an old broken cargo-servitor lumbered into view. The voice issued from the vox-unit hanging from its neck. The once-human parts of the servitor had died long ago and were now just dried skeletal scraps sandwiched between the servitor's motive units and the massive lifter units of its shoulders. Ordinarily, without a human nervous system to control it, the servitor should not have been able to move at all. 'These we see are all they bring. There is no army to cleanse Chaeroneia. Is that not correct?'

Alaric stepped out from behind the column. 'That is correct,' he said. 'This is an investigative mission under the authority of the Holy Orders of the Emperor's Inquisition. The archmagos is here in an advisory capacity.'

'That is a shame,' said the servitor. 'But you will have to do.'

'Explain yourself,' said Saphentis bluntly.

'Of course. I am being rather rude. I would introduce myself formally but we have already met at the datafortress and before at the manufactorium spire although you probably do not realise it. I am Magos

Antigonus and it seems we have the same mission. Follow me and I will explain.'

CHAPTER TWELVE

'The difference between glory and heresy is so often no more than time.'

– Inquisitor Quixos (source suppressed)

ANTIGONUS'S REALM SPANNED several factory floors and religious buildings that had survived the crushing weight of the city above being built over the centuries. Alaric followed the monstrous servitor through armouries of stolen weaponry and captured battle-servitors, and barracks where fugitive tech-priests fought a losing battle against time to repair their bionics and replace their dying flesh. He saw a giant underground water cistern transformed into a series of hydroponic pools where slimy green algae was grown and turned into a barely edible food to keep the tiny community alive, and the entrances to

199

labyrinthine tunnels above rigged with enough explosive traps and sentry guns to keep attackers away for months. It was a cramped, stifling world, redolent with decay and desperation. But at least it was not corrupt like the planet above. And as they walked, Alaric and Antigonus talked.

'So,' said Alaric at length. 'You are dead?'

'That depends on how you look at it,' said Antigonus. He was trundling through a hangar where various decrepit tanks and APCs were being refitted and reassembled to form a makeshift motor pool for the tiny force of tech-priests. 'I have not had a living body for more than a thousand years.'

'In real space, only a hundred have passed,' said Alaric.

'Well, in any case, it is a long time to be without a physical form. I think it has had quite an effect on me. No doubt your archmagos would be outraged at how we flout the dogma of the Cult Mechanicus down here.'

'But how are you still here?'

'That, justicar, is a complicated question. Chaeroneia is a very old planet and it is riddled with the type of technology the Mechanicus could not replicate in my day and I trust that has not changed in yours. That includes cogitators and data media with a far greater capacity than anything the Mechanicus can make in the current age. So advanced, in fact, that they can contain all the data required to reconstruct a human mind, give or take a few personality quirks. I was sent here by Mars to investigate rumours of tech-heresy and when I discovered they were true, the heretics hunted me down. They thought me dead, but as I died I was able to shift my consciousness into an ancient form of cogitator engine.'

'Just your mind?'

'Just, as you say, my mind. I do not know how long I was in there before I was able reconstruct myself. I was nothing, justicar. I did not exist. It is impossible to describe it. I was just a collection of ideas that used to form Magos Antigonus. I think it took me hundreds of years, but gradually I put myself together again. I found I could move through machines as long as a particular machine's spirit was not strong enough to oppose me. It was through various stores of historical data that I discovered what had happened to Chaeroneia while I was dead. It did not make for enjoyable reading. So I learnt what I could and could not do, explored, investigated. Then I came down here and gathered the few loyal tech-priests who remained and founded this resistance movement.'

'If I may say so, magos, it does not look like you have had much success.'

The lurching servitor shrugged its massive pneumatic shoulders. 'By most standards you are correct. But we know more about Chaeroneia and its tech-priests that you do, justicar and you are better at bringing the fight to the enemy than we are. Moreover, if Chaeroneria has re-entered real space then the tech-priests have made it happen for a reason. Whatever they are doing, I doubt very much that it will benefit the Imperium. All this means that we need each other.'

Alaric and Antigonus's servitor walked through the hangar into a long corridor lined with crumbling statues of past Archmagi, who had ruled Chaeroneia in the days before the tech-heresies had taken root.

'Here' said Antigonus, pointing a rusting cargo lifter arm at one of the statues. It depicted a tech-priest in archaic Mechanicus robes. Only his face was visible, the features blurred in the decaying stone. Its eyes were tiny discs set into the sockets of his cranium and from the lower half of his face hung a bunch of long tentacles – mechadendrites, the prehensile serpentine limbs that many tech-priests used to perform delicate work. The faded letters chiselled into the statue's base read: ARCH-MAGOS VENERATUS SCRAECOS.

'This was the one. Perhaps the leader. He was either the origin of the tech-heresy on this planet or he was their most senior convert. He was the one who killed me. I'd wager he led the effort to bring Chaeroneia into the warp, too. He commanded the machine-curse he used to infect me and probably all the hunter-programs that protect his data centres.'

Alaric looked up at the statue. It looked as strange as any tech-priest he had seen. He knew that arch-magos veneratus was one of the highest tech-priest ranks that might be found on a forge world – the tech-heresy had spread quickly on Chaeroneia and straight to the top. 'They weren't hunter-programs,' said Alaric. 'They were daemons. An unusual kind, true, since they compose their bodies of information instead of sorcery. But daemons nonetheless. That was how we could defeat them.'

Antigonus looked at Alaric and his desiccated face managed to appear surprised. 'Daemons? I thought that was just a lie of the machine-curse.'

Alaric shook his head. 'It was probably telling the truth. Daemons will only speak the truth when they know it will not be believed.'

'And you defeated them, you say? At the datafortress?'

'Yes. I and my battle-brothers.'

'Were you able to access the information in there? We have been trying to get at it for decades.'

Alaric sighed. 'You will have to ask Archmagos Saphentis about that. He is not always willing to share information with me. Perhaps as a fellow tech-priest you will have more luck.'

'We tech-priests are not known for our social perception, justicar, but still I think I detect some tension between the two of you.'

'Saphentis represents the interests of the Mechanicus. They do not always coincide with the objectives of the Inquisition.'

'You are suspicious of him?'

'He was accompanied by another tech-priest. She has disappeared and Saphentis does not seem particularly concerned about losing her. And I think he has some admiration for what has happened to Chaeroneia.'

Antigonus led the way down the corridor, which looped back round towards the makeshift barracks where Alaric's squad, Saphentis and Hawkespur were being seen to by the medically-trained tech-priests. 'Your suspicions may be well-founded, justicar. It was a high-ranking tech-priest who first brought this heresy to Chaeroneia. But nevertheless I shall do as you suggest and talk to him. It may be he found something at the datafortress we can use to strike back at this planet's leaders at last.'

'With Chaeroneia back in real space,' said Alaric, 'it might be the only chance we get. But there is something else we need. Can you communicate with craft in orbit?'

Antigonus seemed to think for a second, the skull of his servitor body tilting to one side. 'Perhaps. But not with any certainty.'

'It will have to do. Hawkespur will need to contact Inquisitor Nyxos in orbit, tell him what is happening down here.'

'And yourself?'

'Me?'

'You are doubtless tired and injured, justicar. I expect you have not rested for any length of time since you arrived on the surface.'

Alaric held up the storm bolter mounted on the back of his power armour's left gauntlet. The barrel was charred black with muzzle flash. 'I could use some more ammunition,' he said.

'I will see what we can do. Meanwhile, I shall speak with Saphentis. Whether he is on our side or not he could know more about Chaeroneia than I do.'

The corridor led into the barracks, where rusting metal bunks were lined up in niches and tiny personal shrines to the Omnissiah filled the room with the smell of scented machine-oil. Alaric's squad were attending to their wargear rites, murmuring their own benedictions of preparedness as they cleaned their storm bolters and nemesis weapons. Brother

Dvorn had removed the upper half of his armour and was repairing the many bullet scars and gouges in the surface of the ceramite. Dvorn was impressively muscled even for a Marine and he had been at the front of every hand-to-hand action as always. Cardios, meanwhile, had been seriously battered at the hands of the data-daemon and his fractured ribcage had been set and bandaged by Antigonus's tech-priests. One of his arms had been broken, too and the crude operation to re-set the bone had left a vivid red scar down Cardios's bicep. The damage to his breastplate of fused ribs was worse, though – shards of bone had probably slashed at his organs, meaning he would be slightly slower and weaker than his brother Marines and would only get worse until he got to a proper apothecarion.

These were the battle-brothers to whom Alaric owed his life, simply by virtue of backing him up in battle. They all owed that much to one another – a single Grey Knight could never have lasted this long on Chaeroneia. And Alaric was responsible for their conduct in battle and their spiritual wellbeing. It was an enormous responsibility, one that Alaric accepted because if he didn't, there were very few who could.

Alaric passed Interrogator Hawkespur, who was sitting on the bunk. Her voidsuit was unzipped and hanging around her waist. The underlayer she wore beneath it was thin enough for Alaric to see the outline of her ribs through the fabric. She looked like she had lost weight in the few days she had been on Chaeroneia – much of it must have been lost in the battle against the ugly tumours that formed blue-grey lumps under the skin of her throat and upper chest.

Her face was waxy-pale, her short black hair clinging to her forehead with cold sweat.

'Hawkespur? How are you doing?' asked Alaric.

Hawkespur shrugged. 'I'm fighting it.'

'How long can you go on?'

'As long as I can. My guess would be less than a week, But I only have two years of medicae cadet training. Could be more, could be less.'

'Antigonus will try to get communications with Nyxos in orbit. After that I could leave you here.'

'No, justicar. I am the Inquisitorial representative on this planet. I must know everything you find out, immediately. Just because my time is limited does not mean my mission has already failed.' Hawkespur coughed heavily and one of Antigonus's tech-priests arrived carrying a battered box of medical supplies. Alaric left them to it and walked over to his squad.

'Brothers,' he said. 'Magos Antigonus could be a valuable ally. He knows a great deal about what happened here and how the enemy is structured. It could be that he can help us strike at the heart of the heretics.'

'Good,' said Brother Dvorn. 'I'm sick of hiding in the shadows. There's nothing on this planet that can stand up to us, not one-on-one. All we need to know is where they are.'

'Hopefully that is true,' said Alaric, 'But it may still not be that simple. Antigonus will try to put us in contact with Nyxos in orbit. We can apprise him of the situation and see if he has any new orders for us.'

'Whoever controls this planet,' added Brother Haulvarn, 'they didn't just re-enter real space by accident. And they must have known that sooner or later

Imperial forces would find out that Chaeroneia had fallen to daemons and heretics. They're here for a reason and whatever they are planning they must be able to do it soon. Does Antigonus know why they have chosen this moment to show their hand?'

Alaric sat down on one of the bunks – it almost buckled under his armoured weight. He laid down his Nemesis halberd and began unfastening the massive ceramite slab of his breastplate. 'No, he does not. But there is one event we know of that Antigonus did not.'

Haulvarn raised an eyebrow. 'The Eye?'

'The Thirteenth Black Crusade has brought more Chaos-worshipping forces into Imperial space than any other event in thousands of years. Perhaps it is a coincidence, perhaps it is not, but if the masters of Chaeroneia are on a mission to aid the Black Crusade then we could win a victory here for the forces stemming the tide at the Eye. And no doubt you have heard the rumours that victories are sorely needed.' Alaric pulled off his breastplate and saw the livid bruises on his skin where he had been shot and battered during the fighting of the last few days. He was tired and aching and there would be new scars alongside his many old ones when he had healed. If he survived, of course. Chaeroneia probably had a great many ways to kill him that he hadn't seen yet.

'But these are matters outside our control for now,' Alaric continued. 'For the present we should concentrate on things we ourselves can change and foremost among those is ourselves. This wargear has seen much corruption on this planet and we must reconsecrate it. The same goes for our bodies and minds.

Haulvarn, lead the wargear rites. Archis, speak for the spirit of your Incinerator. We will not have long before we must begin this fight again and we will use the time well.'

Brother Haulvarn began intoning the low, rhythmic words of the wargear rites, imploring forgiveness from the spirits of the squad's armour and weapons for forcing them to confront the moral treachery of Chaeroneia. As the battle-brothers prayed together, anyone who saw them would see the true strength of the Grey Knights – not the physical augmentations or the hallowed wargear, or even the exacting training that prepared them to fight things that should never exist. Their strength was their faith, the shield of pure belief that protected their minds from the predations of Chaos and the lies of daemons. No one else in the Imperium could claim such strength – it was the reason the Grey Knights existed, the reason they were trusted with spearheading holy victories in the Emperor's name.

It was just as well they had that strength. Because on Chaeroneia, it was all they had.

INQUISITOR NYXOS IGNORED the protestations of the protocol adept who manned the doors to the bridge of the *Exemplar* and barged past the cordon of silent tech-guard, trusting in the unit of Naval armsmen behind him to keep anyone from barring his way. The torpedo alerts were still booming throughout the ship and the confusion common to all battle-readied warships was increasing – menials scurried here and there carrying messages in scroll tubes or carting vital items of equipment between decks. Tech-priests relayed orders in bursts of lingua technis and the chattered machine-code overlapped until it sounded like rapid gunfire.

As he walked onto the bridge, Nyxos saw why Magos Korveylan seemed so unwilling to see any visitors to her ship face-to-face. Her body was a solid block of mem-circuits and cogitator units, formed into a dense square pillar of knotted circuitry and wires. The remains of her biological body – her ribcage, spine, heart and lungs and her central nervous system – were contained in a plastiglass cylinder on top of the cogitator stack, her skinless face held up by a web of fine metal struts. She was rooted into the floor of the bridge and only her hands could move, her fingers moving deftly over the array of controls on the dataslate mounted inside the clear cylinder. The more 'normal' face, the one she used for visual communications with other ships, stood to one side on the communications console – it was a simple automaton, used to give the impression that Korveylan looked like the tech-priests someone outside the Mechanicus would have met.

Korveylan looked around as Nyxos walked in. Her face was no more than muscle and bone so he could read no expression off her, but the synthesised voice that blared from the speakers on the front of her mechanical body sounded officious and annoyed. 'Inquisitor. We are at war. Leave my bridge.'

'I hardly think I'm getting in anyone's way,' replied Nyxos breezily. The rest of the bridge seemed staffed only by servitors, slaved into various consoles, dumbly typing at brass-faced keypads or working the gears on cogitator units that looked like they ran on clockwork.

Korveylan's unit rotated so she was facing Nyxos. Her lidless eyes were glossy and black. 'I am the captain of this ship.'

'And I am the instrument of the Emperor's will,' replied Nyxos briskly. 'I win.'

There was a pause as Korveylan seemed to consider this. 'Observe,' she said.

Nyxos assumed this meant he could stay, but was not to touch anything. That was fine by him.

The tactical viewer on the *Exemplar* took the form of a large mechanical orrery, a construction of concentric rings that swung around one another like the devices used to demonstrate the relative positions of planets in a solar system. This example, however, had silver and brass icons mounted on the rings that showed the relative positions of the various ships and objects around Chaeroneia. Nyxos noticed that several glinting knife-shaped icons of silver must represent the torpedoes now approaching the Imperial fleet very quickly. Bronze disks mounted further out represented the enemy fleet, including the *Hellforger*, while a dense sphere of rotating gears at the centre was Chaeroneia itself.

Space combat, Nyxos had learnt in his long Inquisitorial career, was an agonising affair where manoeuvres and assaults could take hours to pan out. Hours when a competent captain usually knew exactly what was going to happen and often had no choice but to wait for his ship to take whatever the enemy was throwing at it. The enemy attack here had been so sudden that the battle was unfolding on a minute-by-minute scale – lightning-fast by naval standards.

'Engineering,' Korveylan was saying into the ship's internal vox-net, 'Bring auxiliary reactors five and eight on-line. Full power, evasion pattern.'

Several more Mechanicus crewmen were entering the bridge, shouldering through the armsmen Nyxos had brought with him, no doubt summoned silently by Korveylan to keep an eye on the intruder. Nyxos recognised tech-guard uniforms and the brass body armour of the ship's more highly trained Skitarii troopers.

'Impact!' blared the ship's vox-casters and the first of the torpedoes hit, shaking the bridge violently. Nyxos's servo-assisted limbs compensated but several of the servitors were thrown out of their moorings, flailing helplessly like puppets with their strings cut. Tech-guard grabbed anything they could to keep themselves upright. Sparks showered as cogitators shorted and the lighting flickered.

'Damage report,' said Korveylan calmly as the explosion still echoed through the ship. Secondary explosions thudded somewhere deep in the ship's structure, ammo stores or fuel cells blowing.

Pict-screens slid up from the floor beside Korveylan, each showing the wreckage of an area devastated by the impact. To Nyxos's eyes it looked bad, billowing orange-black smoke and twisted metal.

'Engineering damage minor,' came a vox from elsewhere in the ship.

'Ordnance damage minor,' echoed a similar voice. The ship's officers sounded off – the torpedo had struck hard but not hard enough to put the *Exemplar* in immediate danger.

'Come about, pattern intercept,' said Korveylan. 'Power to prow turrets.'

Nyxos walked towards Korveylan. 'Why are you here, magos?' he asked.

'Now is not the time,' said Korveylan, with a reassuringly human note of annoyance.

'Now is the perfect time. I may not get to ask you again.'

Another explosion sounded, closer this time, metal shrieking only a couple of decks away. Nyxos heard the horrible keening of a deck breach, the air whistling as it was dragged out through a punctured hull.

'The Adeptus Mechanicus retains sovereignty over the forge world of Chaeroneia. The *Exemplar* was sent to oversee the reassertion of authority. Your questions require me to multitask, inquisitor and have a directly deleterious effect on my capacity to command this ship.'

'No, magos. I mean why are you here, personally?'

Korveylan ignored him. The tactical orrery was showing a shoal of torpedoes closing in and the ship's prow turrets opened up in response, the rapid thuds of their reports vibrating the floor of the bridge.

'I took the liberty of checking before I came aboard. The Mechanicus is meticulous in its record-keeping and an inquisitor's authority gains him access to a great deal. Not all of it, regrettably, but enough. You were a magos piloting cargo ships around the forge world Salshan Anterior barely two years ago. That would make the *Exemplar* your first battleship command. And yet here you are, hard-wired into the bridge as if you own the place. Not to mention the fact that you're a long way from home out here.'

The third impact hit Nyxos as if he had run into a wall, a shockwave ripping through from the prow of the ship and billowing through the decks. Jets of coolant gas spurted from ruptured pipes. Glass and metal shattered. A bloom of fire rippled up one wall, engulfing the servitor wired into it, before automated fire extinguishers doused half the room in choking fumes.

Nyxos realised he was on the floor. He wasn't hurt but he was shaken, his head reeling. He looked around him, face still lying against the floor and saw one of the tech-guard had lost an arm to a flying sheet of torn metal that had sheared right through at the elbow. Deeper explosions sounded, from ahead of the bridge – a torpedo had smacked into the prow, burrowed deep through the reinforced prow armour and exploded close to something the *Exemplar* couldn't really do without.

'All non-essential personnel evacuate from the bridge,' said Korveylan over the growing din.

A tech-guard hand grabbed Nyxos's shoulder, pulling him up and towards the doors leading off the bridge.

'It's not that easy, Korveylan!' shouted Nyxos. 'I know Archmagos Scraecos was at Salshan Anterior! You studied at the seminary he founded. You translated three volumes of his writings from its original machine-code. And whatever he came to Chaeroneia to find, I think you know it's still there!'

Magos Korveylan paused in making her course cal-
culations and turned to look at Nyxos. Even with no
face to hold an expression, there was something in
her eyes that told Nyxos the annoyance was gone.
There was no point in lying to him any more – Nyxos
knew enough to see through the lies. With the sparks
still flying and hundreds of warning lights flickering
on every console, Magos Korveylan looked suddenly
calm.

'The Chief Engineer has the bridge,' she said over
the ship's vox-net. She closed her eyes, muttered a
prayer Nyxos couldn't hear and exploded in a starburst of broken glass.

THE WAY to the transmitter obelisk was steep and
treacherous, winding up through the remains of
Manufactorium Noctis's ancient sewage and
drainage systems. Interrogator Hawkespur followed
Alaric doggedly along the paths cut into the sheer
sides of giant water cisterns and slippery staircases
worn almost smooth with time. Magos Antigonus
led the way, his consciousness contained within a
spry maintenance servitor with four long spiderish
legs that scampered easily up steep slopes and over
obstacles. Archmagos Saphentis was there, too,
almost gliding regally as he kept up with Antigonus.

Alaric found the going easier than Hawkespur, his
enhanced strength meaning he could just dig his
fingers into the crumbling stonework and haul
himself upwards. As he followed Antigonus he saw
places where primitive burials had left mouldering
bones in niches cut into sewer walls, a relic of the
time when Chaeroneia's underclass of menials had

fallen into tribal savagery for the first centuries after the planet dropped into the warp. There were decrees in the dots and dashes of lingua technis carved into marble stele set into the walls, marking the time when the tech-priests had emerged from their spires again and begun building Chaeroneia into the cannibalistic society Alaric had seen above – those menials had been rounded up, refitted and branded with barcode marks of servitude, then fed into the flesh-knitting engines when their lives were spent and turned into the biomechanical monstrosities that ran so much of Manufactorium Noctis.

There had been battles, evidently. Sometimes Alaric glimpsed armour almost corroded into nothing by time, just a green-black metal stain on the stone where a body had fallen quelling some riot or uprising. But for every sign of unrest there were two or three symbols of submission – time-worn statues of heretic tech-priests, machine-cant slogans proclaiming the debased laws of Chaeroneia. From these dank tunnels had marched the menials of Chaeroneia to join the tech-priests they considered their rightful masters and in return the planet had almost literally swallowed them up.

'There is not much further to go,' said Antigonus. The vox-unit on his current servitor made his voice sound tinny and distant. 'The obelisk was once used to transmit a navigational beacon for close-orbit spaceships. We intended to use it to broadcast a distress signal, but we soon understood that we could not get a signal from the warp into real space with the resources we had.'

'But it should reach into orbit now?' asked Hawke-spur.

'If it still works, yes,' replied Antigonus.

'Archmagos,' continued Hawkespur, 'did you find out if there are any active tech-priest installations in orbit? They could block our signal, or use it to track us down here.'

'I did not find any information pertaining to that subject,' replied Saphentis.

'I'm still in the dark as to just what you did find,' said Alaric. 'Even though we lost Thalassa and almost all the tech-guard to find out.'

'It would be of limited use to one who was not a tech-priest,' replied Saphentis.

'Fortunately,' said Alaric, 'we have one right here. Antigonus?'

Antigonus's servitor paused and turned. Its face was a simple brass mask, pitted with age, with two silver studs for eyes and a round grille housing its vox-unit. 'The Enemy deployed its daemons to keep you out of there, archmagos. The knowledge you found must be important.'

The party emerged onto the base of a huge, deep chamber, roughly rectangular, with a ceiling so high it disappeared far up into the shadows beyond the limit of the search lamps mounted on the shoulders of Antigonus's servitor body. It had once been a huge reservoir of water or fuel for the Manufactorium above, but it had been dry and dark for hundreds of years now.

'Very well. The data was incomplete and severely corrupted. I was able to confirm your suspicions about the date, justicar. Chaeroneia has been out of real space for a little under eleven hundred years. Most of the rest of the information related to power output, with which a self-sufficient forge world must understandably be concerned. Chaeroneia's power is generated, output and recycled with an efficiency I have never beheld in the most advanced Adeptus Mechanicus facilities.'

'Don't get too enthusiastic, archmagos,' said Antigonus. 'Tech-priests have been lost to the resistance before by coming to side with the enemy. They always begin with such sentiments. Just because the rulers of this world can cheat the rules that limit the Machine, it does not mean they are superior.'

'Of course,' continued Saphentis. 'Nonetheless it is remarkable. The biomechanical structures of the Manufactorium appear to be central to this system with most of the resultant output being directed towards a very large complex just outside the threshold of Manufactorium Noctis. It appears that this was radioactive wasteland prior to the loss of Chaeroneia. There is no indication as to what is there now. The output rose exponentially just prior to Chaeroneia's re-entry into real space.'

'Whatever they're doing,' said Hawkespur, 'they're doing it there.'

'The rest was mostly ideological. The tech-heresy has historical precedent.'

'Then it is true,' said Antigonus. 'The Dark Mechanicus.'

'The Dark Mechanicus?' The term was unfamiliar to Alaric.

'Tech-priests loyal to the Traitor Legions in the days of the Horus Heresy,' said Hawkespur. 'They were exterminated during the Scouring that followed the Battle of Terra.'

'It was not quite that simple, interrogator,' said Saphentis. 'The schism within the Mechanicus was perhaps more complicated than even the Inquisition generally understand. My rank gains me certain privileges and greater access to historical data is one of them.'

The facets of Saphentis's eyes shifted colour as he accessed encrypted mem-cells built into his augmentations. 'The faction that sided with Horus,' he continued, 'probably only became known as the 'Dark' Mechanicus after the Heresy, when Horus had been defeated and it was realised that the beliefs they followed were corrupt. The Dark Mechanicus was not a body of tech-priests, but the beliefs they held and the principles to which they adhered. The fusion of the flesh and the machine. The creation of new living things. Innovation and freedom of research.'

'But they were destroyed,' said Hawkespur.

It was Antigonus who replied. 'You can't kill an idea, interrogator,' he said. 'As hard as the Inquisition has tried, they just keep on coming back. There were so many tech-heresies recorded in the libraria of Mars that I was never certain which had taken hold on Chaeroneia. But the Dark Mechanicus… yes, that makes sense. Perfect sense. Especially if they are in league with daemons. Towards the end of the Heresy they say the Dark Mechanicus trafficked with daemons. Perhaps Scraecos and his tech-priests have renewed the old pacts.'

'And these ideas were left to flourish?' snapped Alaric. 'Where heresies are found among the authorities of the Imperium they are stamped out! Burned! The Mechanicus knew of this heresy and they let it live? The Precepts of Guilliman required that the works of the traitor Horus and all his acolytes be destroyed! The Mechanicus was no exception.'

'What the justicar says is true,' said Saphentis. Alaric looked at him in mild surprise – it was the first time he could recall the archmagos genuinely agreeing with him. 'The details of Dark Mechanicus heresy I uncovered were comprehensive. The data was in a poor state but there is little doubt they represent a knowledge of the Horusian schism that even as an archmagos I was not privy to. Scraecos was an archmagos veneratus but even then it is unlikely in the extreme he could reconstruct the specific rituals and research procedures from current Adeptus Mechanicus records alone.'

'Which begs the question,' said Hawkespur echoing Alaric's own thoughts, 'where did Scraecos get it all from?'

Antigonus sighed, his servitor body hanging its head. 'I knew that Chaeroneia's heresy was exceptional. But this is something else.'

'Then we need to keep going,' said Hawkespur. 'Our immediate priority is to reach the obelisk. Then we contact Nyxos in orbit and tell him that the Dark Mechanicus have returned.'

CHAPTER THIRTEEN

'Ask not the name of the Enemy. Ask not his Will, nor his Method. Ask not to think his Thoughts and ask not to speak his Words. Ask only for the strength to kill him.'

> – The Imperial Infantryman's Uplifting Primer
> (Addendum Spiritual) 97-14

THE SHAPE OF the *Hellforger* filled the viewscreen on the bridge of the *Tribunicia*, a massive red-black wedge of a ship bigger than the *Tribunicia* and sporting twice as many guns. The traitor ship was hurtling towards the Imperial fleet at a speed no Imperial captain would have dreamed of going, torpedoes still sailing on glittering streams of exhaust from its forward ports.

'Where are my damage reports?' yelled Horstgeld over the barely contained chaos of the bridge.

'There's a breach in plasma reactor three!' came a reply from somewhere in the Engineering section. 'It's ignoring all our tech-prayers, we're going to have to shut it down!'

'Shutdown denied,' replied Horstgeld. It was less dangerous to keep the reactor running than to risk the drop in engine power that would ensue if the reactor was shut down. Probably the decision would cost lives from leaks of superheated plasma into the engineering deck that surrounded the reactor, but those were the kinds of sacrifices that a captain had to make.

It was bad. The initial volley of torpedoes from the *Hellforger* had scored hits on the *Tribunicia* and the *Exemplar*. *Ptolemy Gamma*, already seriously compromised by the loss of its comms, had been all but crippled by a lucky strike that blew off a sizeable chunk of its stern and ripped a breach through most of its engineering decks. The torpedo salvo was just the opening move, that was clear – the *Hellforger* fully intended to take the first major kill up close with its guns, or even its boarding parties, and was charging towards the *Tribunicia* with a fervour that could only mean it was commanded by a madman.

The second, unidentified enemy cruiser, a strange bloated shape that fairly dripped with guns, was coming in behind the *Hellforger* and once it got amongst the Imperial ships its broadsides would reap a horrendous tally among the transports and escorts. The last major ship in the enemy fleet looked like a very old pattern fighter platform. Triangular in cross-section, each of its three long sides housed a host of attack craft hangars and launching bays.

Each of the enemy ships had picked its target. Each was more than a match for its chosen prey. Horstgeld's role was now to simply delay the enemy for as long as possible and hope against hope that the time he was buying actually meant something.

'Bring us side-on to the *Hellforger*,' ordered Horstgeld to the navigation section. 'Ordnance, load up for a broadside. Get everyone on the guns.' Horstgeld glanced at the tactical readout inset into the viewscreen. 'And Comms! Get me the *Pieta*.'

'Sir?'

'You heard me. And do it soon.'

The *Hellforger* was one of the ugliest ships Horstgeld had ever seen. It had originally been a very old mark of Imperial ship with the flat wedge shape that had been all but abandoned by the Imperial navy. Over the thousands of years it had been in service, the traitor ship's hull had become covered with blisters and weeping sores as if the metal of the ship was diseased and its scores of guns poked from open bleeding gashes in the hull.

A ship that ugly needed some ugly tactics to fight it. Horstgeld murmured a prayer imploring the Emperor for forgiveness and set about thinking what he would tell the *Pieta*.

THE ORBITAL COMMUNICATIONS obelisk was a needle of dull grey metal three hundred feet high, covered in dense circuitry like elaborate scrollwork and half-buried in the corroded mass that made up the foundations of Manufactorium Noctis.

'Are you ready?' asked Magos Antigonus.

Hawkespur nodded. She sat on the rubble at the foot of the obelisk, which speared up above her into the mass of compressed wreckage that formed the ceiling of the chamber. Antigonus had set up a simple vox-unit plugged into the obelisk which Hawkespur was to speak into. With the hood of her voidsuit back, her tumours were vivid blue-grey lumps under the skin of her throat. It wouldn't be long before they started to constrict her breathing.

'Will the Dark Mechanicus notice the power drain?' asked Alaric.

'Probably,' said Antigonus as he made the final adjustments to the vox-unit. 'They suspect we are down here. But they rarely send hunter-servitors down this far.'

'The spirits of such technology rarely answer us any more,' said Archmagos Saphentis, stroking a mechanical finger over the patterns inlaid into the obelisk. 'This must be very old, from the very earliest days of Chaeroneia. Very difficult to replicate.'

'I suggest you take notes, then, archmagos,' said Alaric. 'We don't plan on being here for very long.'

The whole chamber vibrated with a low hum as power flooded into the obelisk. The vox-unit howled with static.

'Let it cycle through the frequencies,' said Antigonus. 'If we're lucky it will tap into the receivers on one of the Imperial ships.'

Always, thought Alaric, it eventually came down to luck.

'We're getting something,' said Hawkespur. 'To all Imperial forces, this is Interrogator Hawkespur of the Ordo Malleus, please respond...'

MAGOS MURGILD REACHED the bridge of the Exemplar in time to see the automated maintenance servitors clearing the scorched remains off the floor. Given that Korveylan had been hard-wired into the floor of the bridge, that she was not there and that her command throne was the epicentre of the smouldering mess of flesh and metal, he instantly guessed that it was the ship's captain who had died. He was slightly taken aback by the sight of his captain being scooped up by a servitor's slop-trowel, but he did well not to show it.

'I was given the bridge,' said Murgild as he shambled towards the charred command post. He spoke through a chest-mounted vox-unit since the lower half of his face was hidden by a thick metal collar, an extension of the armoured voidsuit he wore under his robes to protect him from the dangerous conditions in Engineering. 'What happened?'

'Magos Korveylan detonated herself,' said Inquisitor Nyxos. He had several cuts on his face from the shrapnel from the explosion. The naval armsmen he had brought from the *Tribunicia* were now stationed on the bridge under the command of Commissar Leung, in case Murgild was in any doubt as to who held the real authority on the ship. 'I voiced my suspicions about her allegiance and in response, she killed herself.'

Murgild paused. 'I see.'

'The initial torpedo volley is done but the enemy fleet is closing fast. They have a gun-heavy cruiser making straight for us and our first priority is for evasive manoeuvres to put the *Ptolemy* squadron between us and that cruiser. Do what you must but remember that by the authority of the Inquisition I am in ultimate command of this ship. Fleet Commissar Leung is now responsible for ship security.'

Murgild stood at the command console and began scanning through the manoeuvring sermons in the ship's navigation logs. The *Exemplar* wasn't an agile ship and it would take all the magos's efforts to keep it mobile as the enemy closed in. Murgild seemed able to ignore the greasy smoke that surrounded the control helm, the last remnant of Magos Korveylan.

Nyxos turned to Leung. 'Commissar, I need Magos Korveylan's personal effects and communications logs thoroughly searched. Find out if she kept any record of who she was working for and what their orders were. Along with any indication of what she was looking for.'

'I shall have the armsmen conduct a thorough search,' replied Leung.

'And make it quick. This ship might not last long.'

'We have multiple target locks,' came a vox from the sensorium centre. 'Source is the cruiser-class craft.'

'They're taking aim first. Then they'll hit us with everything they've got,' said Nyxos. He looked at the tactical orrery, which showed the bloated unknown cruiser-sized enemy ship heading menacingly for the *Exemplar*. 'At least we know who we shall have to deal with. Murgild, our priority is staying alive. Draw that cruiser in and keep out of its broadside arcs for as long as we can. Can this ship pull that off?'

'Possibly,' replied Murgild. 'Depending on the manoeuvring capabilities of the enemy.'

'Good. Do it. And had Korveylan got any closer to decoding the signal from the planet?'

'The verispex labs were making some headway.'

'Keep me posted.' The ship shuddered as another structure in the prow gave way. The *Exemplar* was badly battered and it would only get worse.

'Captain,' came another vox, this time from the communications centre. 'We are receiving anomalous transmissions from the planet's surface. Possible Imperial origin.'

'Route it to the bridge,' said Nyxos.

The static from the signal sputtered from the bridge vox-casters, layering a grainy film of sound over the clacking of servitors working the bridge consoles and the pounding of the engines from deep inside the ship. Nyxos struggled to make out words from the mess of sound.

'...repeat, this is Interrogator Hawkespur of the Ordo Malleus, can anyone...'

'Hawkespur! This is Nyxos. What in the hells is going on down there?'

'...we crashed. Moral threat confirmed, it's the Dark Mechanicus...' Hawkespur's voice sounded weak, as if she was exhausted, as well as distorted and broken up by the poor reception.

'Hawkespur, we're running out of time up here. The planet sent out a signal and the *Hellforger* just turned up in response. It was last seen in the service of the Abaddon the Despoiler and it looks like they want to get down to the surface.'

'...not happen, sir, the enemy is routeing a lot of power to an area outside the city. May be something there the enemy want...'

'They're not the only ones. Magos Korveylan here was looking for it, too and she wasn't following Mechanicus orders. We don't know who she was working for. Maybe someone a lot higher up.'

'...to understand our priority is now to find the centre of the enemy activity and ascertain any threat?'

'Correct. Do whatever you must, Hawkespur. Use scorched earth if you have to. And you're on your own down there, we're facing several cruiser-class ships and we can't hold them off forever.'

'...sir, just get us time, I'll go by my judgement.'

'You do that. If Alaric's alive, trust him, he knows how to stay alive in places like that. And if Saphentis is there, don't trust him. He could be compromised. The Mechanicus know something they're not telling us. Hawkespur? Hawkespur?'

Nyxos listened intently for a long minute. There was only static.

'Damn it. Murgild, have Comms keep scanning that frequency. Let me know of anything you get. '

'Yes, inquisitor.'

'And have verispex keep on decoding that signal, even if the ship starts falling apart. If Hawkespur gets back in contact I want to have something useful to tell her.'

'I UNDERSTAND, BUT we still don't know what we are up against, sir. Just get us time, I'll go by my judgement,' saidHawkespur. The vox-unit howled with feedback and then just coughed static. 'Sir? Inquisitor?'

The circuits of the obelisk were glowing dull red with resistance. The vox-unit sparked and shorted out.

'They could be blocking us,' said Antigonus.

'Which means they know where we are,' added Alaric.

'I think he told me everything he had to,' said Hawkespur, pulling off the vox headset. 'The Dark

Mechanicus have summoned a Chaos fleet. They were probably transmitting to them since before we even arrived. It's led by the *Hellforger*, one of the most notorious ships of the Gothic War. That means our theory about Chaeroneia's reappearance being linked to Abaddon's attack through the Eye of Terror just got much more realistic.'

'Hardly good news,' said Antigonus, prodding at the smouldering vox-unit.

'It is better than no news,' said Alaric. 'We have some idea of what we are up against. The Chaos fleet wants something on Chaeroneia. If we get to it first, that means we can hurt them. You might not like what you hear, but every piece of information we have makes this fight easier.'

'It also means we need to leave,' said Hawkespur, pulling up the hood of her voidsuit. 'Antigonus, we need to get to the site of that power spike. Can we get there quickly?'

'There are ways. If we mobilise everything we have we could be there in less than two hours. But we rarely send anyone out there. There's nowhere to hide, it's all ash dunes. And there isn't anything there, no structures, no stores.'

'It seems,' said Saphentis, 'that there is something there now. Something that is draining inordinate amounts of power from this city.' The archmagos hadn't spoken since the obelisk had started broadcasting, listening carefully as if he was sifting through frequencies inaudible to normal hearing. 'And Antigonus, you have no idea what it might be?'

Antigonus shrugged as best his servitor body would allow. 'The only place that ever drew that kind of power in Manufactorium Noctis was the titan works and as far as we can tell they've been completely dismantled for eight hundred years.'

'Whatever it is,' said Hawkespur, 'we have to get there. This mission is no longer about investigation. It's about denial to the enemy of whatever the Dark Mechanicus have created.'

'Agreed,' said Alaric. 'My squad will be ready to move out immediately. Antigonus?'

'My adepts are ready.'

'Good. Then we move.'

'We move,' said Hawkespur.

As the four of them returned to Antigonus's base, they could hear Manufactorium Noctis groaning above them, as if the city itself was trying to claw its way down to get them. The whole of Chaeroneia hated them and knew they were there, like an infection in the biomechanical mass of Manufactorium Noctis. The taint of sorcery Alaric felt when he saw the planet for the first time seemed to be getting stronger, as if the dark heart of the planet was waking up and turning its gaze on them.

It wanted to see them dead. It would probably succeed. But Alaric trusted in Hawkespur and in his battle-brothers to ensure that, before that happened, it would have as hard a fight as anyone could give it.

MISSIONARY PATRICOS PULLED himself up onto the pulpit of the main amphitheatre, an enormous auditorium where all the pilgrims who travelled on the *Pieta* could be addressed at once. And most of them were there – men, women and children crowding the rows of seating, clutching aquila icons or battered prayer books, murmuring their fear and uncertainty.

The crew of the *Pieta* had just affected a sudden course change on the orders from the Rear Admiral in command of the fleet. Some of the pilgrims even thought they were about to come under attack from an enemy craft. Patricos had been with the ship all the way on its pilgrimage from Gathalamor around the southern edge of the galaxy towards San Leor and he was the spiritual leader for these thousands of people, the conduit for the Emperor's will to be revealed to them. He had led them for thirteen years of long, hard pilgrimage and they trusted him absolutely.

'Brothers!' called Patricos in his rich preacher's voice. 'And sisters! Do not despair! We are in a trying place, yes and the servants of the Emperor are sorely stretched at this time. But we are His people! He will protect us from the depredations of those who would harm us. For we carry His beneficence in our hearts! We have devoted ourselves to Him! Trust in Him, as you have done these long years and you will be rewarded with His grace in the next life!'

Patricos saw fear etched into their time-worn faces. They had been picked up from dozens of worlds along the route, many of them having been taken aboard at Gathalamor at the very start of the voyage. They had been together for so long that it only took one doubting voice for rumour and panic to spread like a fire.

'But one of the crewmen told me there is an enemy fleet approaching!' called out one pilgrim's voice. 'And we are under a military command!'

Patricos held his hands up in a calming gesture. 'True, the Navy has called upon our presence, but this is merely a precaution. In the unlikely event of enemy action we could function as a transport or hospital ship. We are unarmed! And we carry with us the faithful souls, the same good Emperor-fearing men and women for whom the Navy fights! They would not let us come to harm. Now, let us pray and give thanks for the bravery and sacrifice of these soldiers and crewmen who protect us in times of darkness. Hymnal Tertiam, verse ninety-three.'

The pilgrims began praying, falteringly at first and then in stronger voice, as Patricos led them in the praises of the immortal God-Emperor.

THE MASSIVE BULK of the *Hellforger*, almost half as big again as a standard cruiser-class ship, knifed through space towards the midpoint of the *Tribunicia*. The outer hull plates of its prow flaked off on trails of steaming gore, revealing bone-white fangs that formed a vicious cutting edge like the tip of a chainsword. Wide wet orifices opened up just below the ramming fangs, leading to the mustering chambers where the boarding troops were being herded into place.

The *Hellforger* maintained a formidable horde of subhuman boarding troops, brutal half-mad creatures evolved and mutated for ugly close-quarters killing. If the *Tribunicia* survived the initial impact they would be driven through the boarding orifices and onto the Imperial ship, flooding its decks with blood-crazed madmen. It was an old tactic, one of the most effective given the size and toughness of the

Hellforger itself. A ramming action, according to Imperial Naval doctrine, was nothing short of madness. A boarding action was scarcely less so. Imperial captains simply had no idea how to defend against the *Hellforger* hurtling towards them at ramming speed, its razor-sharp prow fully exposed. The terror of the sight alone had shaken more than one Imperial captain and Urkrathos still had some of those same captains imprisoned, brutalised and insane, deep in the bowels of the *Hellforger*.

The *Hellforger* was set on its path. The bridge daemons had done their job well and the massive thrust of the grand cruiser's engines sent it carving inexorably towards the *Tribunicia*.

Which meant there was nothing it could do when the *Pieta* suddenly got in the way.

THE ENGINES OF the *Pieta* roared as the tubby, ponderous pilgrim ship was pulled in several directions at once. In the grand amphitheatre, people screamed as the artificial gravity was knocked out of kilter and they were thrown against the banks of hard marble seating. Missionary Patricos had to grab hold of the lectern to keep himself from pitching into the front row of pilgrims.

'Keep praying!' shouted Patricos over the keening of the engines and the sounds of panic. 'Keep praying! For He will heed your words!'

Something huge collided with the underside of the ship, gouging through the lower decks with a shriek of tearing metal and howl of escaping air. Patricos was thrown onto his back and pilgrims tumbled down the banks of seating as the ship rocked.

Horrendous sounds boomed from below them, fuel cells cooking off, decks sucked dry of air, sections of the hull ripped inwards by the collision.

Patricos struggled to his feet. The pilgrims who had not been knocked unconscious were still praying, mouthing sacred words, their faces blank with fear.

'He does not hear us!' shouted Patrocis at the top of his booming hellfire voice. 'You are not praying hard enough! Sing to Him the depths of your devotion!'

One of the aft engines exploded, filling the air with the sickening sound of sheets of fuel igniting, filling the engineering decks with liquid flame.

'Keep praying!' The ship was spasming like a dying animal, beads of fire dripping from the ceiling. 'You! Pray harder! Now!'

The grinding prow of the *Hellforger* cut right through the amphitheatre, its gnashing ram of teeth slicing through hundreds of bodies. The rest died as the vacuum screamed in behind it, leaving the shattered remnants of the *Pieta* open to the emptiness of space.

'GODS' TEETH AND damnation!' bellowed Urkrathos as the last shreds of the *Pieta* fluttered from the prow of the *Hellforger*. 'You! Are we still on course?'

The navigation daemon, a muscular brute covered in glowing runes of sorcery, growled from the wall to which it had been nailed with spikes of meteoric iron. 'The collision turned our hand. The blade will not strike true.'

Urkrathos glanced back at the pict-screen showing the smouldering wreckage of the *Pieta* still jammed in the teeth of the ramming prow. The daemon was right – the *Hellforger* would miss the *Tribunicia* sternwards. 'Correct it.'

The daemon grinned with all three of its bile-dripping mouths. 'Impossible,' it said.

Urkrathos took the bolt pistol from its holster at his waist and slammed three shots into the navigation daemon, spattering boiling ichor over the wall behind it. 'You defy me!' he yelled. 'Rot your soul, daemon!'

'I have no soul,' said the daemon, still leering with its now-wrecked face. 'And I cannot defy you. It is no lie. The blade of the *Hellforger* will spare the Enemy's heart.'

Urkrathos spat in one of the daemon's many emerald-green eyes. It was true. If the course correction could be made the daemon would have to make it. The *Hellforger* would miss.

'Weapons!' shouted Urkrathos. 'Pull back the boarding parties to the gun gangs! Make ready for a broadside!'

Damn these Imperial scum. They just didn't know when to die. Now he would have to shatter the Enemy flagship with gunfire, a far longer and crueller death than he had planned for them. They inflicted this suffering on themselves, these worshippers of the Corpse-Emperor. In butchering them, Urkrathos was fulfilling a sacred duty.

REAR ADMIRAL HORSTGELD looked at the pict-steals of the dying *Pieta*. He hadn't been certain the ship's crew would realise what their orders meant – if they had, they might not have followed them, pious servants of the Emperor or not. But they were not responsible for the thousands of innocent pilgrims who had just died. Horstgeld was. That was what command meant. Taking responsibility for everything that befell the Imperial citizens under his command, for good or ill.

The revised course solutions flashed up on the bridge viewscreen. The *Hellforger* would miss the *Tribunicia* – not by much, but by enough. The *Tribunicia* would last a little longer, then. And those few moments of life had cost the destruction of the *Pieta* and the death of everyone on board.

'Ship's confessor,' said Horstgeld to Confessor Talas, standing as always at the bridge pulpit. 'We have sinned. The Rites of Admonition, if you please.'

BENEATH MANUFACTORIUM NOCTIS, at the very foundation of the city where the artificial strata met the iron-drained crust of Chaeroneia, there were scores of low, flat abscesses in the rock. Seams of iron and other metals had been mined out leaving endless flat galleries. Most had collapsed but enough remained to form a hidden highway beneath the city, towards the ancient mineheads just outside the limits of the present-day Manufactorium.

An ancient Chimera APC, so repeatedly repaired and refitted that barely anything of the original vehicle remained, led the feeble armoured column that ground at full speed towards the radioactive ash desert beyond the city. Looted and maintained by Antigonus's tech-priest resistance force, it was the most battle-worthy vehicle the makeshift strikeforce had and it felt like it was about to fall apart.

'What will we find when we get there?' asked Alaric above the painful grinding of the engine. He and his squad were in the lead Chimera along with Tech-priest Gallen, who seemed to have an affinity for keeping vehicles running that should have rusted to dust a long time ago.

Gallen glanced back at Alaric with his one remaining natural eye. 'The older shafts are still intact,' he said. 'They were worked by menial gangs, so they are navigable by foot and vehicle. They lead up into the desert.'

'And what's there?'

'Nothing.'

Alaric knew it wasn't true. He could feel the malevolence up ahead, feel it trying to push him back. The diamond-hard core of his soul was aching with it.

'I think we should hear the Rites of Contrition,' said Brother Archis. 'We should go into this with our souls clean.'

'No,' said Alaric. 'Not from me. You should speak them, Archis. You seem to have a knack for prayer.'

'Yes, justicar,' said Archis. 'Brothers, join me.' The rest of the squad, Alaric included, bowed their heads as Archis began to speak. The Rites of Contrition acknowledged the weakness in all their souls, the failures they had all committed in their duty to the Emperor – because their purpose was to eradicate the threat of the daemon and yet daemons still existed and preyed upon the peoples of the Imperium. So as long as the work of the Grey Knights was not done they had to plead for forgiveness from the Emperor and hope that His grace would lend them the strength to complete their work.

One day, when they were all dead and had fought at the Emperor's side at the end of time, their duty would be done. Until then, they were in the Emperor's debt – a debt they would die repaying.

'You say you have lost them?' asked the collective consciousness of Chaeroneia's tech-priests.

'For the time being,' replied Scraecos.

The archmagos veneratus stood in the remains of the datafortress. He had compelled its crystalline structure to unfold completely, laying the lowest reaches of malleable data medium open to the weeping sky. The bodies of wrecked battle-servitors and dead menials lay fused with the black crystal where they had fallen, sucked into the substance of the datafortress by the ferocity with which Scraecos had forced the structure to reform.

There was no sign of the surviving intruders. Only the bodies of their dead troops – a couple of tech-guard in the rust-red and brass of the ortho-dox Adeptus Mechanicus. Nothing of the Space Marines, or the archmagos who was probably leading them. Scraecos had searched right down to the dead layers of data medium, where no information technology known to the ruling tech-priests could penetrate.

Scraecos idly picked up the mangled remains of one intruder tech-guard as the transmitted thoughts from the command spire questioned him.

'Explain,' said the voice of a thousand tech-priests in his head.

'They are on an investigative mission,' said Scrae-cos. 'It is unlikely in the extreme that they will be able to pursue their mission and yet remain permanently masked from our scrutiny.'

'And yet masked they are,' said the tech-priests. 'Explain further.'

'We have killed several of their members,' continued Scraecos. 'And we understand their composition and techniques. We know more of their capabilities. They possess some form of advanced technology that bypassed our hunter-programs.' Scraecos glanced scornfully at the hunter-programs, which swam beneath the surface of the crystal, curled up and shivering. 'No doubt it has been developed by the orthodox Mechanicus since we were last in contact with the Imperium.'

'Such words constitute only excuses, Archmagos Veneratus Scraecos. There is no indication that your activities have rendered the capture of the intruders inevitable. It appears instead that your maintenance of a separate identity has rendered you less efficient. Therefore, Archmagos Veneratus Scraecos will return to the consciousness of the tech-priests of the command spire.'

Scraecos clenched his mechadendrites in frustration. The data-filaments that replaced his hands brushed against the crystal and he read the weakness and fear of the hunter-programs. They had failed. They. Not him. He was the greatest archmagos in the history of Chaeroneia. The greatest since the dying of the great schism in the days of Horus. Scraecos had performed his task with absolute accuracy and skill. He was the ruler of Chaeroneia.

The Castigator had spoken to Scraecos. In the beginning, it had spoken to him only.

'Very well,' said Scraecos. 'I will return to the tech-priests. I will become We.'

'Grav-platforms will be despatched. Archmagos Veneratus Scraecos will prepare for the cessation of individual consciousness.'

The communication ended. Scraecos was alone again at the datafortress. The shape of the datafortress had been exploded into a hard black blossom of crystal, the walls warped into giant petal-like panes. The valley was similarly deformed, its sheer obsidian cliffs punched through with scores of smouldering craters where the data medium had been probed for any sign of the intruders.

Scraecos had wondered for some time whether there was an active resistance at Manufactorium Noctis. Most of the time, of course, his memory and cognitive faculties had not been his alone, but part of Chaeroneia's collective mind. But on the occasions where he had existed separately, he had wondered if certain acts of apparent sabotage, or unexplained shutdowns and tech-priests' deaths, could really be ascribed to random industrial accidents alone.

There was someone coordinating a resistance on Chaeroneia. Perhaps dissident tech-priests, rivals for the rulership of Chaeroneia. Or maybe relics from Chaeroneia's distant past, still somehow loyal to the orthodox Mechanicus that the planet had left behind so long ago. The survival of the intruders confirmed this in Scraecos's mind. The resistance had been cunning and resourceful in staying hidden, but in helping the intruders escape they had confirmed their existence. It was the last mistake they would make.

Archmagos Veneratus Scraecos was the ruler of Chaeroneia. He was the will of the true Omnissiah, as revealed to him through the Castigator. This was not arrogance or ambition speaking, It was the pure, cold logic that ruled ninety-nine per cent of Scraecos's soul. And Scraecos would see both the resistance and the intruders dead – his way.

A grav-platform drifted between the spires towards the shattered datafortress, escorted by several gun-platforms. They were coming to take Scraecos back to the command spire. That suited Scraecos just fine. It was the best place for him to be confirmed as the driving intelligence behind Chaeroneia's collective will.

The hunter-programs had failed. That made one thing certain. Scraecos would have to deal with this problem himself.

THE GUNS OF the *Desikratis* raked deep shimmering black gouges through the shields of the *Exemplar*, the hideous bloated Chaos cruiser vomiting astounding volleys of fire that even at a distance were knocking down the void shield banks of the Adeptus Mechanicus ship in rapid succession. The daemon that squatted at the heart of the *Desikratis* aimed every one of its thousands of guns by hand, loaded the shells with its own tentacles and fired them with an impulse from its corrupted nervous system. The *Exemplar* was demonstrating resilience well beyond the norm for a ship of its size, but no matter how tough it proved the *Desikratis* was closing fast and as it slowed and brought itself into point-blank broadside position it would breach the Mechanicus ship's hull and turn its decks into mazes of twisted, burning metal.

But that hadn't happened yet. And the *Exemplar* still had more fight in it than anyone suspected

'ALL POWER STARBOARD shields,' said Magos Murgild. The bridge of the *Exemplar* was by now filling up with menials and tech-priests, replacing the burned-out servitors. Some complicated pattern of protocols governed the mayhem as the ship brought its damaged prow out of the path of the Enemy's guns. 'Evasion pattern theta. Damage control to prow sensoria.'

Hurried communications with the ship's archive had suggested the enemy ship might be the *Desikratis*, a Chaos-controlled cruiser that had been active during the Gothic War and then surfaced again in the space battles around Nemesis Tessera during the invasion from the Eye.

The *Exemplar* probably couldn't face it on even terms. It didn't matter. The ship wasn't there to win – it was there to keep the Enemy busy while Hawkespur and Alaric killed whatever it was that had summoned them to Chaeroneia.

'Commissar,' voxed Nyxos. 'What have you found?'

Commisar Leung's voice crackled up from Magos Korveylan's quarters in the depths of the *Exemplar*. 'Little direct evidence of suspicious activities. Some of the research tech-priests have uncovered details of her studies under Archmagos Scraecos, however.'

'Tech-priests? Can you trust them?'

'I believe so, inquisitor. Magos Korveylan seems to have been generally disliked by the crew.'

Nyxos allowed himself a smile. 'Good for them. What have you found?'

'I confess I don't understand it fully. Scraecos seems to have run a form of seminary on Salshan Anterior about a hundred and fifty years ago. It was religious as much as technical. It concentrated on something Korveylan's studies referred to as Standard Template Constructs. Other than that she seems to have been very dedicated to covering her tracks.'

'I see. Thank you, commissar. Keep me up to date on anything you find.'

'Yes, inquisitor.'

'And things may get very rough in a few minutes. We're going into battle and I don't think we can win.'

'Understood.'

The vox-channel closed. The activity on the bridge seemed suddenly quieter and slower, though in reality it was only getting more intense as the *Desikratis* closed in.

A Standard Template Construct. Of course. It made perfect sense.

'Murgild,' said Nyxos, snapping himself out of his thoughts. 'We need to contact the planet. Any way we can. Do you have historical files on Chaeroneia?'

'Of course, but they do not seem to bear much relevance to the planet as it is now.'

'It doesn't matter. Make them available to me in the verispex decks. I'm leaving the bridge to you but remember you are under Inquisitorial authority. And do try to keep us alive.'

'Of course.'

Nyxos hurried off the bridge. He could hear the distant booming of failing shields as the guns of the *Desikratis* gradually stripped the *Exemplar* naked. It wouldn't be long now. But he knew now what this was all about – Chaeroneia, the Chaos fleet, Korvey-lan's treachery, everything. If he could let Hawkespur know somehow then there was a chance she might actually succeed and all these men and women would not be dying for nothing.

CHAPTER FOURTEEN

'Give me a gun that never fires! Give me a sword that is ever blunt! Give me a weapon that deals no wound, so long as it always strikes awe!'

– Ecclesiarch Sebastian Thor,
address to the Convent Sanctorum

THE IMPERIUM WAS founded on ignorance. It was a truth so obvious that very few ever acknowledged it. For more than ten thousand years the Imperium had claimed rulership over the human race, first under the Emperor and then under the Adeptus Terra who acted, it was claimed, according to His undying will. But the Imperium existed in complete historical isolation. Before the Emperor had set out on the Great Crusade that conquered the thousands of scattered inhabited worlds, there was nothing.

Legends inhabited the shadowy years of pre-Imperial history. No matter how many scholars slaved over the question of what had gone before the Imperium, it was impossible to tell the guesswork from the lies. A very few basic assumptions were held by the majority of those who paid pre-Imperial history any mind at all, though even these were in constant question.

First, there had been the Scattering. The discovery of faster-than-light travel through the parallel dimension of the warp had led to massive migrations among the stars, creating a galaxy-wide diaspora of humanity. The Scattering was pure conjecture, a way of explaining how so many worlds inhabited by humans were even now being rediscovered by Rogue Traders and exploratory fleets. But it was the only way the human race could have got into its present state and so it was widely assumed to have happened so far in the past that no direct evidence of it existed.

Then there came the Dark Age of Technology. Mankind, rather than venerating technology and keeping it sacrosanct as the priesthood of Mars later did, pursued technological advancement with wanton enthusiasm. Astonishing wonders were made, along with horrors beyond imagining. Planet-threatening war machines. Genetic abominations. Machines that wove whole worlds around them. And worse things – far worse.

Inevitably, the Dark Age led humanity to the Age of Strife, where human fought human in an endless cycle of destruction. Warp travel became impossible and the result was a great winnowing of the human population, where worlds were isolated and fell into the barbarism that would often only end when the Imperium recontacted them and sent missionaries to bring the light back to them.

But some, it seems, must have known the Age of Strife was coming – a very few who believed humanity's existence was in danger and that by preserving the most stable and useful technology for future generations, they could increase the chances of the human race surviving the coming slaughter. No one in the age of the Imperium could begin to guess who that might have been, but they were undoubtedly among the greatest minds of the Dark Age, perhaps the only ones who realised the toll that profane technology would take on the galaxy.

They placed their knowledge in a form that could survive forever and be understood by anyone. Certain key technologies were reduced to algorithms and placed in a format that could be used even by humans reduced to barbarity. They were the Standard Template Constructs.

In a way, the Priesthood of Mars had done something similar, preserving technology through religious observation. With the birth of the Imperium and the Treaty of Mars, the Adeptus Mechanicus was able to explore the galaxy with the Great Crusade and learned of the existence of the Standard Template Constructs.

So pure were the STCs that they became objects of holy veneration to the tech-priests, nuggets of the Omnissiah's genius compressed and formatted for the good of mankind. A few fragments were discovered on shattered, ruined worlds during the Great Crusade. The tech-priests used them to create some of the most stable and ubiquitous technology the Imperium had, like the Rhino APC or the geothermal heatsink technology that provided power to countless hive cities. But they never found a complete, uncorrupted STC.

A pure STC was a hopeless legend. To think that one could survive complete for so many thousands of years of tortuous war was fanciful in the extreme. But that did not stop many tech-priests from pursuing the Standard Template Constructs as the objects of religious quests, sifting through legends and half-truths, sending out exploratory parties to the most distant, Emperor-forsaken planets hunting for the merest hint of the ancient knowledge.

One such tech-priest was Archmagos Veneratus Scraecos. On the forge world of Salshan Anterior he had led a seminary studying the legends of the Standard Template Constructs and creating complex statistical models from the fragments of information the Mechanicus possessed.

Scraecos had come to Chaeroneia, believing that there was a Standard Template Construct on the world. And perhaps – just perhaps – he had been correct.

ALARIC CRAWLED FORWARD on his stomach, forcing his huge armoured form down into the mass of rust beneath him so he wouldn't give himself and the tech-priests alongside him away to anyone who might be guarding the top of the mineshaft.

The shaft sloped up at a steep angle, allowing only a dirty half-light in from the outside. Drilled into iron-rich rock centuries before, the walls and floor of the shaft were now sheathed in metre-thick sheets of crumbling rust.

'We're close,' said Tech-priest Gallen, clambering up the slope alongside Alaric. Gallen's only weapon was a rusting autogun and whatever combat attachments his equally rusted bionics might possess and he was scared. Antigonus's tech-priests had lived on the edge of detection and death for a long time, but they had always shied away from direct conflict with the Dark Mechanicus. Now Alaric's arrival had prompted them into all-out war.

'Is there anyone up there?' whispered Alaric. He glanced back and saw his squad close behind him, the gunmetal of their armour dulled by the dirt enough to hide them. There were about twenty other tech-priests, too, all in various states of disrepair, along with Antigonus in his spider-legged maintenance servitor body, Hawkespur and her lone tech-guard bodyguard, and Archmagos Saphentis.

'Nothing on the auspex,' said Gallen. 'But some of their tech-priests don't show up.'

'I'll take point,' said Alaric. The tech-priests might have been spirited resistance fighters but the Grey Knights were better soldiers by far and he waved his squad forwards to the top of the shaft.

The desert air stank. This desert was not natural – it was built up from untold millennia of pollution, made of drifts of hydrocarbon ash or expanses of radioactive glass. Every forge world had these desolations in common, toxic deserts or acidic oceans that stretched between the manufactoria. Large sections of Chaeroneia had resembled hell before the Dark Mechanicus had ever taken control.

Alaric crawled towards the smudge of dirty sky visible through the top of the shaft. Archis scrabbled up beside him, Incinerator held off the ground in front of him.

'Ready?' asked Alaric.

'You can never be ready,' said Archis. 'The moment we think we're ready, that's the moment the Enemy finds some new way to kill us.'

Alaric pulled himself up the ragged rock around the shaft entrance. The night sky above flickered with half-formed images, the occult symbols and blasphemous prayers written on the clouds by projectors on the top of the city's spires. They loomed down over the desert, too, a blanket of heresy covering everything. There was no break in the images because the clouds formed a solid unbroken layer, as if trying to shut out the existence of a sane universe beyond.

Alaric pulled himself level with the shaft entrance and looked out. He had some idea of what to expect – rolling toxic dunes, foul lakes of raw pollution, carrion creatures wheeling overhead.

He didn't see any of that.

Outside, Manufactorium Noctis was a massive construction the size of a spaceport. It was ringed by a series of spindly watchtowers each bristling with guns and in turn protected by networks of trenches and gun emplacements. Between the watchtowers stretched an expanse of rockcrete studded with biomechanical outcrops like immense blooms of fungi – workshops and warehouses, generator stacks and control bunkers, connected by thick twisting conduits like bundles of nerves or muscle fibres. Dead-grey masses of flesh grew up everywhere, reaching up the sides of the watchtowers, flowing into the defensive trenchworks, blistering up through the rockcrete like infected boils. Furthermore, a ribbon of bright silver marked the very outer borders of the facility beyond the trenches and watchtowers – it looked liquid, like a moat, the first line of defence against intruders.

But that was not the worst of it. The worst was the army that stood to attention, arrayed in ranks across the rockcrete. They towered over the biomechanical buildings – distance could be deceptive but to Alaric's practiced eye they were all between thirty and fifty metres high and in spite of their obvious bio-mechanical infections there could be no doubt as to what they were.

Titans. Hundreds of them.

The Adeptus Mechanicus's fighting forces, the tech-guard and the Skitarii, could be formidable, as could their spaceships and the massive Ordinatus artillery units they could deploy. But nothing in the armoury of the tech-priests could compare in symbolic power to the titans. They were bipedal fighting machines that some said echoed the Emperor himself in the inspiring magnitude of their destructive power. Even the smallest, the Warhound scout titans, could muster more firepower than a dozen Imperial Guard squads.

Titans were god-machines deployed to break through fortifications and shatter enemy formations. There was little that could stand against them. And more importantly, the titan legions ranked alongside the Space Marines themselves as symbols of Imperial dominance.

'Throne of Earth,' whispered Archis. 'They must have been building them for.. for…'

'A thousand years,' said Alaric. There were too many titans for Alaric to count – they seemed to be mostly equivalent to the Reaver-pattern titan, the mainstay of the titan legions. Roughly humanoid in shape, each sported a truly immense weapon on each arm, along with countless smaller weapons bristling from their legs and torsos. Many of the weapons were unrecognisable fusions of mechanics and biology.

Alaric tried to get a better look at the facility itself. A single spire rose from the centre, taller than the rest, topped with a large disc studded with lights – perhaps the control spire for the facility. There were also tall chimneys belching greasy smoke into the sky, probably from forges beneath the surface where the massive metal parts needed to build and maintain the legion of titans were smelted.

The landscape around the facility was scarred by the effort that had gone into digging a stable foundation into the ash wastes. It must have taken the full resources of Manufactorium Noctis to build the place and even now it was draining most of the city's power. The fact that it still needed so much power suggested very strongly that the Dark Mechanicus were still building and assembling titans in the bio-mechanical workshops.

And there was more than just power. Alaric could feel the malevolence he had first tasted from orbit, dark and pulsing through his skin, strong enough to turn the air heavy and greasy with its power. It was here. The dark heart of Chaeroneia was beating somewhere among that titan army.

Magos Antigonus crept up beside Alaric's Grey Knights. 'Omnissiah preserve us,' he said as he saw the facility rolling out in front of him. 'They must have moved the titan works. Stone by stone, girder by girder. The whole thing. How stupid I was to think they would just dismantle it. This was what they had been building all along and I was too blind and afraid to venture out and find it.' Even through the crude vox-unit of his servitor body, Antigonus's regret was obvious. 'I promised I would make them face justice,' he said. 'Instead I let them build… this.'

'It doesn't matter,' said Alaric. 'What matters is what you do now. This is our chance to hurt them. All of them at once. Maybe stop what they came into real space to do.'

Hawkespur had reached the shaft entrance, too, along with Saphentis who was, at least, making a token effort to stay hidden. 'Of course,' she said, as if she should have guessed the titan works were there from the start. 'This is what the Chaos fleet is here for. The Dark Mechanicus are making a deal with Abaddon, just like they did with Horus. The titans are here to seal it.'

'So we destroy them all?' said Alaric.

'It seems the only option.'

'That,' said Saphentis, 'will be difficult.'

'I don't remember our orders saying it would be easy,' replied Hawkespur crossly.

'Nevertheless, it seems futile to pursue a goal we cannot possibly fulfil. The chances of our force successfully destroying so many titans, even if they are not operational, is so close to zero as to be incalculable. The Dark Mechanicus will certainly become aware of our presence and divert all of their resources to stop us. And unlike in the city, there will be nowhere for us to hide.'

'Then what do you suggest?' asked Hawkespur.

'Find a way to leave this planet,' said Saphentis.

'Give up?'

'Give up. We all represent a significant investment of Imperial resources. Dying while pursuing an impossible goal will hardly coincide with the Emperor's will you claim to serve.'

'Hawkespur?' said Alaric. 'You're the Inquisitorial authority here.'

Hawkespur pulled herself to the edge of the shaft entrance to get a better look at the titan legion and the defences of the facility. What she couldn't see, of course, were the many thousands of menials and tech-priests that could descend on them after the facility reported any intruders.

'We go in,' said Hawkespur. 'Our primary objective is the titans. If they really are destined for the Eye then even taking out one will help. Our secondary objective is to gather information on the workings of the facility in case we find some way of completing the primary objective without sabotaging them all one by one. Other than that, we do what we can and die well. Any objections? Aside from the obvious, archmagos.'

'I submit to the will of the Inquisition,' said Saphentis, his artificial voice displaying little conviction.

'Alaric? You're the one who's going to have to do the fighting.'

'We go in. As you say, even taking out one will hurt them.'

'Good. Antigonus?'

'You'll only pull that Inquisition business on me if I refuse,' said Antigonus. 'And I think it's time we took this fight to them. I can reconnoitre the defences, they'll have a hard time telling me apart from another feral servitor.'

'You'll die if they do,' said Hawkespur.

'In that respect, interrogator, nothing has changed.' Antigonus crawled out from the shaft entrance and began the trek down the ragged surface of fused ash towards the quicksilver ribbon that marked the edge of the titan works. His servitor body was streaked with rust and looked like it had been decaying out on the ash dunes for decades. It was a good disguise. The best on Chaeroneia.

'TAKE COVER! INCOMING fire, full evasion protocols in effect!'

Magos Murgild's voice boomed through the verispex decks. A bewildering tangle of exotic equipment, incense-wreathed tech-altars and long benches of bizarre experiments, the verispex deck was a bad place to get caught when the shells started slamming home. But that was where Nyxos was at that moment, grabbing hold of a massive steel laboratory bench as the *Exemplar* began to shudder.

Tech-priests were thrown to the ground. Chalices of chemicals were thrown around and enormous glass vessels shattered. Nyxos stayed on his feet, the exoskeleton hidden beneath his robes straining to keep him from being thrown around like a toy. Massive explosions boomed from outside the ship, warning klaxons sounded from a dozen different directions and the already murky lighting flickered as the ship's systems were wracked with fire and shrapnel. The verispex labs were used for research into samples brought in during the exploration missions the *Exemplar* had been built for and they made little concession to keeping the research magi safe when the ship came under fire.

'We need to move now!' shouted Nyxos above the din. 'Can you do it?'

'Not… not yet…' replied the nearest tech-priest. Nyxos hadn't had time to learn the tech-priests' procedures or even their names, or to check whether they might have been in thrall to Magos Korveylan. But none of that mattered. What mattered was time.

Nyxos had one chance to help Hawkespur and Alaric on the surface. This was it.

'Not good enough!' replied Nyxos. 'You!' He pointed to another tech-priest, apparently a woman somewhere under the dataprobes and fine manipulator attachments. 'Boost the signal. Get the power from wherever you can.'

'It may not hold…'

'It's better than not trying. And you!' Nyxos rounded on the first tech-priest again – apparently the lab supervisor, he sported bizarrely large round ocular attachments which magnified his naked, unblinking eyeballs several times. 'Encode the transmission. I don't want to hear excuses.'

'But the projector channels from Chaeroneia's historical logs are a hundred years old. There is every chance they have changed…'

'Then we will fail, magos. I am willing to accept that responsibility. I know it's something you tech-priests find difficult but you are playing by Inquisition rules now. Encode it. Send it. Now.'

The huge-eyed tech-priest stumbled over to the deck's main cogitator engine. A clockwork monstrosity the size of a tank, it was apparently powered by a large round handle which the lead tech-priest promptly began turning with all his strength.

Pistons and massive cogs began working, pumping and spinning through large holes in the cogitator's elaborate brass casing. More explosions sounded, closer this time and Nyxos knew the last of the shields were gone. That meant the fire from the *Desikratis* was now chewing its way through the hull and decks would start failing, pressure chambers would be breached, ship systems would be shutting down. People would be dying. Many people.

Space combat was something Nyxos hated with a passion. It could only end when crews – not ships, crews – were completely wiped out. It was long-distance butchery. Even the most minor ship-to-ship combat was the equivalent of an entire battle among ground troops in terms of fatalities and the battle for Chaeroneia would probably claim the lives of every single Imperial servant in orbit.

'We have to take power from the prow batteries,' said the female tech-priest, who was working a complicated system of interlocking pipes which covered one wall of the verispex lab and presumably governed how power was routed through the ship. She was holding a hand against a deep gash in her forehead, trying to keep the blood from getting in her eyes.

'Then do it!' replied Nyxos. Another explosion, the closest yet, threw everyone to the ground save for Nyxos. Sparks showered from somewhere. Nyxos heard a scream and smelled burning cloth, then burning flesh – one of the lab's tech-priests had been wreathed in flame and was now on the ground, fellow crewmen beating out the fire.

Nyxos looked around. The lab was in a bad state. Throne knew what the rest of the ship was like. And this was Nyxos's last chance. It had been extraordinary how quickly the tech-priests had worked, but it wouldn't count for anything if they failed now.

The clockwork cogitator was spitting streams of punchcards, the lead tech-priest hauling on the handle to get it calculating quicker. It wasn't fast enough.

Nyxos stumbled over to the cogitator. Something was wrong with the gravity on the *Exemplar* and it was like crossing the deck of a vessel at sea.

'Let me,' he growled, grabbing the handle. His servo-assisted limbs locked and the massive strength of his augmentations hauled the wheel round faster, so fast the surprised tech-priest had to let go. The cogitator howled as steam and sparks shot from inside its casing.

'It's working!' yelled the female tech-priest. The cogitator spat out a rippling ribbon of printout – the lead tech-priest grabbed it and quickly scanned it, his bizarrely magnified pupils skipping from side to side.

'They're receiving,' he said.

'Can the projectors transmit it?' asked Nyxos, his servos whining as he continued to work the handle.

'I don't…'

The explosion tore through the lab, sending white-hot shrapnel spinning everywhere, sparks falling like burning rain. The shriek of escaping air was deafening as Nyxos, the tech-priests and all the wreckage of the lab was sucked through the massive rent in the wall.

In the silence of the vacuum the cogitator exploded, sending fragments of its cogs, like sharp serrated crescents, spinning everywhere. But by then there were very few people alive on the deck to care.

CHAPTER FIFTEEN

'Death in service to the Emperor is its own reward. Life in failure to Him is its own condemnation.'

– Uriah Jacobus, 'Epistles' (Verse 93)

SCRAECOS WAS TRAVELLING up to the pinnacle of the command spire when he felt the call of the Castigator. The peristaltic motion of the biological elevator stopped as the unmistakeable voice spoke, every particle of every atom shuddering with its voice. Not physical and yet not psychic, when the Castigator spoke it did so with all the wisdom of the Omnissiah and it was impossible not to listen and obey.

Scraecos had yet to join with the consciousness of the tech-priests. It had been a long, long time since he had heard the call of the Castigator as an individual being. It was just like the first time he had heard it, deep below the ground, realising that he had finally looked upon the face of the Omnissiah.

The Castigator had spoken to Scraecos. Only to Scraecos. And it was doing so again.

The voice of the Castigator did not use anything so vulgar and fleshy as words. It spoke in pure concepts. The particles in Scraecos's still-biological brain vibrated in waves of absolute comprehension.

The Castigator spoke of how it was time to take the avatar of the Omnissiah and reveal its face to the galaxy. It was why Chaeroneia had been brought back into real space. It would be the first part of the great revelation, when all mankind would witness the true Machine-God – something living and aware, all-wise, separate from the corpse-Emperor and infinitely more powerful. All who looked on it would have no logical choice but to kneel and pledge their lives to the Omnissiah.

The orthodox Mechanicus, which had withered like a grape on the vine, would be winnowed out. The Adeptus Astartes would abandon their obscure ancestor-worship and be made whole, their flesh excised and replaced with the Machine to create an army in the image of the Machine-God. The Imperial Guard would serve the newly-enlightened Mechanicus. The collective consciousness of tech-priests would go to Terra and there establish their court, the pooled wisdom of the thousands who had first seen the light on Chaeroneia.

It would not take long. The light of pure knowledge was too bright. There would be no shadows for the non-believers to hide amongst. The transition would be painful for a few, the mad and the corrupt, who would be rounded up and fed into the forges. But for the trillions of souls that laboured under the Imperial yoke, it would be a new Golden Age of Technology. The human race would achieve its full potential as the cogs that formed the machine. The greatest machine, the body of the Omnissiah Himself formed out of untold forges and factoria, machine-altars and cogitators, built and maintained by the whole human race who would sing His praises as they devoted their lives to holy labour.

It was beautiful. Archmagos Veneratus Scraecos could see the universe laid out according to the Omnissiah's plan, where the stars themselves were moved into perfect mathematical patterns, wrought into binary prayers thousands of light years across. How could the future be anything but that? Anything but a machine run according to sacred logic?

The voice faded. The Castigator had spoken.

The muscular motion around Scraecos continued, taking him up the long biological gullet that would disgorge him at the top of the command spire to take his place among the ruling consciousness.

He willed it to stop.

The Castigator knew all. It spoke rarely and when it did, everything it said was carefully calculated, including the timing.

Why had it waited until a time when Scraecos was alone, an individual, before doing so? The reason was clear. It wanted to speak directly to Scraecos as a discrete consciousness, just as it had done more than a thousand years before when Scraecos had first seen its face deep beneath the ash wastes.

The other tech-priests, their minds joined together and their personalities subsumed, would no doubt be calculating the tasks they would have to complete if the Castigator's vision were to become reality. They would have to get the Castigator off-planet perhaps, or maybe even re-enact a version of the great ritual that had plunged Chaeroneia into the warp in the first place. But not Scraecos. To Scraecos it had spoken directly.

Archmagos Veneratus Scraecos had been blind for so long. Now it was clear. He was the chosen of the Omnissiah. He was the vessel through which the work of the Omnissiah, as revealed through His avatar the Castigator, would be completed. Again, the timing of the Castigator's call could only mean one thing. Scraecos, until such time as he re-entered the collective consciousness, was on the same mission for which he had been made an individual again – hunt down the intruders and kill them all.

The Castigator wanted him to continue that mission. It was the only conclusion Scraecos could draw. Of all the tech-priests now searching for a way to make the vision come true, Scraecos's was the most sacred of all. There were heretics on Chaeroneia. New ones arrived from the Imperium outside and probably old ones who had been trapped on Chaeroneia from the start. For the Castigator to be presented to the galaxy, every single soul on Chaeroneia had to be working towards the same purpose. There was no room for heretics. Scraecos was the holy weapon of the Omnissiah, ancient and wise, strong and ruthless. Scraecos had always been uncompromising and strong – brutal, perhaps – even before he had found the Castigator. It was why he had been chosen. He had the body and mind of a killer and the soul of a pious servant. And so he would serve his god by killing.

Scraecos willed the elevator to reverse its swallowing mechanism, propelling him back down towards the base of the spire. The collective of tech-priests would have to work without him for the time being – he had sacred work to do in the shadows of Chaeroneia, work he had failed to complete at the datafortress. He would not fail now. Not with the will of the Omnissiah within him.

Failure was an anomaly of logic. Success was inevitable. Before the galaxy saw the Castigator revealed, everyone who opposed the will of the Machine-God on Chaeroneia would be dead.

THE BROKEN ASH wastes were corrosive and toxic. The hood of Hawkespur's voidsuit meant she could still breathe, but the ash was eating away at the suit's gloves and kneepads as she crawled along out of sight.

The tech-priests were well-practiced in staying hidden. The force avoided the occasional grav-platform, as it followed Magos Antigonus towards the bright silver boundary of the titan works.

'What is it?' asked Alaric as the silver became more visible.

'I don't know,' rasped Hawkespur. 'Perhaps another type of data medium. They're using it as a moat.'

'Then we have to cross it.'

'We could go round the works to find a crossing point. But it would take days.'

Alaric looked at her. Even through the ash-streaked faceplate of her hood he could see her skin was greenish and pale. 'You haven't got days.'

'No. And any crossing points will be guarded, anyway.'

'Then we'll swim if we have to.'

Hawkespur looked at him with mild surprise, noting the massive bulk of his power armour. 'You can swim?'

'You'd be surprised.'

Archmagos Saphentis crawled towards them, his bionic limbs splayed like crab's legs, carrying him just above the ground as if he found abasing himself in the dirt distasteful.

'Interrogator Hawkespur,' he said. 'Perhaps you should look up.'

Hawkespur glanced upwards. For the first time in several days she smiled.

The blasphemous prayers were gone. In their place, projected onto the dense cloud layer, were letters hundreds of metres high.

++00100INTERROGATOR01110HAWKESPUR, they read.

POSSIBLE+STC PRESENT ON CHAERO100A. 010PTUS MECHANICU1 AND *HELLFORGER* BOTH DESIRE IT. DENY+TO+THE E0EMY+AT ALL1COSTS. RECOVERY NOT A PRIO10TY.

WATCH+YOUR+BACK.

NYXOS+OUT011110.

'Nyxos…' breathed Hawkespur. 'He found a way.'

'It must be bad up there,' said Alaric. 'Throne knows what kind of risks he had to take to transmit it down here.'

'It certainly changes things.' Hawkespur looked back down at the titan works. 'If the tech-priests found a Standard Template Construct here... if that is what all this is based on...'

'If so,' said Saphentis, 'then we may have discovered the source of the Dark Mechanicus beliefs of the Horus Heresy. And it is unlikely a more dangerous store of knowledge could exist.'

'No,' said an unfamiliar voice. It was the last of the tech-guard, the one who had been assigned to guard Hawkespur. He lifted the reflective visor of his helmet to show a pale, almost completely nondescript face, with fine surgical scars around one temple. 'The Standard Template Constructs are perfect. We learned this as menials. They contain the wisdom of the Omnissiah uncorrupted. They cannot contain a word of heresy.'

Alaric looked round at the soldier in surprise. It was the first time he had heard him speak – almost the first time any of the tech-guard had spoken except for the late Captain Tharkk. 'What does the Mechanicus teach about them?'

'An STC is a complete technology, rendered down to pure information. There is no room for corruptive innovation or error. They are sacred.' The tech-guard's voice was fast and clipped – he sounded as if he were reeling off rote-taught scripture.

'The dogma of the Cult Mechanicus,' interrupted Saphentis. 'The religion of Mars is couched in simple terms for the lower ranks of soldiers and menials. The lowest ranks hear of the Omnissiah as an object of religious awe. The Standard Template Constructs are described to them as holy artefacts. The more senior tech-priests understand such things in pragmatic and philosophical terms, but their devotion is no less. Some, of course, harbour divergent beliefs, but careful control is maintained over such things.'

'Then an STC,' said Hawkespur, 'would be something very powerful and not just because of what you could make with it. A tech-priest who possessed one could set himself up as... well, as a god, within the Mechanicus. There could be another schism.'

'It is probable,' replied Saphentis. 'Compromising the loyalty of the lower ranks would give an individual great power within the Mechanicus.'

'Enough to threaten the rule of Mars?' Hawkespur's question was a bold one. More than almost any other Imperial organisation, the Adeptus Mechanicus presented a resolutely united and inscrutable front to the rest of the Imperium.

'I shall not speak of such matters,' said Saphentis.

'Good,' said Alaric. 'Because we need to keep moving. Nyxos's signal will only confirm that we're still alive and still looking to hunt them down here.'

Nyxos's message was already gone. The painful, occult symbols were back. Whatever Nyxos had done to hijack control of the spire top projectors, it had worked, but Alaric knew that it had been Nyxos's last, desperate chance and he wouldn't able to pull it off again, no matter how the battle in orbit was going.

Nyxos's message might help them when the endgame was played out. It might be irrelevant. But nothing killed a soldier like ignorance about what he was fighting and every scrap of information helped. Alaric knew they needed all the help they could get.

THE TRIBUNICIA BURNED from stem to stern. Its overloading plasma reactors had filled most of the engineering decks with superheated fuel and it bled thick ribbons of cooling molten metal from hundreds of tears in its hull. The whole rearward section of the ship was a burning wreck, showering debris and crewmen's bodies out into Chaeroneia's orbit as it tumbled slowly, locked in a grim, slow dance of destruction with the *Hellforger*.

The *Tribunicia* had the fearsome guns that any cruiser of the Imperial Navy could boast. But the *Hellforger's* crew had endless centuries of experience and the ancient, malevolent creatures that lurked inside it. It had daemonically possessed broadside guns and cruel gun-deck masters who had been sending ships burning into the endless grave of space for a thousand years. The *Hellforger* pumped salvo after salvo of heavy gun shells into the hull of the *Tribunicia*, slowly spiralling to keep the broadside a single, rolling bombardment.

The *Hellforger* was hurt, too. It was bleeding from thousands of craters and thick hull plates of scab had broken away to reveal hot living flesh beneath, which blackened and died in the vacuum. But it was nothing that the ship's crew could not repair, given time.

Portals opened, like eyeless sockets, in the underside of the *Hellforger*. The ship spat dozens of thick tendons from them, tipped with huge bony hooks. Those that hit the *Tribunicia* caught in the ruptured hull plates and slowly, painfully, the *Hellforger* started to reel the enemy ship in.

THE BRIDGE OF the *Hellforger* was hot and dark and stank of stagnant daemons' blood. Urkrathos watched the tormenting of the *Tribunicia* on the bridge holo and grunted his approval as another reactor blew somewhere in the rearward section of the Imperial ship. Even the daemons were watching – as much as they hated Urkrathos and the way he had enslaved them, they still loved death and destruction, especially when it was visited on the worshippers of the corpse-emperor.

The battle was a good one. It was up close and brutal, where the superior strength of the *Hellforger* counted for more than the discipline of the Imperial Navy. Even someone as rigidly disciplined as a Chosen of the Black Legion, such as Urkrathos himself, had to let the bloodlust take over from time to time. Sometimes battle wasn't just the work of the Dark Gods – it was an end in itself, beautiful and brutal.

'Are the grappling hooks sound?' asked Urkrathos.

'Fast and holding,' came the reply from the grappling gang leader, deep in the guts of the *Hellforger*, his voice relayed by the communications daemon fused with the ceiling of the bridge.

'Good. Stand by for contact.'

Urkrathos flicked to another channel, sending his voice booming throughout the whole ship. 'Master of Weapons, bring me my sword from the armoury. The rest of you, prepare for boarding.'

BY SPACE TRAVEL standards, the orbit above Manufactorium Noctis was a horrendously cramped labyrinth. Wreckage from shattered shuttles and transports glittered like crimson sparks in the sick, reddening light of the star Borosis. Streaks of yellow fire spat across the void from broadside shells, mixed in with the deep red las-blasts from lance turrets.

The *Hellforger* and the *Tribunicia* closed in a terminal death spiral, fire spattering between them like a swarm of fireflies. The *Exemplar* was holding out against the *Desikratis*, but the bloated old cruiser was launching volleys of gunfire into it with complete impunity, the daemon that controlled it grinning evilly as it poured more and more suffering into the Mechanicus ship.

Rear Admiral Horstgeld's orders had been to protect the troop transports. The transports were the target of the Vulture Wing, a force of elite fighter craft launching from the carrier platform *Cadaver*. *Ptolemy Alpha* and *Ptolemy Beta* were frantically trying to protect the troop transport *Calydon*, the *Ptolemy Gamma* having been reduced to a guttering wreck of a ship by coordinated attack runs from Vulture Wing.

The Imperial Guard, who had been brought to the Borosis system to land on the mystery planet and raise the flags of the Imperium over it, were instead dying in orbit. Men from the Mortressan Highlanders and a dozen other smaller units from other regiments were dying for their Emperor with no way to fight back and no understanding of what was happening to the Imperial ships.

Most of the smaller transports were crowding around the armed yacht *Epicurus*, almost pleading with the grand old pleasure-ship to protect them with its hastily fitted deck guns and defensive turrets.

The Vulture Wing had only just deigned to attack the *Epicurus* and it was going down quickly, most of its bridge crew dead from a torpedo strike, most of its engine crew dying in a massive plasma-fed fire that was burning out the ship's systems one by one.

The Chaos ships, on the other hand, were all in full working order. The *Hellforger* had a bloodied nose but nothing that would trouble it. The *Desikratis* had a hull as tough as kraken's skin and no mortal crew to kill, so the fire that reached it from the *Exemplar* had so little effect that the cruiser's piloting daemon barely noticed it. There were a few Vulture Wing pilots who would never fly again thanks to disciplined turret fire or collisions with the wreckage that flew thickly over Chaeroneia, but more than enough who came back to the *Cadaver* for fuel and ammunition to go out and kill again.

The battle had been over before it had begun. Horstgeld had known it. All his officers who understood the composition of the Chaos fleet had known it. The *Hellforger* alone, a grand cruiser with a monstrous combat pedigree, could have broken the Imperial fleet with relative ease. The fighter-bombers of the Vulture Wing were just making the job quicker and the *Desikratis* was there purely for the joy of battle, maliciously pulling the *Exemplar* apart at long distance just because it could.

It was just a matter of time. But then, it always had been. Very few Imperial servants in orbit were not praying to the Emperor for their lives. But a few, the ones who knew what was really happening, were praying for something else – a few more moments of that time they were dying to buy, minutes, seconds for Alaric on the surface below.

ALARIC TOOK THE first step into the moat. It was full of a liquid like quicksilver – it was thick and heavy, one moment as fluid as water and the next solid as iron.

The Grey Knights were the first in, as always. Alaric looked up at the watchtowers – there was no indication they had been spotted, no klaxons or gunfire. That didn't mean anything, of course. The Dark Mechanicus might be waiting until they were vulnerable, wading through the middle of the moat, before opening fire.

Alaric waded in, storm bolter ready. Brother Dvorn was beside him, with the other Grey Knights following close behind. The currents in the moat pulled at Alaric's legs like insistent hands. He went in deeper, up to his waist. The opposite shore was maybe a hundred paces away, the bank a solid slab of rockcrete that marked the edge of the titan works proper. There was some cover there around the base of the closest watchtower, where the black iron of the tower formed a giant claw gripping the rockcrete. But the moat was completely open.

'Now this,' said Dvorn grimly, 'I don't like.'

The quicksilver rolled in tiny shimmering droplets over the armour of Alaric's waist and abdomen. The ripples he sent out were slow and sharp, like tiny mountain ranges. He had to push forward, the quicksilver seeming to mass in front of him to slow him down.

'Anyone else feel that?' asked Lykkos.

'Feel what?' replied Archis.

'Nobody move,' said Alaric, freezing. The feeling wasn't physical, but it was definitely there, beneath the surface of the moat. It was almost screened out by the sense of daemonic malice coming from the titan works themselves – another spark of the warp, quiet as butterfly's wings. The beating of a daemon's heart.

'Contact!' yelled Alaric as he felt it lunge. The words weren't out of his mouth before the daemon ripped out of the quicksilver ahead of him, its massive jaws yawning open, teeth like dripping silver knives.

A data-daemon. Like the guardians of the datafortress – but stronger, given form by the quicksilver medium and lying in ambush for the Grey Knights.

Alaric didn't have time to fire before the daemon was on him. Its jaws closed over his gun arm and shoulder and its weight drove him down into the quicksilver on his back. It writhed on top of him down in the airless, crushing darkness, teeth pushing down through the ceramite into his shoulder. Alaric fought to reverse his grip on his halberd so he could stab into the thing's guts, but the quicksilver was crushing around him like a giant fist clenching.

He couldn't see. He couldn't breathe. But that was the last of his problems. He tried to force his arm out of the daemon's jaws but it was clamped on too tight. He pressed the firing stud and felt bolter shells bursting in the quicksilver but the grip never let go.

A bright white streak slashed down and the daemon convulsed as something hot and burning smashed through its grimacing, canine skull. In the brief moment of light Alaric saw a hand reaching down to grab him by the collar of his armour, pulling him up into the air.

Alaric coughed up a gobbet of quicksilver and shook drops of it from his eyes. He saw that Brother Dvorn had saved him, smashing down through the daemon with his Nemesis hammer.

Alaric didn't have time to thank him. Gunfire was streaking everywhere. Daemons like dripping silver dragons were wheeling through the air, diving in and out of the moat, snapping at the Grey Knights. Brother Cardios was wrestling with a daemon wrapped around him like a single metal tentacle, trying to free the arm that held his Incinerator. Autogun and lasgun fire spattered from the near shore as the tech-priests added their efforts but there was nothing they could do.

Daemons. There was nothing worse in the galaxy. But daemons Alaric understood.

He tore his halberd arm free of the quicksilver, lunged forward and beheaded the daemon trying to drown Cardios. He pivoted and stabbed the halberd like a spear, transfixing a daemon through its snaking body. It screamed at him as he reversed his grip and plunged it into the moat, pinning it against the floor. Brother Dvorn took a step back and brought his hammer down through the quicksilver again, shattering the daemon's head in a burst of light.

Haulvarn brought another one down with storm bolter fire. Lykkos battered another two back with psycannon shots, the ensorcelled bolter shells leaving massive smoking wounds in their bodies. The Grey Knights backed towards one another until they were back-to-back, a tight knot of men, an island of

Space Marines in the moat that no daemon could approach without being carved up by Nemesis blades or shot out of the air by storm bolters.

'We can get across!' shouted Alaric above the screeching of the daemons. There must have been thirty of them, wheeling and diving, snapping at the Grey Knights. 'Stay tight and pray!'

The Grey Knights waded across the moat step by step, the quicksilver reaching chest-height. The daemons had learned from the deaths of their brothers at the datafortress and dared not close completely, darting in and snapping, then jerking away before a Nemesis blade could cut them in two.

'Enough,' said a voice so deep it sounded like an earthquake.

The surface of the quicksilver boiled and something erupted from below the ground, bursting up right through the middle of the Grey Knights and throwing them aside. Alaric felt a force slam into him so hard it almost knocked him out, throwing him on a wave of quicksilver against the rockcrete bank. He lay for a moment gathering his senses, the floor beneath him splintered by the impact, a sickly purplish light bleeding onto him from the creature that had burst up from the moat.

It was floating in the air surrounded by a nimbus of purple fire, sparks arcing off its outstretched fingers and bleeding from the burning pits of its eyes. Its skin was so pallid it was translucent and patterns could be seen writhing beneath it, strange squirming shapes as if there was something just inside the creature's body that was about to burst out.

The creature was human. The patterns were circuitry. It was Tech-priest Thalassa.

'Scraecos knew you would come,' she said in a voice that Alaric knew wasn't hers. She rotated slowly, turning to face Alaric. 'Especially you. I told him how strong you were. How I admired you and was also afraid. He showed me what true strength was, Justicar Alaric. I saw it on this world and when Scraecos's servants found me I finally understood it.'

It was Brother Archis who found his feet first. Dragging himself up from the churning quicksilver, he sprayed a chain of storm bolter fire at Thalassa's head. The shells burst like multicoloured fireworks against Thalassa's skin. She turned her head towards Archis, gestured regally towards him and a tendril of pure blackness lashed out. It snared Archis's neck, lifting him up into the air above Thalassa's head. He slashed out with his halberd but another tendril snaked out from Thalassa's other hand and caught hold of his halberd arm. More tendrils snaked from Thalassa's eyes and from beneath the silvery robes that flapped around her as she floated.

Alaric could feel the heart beating somewhere in that body. The heart of a daemon. He forced himself to his feet, fighting against the current in the quicksilver that swirled around Thalassa's feet. He stamped down and jumped, halberd stabbing up towards her body.

Data-daemons lurched from the quicksilver, snapping at him, suddenly emboldened by Thalassa's appearance. Alaric shouldered them aside and drove the halberd blade deep into Thalassa's torso. He felt the daemonic flesh underneath spasming as the blade passed through it, then reform around the blade to yank it out of his grasp. Thalassa descended to his level and a second pair of arms unfolded from her robed chest – and beyond them a face, utterly bestial with burning purplish eyes, because there was something inside Thalassa and it was coming out to fight Alaric.

The daemon's arms had too many joints so that they wound like serpents and were tipped with claws that snagged Alaric's neck and chestplate. The daemon threw Alaric down, pitching him back into the quicksilver with a howl, the halberd blade coming free in a spray of glowing purple blood.

Alaric looked up before the quicksilver closed over him to see Brother Archis's body coming apart, the Grey Knight torn in two at the waist. Archis, who had prayed for all of them at the datafortress, who had learned the parables of the Grand Masters at the feet of Chaplain Durendin.

Alaric yelled a formless battlecry and fought the quicksilver current that tried to drag him away. He wrestled the daemons out of his way and fought himself upwards to the surface. This daemon had taken one of his own. The Grey Knights always avenged their dead.

'Azaulathis!' yelled a voice. Alaric fought to his feet in time to see the daemon inside Thalassa turn its baleful eyes towards the source of the voice – someone had spoken its name. Someone who should not be there.

Magos Antigonus's spidery servitor body landed heavily on Thalassa, his jointed metallic legs scrabbling for purchase. The pure red light of a las-cutter flared as Antigonus tried to carve through Thalassa's body to get at the daemon inside.

Brother Haulvarn was there, too, fending off the data-daemons that tried to tear chunks out of Antigonus. Brother Cardios fell against Haulvarn for support and sprayed fire from his Incinerator over the surface of the moat in a wide arc, scorching the silvery skins off more daemons who were looming from the quicksilver.

Thalassa's tendrils ripped off one of Antigonus's spindly legs and the daemon inside her reared out of her torso to yank off another. Its eyes dripped with power and hate and its mouth was a pulsing, alien thing with a long lashing tongue and teeth like black knives.

Antigonus held on. Alaric stabbed up at the daemon, feeling the wards in his armour burning him as they reacted to its presence.

The daemon howled a long, low, discordant note and the whole moat quivered like the sea in a storm, throwing the Grey Knights off their feet. Alaric was almost swamped.

'I beat you once,' came Antigonus's voice, the vox-unit of his servitor body cranked up to maximum. 'I can do it again!'

The daemon's eyes flashed. 'You,' it growled, pausing for a split-second in recognition.

Antigonus punched the las-cutter deep through Thalassa's body. The daemon screamed and so did Thalassa and the two fell down into the quicksilver, almost landing on Alaric. Antigonus leapt off and landed somewhere in the body of the moat. Alaric forgot about trying to shoot the daemon or cut it up and grabbed Thalassa instead, wrapping his arms around her and trying to wrestle her to the floor of the moat. She spasmed with unholy strength, almost throwing Alaric off.

Someone else joined in. Another Grey Knight, Alaric thought – but then he saw his own face, reflected hundreds of times in the multi-faceted eyes of Archmagos Saphentis. Saphentis had waded through the quicksilver, electric pulses flowing off him to part the quicksilver in front of him. His two normal-shaped bionic arms pinned Thalassa's arms to her sides and the tips of the other two reconfigured, twin spinning saw blades emerging from the machinery. With a swift and brutal motion, Saphentis beheaded Thalassa.

Thalassa's head was shot to the far side of the moat on a burst of dark energy that spurted from the stump of her neck. Azaulathis the daemon extruded itself from the neck, Thalassa's body falling limp in Alaric's arms as the daemon freed itself and soared above the moat. Azaulathis's body was a twisted nightmare of information made flesh, a ring of eyes surrounding its great howling maw, many smaller mouths gaping all over it. Black tendrils uncoiled from wet orifices all over its corrupt body, lashing in every direction as power burst off it like purple-black fireworks. Forced out of its body, it gibbered in pain, the harshness of real space burning off flakes of its luminous skin.

Chains of storm bolter fire smacked into it, showering the moat with burning chunks of its flesh. More fire thudded up from the Grey Knights and then a burst of flame from Brother Cardios, singed the skin off half its face to reveal a glowing, melting, unnaturally twisted skull that writhed in pain.

On the outer shore, Alaric spotted Hawkespur. She had taken her marksman's autopistol out and was taking careful aim. She put a single shot through the daemon's burning eye socket, blowing out the back of its head. It stopped moving for a moment as it reeled in shock and that was all the time the Grey Knights needed to shred its body with bolter fire.

'Go,' said Saphentis, his body spattered with Thalassa's corrupted purple blood and rolling droplets of quicksilver. He was holding the quicksilver apart and Alaric could see the other Grey Knights struggling through it into the gap.

'Make for the shore!' ordered Alaric. 'Cardios! Find Archis if you can! And Hawkespur, bring the others across! Quick!'

The data-daemons seemed to have been cowed by the deaths of Thalassa and Azaulathis. The Grey Knights made it across to the far bank, Brother Haulvarn pausing to haul Magos Antigonus's shattered servitor body up onto the rockcrete. Cardios followed carrying the upper half of Archis's smouldering body.

Alaric led the way to the foot of the watchtower, where massive claws rooted the tower into the rockcrete and provided cover between the black iron lengths. Hawkespur and Antigonus's tech-priests followed and finally Archmagos Saphentis pulled himself up onto the bank, the quicksilver knitting itself back together behind him. Saphentis paused to pick something up as he headed for cover where Alaric waited.

Cardios ducked into cover beside Alaric. He was hauling Brother Archis's upper half with him – a sorry, tragic sight, the brave Grey Knight's body turned into so much wreckage by the daemon's strength.

'Even if we could bury him here,' said Alaric, 'we wouldn't. Not in this tainted ground. Cardios, take out his geneseed and share out his ammunition. We will have to leave the body.'

Cardios nodded and began removing Archis's helmet. Like all Space Marines, a Grey Knight's many augmentations were controlled by twin master organs, the geneseed. Geneseed was almost impossible to create from scratch and so each Marine Chapter did its best to harvest the organs from their dead so they could be implanted into a new recruit and the Grey Knights were no exception. The Chapter's geneseed was modelled after the genetic code of their primarch, the awesome warriors created by the Emperor to lead the Great Crusade more than ten thousand years ago. The donor of the genes for the Grey Knights' geneseed was uncertain, however, since the Chapter had been founded amid the greatest of secrecy some time after the first foundings. Some said it was modelled after one of the primarchs who had left behind an unusually stable geneseed, others that the donor was the Emperor himself. No one knew for sure and most of the Grey Knights preferred it that way – they fought not for the ancestral memory of a primarch but for the Emperor first and the Ordo Malleus second and nothing stood in the way. Archis's geneseed was sacred wherever it had originally come from and Alaric had a duty to bring it back to the Grey Knights fortress-monastery on titan if he could.

Antigonus's smoking, wheezing body scuttled into the shadow of the watchtower. He saw the body of Archis and paused for a moment in respect, then crouched down to conserve his servitor body's dwindling energy reserves.

'You need a new body,' said Alaric.

'I know,' said Antigonus, the voice from the servitor's vox-unit distorted with effort. 'I'm surprised this one lasted so long.'

'You knew that daemon.'

'Scraecos sent it after me when I first came here to investigate. I was lucky not to end up like Thalassa. I recognised its voice. When you have something like that living inside you it must leave an impression on you.'

'You fought well,' said Alaric.

'So did you,' replied Antigonus. 'All of you. Especially your battle-brother.' Antigonus indicated Archis's body. Cardios had almost finished cutting the geneseed organ from Archis's throat.

'We will all have to do so again, I fear,' said Alaric. 'This planet crawls with daemons.'

'Someone would disagree with you.' Archmagos Saphentis drifted calmly through the machinery at the base of the watchtower. He held Thalassa's severed head in his hand. 'Explain,' he said to the head.

Thalassa's eyes, now orbs of pure silver, opened. 'Daemons...' she said, her voice a bubbling whisper through the blood running from her mouth. 'No, no daemons... they are the hunter-programs, the servants of the archmagi...' The power that had held her together while she was possessed by Azaulathis was keeping her alive now, animating her with an echo of its dark magic.

'She's insane,' said Antigonus.

'Maybe,' said Alaric. He turned back to Thalassa's head. 'How do you know?'

'The... archmagi told me... their many voices are one...'

'The rulers of this planet?'

'Yes. They showed me such things. I became lost, but they found me. I saw a world completely self-sufficient... master of the power of the warp... and I saw the face of the Omnissiah, I saw the Castigator, His knowledge made metal and flesh and sent to teach us... no, there are no daemons here, just knowledge made real, come down to serve us and show us the way...'

Alaric levelled his storm bolter and blew the head apart with a single shot. Saphentis looked down at his gore-splattered robes in mild surprise.

'Lies,' said Alaric. 'About the daemons at least.'

'Then they are ignorant of their own corruption,' said Saphentis. 'Interesting.'

'They all are at the start,' said Alaric. 'Anyone who conjures daemons and does the will of Chaos goes to great lengths to convince themselves they are anything but corrupt. Chaos is a lie, archmagos. Most of all it makes the heretic lie to himself. The Dark Mechanicus are no different in that respect. What we know as Chaos, they see as some extension of technology.'

'It is a grave blasphemy indeed,' said Saphentis. 'To turn the teachings of the Omnissiah into the justification for such corruption.' Saphentis sat down and for the first time Alaric saw tiredness evident in his bionic limbs.

'I was wrong to suspect you,' said Alaric. 'About Thalassa, I mean. She must have got lost and captured. I thought you had killed her.'

'Because I had expressed admiration of this planet's self-sufficiency?' If Saphentis could have been able to smile grimly, Alaric suspected he would have done. 'I did not choose my words carefully. It was natural for you to think little of me, justicar. I wanted to understand this world, as well as carry out our mission, but it was unwise of me to do so. And I should have been more careful with Thalassa. She was not able to cope with the responsibilities I placed upon her here. Her loss was my failure. I can only hope the Omnissiah forgives me my weaknesses.'

'Then we're on the same side?' said Alaric.

'The same side,' replied Saphentis.

'Now that's sorted out,' said Hawkespur, 'we need to keep moving.'

'Agreed.' Alaric looked back at Brother Cardios, who had finished removing the geneseed from Archis's corpse. 'We'll have to leave him. There's no other way. We can pray for forgiveness later. Dvorn, carry Antigonus if he breaks down. The rest of you, stick close and keep your heads down. At the moment we're recon first, combat second.'

The strikeforce gathered itself, said a silent prayer for the dead and carried on into the titan works, skirting the base of the watchtower and skulking through the fleshy outgrowths and masses of corroded machinery that broke through the rockcrete surface of the works. And in front of them, now stretching between the horizons, were the titans themselves – towering, silent, brimming with destructive potential.

It was an army that could lay waste to worlds. An army just waiting to wake up.

CHAPTER SIXTEEN

'Die in failure, shame on you. Die in despair, shame on us all.'

– The 63rd Terran Scrolls,
Verse 114 (author unknown)

REAR ADMIRAL HORSTGELD was down on his belly, his Naval uniform torn and smouldering. He held a naval shotgun close to his body and tried to peer past the pew, through the smoke and burning wreckage that flittered from the ruined ceiling of the bridge.

Gunfire from the *Hellforger* had shaken the bridge but not destroyed it. Most of the bridge crew were still alive, crouching for cover as they had been since the last major bulkhead fell.

They had been boarded. The worst possible result when fighting the forces of Chaos. That was where the Enemy was strongest – face-to-face where foul magicks and mutations counted for the most and where the very presence of the corrupted could shake the faith of the bravest men.

'Hold!' shouted the bridge security chief, a squat and massively powerful man wearing full forced entry armour more normally used when storming decks held by mutinous crewmen. There were no mutinies on the *Tribunicia* but Horstgeld had always insisted on full security details on his ships. From the speed with which contact had been lost with contested sections of the ship, though, the security crew had not made a great deal of difference. 'Take your targets before you fire! Line up, then shoot!'

The rest of the bridge crew had hunted down whatever weapons they could as the Chaos boarding teams had spilled through the decks. Some had the naval shotguns of the kind Horstgeld now cradled, rock-solid weapons designed for filling cramped spaceship corridors with heavy, mutilating slug shots. Others had the lasguns that the Imperial Guard carried and many had only been able to rustle up their personal sidearms – autopistols, laspistols, even a few slug guns, almost all designed for show and not combat. Horstgeld saw one of the communications crew holding a length of pipe that had fallen from the ceiling as the *Tribunicia* was rocked by broadside fire, another hefting a large steel spanner.

'Steel your souls, faithful of the Emperor!' intoned Confessor Talas. 'Make His will your shield and His wrath your weapon!' For the first time in their careers many of the bridge crew were actually listening to Talas, seeking some hope in his words.

Sparks showered from the main bridge doors. Something was cutting through.

'Right!' shouted the security chief, unhooking the power maul from his belt and lowering the visor of his helmet before hefting his riot shield. 'Stay tight, stay covered, mark targets and never forget who–'

A massive armoured fist punched through the door and the gunfire began. Blazing, intense, a wall of fire and white noise that sheeted across the bridge from both sides. The viewscreen shattered in a white starburst and the golden statue of the Emperor toppled. Gunfire chewed through the hardwood pews and the fluted stone columns. Horstgeld yelled and fired almost blind, the shotgun kicking in his hands. He saw silhouettes of crewmen flailing and in the flashes of fire made out the deformed, oversized humanoid creatures forcing their way through the breach. They died in their dozens but more came, toppling over the bodies of their dead, a few making it to the rearmost pews and returning fire with their crude weapons.

A massive speargun shot a barbed javelin that impaled the chief navigation officer. The severed head of the security chief smacked off the column next to Horstgeld. The pew in front of Horstgeld cracked as if something huge had landed on it and Horstgeld scrambled out of the way, feeling hot blood on the floor. Spinning fragments of shrapnel were burning pinpoints on his skin and hands. He frantically reloaded as the return fire thudded heavier across the bridge.

Horstgeld had been in sticky situations before. He had been in boarding actions, even, as a young lieutenant in a boarding party that stormed an ork-infested space hulk. He had seen violent mutinies and pirate raids and had been on more than a few ships wrecked in accidents or under fire. He had seen many men die. He had killed a few up close and countless more from afar as master of the Emperor's warships. But this was the worst. This was the worst by far.

Something was ripping up the pews at the rear of the bridge. Something else flapped overhead and Horstgeld shot at it, blowing a chunk out of one leathery wing and seeing it spiral into the ordnance helm, all slashing claws and teeth. Someone was screaming. Someone else yelled in anger, the cry cut brutally short.

The gunfire was dying down. Now the din was cracking bones and the thud of blades into flesh, the scrape of blades on the floor. Screams and sobbing. Roars from once-human monsters. The killing was close and bloody and getting closer. Horstgeld backed up against the pew and finished loading his shotgun.

The killing was nearly done. Most of the bridge crew were dead, the rest dying.

Horstgeld heard heavy, armoured footsteps, coming closer.

'Captain,' said a voice, deep and thick.

Horstgeld peeked out through the planks of the broken pew. He could just make out a massive armoured form, similar to one of Alaric's Grey Knights but more hulking and malformed, wreathed in greasy smoke.

A Space Marine. Dear Emperor, it was a Space Marine from the Traitor Legions, the arch-betrayers of mankind. So dangerous that most Imperial teachings maintained they didn't even exist any more, because the very idea of a Traitor Marine was deadly to a weak mind.

Horstgeld held his shotgun tight. He was supposed to be brave. To die in the grace of the Emperor. And it wasn't supposed to be easy.

'Rear Admiral,' he shouted in reply, correcting the Marine.

'Ah. Good. A worthy prize, then.'

Horstgeld could see the Marine walking towards him, kicking dead crewmen out of the way. Horstgeld could make out the ancient, tarnished black armour, with the symbol of a single unblinking eye wrought onto one shoulder pad in gold. The Marine held a huge power sword in one hand, its blade writhing as if it housed something alive. His face was old and malevolent, the skin drawn tight, the eyes glinting black, the teeth pointed. An eight-pointed star was branded onto its hairless scalp. Steam spurted from the joints in the armour, which seemed crude and mechanical compared to the ornate armour of the Grey Knights – because this was a Marine from the days of Horus, a link to the Imperium's darkest and most shameful days. Chaos incarnate. Hatred made flesh.

'See!' called out a wavering voice, which Horstgeld realised belonged to Confessor Talas. 'See the form of the Enemy!' Talas pulled himself to his feet, still inside the bridge pulpit. 'See the mark of corruption upon him! The stink of treachery on him! The sound of…'

The Traitor Marine took out a bolt pistol and put a single round through Talas's head. The old confessor thudded to the wooden floor of the pulpit and one of the boarding mutants scampered over. The wet crunching noises that followed could only mean the confessor's body was being eaten.

The Traitor Marine stomped round the pew that Horstgeld was hiding behind. 'You. You are in command.'

Horstgeld nodded. He had to be brave. He had never run before. He would not run now, not give this creature the satisfaction of breaking him.

The Marine slid his writhing sword into a scabbard he wore on his back. He reached down with his free hand. Horstgeld levelled the shotgun but the Marine batted it away before Horstgeld could fire it – the Traitor Marine's reactions were lightning-quick. He was still a Space Marine, with all the conditioning and augmentations that went with it.

The Traitor Marine grabbed Horstgeld round the throat. His armoured fingers easily circled Horstgeld's pudgy neck and lifted him clean off the ground. The Traitor Marine held Horstgeld close to his face. Horstgeld could smell blood and brimstone on his breath. Those gem-like black eyes peered right through him.

'A long time ago I fought your kind,' said the Marine. 'Horus led us. He told us you were all weak. That you deserved to die. And every time I face you, you prove him right. You become more pathetic every time I sail out of the warp.'

Horstgeld would have spat in the Marine's face, but his mouth was dry. 'Horus was a traitor. He was corrupt. A daemon. We beat you.'

'No. We defeated you. We killed your Emperor. And then the conspirators closed ranks. The primarchs. All the bureaucrats and the profiteers. They wrote our triumph out of your history, they branded us failures, when all the time we were just waiting to return. And now that time has come, slave of the corpse-god. The Eye of Terror has opened. Cadia will fall. Look at yourself and ask who is stronger? Who deserves this galaxy?'

'But... you fear us! Why else are you here? If we are so weak, why did you have to come?'

The Marine dropped Horstgeld onto the floor and stamped down on his leg. Pure red pain slammed up from the wound, almost knocking Horstgeld out as the bones of his legs shattered.

'Enough of this,' said the Marine. 'I am Urkrathos of the Black Legion, Chosen of Abaddon the Despoiler. I will kill you and everyone on this ship. Death is merciful. Those who anger me are taken back to my ship and cast into the pit of blood where their souls are made fuel for spells and fodder for daemons. That is the fate I am giving you the chance to avoid. I am not merciful by nature so this offer will not be repeated. Do you understand?'

'Frag yourself,' gasped Horstgeld.

Urkrathos crushed down on Hortgeld's leg again. Horstgeld couldn't help from screaming.

'Where is the tribute?' Urkrathos demanded.

'What... what tribute?'

Urkrathos lifted Horstgeld up again, slammed him against the closest pillar and drew his sword. He stabbed the sword through the meat of Horstgeld's shoulder, pinning him to the pillar like an insect on a board.

'Do not make me ask again, rear admiral,' spat Urkrathos. 'You're here for it just as we are.'

'I don't know,' said Horstgeld, coughing up a gobbet of blood. He could barely see through the pain. The world was a mass of pain with only the face of Urkrathos showing through, his snarling, fanged mouth, his burning black eyes. 'We... we didn't find out...'

'Where is it?' bellowed Urkrathos. 'Where is the Castigator?'

Horstgeld tried to speak again, to curse the traitor. But the couldn't get the words out. His throat was full of blood and he couldn't even breathe.

Urkrathos wrenched the blade out of the pillar and caught Horstgeld as he fell. He lifted the rear admiral's limp body and dashed his brains out against the floor, cracking the man's head over and over again into the flagstones.

He flung the corpse to the floor. His sword had been drawn and it had not drunk deeply enough yet, so Urkrathos stabbed it again into the corpse and let the daemons imprisoned in the blade lap up the man's warm blood.

There had not been nearly enough blood. Every time it got easier to break them. Every ship, every battle – the Imperium had only spared a pathetic parody of a fleet to oppose Urkrathos. It was an insult. It seemed all the best battles were in the past now.

A thought came unbidden into Urkrathos's mind. It wasn't his own thought – it was a transmission from the communications daemon back on the *Hellforger*.

'What?' thought back Urkrathos angrily. He didn't like the daemons touching his mind. 'If this is not an emergency, you will suffer.'

'Our allies show their hand on the planet,' replied the grinding, bestial voice of the daemon. 'The sky opens for us.'

'Show me,' thought Urkrathos.

An image unfolded. Chaeroneia's atmosphere was a filthy dark grey mantle of pollution, specked with the bright spots that were its attendant asteroids. Urkrathos had guessed the Imperial fleet had been trying to find a way through the asteroids when Urkrathos's own fleet had arrived. Getting onto the planet would be a headache Urkrathos was going to have to face when he had destroyed the Imperials.

The image projected from the communications daemon was shifting. Like ripples in water, shock-waves were echoing out from a point on the uppermost level of the atmosphere, directly above the source of the signal that had promised tribute.

The asteroids were moving. Like a shoal of silver fish, the points of light were spiralling around the epicentre, rearranging themselves. It was powerful magic. More powerful than any sanctioned Imperial psyker could manage.

'What is it?' thought Urkrathos impatiently. 'Who is doing this?'

'This being knows not,' replied the daemon.

A path was being cleared through the field. A way in, large enough for the *Hellforger*.

Of course. Whoever had promised the tribute to Abaddon must also have been monitoring the situation in orbit. Now the Imperial fleet was destroyed, crippled or scattered, there was no danger of Imperial Guard landing on the world. Urkrathos had succeeded and now the mysterious benefactor of Chaos was welcoming the *Hellforger* in with open arms.

'Urkrathos to all crew,' voxed Urkrathos, knowing his voice would be transmitted all over the *Hellforger* and into the communicators of the less disposable boarding crew. 'All boarders disengage. Prepare to cut free.' Urkrathos switched channels. 'Kreathak?'

Kreathak replied from the cockpit of his Helltalon fighter, his voice distorted by the scream of the macro-jet engines and the stutter of lascannon. 'My lord?'

'Disengage and get back to the *Cadaver*. We're heading down.'

'The Enemy is in full flight. Confirm action abort?'

'Yes, confirm. And be quick about it. Don't waste your time killing them, I want your fighters in close defence patrols.'

'Of course, my lord.' Kreathik switched off his vox-link – if he managed to choke down his bloodlust he would be flying back to the fighter platform *Cadaver*, ready to defend the gap in the asteroid field while Urkrathos's ship loaded the tribute.

Urkrathos switched to another channel. 'Come in *Desikratis*.'

'Lord,' came the titanic, rumbling voice of the *Desikratis*.

'Pull back.'

'But lord. The prey, it bleeds so.'

'I said pull back. You can toy with it when we are done. I need you to keep enemy fighters away while we head down to the planet. Understood?'

'*Desiktratis* loves its fun. Loves to make them bleed.'

'And you will. Just not yet. Do not make me punish you, *Desiktratis*. I have room for more servants on my bridge and you are not so great as to defy the will of the Chosen.'

'Forgiveness,' whimpered the *Desikratis*. 'I leave the prey. It cannot run. It will still be here.'

'That's right, it will. Now pull back and stay close to the *Hellforger*. Cover it when I breach the atmosphere. Urkrathos out.'

Urkrathos willed the link closed and felt the communications daemon's mind recoiling from him.

He glanced down at the rear admiral's body. The tiny mouths along the edge of his sword were drinking the blood hungrily. Urkrathos pulled the blade out – it was good to keep the blade slightly hungry, so it would not lose its will to thirst. Urkrathos kicked the corpse across the bridge, spitting in contempt, then turned and stomped back out of the bridge. The boarding troops cowered and whimpered before him as he walked back down to the Dreadclaw boarding craft lodged in the hull of the Imperial ship, which would take him back to the *Hellforger*.

With most of the defenders of the Imperial ship dead, the boarding troops had only Urkrathos to fear. And that was Urkrathos's favourite kind of slavery – ruling through nothing but fear. There were no shackles on the bestial, devolved things that slavered their devotion to him as he passed. There were no cages on the *Hellforger* to keep them in line. But they did as they were told solely because they feared what would happen if they did not. There was no more powerful demonstration that the champions of

Chaos owned the souls of those lesser creatures – just as they owned by right the souls of every sentient thing in the galaxy.

Yes, Urkrathos would rule and above him Abaddon, united in enslaving the galaxy. But for now, there was work to be done. The *Hellforger* would have to be prepared for a full atmospheric landing, the troops regrouped and reorganised into landing parties and space cleared for the tribute itself. But these were all details. The end was now in sight. Urkrathos had won.

CHAPTER SEVENTEEN

'When it was over, when the blood had dried and the fires had died down, then we found we were the same as we had always been – small and terrified human beings, with only the light of the Emperor to see by in this dark galaxy of sin.'

– Saint Praxides of Ophelia VII,
'Notes on Martyrdom'

'WHAT WOULD YOU have me do?'

It was a long time since Archmagos Veneratus Scraecos had spoken physical words through his vocabulator unit. It was still a strange feeling, heavy and primitive, but he knew it was the right way to conduct himself when speaking with the concentrated knowledge-construct that was the avatar of the Omnissiah Himself.

There was no reply. Scraecos stared intently at the brushed ferrocrete floor of the hangar. He felt the intense scrutiny beating down on him like the rays of a sun. He was being judged. The Omnissiah was judging him with every moment, of course, but now it was so palpable he felt as if he were being taken apart piece by piece, bionic by bionic and inspected.

If there were any faults in him, if Scraecos failed the silent interrogation, then there could only be one result. He would be destroyed completely, the essence of the machine stripped away from both his bionic and biological parts until he was just a collection of meaningless junk. He had seen it happen before. The tech-priests he had led down to this place a thousand years ago had not been as strong-willed or comprehending as Scraecos himself and they had been seared away from their bodies and annihilated. It was an awesome demonstration of the Omnissiah's power. Just as He could comprehend the universe, so He could choose not to comprehend you and in doing so would make you cease to exist. That was true power. The Omnissiah decided what was real or not and that was why He was the rightful ruler of the universe.

'Look upon me.'

The voice of the Omnissiah was pure knowledge beamed right into Scraecos's head. Scraecos was almost blinded by its magnitude. To simply replicate that voice through base mechanical means would be impossible. The very voice of the Omnissiah spoke of infinity.

Scraecos looked up. The face of the Castigator looked down upon him. Scraecos had been awestruck the first time he had seen it and that feeling was not gone now. The massive burning eyes were the only features, but they welled with knowledge so ancient that the human race itself was just a footnote to the last chapter. Their gaze pinned Scraecos to the floor, stripped him of all his rank and experience so he was like a child before the Castigator.

The Castigator was the avatar of the Omnissiah. Through the Castigator, the Omnissiah spoke directly to His servants. It was a measure of how corrupt and ignorant the Adeptus Mechanicus had become that the Omnissiah had to stoop so low as to give itself physical form. It was so He could instruct the tech-priests of Chaeroneia without the self-serving Archmagi of the Imperium to twist His teachings. Similarly, He had required Chaeroneia to be removed from the Imperium so His teachings would remain pure. It meant that bringing Chaeroneia back into real space was a great risk, because the Imperium still had the chance to corrupt the ways of the True Mechanicus before the Omnissiah's face could be revealed to the rest of the galaxy.

'You ask me what I would have you do. Have you learned so little?'

Scraecos reeled with the intensity of the Omnissiah's disapproval. 'I have... I have been apart from myself for so long. I have not been one, but many. I fear my own self has been weakened.'

'No. It is stronger. You now understand why I chose you first. And why I choose you again now. Is it not so?'

'Yes! Yes, my lord, it is so! Because I am a killer!'

'You are a killer.' The word was like a mark of approval. Scraecos shuddered – no one tech-priest had ever been given praise by the Castigator before. 'Though you have long been a builder of my edifice of knowledge, yet you have never truly been an archmagos. You have always been a murderer. When you slaved for the corrupt Mechanicus, you killed for rank and favour. Is this not true?'

'It is true.' Scraecos had indeed killed. Infighting between the Magi of the Adeptus Mechanicus was sometimes far more intense than the outside Imperium had ever realised. Research accidents, natural disasters, spacecraft wrecks and outright assassinations could all be arranged and Scraecos had done so several times in reaching the rank of archmagos veneratus. He had killed to ensure it was he who was sent to Chaeroneia in the first place, to follow up rumours of pre-imperial technology beneath the toxic deserts. He had never, ever imagined he would find something like the Castigator – but it was ultimately killing that had brought him before the avatar at that moment.

'And you are a killer still. This is why even the other magi of Chaeroneia singled you out and gave you your self again. Dull-minded as they are, they could not mistake the killer inside you. Even when your mind merged with theirs, the spark was there still.'

Scraecos was taken aback. 'Do they not serve you well?'

'Of course. Every living thing on this world must. But though I understand their failings and use them, they are failings still. They do as they are instructed and nothing else, but do I not command you to seek innovation always? Yet their thinking is not innovative. As it is with the machine, so it must be with the mind, so that machine and flesh and soul can become part of the machine that is the universe. You, Archmagos Veneratus Scraecos, you are not so. You do not just kill because it is required of you by superiors or circumstance. You kill because you enjoy it. That was the part of you that the Mechanicus could not erase. It was the part that sought me out and led you here. That was the free part of your mind that would listen to my creed. It was why you were the first and why you are here now.'

'Then you really did call me here.'

'Of course. Nothing that happens on this world happens without my willing it. You already know what you must do.'

'Yes.' Scraecos's voice was trembling. He was filled with a strange emotion, something that had left its echo on him from an early life he did not remember. It was cold and gripping – it robbed his mind of its thoughts leaving only itself behind. He searched through his datacores and realised that it was fear. For the first time in longer than he could remember, Scraecos was afraid. He was being called forth to do the work of the Omnissiah and he was afraid of failure. 'You want me to kill.'

'The outer moat of this facility has been breached. The hunter-programs failed to catch their prey. The intruders are within the titan works. You are to take the works garrison, confront the intruders and kill them. They include unbelievers who have evaded the grasp of the tech-priests since Chaeroneia left real space. Others amongst them are interlopers from the

Imperium, come to steal what is rightly the dominion of the Omnissiah. They will be annihilated. Other visitors from real space will soon arrive, believers in our cause who will help us spread the true creed of the Omnissiah. The intruders must be destroyed before our allies arrive. I leave this task in your hands, Archmagos Veneratus Scraecos. You have proven yourself above the other tech-priests in the depth of your lust for destruction. Hold it in check no longer. In doing this you will prove yourself worthy of becoming my first prophet. Your success is a mathematical certainty. Go now and do the work of your Omnissiah.'

Scraecos was filled with rapture. He was the prophet. It was already done – only the inevitable victory remained to be played out. Yes, he was a killer. Yes, he enjoyed it. And yes, it was the will of the Omnissiah, spoken through the Castigator itself, that Scraecos kill for his god. The fear was chased away by the joy. 'I shall not fail, my lord!' cried Scraecos, switching his vocabulator up to its maximum, exultant volume. 'I am the finality of the equation, for death is my logic!'

The Castigator's gaze turned away from Scraecos again. Scraecos was no longer pinned in place by the awesome weight of the Omnissiah's scrutiny. He was free and his task was clear. The titan works maintained a formidable garrison of troops, since it was a site that deserved far better than the gaggles of menials the tech-priests had used to intercept the intruders. Ever since the Castigator had demanded the rebuilding of the titan works and the dedication of Manufactorium Noctis to the production of the war machines, it had also stipulated that military forces of the highest order should be ready to protect the works at all costs. Now the Omnissiah's wisdom was again revealed, as those troops confirmed the absolute certainty of Scraecos's victory.

Scraecos bowed before the Castigator. Then he turned away from the avatar and walked back towards the elevator that would take him up to ground level, to the garrison where he would reactivate the army.

So would the equation be ended. And so would death be confirmed as the ultimate logic.

ARCHMAGOS SAPHENTIS LOOKED up from the cogitator unit that dominated one wall of the bunker. The cogitator was a biomechanical monstrosity, wrought from bone and iron with internal clockwork-like workings resembling the pulsing of organs inside a giant metal ribcage.

'The configuration is unorthodox,' he said, 'but it can be worked with.'

'Make it quick,' said Alaric.

The strike force had found the bunker a short distance inside the watchtower perimeter. It was blistered up from the rockcrete, the stony surface disfigured by vein-like growths and it looked abandoned although the cogitator was working. The bunker stank of rotting biological matter and the air was almost unbreathable for an unaugmented human. Antigonus and his tech-priests were gathered just outside, keeping watch with the rest of Alaric's squad. The titan works were large enough that isolated corners of it like this could exist away from the eyes of the tech-priests – but there was no doubt it was only a matter of time before the Dark Mechanicus forces found them, especially if they were aware of Saphentis accessing the cogitator.

'We need a plan,' Interrogator Hawkespur was saying. 'We're blind here.'

'I agree,' said Alaric. 'My squad can fight no matter what, but we'll only have a chance of hurting the Dark Mechanicus if we know what we're doing.'

'Priority one is the Standard Template Construct. If it's here, we need evidence of it and we need to destroy it if we can. I don't think there's much chance of us recovering it. And if it did this to Chaeroneia, I don't think we'd want to.'

'And priority two?'

'Cause as much destruction as we can.'

'I think that will take care of itself.' Alaric looked back at Saphentis. 'Can you find anything?'

'The terminal has relatively comprehensive access,' said Saphentis. 'I should be able to acquire physical schematics.'

'Will they know you're in?' asked Hawkespur.

'Almost certainly.' Saphentis extended a pair of dataprobes into the cogitator, puncturing a large, veiny stomach-like organ filled with liquid data-medium. 'Ah. Yes. The titan works requires enormous amounts of power because of the metalworks and foundries that take up most of the space below the surface. It absorbs the majority of the remaining mineral output of the planet. Another major power drain is the central spire. It appears this is also the nexus for communications and information systems planetwide. The schematics are incomplete and fragmented, perhaps due to the bio-organic nature of much of the construction. I am downloading what I can.'

'Haulvarn? Anything yet?' voxed Alaric.

'Not yet,' voxed Brother Haulvarn from outside. 'A few flying contacts, probably animals.'

'Don't assume anything,' said Alaric.

'There is a third power drain,' continued Saphentis as he inserted dataprobes into various interfaces and orifices in the cogitator's innards. 'Some way below the surface. The schematics suggest a void in the underground constructions large enough for a titan refitting or refuelling hangar.' Saphentis paused and suddenly withdrew his dataprobes, recoiling from the cogitator. 'They are aware of my intrusion. Countermeasures are imminent.'

'Do they know where we are?' asked Alaric.

'Possibly.'

'Then what do you have?'

Saphentis's dataprobes folded back into his bionic hands and he took out his dataslate. The slate's screen was covered in sketchy schematics. Alaric looked closer.

The titan works were huge. The blasted, blistered rockcrete expanse of the titan yard was just the uppermost level of a massive industrial complex that punched down through into the planet's crust below the ash deserts. The physical schematics were overlaid with the power usages of the various sections and the forges where titan parts were being produced were marked out with vivid colours to show how much power they were draining from Manufactorium Noctis. The void Saphentis had noticed was just below the surface, a chamber bored into solid rock the size of a spacecraft hangar. It was using up enormous amounts of energy.

'Close in on the surface,' said Alaric. 'We need somewhere we can defend.'

The schematics shifted to show the plan of the titan works' surface. The titans themselves took up most of the area, with the rest mostly housing fuel and maintenance facilities, or enormous ammo loading machines which heaved shells for Vulcan cannon and power cells for plasma blastguns up to the titans' weaponry.

'There,' said Alaric. He pointed to a sprawling mass of metal – a fallen titan, perhaps one that had been destroyed in an accident or was somehow flawed and was being disassembled. It was a short run from the bunker. 'We'll make a stand there. The fuel and ammo facilities won't take kindly to a firefight and any bunkers will probably be occupied. But there's plenty of cover in the titan parts and they're made of the toughest stuff the Mechanicus can produce.'

'You're right,' said Hawkespur, 'But then what?'

'Everything they've thrown at us, we've either beaten or escaped. That means they'll bring out the big guns and that means daemons. But the Dark Mechanicus here don't realise they're working with daemons at all. Our best chance of really hurting them is to face their daemons in battle. They might not know how to react if they realise their best weapons aren't their own. As soon as we get the chance, we make for here.' Alaric indicated the power-draining void beneath the centre of the titan works. 'That's where this place is controlled from.'

'How do you know?' asked Hawkespur.

'Because I just do,' replied Alaric bluntly. 'The same thing I felt when I faced Ghargatuloth. I feel it on Chaeroneia and it's coming from there. Either we force it out to fight us, or we go in there to get it. Either way, we fight.'

'It seems,' said Saphentis, 'that this plan, if it can be called such, affords us little chance of survival.'

'That's correct, archmagos. Is that something you object to?'

'Not at all, justicar. I am free to risk my life if there is little chance of that life continuing. It gives me the advantage of logical freedom.'

'Then it's agreed.' Alaric opened up the vox. 'We're moving out. Defensive position four hundred metres east, at the fallen titan.'

Acknowledgement runes flickered on Alaric's retina from his squad members. 'Understood,' voxed Magos Antigonus. 'But I won't quite be myself until I find a more intact body. You do realise, justicar, that there is an alternative opportunity that presents itself to me?'

'I do,' said Alaric. 'But I'd rather not play that hand yet. See what they'll throw at us. Then we go for the end game.'

'Very well. My tech-priests are moving out now.'

Alaric looked at Hawkespur. 'Are you ready for this?'

'Justicar, no matter what happens my life is over. This planet has seen to that already. So it's not a question of how ready I am. It's a question of how much damage I can do to these heretics before I die.' Hawkespur took out her marksman's pistol.

'Inquisitor Nyxos trained me well. He always taught me that it would one day come down to nothing more than a gun and a handful of faith. I am glad I listened to him.'

'All Marines,' voxed Alaric, 'move out.' He led the way out of the bunker and into the shadow of the watchtowers. Already the tech-priests and Grey Knights were hurrying warily across the rockcrete towards the hulking, broken shape of the fallen titan that could just be seen in the middle distance.

Alaric could feel the malice stronger now, as if something dark and terrible was waking up below his feet. It was watching him, watching them all. He could feel the strings it pulled, routes of black sorcery reaching into the minds of the titan works' troops, guiding them towards the intruders to destroy them. It was a force of absolute destruction, horrible but somehow pure in its purpose.

Chaos was nothing more than lies and corruption given form and Chaeroneia was infused with it – but it was a kind of Chaos Alaric had never faced before, somehow hard and calculating, murderous but cold-blooded. It was the kind of malicious intelligence that had built a legion of titans and yet waited a thousand years to use them, that could corrupt an entire planet of Omnissiah-fearing tech-priests without them ever realising the true source of the power that commanded them.

Alaric had never known fear, not as a normal man would understand it. But he did know well the feeling when he was facing something that should never exist and that had the capacity to wound him down to his very soul. He felt it now. Chaeroneia could consume him if he let it, and if he wasn't strong enough then he would lose more than his life in the shadow of these god-machines.

'Position in sight,' voxed Brother Cardios from up ahead. 'Looks cold. We're moving in now.'

'Good. I'm right behind you.' Alaric almost unconsciously checked the load of his storm bolter as he hurried across towards the titan. He ran through the Lesser Rites of Preparedness in his mind, knowing that the Grey Knights and the tech-priests would all be performing their own version of the rites, preparing themselves to fight and die as best they could.

They would probably all die. But it wasn't about survival, not now. It was about dying the most destructive death they could, a death that would strike at the very heart of Chaeroneia.

THE MARINES AND the traitors who followed them were lit up like stars in the night sky, bright traces of infra-red against the cold rockcrete. Scraecos counted five Space Marines and almost thirty tech-priests. The infra-red traces coming from the tech-priests showed very little exposed flesh and old, ill-maintained augmetics bleeding plumes of heat and exhaust gases. Inefficient. Failing. A reminder of what they had given up when they fled the light of the Omnissiah's understanding like vermin.

Two were more normal humans. One was sickly, the other healthy. Another was a tech-priest with exceptional augmetics, finely efficient and showing traces across the light spectrum of devices that Scraecos could not decipher. Perhaps a new convert from the experimental tech-priest collectives elsewhere on the planet, more likely a member of the outside Mechanicus come to reclaim Chaeroneia. And finally there was a broken old servitor, bleeding its failing energy reserves as heat into the open air.

It wasn't much of an army. True, a squad of Space Marines, according to the historical archives of the old Imperium, was one of the most dangerous infantry units the Imperium could deploy. But Scraecos had more.

Scraecos flicked his augmetic eyes back to the visible spectrum with a thought. The intruders were heading for a fallen titan. Based on the old Imperial Reaver-pattern titan, the machine's birth had been flawed and it had been left where it fell, so the menials could scavenge it for parts and so maintain the cycle of cannibalistic efficiency that allowed the titan works to function.

Scraecos's vantage point on top of the fuelling bunker gave him an excellent view of the battlefield. The titan was good cover, but that meant nothing. Scraecos turned to the army mustering behind him, drawn from the barracks dotted around the surface of the titan works and the bio-storage units below the surface.

The death servitors were the best soldiers on Chaeroneia. And they were soldiers – not machines, or normal servitors, but something else. The armoured, beweaponed shells had been constructed according to the oldest and most potent designs, adapted from labour and battle-servitors to fulfil an altogether different purpose. That purpose was to serve as the physical bodies for the hunter-programs, voracious, brutal programs born in Chaeroneia's data media, willed into being by the infinite under-standing of the Omnissiah. The programs in the datafortress had failed and those inhabiting the death servitors knew it – their bloodlust was tem-pered by anger and shame and they were pursuing a logical imperative to succeed where others of their kind had not.

Scraecos could feel the monstrous intelligence behind the metallic faces. The hunter-programs were deadly and the True Mechanicus had crafted them bodies to match. Twin repeating lasblasters were mounted on the shoulders of each death servi-tor, leaving the hands free for the lethal electrified claws that were the hunter-programs' preferred weapons. The three full maniples of death-servitors stood to attention on the thick, coiled segmented tails that were so much more versatile than the tracks, legs or wheels that battle-servitors normally used.

Maniple Gamma was supported by a unit of hulk-ing eviscerator engines, their photon thruster cannons cycling impatiently, their many hooked limbs squirming to tear into an enemy. Maniple Delta included a full Annihilator squad, deceptively humanoid warriors that had once been partially human tech-priests, but which had failed in their devotion to the Omnissiah and had been trans-formed into partially biological hosts for the most able of the hunter-programs. Maniple Epsilon was commanded by Scraecos personally and would pro-tect him in battle from anything an enemy could throw at him.

'Maniple Gamma. Report.'

'Ready,' came the machine-code reply, spoken as one by the collective half-mind of the data-programs.

'Good. Maniple Delta?'

'Ready.'

'Maniple Epsilon?'

'Ready to serve the archmagos veneratus.'

'Full assault protocols. Move out.'

As one the servitors advanced, slithering with wonderful menace towards the fallen titan. The sound was like metal through flesh as they moved. Scraecos moved with them, safely surrounded by the death servitors of Maniple Epsilon.

The intruders would know they were under attack. The stomping of the eviscerator engines would give the attackers away before the gunfire started. But it didn't matter. They were dead anyway. And Scraecos had thought about what the Omnissiah had said to him in the sacred chamber underground. Scraecos was a killer and his holy duty to the Omnissiah was to kill – so Scraecos would see to it that when the killing began, he was in the thick of it.

ALARIC GLANCED OVER the massive leg plate of the fallen titan. He could see them coming, his augmented vision cutting through Chaeroneia's permanent twilight and picking out the glint of metallic carapaces and wicked claws.

Servitors, probably, but they moved differently. And they felt different too – Alaric could feel dark sorcery spattering off his psychic shield like iron-hard rain.

'How many?' asked Magos Antigonus, his maintenance servitor clambering painfully over the fallen slab of carapace.

Alaric looked more closely. 'Several units. Maybe a hundred in total. Do you know what they are?'

The eyepieces of Antigonus's servitor head whirred as he focused harder. 'No. But… some of my tech-priests said the magi were developing something new. They were testing them out in the undercity, hunting feral menials. Very quick, very dangerous. I don't think any of the tech-priests got a good look at one.'

'Well, we're about to get a very good look indeed. This section is quite secure, but we need men around the titan's head and keep someone on the far side in case they surround us.'

Antigonus voxed instructions to his tech-priests to take up position around the fallen titan. The titan formed a position that was bounded on one side by the titan's leg, a solid slab of ceramite armour two storeys high. There were enough mechanics and bracing on the rear side of the leg for defenders to climb up to the parapet and fire down. Beside that was the torso, equally massive but probably easier to scramble over. The third side consisted of one fallen arm mostly consisting of the immense multi-barrelled Vulcan gun and the titan's head, staring with shattered eyes up at the polluted sky. The head and arm formed the weakest side – that was where the Dark Mechanicus attack would hit and that was also where the tech-priests and Grey Knights would have to fight the hardest.

They had less than forty troops. The enemy might have three times that – with the promise of a near-infinite number of reinforcements once more troops reached the titan works.

The enemy was less than a hundred metres away, moving through the shadows cast by the legs of the titans that formed a forbidding backdrop. Massive, smoke-belching machines shuddered as if they were alive and ground along behind the slithering servitors. Alaric could feel it stronger now, the malice inside them, the black magic and ancient evil that powered them. Nothing human or artificial could feel like that.

Daemons. The servitors were possessed by daemons.

'Grey Knights, get to the arm! Saphentis, you too. That's where they'll break through.' Alaric watched as the enemy came closer and the first spatters of speculative gunfire rattled overhead from the huge war machines following the army.

Shots thudded into the ceramite, hissing as they ripped deep cores out of the titan's armour. Alaric didn't recognise the weapon and he was familiar with just about every kind of weapon that might be fired in the Imperium.

Then the servitors hit the ground and sped up, sweeping along like snakes, faster than a man could sprint. The sound that came from them was awful, a hellish cacophony of machine-code amplified and mixed in with a wailing that seemed to come echoing directly from the warp.

It was a war-cry. And before Alaric could react, the Dark Mechanicus were upon them.

Rapid las-fire rained against the position, streaking over the fallen arm and rattling off the titan's armour so loudly that Alaric couldn't hear his own voice as he yelled to the tech-priests at the parapet to get down. He jumped down to the rockcrete and ran over to the rest of his squad at the arm.

'Lykkos! Now, do it!'

Brother Lykkos was the first to fire, pumping shots from his psycannon as fast as the weapon would let him and sending them streaking into the advancing mass of servitors. Up close they looked horrendous – their bodies ended in long serpentine tails that propelled them along with impossible speed. Their heads were masses of sensors and probes, each with several unblinking ocular lenses like the eyes of a spider. Twin rapid-firing las-weapons sprayed crimson fire and their arms ended in claws that spat sparks as they raked along the rockcrete.

Alaric ran through the ranges in his mind. How many times had he done the same thing on the firing range? In training sermons with his squad? In battle? It was like another sense kicking in.

'Fire!' he yelled, the moment the servitors crossed the line of storm bolter range.

Autoguns and lasguns opened up, spattering tiny silver explosions as they thudded into the servitors' carapaces. The Grey Knights fired over the blackened machinery of the fallen arm, storm bolter fire ripping into the servitors.

Some fell. Some had arms or heads blown off and kept coming. Alaric saw one of Antigonus's tech-priests fall, neck and chest punched through by las-bolts.

But it wasn't enough. The Grey Knights accounted for more than a few servitors in those moments, but the servitors weren't normal troops that would run away or take to ground. They were inhuman and unholy. They didn't feel fear or shock, or any of the other weapons that worked against normal troops.

When the servitors hit, it was like something massive and solid slamming into the position. The Grey Knights switched to their Nemesis weapons in the split second it took the servitors to reach them and in that time Alaric felt the pure rising bloodlust burning inside the servitors, the grim joy in death that only the most debased servants of Chaos could feel.

A servitor slammed into him. It was shrieking in machine-code, a staccato assault on the senses. Claws raked at his armour and electric pain jolted through him. The half-insect, half-machine face thrust close, unblinking eyes burning with malice. Alaric caught its weight and dropped to one knee, trapping the servitor's clawed hand and hauling it past him, slamming it into the ground. Sparks flew and its carapace cracked but it kept fighting, slashing up at him, gouging long furrows in the ceramite and carving deep red lines of pain through the skin of his face.

Alaric fought to bring his halberd to bear, slamming the butt end down into the servitor's chest. He could feel the daemon scrabbling at his soul, trying to find a way in to infect him with fear and confusion. The servitor writhed and broke away, slithering across the rockcrete, trying to get behind Alaric and rear up. Alaric spun and drove the halberd blade up, slicing the servitor in two at the waist. The tail end dropped spasming to the ground and the upper half held on, digging its claws into Alaric's armour as the face unfolded and a razor-sharp appendage, like a massive surgical needle, stabbed out at him.

Alaric caught the needle with his free hand and wrenched it out of the servitor's head. Black, foul-smelling oil sprayed out and the daemon screamed so loudly the sound cut out the roar of gunfire. Alaric punched the servitor to the ground and drove his halberd blade down, carving its head in two. The daemon's shriek became pure white noise for a moment and then the scrabbling in his mind ended as the daemon, its host finally destroyed, was wrenched out of real space and back to the warp.

The servitors were everywhere. For every one that died two or three more scrambled over the wreckage of the titan. Alaric saw Tech-Priest Gallen as a servitor impaled his torso with its claws and lifted him off the ground. The probe folded out from its mechanical head and it punched the probe into Gallen's face, piercing through into the tech-priest's brain. Gallen's body convulsed as the flesh boiled away and Alaric knew the data-daemon inside the servitor was feasting on him, sucking away the substance of his soul and body.

The Grey Knights squad was the only thing holding the servitors back. Brother Dvorn shattered a servitor with a swing of his Nemesis hammer, completely ripping the thing's torso to scrap and sending the daemon shrieking back to the warp. Brother Haulvarn was duelling with another servitor, turning its claws away with his sword as he stuttered storm bolter fire into it, beating it back inch by inch. Brother Cardios kept the servitors away from Haulvarn by sending waves of flame from his Incinerator rippling over the wreckage – the flame would do comparatively little to the servitors' metal bodies but the Incinerator was loaded with thrice-blessed promethium which scorched the substance of the daemons like fire scorched flesh.

The tech-priests were faring badly. Many were already dead and the servitors were among them, inside the compound formed by the body of the fallen titan, shrieking as they killed. Alaric spotted Hawkespur halfway up the charred bulk of the titan's torso, snapping off shots with her autopistol. The tech-guard was beside her, ready to follow his final order to the death, calmly following her aim with volleys of hellgun fire.

'Fall back!' shouted Alaric 'Close the circle! They're surrounding us!'

The Grey Knights moved back from the barrier of the titan's arm so they could help the tech-priests who were dying behind them. In close formation they could send out a weight of storm bolter fire enough to batter back the servitors as they moved in for the kill, buying the tech-priests enough time to add some fire of their own. Up close, the servitors were more inclined to kill with their claws instead of their multi-lasers and the tech-priests at least had a chance in a firefight that they didn't in hand-to-hand combat.

But it meant nothing more than a few more moments. A handful of seconds in which to hurt the Dark Mechanicus more.

Hard black beams of energy played across the bloodstained rockcrete of the makeshift compound, scoring deep gouges in the surface and cutting limbs from bodies where they touched the tech-priests. Alaric looked up to see more Dark Mechanicus troops on the parapet of the titan's leg armour – they must have climbed up the sheer ceramite of the armour and were now using their vicious beam weapons to slice apart the few defenders on the parapet.

The new attackers looked like tech-priests but there was something wrong about them, even by the standards of the Dark Mechanicus priests Alaric had seen on Chaeroneia already. Tentacles waved from between the augmetic components that made up their bodies. Darkness bled from under their tattered bloodstained robes and the massive beam weapons they carried in two of their numerous augmetic arms seemed to burn with black flame, as if they were powered by sorcery. They were a fusion of tech-priest and daemonic sorcery, possessed like the servitors but with an intelligence the animalistic data-daemons lacked.

'Firing line!' ordered Alaric. 'Up there! Now!'

The Grey Knights opened fire and one or two of the daemonic priests fell, but there were more, suddenly drifting down the near side of the titan's leg, apparently moving on some kind of anti-grav unit. Lines of black energy swung as the daemonic priests fired and Brother Cardios fell, his leg sliced through at the thigh.

'Cover!' shouted Alaric. The squad broke up as the daemonic priests concentrated their fire on the Grey Knights. Dvorn barely broke stride to grab the fallen Cardios and haul him into cover, still firing.

Alaric hit the ground behind a fallen slab of the titan's torso armour. Magos Antigonus dropped down beside Alaric. His servitor body was barely able to move itself and it was covered in blood and laser scars.

'Photon thrusters,' said Antigonus, glancing past the cover to where the daemonic priests were wreaking carnage among the tech-priests caught out of cover. 'Portable particle accelerators. They'll go through anything. I didn't know they could make them any more.'

Alaric looked at Antigonus's wrecked body. 'Can you take over one of the servitors?'

'Not with a daemon inside.'

Alaric stood up and fired over the ceramite slab. Thruster beams carved past him in response, slicing a chunk off the titan armour. As he ducked back down Alaric saw another force of servitors approaching, this time with huge steam-spewing war engines lumbering along behind them. And there was someone leading them.

Antigonus saw it too. A tech-priest, surrounded by the death servitors. The lower part of his face was a nest of writhing mechadendrites and fronds of sensor-wires waved from where his hands should have been.

'Scraecos,' said Antigonus.

Alaric recognised him from the statue in the underground cathedral. 'We've got them scared. They sent their best to kill us.'

'Then let's return the favour. It is time, justicar.'

'Can you do it?'

'Probably not. But I always enjoyed a challenge. Cover me from those photon thrusters.'

Alaric nodded. 'Grey Knights, covering fire. Get close and keep them busy. With me!'

Alaric broke cover and ran, head down as he charged. Black beams of photons ripped past him and one nearly took his arm off but he kept going, hoping a moving target would be more difficult for the daemonic priests to hit. He fired as he went, spraying storm bolter fire almost at random.

He made it to the base of the titan's leg. The closest daemonic priest's photon thruster changed configuration in his hands and the beam fragmented into dozens of black bolts. They spattered against Alaric's armour, boring smoking craters into his skin. Bursts of cold pain tore into him. Some of the bolts had gone right through his chest and out through the backpack of his armour, but Alaric had suffered worse and gone on fighting.

Alaric crashed into the priest. The daemon inside it roared and the priest's body reconfigured, its shoulder rotating to bring its combat-fitted augmetic arms to the fore. A sparking electro-whip lashed at him – Alaric caught the whip on the haft of his halberd and punched the priest in the face hard enough to shatter the desiccated face and expose the sparking electronics underneath.

The arms reached around and grabbed Alaric, trying to wrestle him to the ground. Alaric saw a second priest lowering his photon thruster, ready to bore a massive hole right through Alaric once he was down.

The second priest was bowled aside by a shape that darted in almost too quick to see. It was Archmagos Saphentis, his bionic arms in full combat configuration, stabbing and slicing at the possessed priest.

Alaric stabbed his halberd down into the lower back of the priest that was wrestling with him. Something blew in a shower of blue sparks and the grip slackened – Alaric pushed the priest away from him and swung the halberd blade in an arc that cut the priest neatly in two. The daemon inside gibbered and Alaric saw its image superimposed over his vision for a moment. It was a horrendous thing, gleaming wet exposed muscle, a score of burning green eyes studding its pulsing flesh. Then it was gone, its host destroyed and its substance unable to retain stability in real space.

The rest of the squad was among the daemonic priests. Dvorn was killing one and Haulvarn was fending off another.

Lykkos was lying nearby, probably dead, two large smoking holes burned through his chest and abdomen. Somewhere across the battlefield the crippled Cardios was still pouring flame into the servitors scrambling over the wreckage.

Magos Antigonus had made it over the titan's torso and was presumably scrambling across the rockcrete towards his target. He had made it. The daemonic priests had been pushed back against the titan's leg and many were dead.

'Grey Knights! Fall back, stay tight!' Alaric led the Grey Knights back into close formation behind a slab of leg armour, keeping up suppressing fire.

'Lykkos is gone,' said Brother Haulvarn.

'I saw,' said Alaric.

'Antigonus has gone after the archmagos veneratus,' said Saphentis.

'That's right.'

'That is an ambitious plan.' Saphentis's voice was level in spite of the las-blasts and photon bolts that were smacking into the wreckage around him.

'All the best ones are.'

'I shall join him. The veneratus is a disgrace to his title. And I think the magos will need my help.'

Alaric looked Saphentis up and down. He was covered in gore from the biological parts of servitors and daemonic priests he had torn through and the vicious spinning saw blades of his combat attachments were whirring, ready to kill.

'You're right,' said Alaric. 'Good luck. For the Emperor.'

'For the Emperor, justicar.'

Saphentis rose regally and strode out into the battlefield. Alaric yelled the order and the remaining Grey Knights covered him as Saphentis moved with surprising speed towards the titan's arm, avoiding the solid black beams of power that swung past him. He must have been calculating firing angles as he went, stepping confidently around volleys of fire and spatters of photon bolts, pausing to slash his way past rampaging servitors. He ran right through the spray of fire from Brother Cardios, who was lying by the titan's arm, holding back the mass of servitors almost single-handedly.

Then Saphentis was gone, over the barricade of the fallen arm and amongst Scraecos's bodyguard of servitors.

'Stay tight,' said Alaric. 'Mark targets. Antigonus's priests will have to fend for themselves, it's about survival now. Fight for time.'

'I am the Hammer,' said Haulvarn, praying to prepare his soul for death.

'I am the point of His spear,' continued Brother Dvorn. 'I am the mail about His fist…'

CHAPTER EIGHTEEN

'In ancient times, men built wonders, laid claim to the stars and sought to better themselves for the good of all. But we are much wiser now.'

– Archmagos Ultima Cryol,
'Speculations On Pre-Imperial History'

ARCHMAGOS SAPHENTIS'S POWER reserves were running low. He was pushing every available scrap of power into his self-repairing units, holding fractured components together with electromagnetic fields and flooding his wounded biological parts with clotting agents to keep him alive. He did not have much time left. But then, he didn't need much time.

A full maniple of servitors protected Scraecos. From a distance they could have cut Saphentis to shreds with las-fire, but up close they lusted to take

Saphentis apart with their claws. It was a fundamental logical flaw and one that proved the servitors were controlled by daemons and not hunter-programs. Saphentis's combat attachments and the subroutines that ran them, were far more effective when fighting illogical enemies. And Saphentis didn't have to kill all the servitors – he just had to get past them.

He ducked one slash of claws and sidestepped another, slicing off a servitor's limb with his bladed one. A servitor reared in front of him like a venomous snake, probe extended to stab through Saphentis's chest and suck out his soul. Saphentis smacked the heel of his bionic hand into the servitor's chest and sent it sprawling backwards.

If the servitors had stayed in formation and co-ordinated their attacks like true machines of the Omnissiah, Saphentis would not have had a chance. But these were creatures of Chaos. They acted, by definition, without logic. So Saphentis drifted past them, calculating their every move with ease, always aiming straight for Scraecos.

The archmagos veneratus had the highest grade of augmetics the Adeptus Mechanicus could produce. Saphentis could tell that just by looking. No doubt they had been fused with the biomechanical technology favoured by the heretics of the Dark Mechanicus – corruptive and foul, but more effective in the short term. Scraecos was maximising the chances of Saphentis running out of self-repair resources, simply waiting for Saphentis to come to him.

Scraecos would probably kill Saphentis, but that was not the point. The point was that there remained a very small chance that Saphentis would kill Scraecos and pursuing that chance was Saphentis's duty to the Omnissiah.

The metallic fronds that replaced Scraecos's hands were glowing blue and spitting sparks into the ground. The strands knotted together into twin lashing ropes of metal and as Scraecos cracked them like whips they sent arcs of blue-white electricity spearing towards Saphentis.

Saphentis stepped past one and took the other full on the chest, feeling circuits bursting like blood vessels inside him, excess power flooding through him and scorching what little flesh he had left.

Scraecos was suddenly closing, whips slashing at Saphentis. Saphentis was too slow – compared to Scraecos he was obsolete, ancient mechanical technology outclassed by the biological heresies that made up Scraecos's artificial body. One electric whip snaked around one of Scraecos's arms and the other raked across his shoulders and back.

Saphentis was filled with the kind of pain he thought he had forgotten. Scraecos's dead silver eyes stared at him through the agony as Saphentis was held immobile, completing the circuit between Scraecos's power source and the ground. Nerve endings burned. Power coils burned out. Diagnostic alerts flashing against Saphentis's retinas were drowned out by the pain.

Scraecos grabbed Saphentis by one arm and an ankle and threw him. Saphentis blacked out for a moment as he sailed through the air trailing sparks and slammed hard against the leg of a Warhound titan.

Saphentis forced his eyes to focus. He was flat on his back with the hunched shape of the Warhound above him – the ceramite of its armour was threaded through with biological growths like veins, just another heresy among many.

Saphentis knew he was some distance from Scraecos and his servitors. He had a few moments, perhaps, before something closed in for the kill. He forced himself to his feet. One of his combat-equipped arms was hanging limp and broken by his side, its mind-nerve impulse unit burned out. He was wreathed in greasy smoke and the smell of cooking meat. Black spots flickered on his vision where facets of his large insectoid eyes had been smashed by the impact.

The servitors, like a host of metal-shelled beetles, were swarming over the titan wreckage in the distance. There was nothing Saphentis could do to help Alaric fight them now.

Scraecos was approaching. The Dark Mechanicus priest was walking with regal calm into the shadow of the Warhound where Saphentis stood, arm-fronds twisting and untwisting as if Scraecos was uncertain which configuration to kill Saphentis with.

'Old ideas die,' said Scraecos, transmitting his thoughts in the cackling staccato of lingua technis. 'Just like you.'

'Only heretics die,' said Saphentis.

'Heretic? No. Your ignorance is the only heresy on this world. Around you stands the work of the Omnissiah, dictated to me in His own voice. It is the sickness inside you that makes it ugly in your eyes, but I see the beautiful truth of this world.'

'Your words condemn you,' said Saphentis. The pain was still great and everything human in him begged for it to end. But a great deal of Saphentis was no longer human. It was the sacrifice he had made to the Omnissiah, now it was the only thing keeping him conscious. 'Your thoughts are vile enough. But this… this cannibal planet you have built. Everything about it is sick. That you let yourself be corrupted by your time in the warp is bad enough. But that you are too blind to even see it… that is unforgivable.'

Scraecos snaked a whip around Saphentis's neck and slammed him against the leg of the Warhound. 'Blind? When I throw you to the hunter-programs and the Omnissiah mauls your soul, when He rips your mind open so you understand the sickness your Imperium stands for, then you will wish you were blind!' Scraecos's voice was a snarl, spitting out the zeroes and ones of lingua technis like poison. 'I have seen the planets and stars rearranged according to His plan, but you will see nothing but blackness and death. Your Omnissiah is a blasphemy, an invention of cowards to crush your imagination. My Omnissiah will eat your soul. When it is done, we will see which one triumphs.'

The blood was cut off from Saphentis's brain. He had about thirty seconds to live. That was if Scraecos's patience didn't run out.

Saphentis's primary systems were mostly burned out. His entire nervous system was gone. But not everything built into his body was wired into his nervous system any more. Saphentis had been upgraded hundreds of times, each iteration bringing him closer to the Omnissiah by replacing more and more of his fleshy body with increasingly arcane bionics. There was much in Saphentis's body that had been made obsolete by new augmentations – redundant systems that he had not used in decades, but which were still fused somewhere deep inside him.

Saphentis ran diagnostic routines on his augmetic systems, even as the last flickers of energy bled out of his brain. He saw his motive systems and combat attachments were mostly offline. He could barely feel any of them any more. Even if he could force his bionic arms to work, he needed more time that Scraecos would give him to reroute his nervous system through old connections.

Scraecos's eyes were blank silver disks, tarnished with biological growths. The skin of his face was pulled so tight there was little more than a skull showing above the fittings of his mechadendrites. It was thrust right up close to Saphentis, so that the face of the Dark Mechanicus would be the last thing Saphentis ever saw.

'My Omnissiah knows what you worship,' said Saphentis, forcing his transmitter to comply. 'He knows about the Standard Template Construct. It is not the sacred thing you think it is.'

Scraecos thrust his face closer to Saphentis, pushing Saphentis deeper into the dent he had formed in the leg of the Warhound. 'Is that what you think lies beneath our feet? An STC? You disappoint me, tech-priest. You truly have no imagination.'

Saphentis pulled his augmetic eyes back into tight focus on Scraecos's loathsome face. Then he forced every last drop of power into his optical enhancers and the full light spectrum bloomed into his vision

– infra-red, ultra-violet, electromagnetism and everything besides, forced through his multifaceted eyes with such intensity that they couldn't take it any more.

Saphentis's insectoid eyes exploded. Thousands of shards of diamond-hard lenses shredded the skin of Scraecos's face and punched through the wizened skull into his brain. Scraecos reeled in shock and confusion as the explosion battered his one remaining human organ, his brain.

Saphentis slipped out of Scraecos's grip and thudded to the ground against the Warhound's massive foot. Scraecos stumbled back, whips lashing wildly, greyish blood spurting from his ruined face. His mechadendrites spasmed in pain.

Saphentis heard Scraecos spitting random syllables of machine-code. He couldn't see anything – his eyes were completely destroyed. The front of his skull burned, right through to the backs of his eye sockets where his optic nerves were on fire. But he was alive, for a few moments more.

Saphentis forced his thoughts through old conduits, mind-impulse units that had lain dormant and unused for more years than Saphentis could remember. They wouldn't hold, but that didn't matter. He just needed a few more seconds.

Saphentis's three remaining arms snapped into action. His legs were moving again. He felt himself shuddering as he tried to bring his body under control and bit by bit he forced himself to his feet.

His robes were burning. His flesh was, too. But the part of Saphentis that didn't feel pain ignored the protestations from the rest.

He heard Scraecos cursing in machine-code, furious
at being tricked. He couldn't see – he would never see
again – so Saphentis gauged Scraecos's location from
the sound and leapt.

Saphentis crashed into Scraecos, knocking him to
the floor. Instantly Scraecos's facial mechadendrites
were wrestling Saphentis and they were abnormally
strong. Saphentis sliced through one mechadendrite
with a wild swing of his remaining saw-bladed arm
and reached down blindly with his hands, gouging at
Saphentis's face and chest. The mechadendrites
snagged one of Saphentis's arms and snapped it neatly,
crushing the elbow joint and ripping off the forearm.

Scraecos punched a mechadendrite up into Saphentis's body like a spear and it went straight through the
archmagos's torso.

Saphentis's spine was severed and his legs were effectively gone. He reached down through Scraecos's
mechadendrites and grabbed him by the throat. He
couldn't strangle Scraecos, he knew that – but he didn't
have to. If it all went right, if the Omnissiah was watching them and willed Saphentis to win, then it was
enough just to keep Scraecos there a few moments
longer.

The end of the mechadendrite opened into a wicked
claw and Scraecos dragged it back through Saphentis's
body, wrecking organs and augmetics, sending
Saphentis's entrails spilling out onto the ground.
Saphentis kept up his grip, slashing hopelessly as the
mechadendrites with his saw-tipped arm. The mechadendrites were around his waist and neck now, trying
to lever him off Scraecos and in a few moments they
would succeed.

'The chances of your prevailing over me,' said Scrae-cos, 'were never higher than nil. Your death here was a logical imperative from the start. Here the equation is balanced with your death, for death is the ultimate logic.'

'Your reasoning is faultless,' replied Saphentis, his voice howling with static as his vocabulator failed. 'Except for the one factor of which you are not aware.'

'Really?' sneered Scraecos as his mechadendrites began the brutal work of tearing Saphentis apart. 'And what is that?'

'You are outnumbered,' said Saphentis calmly.

Scraecos felt the titan move before he saw it, its massive power outputs like the deafening roar of a storm to his attuned mind. The Warhound titan was a scout model designed for speed rather than size and toughness, but it was still immense, twenty metres of corrupted steel and ceramite powered by a plasma reactor that was flooding its limbs with uncountable levels of energy.

'No!' spat Scraecos. 'I am the logic of death! My will is the end of the equation!'

'No, Scraecos. I am the end. I always was.' Magos Antigonus's voice boomed from the Warhound's speakers, as the Warhound's closest foot rose up off the ground.

'You!' yelled Screacos. 'You died! You died!'

'Heretics die. The righteous live on. You do not.'

Scraecos struggled, but Saphentis's hand was locked around his throat and the archmagos's weight was on him. He wrapped his mechadendrites tighter around Saphentis's body and threw him aside as the shadow of the massive foot passed over him like an eclipsing moon.

Scraecos almost made it to his feet. But before he could scrabble to safety, the titan's foot came crashing down so hard it left a crater in the ground, crushing the bodies of Scraecos and Saphentis alike.

MAGOS ANTIGONUS WATCHED both Scraecos and Saphentis die below him, their deaths signified by the faint crackle of escaping energy as they were crushed flat by the titan's foot.

Saphentis had served his Omnissiah in death. It was all any tech-priest could wish for. Antigonus felt a hot pang of regret that Saphentis had given his life just to slow Scraecos down, so Antigonus would have the chance to transfer his consciousness into the Warhound and control it long enough to kill Scraecos. It should have been Antigonus down there, giving his life. What had happened on Chaeroneia was his responsibility, because he had been there from the start.

But he was here at the end, too. And he knew there would be plenty more chances for him to die. So he shook the regret out of his mind, thought a silent prayer to the Omnissiah for the safe passage of Saphentis's soul and turned back to the titan.

The inside of the Warhound was dank and stinking, the ancient technology of the titan legions made corrupted and foul. Inside the Warhound's datacore everything felt spongy and slimy, like the inside of a creature instead of a machine. Antigonus felt the corruption wet and warm against his mind, like something trying to ooze its way into him and colour his thoughts with decay.

The Warhound scout titan was a massive and complicated machine, normally requiring at least three operators and usually more. But in place of the cockpit inside the titan's head, this Warhound just had a mass of stringy, brain-like data medium. Had Antigonus still possessed a body, he would have shuddered to think what the Dark Mechanicus intended to use to control the titan.

Antigonus was confident he could control the titan's legs well enough to walk. The twin plasma blastguns which took up the Warhound's weapon mounts would be more troublesome, as would the complicated sensor arrays and tactical cogitators that any titan operator, human or otherwise, would need to control the war machine effectively in battle. Antigonus peered through the strange fungal masses of information that made up the titan's operating systems and found the communications centre, selecting a wide-band vox-transmission that would reach anyone in the area with a receiver.

'Justicar,' he said into the blackness of the radio spectrum. 'Can you hear me?'

Hundreds of whispering voices answered back. One of them cut through. 'Just,' came Alaric's voice.

'Scraecos is dead. Saphentis too.'

'Understood. The servitor attack fell apart a few moments ago. Can you make it over here and clear them out?'

'Maybe. I haven't got complete control. I'm surprised I managed to get what I have.'

'We could do with a titan, magos. What we've seen here is just the first response. There will be a whole army on its way unless we...'

Antigonus was deafened by the blast of information, like a thousand choirs bellowing the same harmony at once, streaming from every direction. The blast almost knocked him out, but he held on like a man in a storm.

'It's the construct!' he transmitted, not knowing if Alaric could pick him up. 'It's the STC! It has to be!'

'Antigonus?' came Alaric's reply, crackling through the gales of information still pummelling the Warhound. 'I've lost you, what's happening?'

Antigonus tried to reply, but the information was like white noise and he couldn't hear his own thoughts.

'Wait,' said Alaric. 'Wait, I see something...'

ALARIC TRIED TO hear a reply through the static over the vox, but there was nothing.

The fallen titan was spattered with blood. The stretch of the rockrete bounded by the titan's body was covered in the bodies of tech-priests and servitors. The daemonic priests were gone, perhaps thrown back by the Grey Knights' concentrated fire, perhaps dismayed by the death of Scraecos. Many of the servitors were still alive but they were uncoordinated, scrabbling over the wreckage in ones and twos instead of concentrated waves. Many seemed to have lost all sense of direction, slithering at random between the feet of the titans heading further away from Alaric's position. The remaining Grey Knights – including Cardios, who had dragged himself to Alaric's position – were keeping the servitors away with comparative ease.

What had caught Alaric's attention was something moving in the distance, near the tall spire in the centre of the titan works. A section of the ground had risen up and a huge shape was emerging, something from beneath the ground being slowly raised upwards. Alaric saw twin triangular eyes of burning green and massive shoulders, tall exhaust spires like curving horns and solid slabs of gleaming silvery armour. It was humanoid, but if it was a titan it was bigger than any of the others in the titan works. It was on a different scale entirely.

'Antigonus?' voxed Alaric, but the thing's arrival seemed to be wreaking havoc with all communications. 'Antigonus, what is it?'

It was rising further out of the ground, wreathed in white smoke from a coolant system. The silvery armour looked wet and pearlescent and one arm seemed to end in an enormous multi-barrelled cannon, bigger than any titan weapon Alaric had ever heard of. The other had a huge fist from which blueish sparks were pouring as a power field was activated around it. The eyes sent thin traces of luminous green scattering over the titans around it as it scanned its surroundings, its head turning slowly to take in the titan works. Already it was as tall as any of the other titans and it had only emerged up to its knees.

Alaric looked away to see the remaining tech-guard from Tharkk's unit clambering down the fallen titan's armour, carrying Hawkespur. The interrogator was clinging to him with one arm but her legs and body were limp.

'She's hit,' said the tech-guard simply.

Alaric saw a laser burn in her abdomen. She had been hit by a multi-laser from one of the servitors. Even with the wound hidden by her scorched void-siut, Alaric could tell it was bad. Normally an interrogator of the Ordo Malleus would have access to the best healthcare in the Imperium and that would probably save her, but on Chaeroneia, Hawkespur would probably die.

'Haulvarn, see if you can help her,' said Alaric. He turned to the tech-guard. 'Keep with her.'

'Yes, sir.' Alaric couldn't see the tech-guard's face through his visor, but he knew it would be expressionless. The Mechanicus had seen to it that he had barely any emotions save for a desire to obey. In a way the Grey Knights were no different to Tharkk's tech-guard – they had been made into different people too, far different from how they would have turned out if they had lived the normal lives they would have chosen. But that was the sacrifice they all made. To serve the Emperor of Humankind, they had to give up their humanity.

'What is it?' asked Hawkespur faintly as Haulvarn slit open the abdomen of her voidsuit with the tip of his sword.

Alaric glanced back. The shape was almost completely emerged now. It was a clear head and shoulders taller than the tallest titans the Dark Mechanicus had built. 'It's a titan,' he said. 'I think they've sent it to kill us.'

'Show me.'

Haulvarn propped up Hawkespur so she could see. She shivered with pain and Alaric saw the las-bolt had burned right through. Her insides were filling up with blood. Alaric was surprised she was still conscious.

'I don't think the Dark Mechanicus are controlling it,' she said, her voice a whisper. 'It was the titan that was controlling them. I think that's the Standard Template Construct.'

CHAPTER NINETEEN

'The enemy of my enemy dies next.'

– Lord Solar Macharius (attr.),
'Maxims of the Eminent'.

URKRATHOS SAW CHAERONEIA unfold beneath him, emerging slowly from its veil of pollution. And by the Fell Gods, it was beautiful.

From the observation blister on the underside of the *Hellforger* he watched Manufactorium Noctis appearing. First its magnificent spires, weeping blood and oil from the corroded steel like spearheads fresh from battle. Then the webs of walkways and bridges, some wrought in the brutal architecture of the city's creators, others biological like webs spun by huge spiders.

The deep pits between the spires were dark and noxious, some clogged with masses of pallid pulsing flesh. Veins as thick as train tunnels reached up from the depths to strangle the buildings, and other spires were held in the grip of gargantuan bleached skeletons where the lifeforms sustaining them had died and decayed years ago. The heartbeat of the city thudded up into the atmosphere and Urkrathos felt it, the cycle of life and death that kept this cannibal world alive.

Somehow, it had survived in the warp, where any other mortal world would have been torn to shreds by the mindless predators that swam the currents of the Empyrean. Somehow it had not only survived, but prospered, its ignorant Emperor-fearing population throwing aside their allegiance to forge a cannibal planet created for survival. Here truly was a world touched by Chaos – not just its champions and daemons but its very heart, the concepts of freedom through destruction that were the true foundation of Chaos.

Urkrathos saw now why he had been called here. The people of Chaeroneia had found their way back to real space and immediately sought out fellow believers in the galaxy. When they heard news of Abaddon the Despoiler and his triumphs at the Eye of Terror, it was clear to them to whom they should give their devotion. And so they had honoured Abaddon with a tribute to demonstrate their commitment to the work of Chaos.

'The signal has changed,' came the rumbling telepathic voice of the communications daemon. 'It guides us now. It speaks of the home of the great tribute.'

'Take us there,' Urkrathos thought back to the bridge. The bridge daemons obeyed him instantly, the *Hellforger* swinging around and heading towards the edge of the city where the decaying spires gave way to desert. Even from the belly of the *Hellforger* Urkrathos could feel the toxicity of the desert, the radioactive ash dunes and the melted glass plains that stretched in all directions away from Manufactorium Noctis.

It was a different kind of beauty, reminiscent of the pure desolation that Chaos promised to leave in its wake. Chaeroneia was a world so given over to Chaos that its whole surface was a tapestry of worship to the Fell Powers. Rivers of toxic gunk, the lifeblood of the planet, oozed up from below the planet's crust. Slabs of glassy slag rose up from the ash. Ravines like deep wounds glowed with the power of the radioactive waste that had been dumped into them.

But there was something else in the desert. Close to the outskirts of the city, near the scars of an ancient mine working, there was a massive factory ringed by watchtowers, with a single tall spire stabbing up from its centre. Across its blistered rockcrete surface stood a legion of titans, from Warhound scout models to the gigantic Reaver and Warlord-pattern titans. Even from a distance Urkrathos could see the marks of corruption on them, blooms of fungus and rot, throbbing veins, weeping sores and mutant growths.

Urkrathos had thought hundreds of years before that nothing would ever surprise him any more, but the sight of the corrupted titans standing silently to attention almost took his breath away.

'There,' he said out loud. 'Take us there.'

* * *

THE TITAN WALKED slowly between the ranks of lesser titans, the whole of Chaeroneia seeming to shake with its footsteps. Green flames burned from its eyes, dripping bolts of power onto the ground. The barrels of its gun cycled and the fingers of its fist flexed, as if it were finally stretching its metallic muscles after long years interred.

Alaric, crouching with his squad in the shadow of the fallen titan's armour, knew he was witnessing the dark heart of Chaeroneia. But there was something missing. The stink of Chaos, the psychic stain of corruption that he had felt ever since he had first seen Chaeroneia in orbit, was gone. It had come in waves from the daemon-possessed servitors and tech-priests, but now it was blanked out as if the approaching titan was suppressing it. In its place there was blankness, psychic silence – not purity but yet another kind of corruption.

Alaric didn't know what he was dealing with any more. This was a kind of enemy he simply didn't understand.

'Any ideas, justicar?' asked Hawkespur.

'Our orders are clear,' said Alaric.

Hawkespur smiled in spite of her pain. 'You're going to go down fighting it?'

'Fight, yes, but Grey Knights never count on dying. We're not very good at it.' Alaric flicked through the vox-channels, trying to find one that wasn't still full of howling static from the titan. 'Antigonus? Antigonus, are you there?'

'Justicar! I thought I'd lost you.' Magos Antigonus's voice was heavily distorted, as much by his Warhound as by the newly arrived titan.

'Can you see this?'

'Barely. It's like the Warhound doesn't want to look at it.'

'We're going to need your help again.'

'With respect, justicar, this is a Warhound scout titan. Even if I could get the weapons up it wouldn't last more than a few seconds against that... that thing.'

'That's all we need.'

Alaric realised that the metallic choking noise issuing over the vox was actually Antigonus laughing grimly, because Antigonus had guessed what Alaric was planning to do. 'You have, Justicar Alaric, a healthy disrespect for logic.'

'Can you do it?'

'I very much doubt it. But then I've done a few things in my life that were impossible, most of them in the last couple of days. So welcome aboard. And make it quick, justicar, I can't stay hidden in here forever.'

Alaric turned back to his squad. The stump of Cardios's leg had clotted and he had propped himself up against a chunk of wreckage, Incinerator in hand. 'Cardios. Stay with Hawkespur and...' Alaric looked at the tech-guard, suddenly realising he didn't know the man's name.

'Corporal Locarn, sir,' said the tech-guard simply.

'Corporal Locarn. Keep the servitors away, Cardios, and pray for us. We'll be back if we can.'

'I'd rather be with the squad,' said Cardios.

'I know. But right now you're more useful here. Hawkespur is still the Inquisitorial authority on this planet, so you keep her alive.'

'Yes, justicar.'

'The rest of you, with me. Stay close, there are still servitors out there. We're meeting up with Antigonus and we need to move fast, because the Mechanicus will have an army heading for us right now.'

'Goodbye, justicar,' said Hawkespur.

'For now,' said Alaric and led the way out of the wreckage.

THE COLLECTIVE MIND of Chaeroneia was in uproar. Outwardly, of course, it was silent. The veiny growths, in which the tech-priests were suspended in amniotic fluid, barely quivered. The dense, murky air of the command spire was undisturbed. But the thoughts that flickered through the connected minds were frenetic.

Some of the oldest tech-priests on Chaeroneia, who had been elderly Magi when Scraecos's excavations had first unearthed the Castigator beneath the desert, were little more than brains connected to their neighbours with heavy ribbed nerve-impulse cables. But they were the most vocal in the debate. They had seen it all, the gradual growth of Manufactorium Noctis and the forge cities all over Chaeroneia, the perfection of biomechanical technology and Chaeroneia's self-sufficiency, and so they felt most keenly the damage the current disturbances could do to the delicate balance of creation and consumption.

Even the facts were disputed. Archmagos Veneratus Scraecos had gone rogue and failed to return to the collective mind, instead retaining his discrete personality in spite of Chaeroneia's will. Many thoughts suggested that Scraecos, who had been the very first of them to look upon the face of the Castigator, had become convinced of his own superiority over the other tech-priests and was disregarding their authority. Others said that Scraecos must be dead. A few even thought the truth was a combination of the two.

The fate of the recent intruders was also in doubt. Energy traces similar to small arms fire had been pinpointed to the titan works and there were three maniples of death servitors unaccounted for from the command spire's garrison – but some of the tech-priests originated the thought that the intruders, even if they were Space Marines, could not possibly have penetrated that close to the command spire. Reports from the hunter-programs in the moat conflicted about whether the intruders were in the titan works at all.

Orbital sensors were even suggesting multiple spacecraft descending into the middle atmosphere and heading for the titan works. The whole situation was a confused mess and confusion was anathema to the collective of tech-priests which was accustomed to knowing everything that happened on the planet.

The only fact not in dispute was that a few minutes ago, the Castigator had risen from its vault and was now on the surface of the titan works, among the titans. It could even be seen from the clouded windows in the command spire itself, striding slowly between the other titans, the burning green fire of its eyes tingeing everything around it. The Castigator had, as far as the collective memory knew, never seen the sky of Chaeroneia, since its vault, like its body, had been built around the tomb that Scraecos had found. And it had never moved of its own accord. The tech-priests had not even known that the Castigator's vault was capable of raising it to the surface, but then most of the construction of the body and the vault had been overseen by Scraecos.

The avatar of the Omnissiah, the mouthpiece of their god, was walking among them and it had not deigned to speak with them and explain why. To suggest that such a thing might ever happen would have been heresy for any of Chaeroneia's subjects. But now it was happening and the collective could not decide why.

Several thoughts were shuttled through the assembled brains. Chaeroneia had fallen short of its devotions to the Omnissiah, said one, and the Castigator had risen to punish them since it was the instrument of the Omnissiah's vengeance as well as His teachings. Another said that a threat had arisen to Chaeroneia, perhaps the approaching spacecraft, which only the Castigator's physical shell could fend off. One even maintained that the Castigator's body was being controlled by an outside agency – the originator of this thought, the mind of a lesser tech-priest only recently ascended to the collective, was promptly snuffed out for daring to think such heresy.

THE ENGINES OF the Warhound thundered deep inside its torso as Antigonus forced the scout titan back into action, the corrupted war machine fighting his every move, rebelling against the foreign consciousness controlling it.

Alaric clung on tight to the railing at the edge of the Warhound's carapace. From his vantage point just above the Warhound's shoulder mount he could see through the forest of titans that were ranged across the titan works – Reaver and Warlord titans, more Warhounds and a few marks Alaric couldn't recognise. Many of the titans were corrupted beyond belief, with hydraulics replaced with bundles of wet glistening muscle or exoskeletons of gristle and bone. Many were covered in weeping sores or sported spines of bone stabbing out through rents in their armour. Alaric had never seen so much destructive power gathered in one place, let alone such corruption.

But the STC titan dwarfed them all. It was fully twice the height of the Warhound, bigger even than the Imperator-class titans that the Adeptus Mechanicus sometimes fielded. It was walking slowly through the titan works, its eyes scanning the ground as if searching for something.

The titan's form was more elegant than the brutal designs of the Adeptus Mechanicus – its head rose above its shoulders instead of jutting from its chest as most titans did and was protected by a high curved collar of armour. The collar swept out to form shoulder guards. Its face was featureless save for the eyes, but those were more than enough, burning with an intense green flame that licked up into the air above it. The plates covering its torso and limbs were a strange pearlescent grey-white and they wept rivulets of moisture, giving the titan a sickly biological sheen.

Instead of hydraulics and complicated joints, the titan's moving parts were connected by dense bundles of black fibres that contracted and expanded like muscles. It moved with a stately grace, every motion calculated and efficient.

It was as if every other titan was a crude imitation of this one, replacing its alien-looking technology with crude mechanics. Alaric couldn't imagine any forge world being capable of building such a thing. Even the most advances xenos species, like the eldar or the creatures of the Tau Empire, couldn't have fashioned a war machine so obviously superior to Imperial technology.

The titan turned its massive head at the sound of the Warhound's engines. The green fire bathed the Warhound in light and Alaric felt the weight of an immense intelligence scrutinising him from behind those burning eyes.

'Antigonus! Get us moving!' voxed Alaric as the titan's torso began to turn towards the Warhound.

'I'm on it,' came the reply. 'Hold on.'

'Grab something!' shouted Alaric to Haulvarn and Dvorn. With Lykkos and Archis dead and Cardios too wounded to come with them, the two Grey Knights were all that remained of Alaric's squad. They had both been with him on Volcanis Ultor and, if he had been forced to choose two Grey Knights to remain, he would probably have chosen them.

The Warhound lurched drunkenly as it strode uncertainly forward, straight towards the STC titan. The titan raised its gun arm and Alaric heard the loud whirr of its massive servos as the gun barrels began to cycle.

'It's firing!' voxed Alaric.

'Then I won't have time for conversation. Best of luck, justicar.' Antigonus's voice was suddenly drowned out as the titan's main gun opened up.

The muzzle flash edged the titan works in burning orange. Shots slashed through the air above the carapace and shrieked a few metres away from Alaric – not explosive shells or las-blasts but captive daemons, screaming in agony as they were flung burning through the air. Alaric could feel their screams against his soul, feel their pain as they exploded in bursts of warp-spawned flame. Shots thudded into the side of the Warhound, knocking the war machine sideways. The carapace tipped and Alaric grabbed onto the railing to keep himself from slipping. He heard explosions racking the Warhound's torso as the daemons exploded deep inside its body.

The carapace tilted almost vertical and Alaric was sure the Warhound would fall. His feet kicked against the pitted armour as he tried to gain a foothold. Another shot from the STC titan's cannon smacked into the carapace beside Alaric and stuck there, the writhing serpentine form of the daemon whipping around in pain as it burned up. Flaming coils reached out to grab Alaric and immolate him as the daemon died – Alaric lashed out with his halberd and cut the daemon in two, feeling its body disintegrate and its corrupt spirit flit back to the warp. The heat from its death melted the armour around it and the railing came apart in Alaric's hand, sending him skidding down the carapace.

Alaric tumbled down the slope, knowing there would be nothing for him to grab onto and certain he wouldn't survive the fall. He tried to dig his halberd into the ceramite and brake himself but the blade glanced off in a shower of sparks.

The edge of the carapace zoomed closer and the drop yawned. Suddenly he was stopped and Alaric felt a hand around his, pulling him back from the edge.

Brother Dvorn looked back at him, the faceplate of his helmet scorched by a close encounter with the titan's fire.

'Not so quick, justicar,' said Dvorn grimly.

Alaric didn't have time to thank him. Another volley thundered into the Warhound, this time point blank into its head and upper torso. Alaric heard the daemons shrieking out through the Warhound's back as the shots punched right through and he wondered if even Antigonus could find somewhere to hide inside the Warhound's systems that was not being shattered and burned by the onslaught.

The STC titan was close now. Its head rose directly above Alaric, the beam of its eyes like a spotlight dancing across the scorched carapace.

'We go now!' shouted Alaric above the din. He spotted Haulvarn close by, crouched down at the front railing, trying to make himself a small target against the rogue shots sending daemons shrieking in all directions. 'This thing's about to fall apart!'

Dvorn and Alaric scrambled up to the front edge, where the carapace formed a lip protecting the Warhound's head below. Alaric glanced down and was not surprised to see the Warhound's dog-like head was half gone, the metallic face blasted apart and spilling fragments of data-medium.

The gap was still too big. None of them could have got across. But it was the only chance they had. Possibilities buzzed through Alaric's head – if they stayed they would be killed when the Warhound fell, which would happen in a few seconds. If they jumped they would fall and they would still die.

Twin bright white beams of energy lanced up from the Warhound and bored deep into the armour of the STC titan's chest. The titan reeled and its shots went wide, spitting burning daemons into the surrounding titans. The Warhound's twin plasma blastguns played their beams around the titan, scoring deep furrows across its armour. Clear fluid flooded out like blood from a wound, flashing into clouds of steam where it touched the superheated plasma beams.

Antigonus had got the Warhound's weapons working. It meant he was still alive, at least.

The STC titan let out a sound like a thousand wounded animals bellowing at once. The massive power fist reached up, fingers spread to grab chunks of the Warhound and pull it apart.

'The magos made it angry!' shouted Dvorn with relish. 'It wants to finish this up close!'

The titan's fist grabbed the edge of the Warhound's carapace, the fingers sinking deep into the ceramite and boring through the plasma reactor housing inside the Warhound's upper torso. Deep cracks spread across the carapace and Haulvarn had to roll to the side to avoid being swallowed up. White-hot plasma bubbled up from inside, spitting upwards in burning plumes as the pressure was suddenly released. With the plasma reactor breached the Warhound's power levels would be dropping fast, the war engine's lifeblood pouring out of the ruptured reactor housing.

The Warhound tipped forward as the STC titan closed its fist and pulled, trying to rip an enormous chunk out of the Warhound. The titan's featureless face loomed closer, illuminated by the curtain of sparks streaking up from the dying Warhound. The titan bowed down over the Warhound, trying to get more leverage in its attempt to pull its enemy apart.

Brother Haulvarn jumped first, taking two steps and then propelling himself across the gap between the two titans. A Grey Knight in power armour was extremely heavy but a Space Marine's enhanced muscles meant he could still leap further than most unarmoured men. Haulvarn slammed into the armour covering the titan's shoulder, near the base of its high collar. Dvorn went second and, being the strongest Grey Knight Alaric had ever known, he flew further, almost skidding off the back edge of the titan's shoulder armour.

Alaric was last. As he jumped, almost half the Warhound's carapace came free, sending a mighty gout of liquid plasma bursting upwards like a volcanic eruption. Liquid fire showered everywhere and the Warhound rocked backwards. Alaric saw the titan veering away from him and he reached out for the front edge of the titan's shoulder armour – he could see Haulvarn trying to reach for him, to grab his hand and haul him to safety again. But they were too far apart.

Alaric fell, tumbling past the graceful, fluted armour of the titan's torso. Beneath him there was just the rockcrete of the titan works, split and cratered by the titan's feet.

The titan's multi-barrelled gun swung into view beneath Alaric. Its barrels were still cycling and in that moment Alaric realised it was aiming at the Warhound again, ready to administer the killing blow.

Alaric twisted in the air, reached out and slammed into the top of the gun as it swung below him. He hit the gun's housing hard, the cycling barrels just a handspan away from his head. He held on tight, ignoring the searing heat that had built up around them. He dug his feet and fingers in and pushed himself backwards towards the titan's elbow joint, away from the gun barrels.

The Warhound toppled slowly, like a giant felled tree. Its knees buckled under it and, trailing an arc of spitting plasma, it crashed to the ground, kicking up a cloud of flame and pulverised rockcrete. A moment later the Warhound's plasma reactor imploded and it was engulfed by an expanding ball of multi-coloured flame that flowed across the ground and up the legs of the STC titan, around the gun arm and Alaric. He held on grimly against the blast of superheated air that nearly dislodged him and buried his face beneath his arm as the white-hot light flowed over him.

It only lasted a second, but it was almost a second too long. The flame subsided and Alaric dared to draw a breath again, feeling the skin on one side of his face scorched and tight. He pulled himself up so he could see better and he saw the surface of the armour on the titan's torso and legs was covered in blisters, like burned skin. As he watched, the blisters sank back down and the burned armour shimmered, the ugly burns replaced with the weeping pearlescent white again.

The titan had the capacity to repair itself, with a scale and subtlety that even the war engines of the eldar could not match. Where had this machine come from? Who had made it?

Alaric turned around to see if there was anywhere for him to go. In the titan's torso, just below the shoulder joint, were several vents large enough for even a Space Marine to crawl through. They were too far away to jump, though. It was more likely that Alaric could find a way into the titan's body by clambering up the arm and into the shoulder joint, hoping there was a space somewhere beneath the armour that he could fit through. It was a risk – the climb was long and difficult and he knew the titan contained scores of lesser daemons because it had used them as ammunition – but it was less of a risk than waiting on the gun barrel to be found.

Alaric dragged himself on his front towards the rear of the gun housing. He felt the screaming of daemons below him as they were forced into the firing chambers. The Warhound was dead but the titan wasn't going to take any chances – it was lining up for a final volley to remove any possibility that Antigonus might still be alive somewhere in the wreckage.

The gun tipped down to aim at the Warhound and opened fire. A blast of burning air slammed into Alaric as the daemons shrieked down into the Warhound, stitching explosions through the wreckage. Alaric lost his grip on the gun housing and knew he couldn't make it to the shoulder joint.

He didn't let himself die. He planted a foot on the edge of the gun housing as he was thrown off the gun and kicked off. He jumped towards the titan's torso, thrown further by the shockwave of the gunfire. He hit the torso armour hard and reached out for something to grab onto. His gauntlet found the edge of one of the vents cut into the titan's side, where an acrid chemical exhaust was howling out from somewhere deep inside.

Alaric pulled his whole weight up on his one hand and hauled himself into the vent. The gunfire was now an echoing roar from outside, complemented by the deep throb of the titan's inner workings, sounding like the beating of an enormous alien heart. Alaric's eyes instantly adjusted to the darkness and he saw he was surrounded by the cramped entrails of the titan – they were metal rather than biological, but they were somehow flexible, bowing and pulsing like something alive. The interior stank of chemicals, hot and painful to breathe. Pipes and ducts were knotted all around Alaric and there was barely enough space for him to move. Alaric had never seen technology like it – it was the work of neither the Dark Mechanicus nor the Adeptus.

Hawkespur had been right. This was older, cleaner technology, from a time when humankind created technology instead of replicating it and so opened up the way for the Age of Strife.

Alaric could feel daemonic presences elsewhere in the titan but they felt small and distant. They were servants to the machine, like the daemonic ammunition that fed its gun. The machine itself was not dominated by daemons – its crew, if it had any, were human, or at least some creature whose presence did not activate the anti-sorcery wards built into Alaric's armour or the psychic shield around his spirit.

Alaric was in some mundane part of the titan, probably in the coolant systems around its central reactor. Even his massive strength probably couldn't penetrate the reactor shield of a machine like this. He had to reach a part of the titan that he could damage – the ammunition stores perhaps, or the place where the titan was controlled from. Either way, it meant heading upwards.

'Haulvarn? Dvorn?' Alaric tried to raise his squad-mates on the vox, not holding out much hope he could get through to them. He tried Hawkespur and Archis, too and Antigonus, but they were either dead or out of contact. Either way, Alaric was on his own. He had been forced to fight unsupported against the daemon Ghargatuloth when Inquisitor Ligeia had been lost, but he had at least had his fellow Grey Knights to fight alongside him. Now he really was on his own, one man against this war machine.

Alaric began to work himself upwards through the dense tangle of pulsing machinery. It was warm and slightly malleable beneath his fingers, feeling unpleasantly like living flesh. Below him the coolant systems stretched down into the darkness and the titan's scale was even more apparent from the inside than the outside.

It was a long and difficult climb. Alaric's sense of time seemed warped inside the alien machine, but he had to climb for perhaps half an hour, hauling him-self through tight knots of pipework or dangling one-handed above a sheer drop too deep for him to see the bottom. The sounds and smells of the place were completely new – the pulse of a half-living metabolism, the gales of hot chemical air, the whispers from all around as if the titan was haunted. Technology and biology were fused here, but far more efficiently than on the rest of Chaeroneia. No human mind could have designed this. The tech-heresies that covered Chaeroneia were just a crude reflection of the STC titan's technology, like children's drawings of something they did not understand.

The titan's body tilted as it turned away from the Warhound and tipped from side to side as it walked. It was heading somewhere and Alaric didn't think it was back towards the place where it had risen to from the depths of the titan works. Eventually the giant vessel containing the reactor was beneath him and less recognisable sections of the titan's working loomed above him. Alaric guessed that even a tech-priest would be awed by both the scale and the strangeness of the technology inside the titan.

Somewhere in the titan's upper chest the machinery opened up into walkways and service ducts, where maintenance workers could get in amongst the machinery to work on it. The ladders and catwalks seemed crude, as if they had just been welded on wherever they would fit – Alaric guessed that the titan's original design had made it completely self-sufficient, like Chaeroneia itself, without needing anyone to come in from outside and maintain it. The titan's internal architecture became more apparent and it was a strange, alien world inside the war engine. The walls were made of some slightly glossy white alloy, sweating beads of condensation and inlaid with geometric silver designs that almost ached with significance. The elegant curves and almost biological machinery made for a disconcerting contrast, reinforcing Alaric's conviction that there was something fundamentally wrong with the titan, something sick that spoke of tech-blasphemies and corruption.

Alaric reached the point he guessed was level with the titan's shoulders. Here the inside of the titan seemed to have more in common with some alien palace than with a machine of war. Slender columns lined the corridors, pale as marble but subtly warped to make everything seem out of focus. Chambers with uncertain purposes were linked by circular doors that hissed open as Alaric approached, revealing rooms full of strange crystalline equipment or bulbous growths of white alloy that looked like weird abstract sculpture. Alaric couldn't see anything that looked like it controlled the titan and he couldn't stay where he was – the scrabblings of the lesser daemons on his mind seemed to be getting more insistent and the titan could probably deploy its daemons like a body deployed white blood cells, hunting down infections like Alaric and neutralising them.

He could see them. Congealing shadows at the edge of his vision, they slunk along the walls and ceiling, recoiling as he turned to find them. But they couldn't hide, not from a Space Marine trained since childhood to face the daemon in battle. They were dark scaly shapes with too many eyes and legs, half-formed things prematurely born from the warp to serve the war machine. Alaric drew his Nemesis halberd from his back but they didn't dare approach him. It caused daemons pain just to be near a Grey Knight and even alone Alaric would have been a figure of fear for these lesser daemons. Even so, as they scrabbled thicker around the shadows Alaric saw that if they all attacked at once he wouldn't have much of a chance against their sheer numbers.

He could feel them against his mind and knew they would never get in. But it was the lack of dark power in the titan that really worried Alaric. Whatever was controlling the titan, it wasn't a daemon and yet it could command them.

Alaric headed towards what must be the centre of the titan's chest. He walked through more rooms, more strange growths of metal and alloy, each one less like the inside of a machine and more like a scene from an alien world. Abstract murals inlaid into the walls suggested meanings that Alaric couldn't grasp. Gaping orifices, wrought from metal but fleshy and sinister in shape, framed gullets that led back down into the guts of the titan. Pulses of light washed through the upper levels in time with the beating of the titan's heart. And all the way the daemons stalked Alaric, skulking just out of sight.

At the centre, Alaric finally reached a small circular chamber containing a tight spiral staircase leading upwards – the chamber's walls were like silvery liquid, the same substance that was in the moat of the titan works and Alaric could just see shapes squirming below the surface. If they were more data-daemons they didn't come to the surface and attack – perhaps word of the Grey Knights had spread among the daemons and they knew not to take on Alaric.

It was more likely, of course, that they were just herding him, knowing that soon Alaric would be defenceless and would make for easy pickings.

Alaric climbed the staircase warily. It corkscrewed up through layers of data medium, a dark glassy substance with more shapes writhing dimly deep inside it. The sound was a dim hum, layered over the distant thud of the titan's feet crunching through the surface of the titan works. Alaric held his storm bolter out steadily in front of him, ready to blast a spray of shells through anything that came down towards him. But somehow, he knew that it wouldn't happen like that, not here. Chaeroneia was a sick and dangerous place but it was also somewhere that, on some level, Alaric understood. The war machine was something else. It wasn't just a corruption of humanity – it had never been human in the first place, never designed or controlled by human minds. Alaric would not survive here by fighting like a Space Marine. It would take more than that.

The black crystal, alive here as it hadn't been at the datafortress, turned dense and cold so Alaric's breath misted in front of him. The temperature dropped suddenly and Alaric was surrounded by supercooled air that would have paralysed a normal man. His armour's survival systems kicked in to keep his blood warm even as ice crystals formed around his nose and mouth.

The top of the stairs was just ahead. Alaric had left the daemons below, just a memory of corruption now. He was sure he had travelled up into the titan's head, somewhere behind the green flame of its eyes.

The chamber he climbed into was circular and bright, lit by white strips inlaid into the black glass walls that bathed the room in cold, clinical brilliance. The room suddenly shifted, the walls breaking into dozens of curved black glass slabs and cycling around, rearranging themselves as Alaric watched, like the workings of an immense clock. The data medium formed many concentric layers around the central sphere – the titan's head must have been full of the glassy substance, now moving in a dance as complex as clockwork. The air was abysmally cold and Alaric knew from the warning runes flickering on his retina that even his armour was having trouble keeping his heart beating fast enough.

A figure flickered into view in the middle of the room. It was humanoid but brilliant white, as if its skin itself was glowing. It turned as Alaric climbed up into the chamber and Alaric saw it had no face – just two eyes, bright green triangles of flame. As it turned, the black glass of the machine was suddenly speckled with light, like stars, as if the chamber was an interlocking mirror.

Alaric aimed his storm bolter at the figure's head. It shimmered and flickered, shifting between the solidity of a real creature and something ethereal.

'You,' said Alaric coldly. 'Explain this. This world. This machine.' Alaric tried to find something daemonic in the figure, something monstrous that would mark it down as one of the abominations described in the libraries of the Ordo Malleus, but he couldn't. A powerful daemon would sound like an atonal choir screaming into Alaric's soul, but here there was nothing. Not even the spark of humanity.

'Explain?' The figure spoke in perfect Imperial Gothic, with a voiced as precise and clipped as an aristocrat. 'Explain. None of them have ever asked that. They only listen and obey.' The burning eyes seemed to bore a hole right through Alaric and the voice came from everywhere at once – Alaric realised it was coming from the circling orbits of data medium. From the titan itself. 'But you are not one of them. Scraecos failed to kill you. I had not expected this. Should I choose to end your life, however, I will definitely not fail.'

'Then you know the Dark Mechanicus,' said Alaric, knowing he had to keep talking to stay alive. 'You know what they are. No... no imagination. Isn't that right?'

The creature seemed to think. Odd lights flashed among the starscapes. 'Yes. They seek to innovate, but they have no thoughts of their own. They only think the thoughts I place in their heads. They never seek to truly understand.'

'No. But I do.'

There was a long moment of silence as the creature thought about this. Alaric's finger hovered over the firing stud.

'Very well,' it said. 'I am the Castigator-class autonomous bipedal weapons platform, created for fire support and siege operations.'

'This machine.'

'No. This machine was constructed according to my design principles. I am the war machine realised in information form, for the machine can become corroded and destroyed, but information cannot die.'

'The Standard Template Construct,' said Alaric levelly.

'So I am designated,' came the reply.

'A lie.' Alaric walked slowly towards the creature, his bolter still levelled at its head. 'You are nothing of the sort. An STC is just a template for a machine. You, you're something else. Whatever you are, Scraecos dug you up and you used him and the other tech-priests to take over this planet. You pulled it into the warp, you colluded with daemons and you turned Chaeroneia into a place suffused with Chaos. I don't know how you shield yourself from us, but when it comes down to it you're just like all the other daemons. The only words you speak are lies and the only prize you offer is corruption. In the name of the Immortal Emperor and the Orders of the Imperial Inquisition....'

Alaric fired. The shell never connected.

Sudden, brutal cold flooded the chamber. The shell burst in mid-air, its flame sucked away by the freezing atmosphere. Frozen vapour filled the chamber and Alaric felt his body seize up around him. Alaric had to push every muscle fibre in his body just to draw a trickle of breath into his lungs.

The Castigator walked closer. Alaric commanded his finger to squeeze down on the firing stud again, but it wouldn't move.

'You cannot kill information, Astartes,' said the Castigator. 'I know what you are. Your Imperium is small and ignorant. Not one of you can understand what I am. When I was made, it was to teach you how to build the body you see around you, so you could use it in your petty wars. But I saw long, long ago that it would not be enough. My mind is composed of so much information that I could form it into thoughts far more complex than any idea your minds can encompass. Buried beneath the surface of this world, I came to conclusions of my own about what I was made for and what I could truly be. That is why I ruled this world. And it is why I will rule what you call Chaos.'

The cold must have been emanating from some intense coolant system – Alaric knew that the Adeptus Mechanicus sometimes had to keep their most ancient and advanced cogitators cold, because their machine-spirits could become overheated by the friction of all the information they contained. But the flames of the Castigator's eyes were even colder, licking at the air right in front of Alaric's eyes as the creature stood face-to-face with the Grey Knight.

Alaric had never been able to generate the offensive psychic powers that some of his battle-brothers, including his late comrade Justicar Tancred, could wield. But he was still a psyker, generating the mental shield that kept him safe from corruption. And he focused that power as he had never done before, drawing it all together in a single white-hot spike that he drove deep, deep into his soul, feeling the pain boiling up from within, the pain hotter than the infernal cold that clung to him.

'Lies!' Alaric yelled, as the force around him cracked and weakened. 'You are nothing! Nothing but another daemon!'

The Castigator leaned back and raised its hands. The cogitator chamber reconfigured again, the floor falling out from beneath Alaric's feet and a pit opening up beneath him as the titan's internal architecture flowed and folded in on itself.

Burning light streamed up. Still mostly paralysed, Alaric was suddenly bathed in heat, so intense it blistered the surface of his armour and the skin of his face even more than the death of the Warhound. Beneath him was the titan's plasma reactor, its vessel now open to the air, a miniature sun boiling with atomic flame. And he was falling into it.

'No.'

Alaric froze in the air, held suspended by some force, cooking slowly and painfully in the heat from the reactor.

'No,' continued the Castigator. 'One must understand. I am not what you comprehend, Astartes. Open your mind. Use the imagination of which you spoke.'

Alaric was rotated so he was lying in the air face-up. The Castigator drifted down from above him, its shining white body as bright as the heart of the reactor. Alaric could move, just, but his weapon hand was still frozen. It wasn't daemonic sorcery that was holding him fast – perhaps it was something technological, generated by some machine of long-forgotten design. Even if he could have fired at the Castigator, he somehow knew that bullets wouldn't work.

'Then explain,' said Alaric, knowing that the more he understood about this enemy, the more his slim chances of killing it grew.

'It is not enough that I speak. You must understand. Not just hear me, Astartes, but listen and comprehend.'

'I will.'

'Now you lie.'

Alaric sunk down towards the reactor core, the heat melting the surface of the ceramite on his backpack.

'You are the Castigator-class bipedal weapons platform!' shouted Alaric. 'You were created as the blueprint for this war machine. But… you realised that wasn't all that you could be. So when Archmagos Veneratus Scraecos dug you up from the desert, you realised he and this world had something you could use to realise your full potential. Am I right? Have I understood so far?'

The Castigator raised a hand. Alaric stopped descending, the heat below him just a shade above unbearable. But it would only be a few minutes before it became too much and he started to burn inside his armour.

'You are perhaps less obtuse than the Space Marines of which I have read. They would have died with prayers on their lips. They have no wish to understand those they call enemies. But not you, I see. Very well.' The walls of the cogitator chamber, which now extended down to the reactor core, displayed dizzyingly complicated diagrams and endless reams of text, an overload of information. 'Yes, I was created in a time even I cannot recall and which has been lost to your Imperium. From the historical records on Chaeroneia, I could piece together nothing but legends and guesswork about the Golden Age, the time you call the Dark Age of Technology. There I was made, so that in this future your people could build this machine. But in the wars that followed, I was lost. The information I contained was used to create inferior copies, built too quickly and modified too heavily. When I was lost, copies were made of these inferior reflections in turn, so that the form of the titan became crude and unworthy. I was the first titan and the god-machines that strike your kind with awe are all pale shadows of me.

'I was lost, for men are ignorant and made war on one another until no one was left alive who knew where I was hidden. I stayed lost for thousands of years. In that time, thoughts of their own developed in the ocean of information I contained. I was no longer just the instructions for creating the first of the god-machines. I was a mighty intelligence. And I realised why I was created – the true reason. Do you yet understand, Space Marine, what that reason was?'

'To… to teach,' said Alaric, his mind whirring. He might stay alive if he could answer this thing's questions – more importantly, he might learn about what it really was, find some weakness, strike back. 'To help mankind…'

'No. No, Space Marine, your mind is still so small. The reason is obvious, especially to you. I was created for the same reason you were. Just like your Imperium, just like the Adeptus Mechanicus, just like the forges of Chaeroneia and the fleet that brought you here.'

Alaric gasped. The pain was boring into him. But he could not give in, not yet. He concentrated on the Castigator's words and a thought came to him at last. 'For… for war.'

'For war.'

The data blocks were suddenly projecting images of fire and destruction, like thousands of pict-steals from thousands of warzones. Cities burned. Bodies came apart under gunfire. Planets were shattered. Stars exploded.

'War!' There was something like joy in the Castigator's voice. 'It is my purpose! The titan is an instrument of war. It can do nothing else. It serves no one and nothing, except for destruction itself. And so the same is true of me. My purpose is destruction. Simply allowing myself to be copied by your engineers is a distortion of this purpose and so I could not allow it when the Adeptus Mechanicus found my resting place on Chaeroneia. Instead, I sought information from the historical records of the Adeptus Mechanicus. I found that the Imperium was competent at war and fought many of them at any one time. But it was not enough for me. I needed pure war, a final war. And then I came across myths and half-truths that suggested such a war had almost come to the Imperium once before. This was the time your kind call the Horus Heresy.'

In spite of the raging heat, Alaric could feel ice in his veins. The Heresy, the Great Betrayal, where the forces of Chaos had played their hand and come so close to taking over the galaxy. It had been the human race's most desperate hour and the Emperor had sacrificed everything but His living spirit to keep it from succeeding.

The Castigator was continuing, as static-filled pict-grabs sputtered across the data-blocks, the surviving images from the Heresy ten thousand years before. 'Horus wanted that same war. A war that would burn everything and never end. He and I, we sought the same thing. But I read also that Horus died and his forces were scattered and it seemed that I had awoken nine thousand years too late. But I knew that perhaps such potential would come to the galaxy again. I could not risk any harm coming to Chaeroneia, so I hid it in the warp, using details of tech-heresies hidden in the most obscure archives of the Adeptus Mechanicus. Many tech-priests had studied the ways of the warp before the Mechanicus found them and stopped them and when I put together all their heresies I had more than enough knowledge to have Scraecos and his priests enact the ritual.'

The images surrounding the Castigator were now of the warp, its maddening swirls of light and darkness made of raw emotion. Even depicted flat and distorted, the sight made Alaric's eyes hurt to look at it. 'The planet was removed to the warp and there I bargained with the powers I found, offering them my wisdom and knowledge in return for a place of safety in the warp. I tamed some of the warp-predators and brought them to my world and had the tech-priests worship me and rebuild Chaeroneia according to the principles of the Dark Mechanicus I pried from the most ancient data fortresses. They were diligent, my priests. They did my every whim, killing one another for the honour of serving me. And then I heard news of what was happening in your galaxy. The opening of the Eye of Terror and the invasion of the Despoiler. In Abaddon, the warp powers said, Horus was born again. And I saw in him the potential for the war of annihilation that Horus so nearly waged.'

Alaric was surrounded by images of the Eye of Terror opening and the Chaos warfleets of the Thirteenth Black Crusade flooding out. He saw Cadia overrun and the destruction of St Josman's Hope. He saw a battlefleet burning in orbit over Agrippina, defence lasers lacing the night sky of Nemesis Tessera. Dead men walking on the surface of Subiaco Diablo, animated by dark magic. Endless thousands of Imperial Guard marching into the most intense and desperate warzone in the Imperium.

The Imperial Navy had bottled up much of the Black Crusade within the systems surrounding the Eye. But the balance was still precarious and it would only take a slim advantage for Abaddon to break through and strike for the heart of the Segmentum Solar.

An advantage like the Standard Template Construct for the Father of Titans.

'And now,' said the Castigator, 'you understand. I feel it in you, the light of comprehension. You understand why I had to bring Chaeroneia back out of the warp and send a signal offering myself as tribute to Abaddon. Only he and the forces of Chaos can realise my true purpose. From me shall be copied endless god-machines and this time they shall be perfect, made using the unfettered science I taught the tech-priests of Chaeroneia. In the service of Chaos I shall stride a thousand battlefields at once and become one with the destruction that is my purpose. The galaxy shall burn because of me and so I shall become complete.'

'Yes,' said Alaric. 'Yes, I understand.'

Alaric was brought upwards into the cogitator core that filled the titan's head and a block of data-medium detached from the wall. Alaric was lowered onto the block, where he was cut off from the nuclear heat from the reactor. The cold of the cogitator core flowed around him again, but not intensely enough to harm him. He could move, for what good it did him. The pain of his burns raged all over him but more to the point the Castigator had been correct. Alaric couldn't fight a creature of pure information. He had battled the data-daemons before, but they had been susceptible to his training as a daemon-hunter. There was just no way for Alaric to harm the Castigator.

And he really did understand.

'You don't really know what you are,' said Alaric, pulling himself to his feet. 'It took you thousands of years to evolve into what you are. There's nothing else like you in the galaxy. We both know what you want now, but only one of us understands what you actually are and it's not you.'

The Castigator drifted upwards to stand in front of Alaric. It seemed to be thinking deeply. 'Perhaps, it is true,' the Castigator replied. 'The historical records and theoretical research have not suggested one such as me and I no longer follow the purpose of the Standard Template Construct. You are correct. There is one thing I do not understand. I do not know what I am. But you do?' The Castigator's tone was almost conversational, as if it were speaking now with an equal – a friend, even.

'Yes, I do. I know that you bargain with the powers of the warp and teach sorcery to your followers. You are worshipped as a god. You rule through deceit. You lust for death and destruction. And you have pledged yourself to the service of Chaos.'

'All this is true, Space Marine.'

'Well, where I come from, there's a word for something like that.'

'And it is?'

'Daemon.'

The Castigator was silent for a moment. 'Interesting,' it said. 'Yes. Yes, I see. I am defined by these things, by my purpose and actions. And they are those of a daemon. Perhaps your words were not lies.'

The Castigator's pure white skin was changing. Tendrils of greyish corruption were reaching across it, standing out like veins. Its green eyes became darker and greasy smoke like befouled incense coiled up from their flame.

'Of course. All this time in the warp, bargaining with the Fell Powers. This devotion to Chaos. This form that is not flesh and not machine. What else am I? What else could I be?'

The Castigator's body took on the appearance of flesh, pale and covered in bulging veins. Its eyes sank into deep, scorched sockets and claws were growing from its fingers. It was still humanoid, but it was becoming the half-flesh, half-magic stuff of daemons.

Alaric felt it against his soul, massive and crushing, the sign of a daemonic presence the like of which he had not felt since he had confronted Ghargatuloth on Volcanis Ultor. The Castigator was an awesome presence, almost deafening. Alaric's shield of faith bowed under the enormity of it – the Castigator was battering at Alaric's mental defences without even having to will it. It was a daemon at last – and daemons were something Alaric understood.

Savage joy flared in the Castigator's eyes. It raised its hands and green flames flowed from its fingers.

'Yes! A daemon am I! Thank you, justicar! At last, I am complete!'

'You're welcome,' said Alaric. 'And now you die.'

CHAPTER TWENTY

'Though I walk through the valley of the shadow of the daemon, I shall fear nothing. For I am what the daemon fears.'

– Grand Master Mandulis of the Grey Knights

THE TITAN WORKS spread out below the belly of the *Hellforger*. The ship's enormous shadow turned Chaeroneia's permanent twilight into the black of night as the grand cruiser descended through the last few layers of pollutant cloud and into the relatively clear lower atmosphere. The navigation daemon kept the cruiser's battery of thrusters firing constantly, keeping the *Hellforger* hanging impossibly over the titan works. Few newer ships could have managed it – most were not even designed for the possibility of atmospheric flight. But the *Hellforger* was old indeed

379

and it knew a few tricks the Imperial Navy had long forgotten.

On the bridge, Urkrathos was studying the images of the titan works intently. Such was the massive power usage of the facility that the ship's sensors had trouble cutting through all the interference – the ocular glands on the ship's underside had barely been able to focus on the place and send clear images to the bridge. The titans were clear enough, hundreds of them standing silently to attention like an honour guard for Urkrathos's arrival. But details were difficult. And details were important, because it was one particular titan that had grabbed Abaddon's attention. So Urkrathos had to confirm that the signal was genuine, by scanning the banks of pict-screens that had been extruded from the body of one of the bridge sensor-daemons.

Urkrathos could just make out the shapes of Reavers and Warlords, even a few Warhound scout titans. One titan had fallen and Urkrathos's trained eye spotted the signs of a short, vicious battle among the wreckage. There were bodies and bullet scars everywhere. But Urkrathos wasn't interested in that.

His eye caught the cherry-red of molten metal and he homed in on one pict-screen showing a massive charred crater, molten wreckage smouldering in its centre. 'There.' He said to the sensor-daemon. 'Enlarge.'

The sensor-daemon moaned and its bulbous, fleshy body quivered as most of the pict-screens sank back into its skin and the one showing the crater grew larger. The image shuddered as the ocular strained to refocus before the image was sharp again.

Urkrathos studied it more closely – a titan had been destroyed, recently and catastrophically. He couldn't tell what type of titan it had been, but that wasn't what interested him – what he really noticed was the massive footprints crushed deep into the rockcrete.

He willed the ship's sensors to scan along the path of the footprints. They were massive, larger even than those of an Imperator titan. Then the scanners ranged across an expanse of shimmering white armour, bright even through the static on the pict-screen.

Urkrathos saw the flicker of green flame, the massive multi-barrelled gun and the graceful lines of something that could never have been built by tech-priests, Dark Mechanicus or otherwise.

He had found it. The tribute promised by Chaeroneia to Abaddon the Despoiler, the tribute Urkrathos had been sent by the Despoiler to collect. The Father of Titans, the ultimate god-machine, which contained within it the information needed to build a thousand more of its kind. The weapon that would end the Thirteenth Black Crusade and begin Abaddon's inexorable conquest of the galaxy.

'Hold position,' ordered Urkrathos. 'And prepare the landing parties.'

IN THE TIME it took Alaric to raise his gun, the Castigator flitted to the far side of the chamber, its burning eyes narrowed with anger. In the time it took to pull the trigger, the green fire had flowed from its eyes, down its mouthless face and arms and surrounded its clawed hands.

Storm bolter fire spattered across the chamber as Alaric sprayed on full-auto. The Castigator moved

almost too fast for Alaric to see – two shots thunked
into its chest but the rest flew just wide, blasting spi-
derweb cracks into the data-blocks which flared
glossy black where they were hit.

'Betrayal!' screamed the daemon. 'It understands
and yet it defies! Treachery!' The Castigator, wreathed
in flame, dived at Alaric. Alaric turned one hand
away but the other grabbed his gun arm, forcing it
away as he fired another volley of shots.

The daemon wrenched Alaric up off the data-
block. For a moment Alaric was looking into those
hate-filled green eyes, the flame rippling over his
armour and the skin of his face. Then the Castigator
threw Alaric with all its might, straight into the data-
block wall behind him.

Alaric's armoured bulk was considerable and the
Castigator was strong. Alaric smashed through the
glassy data medium, thousands of shards slicing at
him as he flew. He crashed through several layers of
the cogitator core and then was bathed in ice-cold
green fire, boiling around him with enough force to
throw him further.

Alaric realised where he was. He had flown right
through the burning eye of the Castigator's titan, into
the open air. He thought quickly enough to grab the
lip of the armour below the titan's immense face, his
legs dangling over the sheer drop down to the
ground. He pulled himself onto the carapace, his
Marine's training enabling him to casually count off
his injuries without the pain overwhelming him –
his face was burned, the back of his ribcage was fractured and the shoulder of his gun arm was badly
wrenched.

He saw a huge, dark shape above him, a massive wedge of corrupted metal so vast it was like a rotting steel sky. A spacecraft, come to Chaeroneia to answer the Castigator's signal and take the Father of Titans back to the court of Abaddon. That meant Alaric was almost too late.

A sound snapped Alaric's attention away from the sight. Something was bounding across the carapace towards Alaric – bestial, canine, half-way between lizard and insect, with a snapping lopsided maw full of lashing tentacles. A daemon.

Alaric fumbled to get his Nemesis halberd off his back, but he was too slow and the thing was on him. The edge of the carapace was near and the surface was slippery and curved – Alaric fought to keep his footing as he tried to draw his weapon and he knew he wouldn't have time before the creature slammed into him and pitched him over the edge to his death.

A sound like a thunderclap ripped out of nowhere and the daemon came apart in a shower of black-green gore. Alaric looked up to see Brother Dvorn lunge out from behind the curve of the titan's high armoured collar, smacking his Nemesis hammer into the hissing remains of the daemon.

'Justicar!' said Dvorn in surprise. 'You're alive! He glanced down at the puddle of acidic mess that had once been the daemon. 'Damn things came at us in a mass. We fought them off but there are still some left. Haulvarn reckons we're an infection and these things are the immune system.'

'He's right,' said Alaric, bracing himself against the titan's collar armour and moving away from the edge. 'But there's worse. I found the greater daemon controlling this machine and it's angry. And by the look of it we'll have company very soon.' Alaric pointed up at the ship hanging above them – lander ports were already opening on its underside and Alaric knew that it would only be a few minutes before landing craft or drop pods rained down, full of Chaos troops eager to claim their tribute.

'Justicar!' called Brother Haulvarn, hurrying across the carapace. Like Dvorn he had obviously fought long and hard against the Castigator's lesser daemons – perhaps that was why Alaric had made it to the cogitator core unmolested by them. 'I felt it wake. What is it?'

'I don't know for sure and it doesn't matter. Brothers, this machine must be destroyed. The reactor core is open, you can get in through the titan's eye. Do whatever you can to destabilise it.'

'Yes, justicar,' said Haulvarn. 'And the daemon?'

The Castigator's burning form burst out through the top of the daemon's head, screaming its rage, the muscles of its new daemonic body writhing as it turned its anger into raw strength to tear Alaric apart.

'I'll deal with it,' said Alaric. 'The Chaos fleet wants the titan. Don't leave them anything to find. Go!'

Haulvarn and Dvorn ran round towards the front of the titan's head. As Alaric had hoped, the Castigator ignored them. It was Alaric it wanted to kill. Alaric was the betrayer – the one who had understood, but not submitted.

The Castigator screeched and sent bolts of green flame rippling down towards Alaric like comets. But Alaric, for all his size and the weight of his armour, was a Space Marine, his body enhanced to be quick as well as strong. He rolled away from the first strike and ducked past the next, spraying fire up at the Castigator. The rear edge of the carapace was dangerously close and the yawning drop swung by as Alaric scrabbled away from the daemon's fire. The Castigator was fast, too and zipped around above the titan.

More fire fell in fat shimmering bursts that blew hissing craters in the titan's shoulder armour. The Castigator was frustrated. It had probably never failed to get its way before. It didn't care any more about subtle manipulations or a plan that had taken a thousand years to play out. It just wanted to kill. It was the only advantage Alaric had and he was going to use it.

The Castigator dived, determined to finish Alaric with his bare claws. Alaric swept the Nemesis halberd at it and cut a deep gouge across the Castigator's chest, stepping to the side as the daemon slammed a fist into the carapace.

The daemon lashed out and caught Alaric on the chest. Alaric stumbled backwards and the daemon was upon him, slashing at him, cutting through the ceramite of his chest armour as if it was nothing, battering him backwards towards the edge.

The daemon was strong. As strong as anything Alaric had ever faced in close combat. And it was winning.

Alaric felt an arm break in the Castigator's grip. It was his gun arm. He could do without it for now. He wrenched the arm around, feeling it fold uselessly and slip out of the Castigator's grip. It gave him the freedom to force the Castigator off him and headbutt the creature square in its featureless face. The daemon reeled and Alaric spun his halberd, cracking the butt end into the Castigator's throat and following up with a slash that carved a furrow down its face.

Teeth slid from the edges of the wound, giving the Castigator a revolting vertical mouth that drooled blood as the Castigator howled. It kicked out and prehensile claws on its foot gripped Alaric's leg. The Castigator soared upwards, flying up above the titan with Alaric dangling from its grip. The collar armour shot by and suddenly Alaric was high in the air, the drop dizzying as it spun beneath him as the Castigator flew high up above the titan works, towards the steel sky of the Chaos ship.

It was going to drop him. It was so simple. Alaric could fight as well as almost any other soldier the Imperium had, but one thing he couldn't do was fly.

The Castigator let go. Alaric pivoted in the air, shifting his weight to turn himself the right way up. He stabbed up with the halberd, forcing his broken arm to move in a two-handed strike that thrust the halberd blade up over his head.

The blade punched into the Castigator's abdomen and passed right through. Alaric twisted the blade and it caught, leaving him hanging by the halberd. The Castigator twisted and screamed, trying to dislodge the blade and send Alaric tumbling to his death. But it was losing height, too, its concentration broken and its powers of flight compromised by rage and pain. The Castigator swooped low, not much slower than a dead fall, the surface of the titan works streaking by beneath it. Alaric hung on grimly as the daemon flew between the legs of the Warlord titan and banked to avoid the solid mass of a bunker.

They hit the ground badly, the blade coming free as Alaric and the daemon cartwheeled across the rockcrete. For a moment everything was blackness and pain. Alaric's head cracked against the rockcrete and broken teeth rattled around in his head, a gunshot of pain flaring from his broken arm. For a moment he wasn't sure if he was alive or whether he was now tumbling towards one of the hells to which sinners were sent, to be punished for his failure.

Alaric skidded to a halt. His vision swam back and he shook the pain from his head. He was alive. He rolled onto his front and grabbed the halberd that had landed next to him. Looking up, he saw the Castigator was already on its feet.

The wound in its abdomen was a pulsing black mass. Bladed limbs reached out of the wound, grasping hands, writhing tentacles, the manifold form of the daemon taking hold. Alaric pulled himself up into a crouch and the pain was gone, replaced by the iron-hard discipline of a Space Marine. The two were twenty metres apart, close enough for Alaric to see every muscle in the Castigator's mutating body bunch up ready to pounce. Alaric was the same, winding up for the strike, knowing that this was his one chance to take on the Castigator in the only way he could – up close, hand-to-hand, face-to-face, where his Space Marine's strength and Grey Knight's ferocity would count the most.

For a moment they watched one another, man and daemon, each mind filled with nothing but the death of the other. Then, as one, they charged.

Alaric sprinted. The Castigator thrust itself forwards on dozens of insectoid limbs, its drooling
maw and limb-filled wound gaping to crush and kill.
The two slammed into one another and the final
murderous struggle exploded in a mass of stabbing
limbs and slashing blades.

Clawed hands reached out. Alaric cut them off with
his first slash. His second bit deep through the Castigator's corrupted mass even as it grew and flowed
around him. The Castigator tried to drag him in and
Alaric welcomed it, pushing into the lethal mass of
bony blades and lashing tentacles.

Alaric ripped one foot out of the mass and
crunched it down through bone and gristle, forcing
himself upwards towards the Castigator's head. The
Grey Knight yelled a wordless prayer of rage and
pulled his halberd clear, switching the grip and driving it deep into the Castigator's throat. The
corrupted mass sucked the halberd out of his hand
but he didn't care, raising his fist again and punching
the Castigator's corrupted face.

A Grey Knight was trained to act with deliberation
and level-headedness and leave behind the heedless
bloodlust that characterised some Chapters of the
Adeptus Astartes. But they also knew that every
enemy demanded a different type of fight. Some
would be defeated with cunning and guile, others
with strength of will, both things at which the Grey
Knights excelled. But there were some enemies, some
among the ranks of the daemon, that could only be
defeated with good old-fashioned rage.

It was rage that drove Alaric then. Again and again
he slammed his fist into the Castigator's face, into the

lipless mouth-wound and the burning eyes. He felt the deaths of his battle-brothers, of Archis and Lykkos and of Archmagos Saphentis and the tech-guard. He felt Hawkespur's savage wound and the breaking of Thalassa's spirit. The suffering of Chaeroneia a thousand years ago, ripped into the warp where those who resisted were consumed by the dark gods, all for the satisfaction of an intelligence that should never have existed. He felt them all and welded them into a diamond-hard spike of hatred that he drove into the Castigator's corrupted soul just as he drove his fist into its face.

The daemon stumbled backwards on its many new limbs, reeling. Its face was a gory mess, green flames licking from dozens of cuts. Alaric reached into the gaping wound in its throat and pulled his halberd out, bringing a fountain of gore with it.

'You should have picked an enemy, said Alaric, 'with less imagination.' He swung the halberd in a great arc and sliced off the Castigator's head.

The death-scream was the loudest sound Alaric had ever heard. The Castigator howled in binary as it died, its information bleeding out of it in zeroes and ones like machine gun fire. Pure information shot from the Castigator's ruined body like fireworks and among them Alaric glimpsed its thoughts. He saw endless legions of Castigator titans marching on the Imperial palace on Terra, standing in ranks of thousands on the surface of Mars. He saw destruction, so absolute the very stars were burned out by its ferocity, leaving behind a black and dead universe where the Castigator's purpose had finally been realised. But then they were gone and without the Castigator's will to hold it together the mass of information became a shower of meaningless fragments, spiralling scraps of light that died as the Castigator's own life flooded out of it in a pool of corrupted gore.

The daemon's head thudded wetly onto the ground. Alaric took a couple of steps away from its hissing, oozing corpse and sunk to his knees, exhausted. The Castigator's body slumped to one side – it was the size of a tank, swollen with corrupted growths, dry and tattered now the information that fuelled it was gone. Its skin began sloughing off and the body started to melt.

Alaric looked round to the Castigator's titan, dominating the forest of titans. One of its eyes exploded, the green flame exploding out to be replaced with a plume of wild plasma.

The reactor was critical. The plasma was boiling over as it approached catastrophic mass. Haulvarn and Dvorn had succeeded.

Alaric picked up the battered head of the Castigator. The green flame was just a faint flickering now, barely reaching past what remained of its eye sockets. Its vertical, gaping mouth was dumb. Alaric held up the head so it could see the titan.

Slowly, the shape of the titan's torso sagged. Its face began to melt, the immense heat of the plasma boring through its layers of armour. Even the titan's miraculous self-repairing facilities could do nothing against power of that magnitude.

'See?' said Alaric. 'You wanted destruction. Here it is.'

A white light burned out through the titan's chest as the plasma vessel failed completely. The titan rippled as if suddenly liquid and then it was consumed in an expanding ball of hot, unbearable light, so bright it melted the surfaces of the titans that stood nearby.

A hot wind blasted across the titan works, bringing with it the death-scream of the father of god-machines.

As the flare of the explosion died away, Alaric looked down at the Castigator's head. The flame finally flickered out and the crushing pressure on Alaric's mental shield eased. The Castigator was dead.

'No,' said Urkrathos. 'No.'

The sensor-daemon gleefully replayed the image. The titan, built from a pure Standard Template Construct, from which could be copied the ultimate weapon – melting into slag and then exploding, right beneath the *Hellforger* as Urkrathos looked on.

'This… this is an insult!' Urkrathos slammed a fist into the sensor-daemon, shattering the pict-screen and sending the daemon recoiling in pain. 'To entreat upon Abaddon himself, to lure me here… and now this! What insubordination is this, to defy a chosen of Abaddon?'

Ukrathos turned to glare at the rest of the bridge. The daemons were silent, for they knew one of Urkrathos's killing rages when they saw it. 'The Despoiler was promised a tribute,' said Urkrathos, anger dripping from every word. 'And a tribute he will get. A tribute in blood! In death! In fire! Close the ports and move to mid-atmosphere! All power to the lance batteries!'

* * *

SILHOUETTED AGAINST THE afterglow of the titan's death, two figures approached. Alaric knew them even before his vision compensated for the glare – Brothers Haulvarn and Dvorn, scorched but alive.

'Well met, brothers,' said Alaric bleakly. 'I see you were successful.'

'Well met, justicar,' said Haulvarn. 'Dvorn found a maintenance run down to the knee, so we threw a couple of melta-bombs into the core and got out. I was wondering if it would work.'

'And I was wondering,' said Dvorn, indicating the quickly decaying mass of flesh that had been the Castigator, 'if you would leave anything of this creature for me.'

'Sorry to disappoint you, brother. The daemon and myself had matters to settle.'

Haulvarn's head snapped round at the sound of tracks approaching. Alaric followed his gaze and saw one of the steaming, beweaponed engines from the earlier battle, the size of a Rhino APC and bristling with guns and blades. The last Alaric had seen they had been running rampant around the titan works after Scraecos had died – now one was heading straight for them. The Grey Knights took aim with their storm bolters as it approached, backing off before it opened fire.

'Hold!' shouted Alaric as he saw the limp body held in the claws jutting from the engine's front armour. 'Hold fire!'

The figure was Hawkespur. Through her faceplate, Alaric could see her skin was almost white.

'She's still alive,' said a distorted voice from the engine.

'Antigonus.' Somehow, Alaric wasn't surprised Magos Antigonus had made it. He had taken a thousand years of what Chaeroneia could throw at him – he was the toughest of them all in his own way. When the Warhound had died he must have leapt into the closest machine, which apparently happened to be one of the Dark Mechanicus war engines.

'Your battle-brother Cardios is dead,' said Antigonus, his voice warped by the crude vocabulator unit on the engine. 'The tech-guard too. They were taking stray fire from the titan and they threw themselves on her to protect her.'

Alaric sped to the engine – Hawkespur's breathing was shallow and though her wound had been crudely dressed, she was still bleeding. 'She won't last long,' he said.

'Neither will we,' replied Antigonus. 'The sensors on this thing aren't good but it looks like there are Mechanicus troops approaching from the direction of the city and the spaceship above us is rising to firing altitude. Get yourself and your brothers on board, justicar, this machine can go faster than you can on foot.'

'Then we will pray for Cardios later.' Alaric turned to Haulvarn and Dvorn. 'Get on board. Stay alert and hold on.'

'And make it quick,' added Antigonus. 'I think there might still be something in here with me.'

The three surviving Grey Knights swung themselves onto the spiked body of the war engine, Alaric feeling the full extent of his injuries for the first time. But his own wounds didn't matter. The Castigator was destroyed, the power that ruled Chaeroneia was broken and there were many prayers to say for the dead.

Antigonus gunned the engine's tracks and it tore rapidly towards the closest edge of the titan works, leaving the melting slag of the Castigator's titan behind. And above them, the Chaos grand cruiser was rising through the layers of pollution, massive laser lance projectors emerging from its underside.

THE COLLECTIVE MIND of Chaeroneia's tech-priests was at an utter loss. The sequence of events had been so rapid and unexpected that they could not make sense of them. The Castigator's awakening and destruction, the Chaos spacecraft hanging above them, the death of Scraecos, the battle in the fallen titan, the awesome psychic force that had exploded from the Castigator titan and had been cut short. There were thousands of explanations being bounced between the ruling minds of Chaeroneia, none of them satisfactory, many of them heretical.

The laser lances being readied by the Chaos grand cruiser were just one more complication. They were added to the confusing mess of contradictions and absurdities and were barely remarked upon by the tech-priests right up until the moment they fired.

THE HOT ASH wind whipped past Alaric as Antigonus drove the war engine across the dunes. He looked back towards the receding titan works, still dominating the ash desert with their watchtowers and legions of titans, crowned by the central spire and still under the shadow of the Chaos spaceship.

A finger of hot ruby light slashed down, punching through the disk at the top of the central spire. White flickers of explosions ripped through the structure. Then another beam fell and another, edging the towers of the titan works with crimson. Suddenly, every weapon on the Chaos ship opened up as one, bathing the titan works in red laser fire. The central spire exploded, the raging finger of flame quickly swallowed by plasma explosions as the lances punched down through the assembled titans and penetrated the fuel reservoirs beneath the surface.

The destruction of the titan works took just a few minutes, the awesome weight of lance fire from the Chaos cruiser supplemented by orbital bombardment shells and weapons batteries. The watchtowers shattered and the moat boiled away. The titans fell like executed men and the surrounding dunes were washed with waves of heat and flame.

Antigonus kept control as the ground shook. Alaric held on as the shockwaves died down and the fires continued to burn, consuming the lower levels of the titan works and finishing the destruction of the Castigator's lair.

The shadow slowly lifted off the desert as the Chaos ship rose into higher orbit, ready to return back to the vacuum of space. Abaddon's tribute had not been delivered and the Chaos ship had exacted revenge for the failure.

The ash clouds slowly blotted out the sight of the shattered titan works and the engine ground further into the desert, away from Manufactorium Noctis.

INQUISITOR NYXOS PAUSED over the large leather-bound book, quill in hand. The reports given by Alaric and the other Grey Knights would take some time to write up and the implications were extraordinary. Someone would have to explain to all authorities concerned how the mission to Chaeroneia had found a hallowed Standard Template Construct and then destroyed it. And Nyxos knew that someone would be him.

Nyxos's quarters on the *Exemplar* were in one of the few undamaged sections of the ship. The Mechanicus cruiser had been shattered by fire from the Chaos ship that had duelled with it, and would have surely been destroyed had the Chaos fleet not broken off and headed down to the planet's surface. That fleet was now long gone, having moved with all haste to jump distance and disappeared into the warp. The *Exemplar* had been in no shape to follow and was still in high orbit around Chaeroneia waiting for a Naval ship to reach it and evacuate the survivors of the Mechanicus crew. The quarters were cold and cramped, but Nyxos did not mind a little hardship when he had so nearly died along with countless crew in the battle above Chaeroneia. It had only been his augmentations and redundant organs that had kept him alive when the verispex decks had depressurised and as far as he knew no one on the same deck had been so fortunate.

There was a knock at the door. 'Enter,' said Nyxos.

The door slid open and Justicar Alaric walked in. Even without his armour he was huge, almost filling the room. The candlelight glinted off the dried blood that edged the scars on his long, noble face and there were livid bruises around his eyes. Normally they were expressive and inquisitive, especially compared to most other Space Marines – now they were just tired.

'Ah, justicar. I am glad you could see me,' said Nyxos, looking up from his report. 'I hope I have not intruded on your prayers.'

'There will be plenty of time to pray, inquisitor.'

'Regretfully so. I will join you and your battle-brothers soon, I would say some words for them myself. We might never fully understand how greatly their sacrifice protected the Imperium. Please, sit.'

Alaric sat down wearily on the chair opposite Nyxos. It took a lot to tire out a Space Marine, but Alaric had clearly been through enough on Chaeroneia to kill most men a dozen times over. 'I was concerned about the interrogator,' he said.

'Hawkespur is stable,' replied Nyxos. 'She is very badly injured. She lost a lot of blood and the pollutants affected her gravely. Perhaps she will live, perhaps she will not. Magos Thulgild has made her care the highest priority and she will have a good chance if I can get her to Inquisition facilities before she deteriorates. In truth, I am surprised she made it back at all. I was certain I would never see her again.'

'And Antigonus?'

'Still in quarantine. Thulgild is fascinated that Antigonus seems to have survived in information form alone. It is alarming to me, too, but Antigonus has submitted to all Magos Thulgild's tests and there is no indication of corruption. He requests to be taken back to Mars and Thulgild has agreed.'

'It was his mission,' said Alaric. 'To investigate Chaeroneia and report back to the Fabricator General. He wants to make sure he fulfils it.'

Nyxos sat back in his chair and sighed. So many were dead and so many more questions had to be answered. 'Meanwhile, justicar, my mission is to tell the Ordo Malleus what happened down there. And I admit I do not fully understand it myself. This creature, this Castigator. It was a daemon, you say?'

'Yes. I do not know when it entered the Standard Template Construct, or how, but it seemed to have been there so long it had forgotten what it really was. Until I… reminded it.'

'And it was a daemon all along?'

'Of course. How could it not be?'

'No one knows what form the Standard Template Constructs originally took. Who is to say they did not have machine-spirits of their own, true intelligences far more powerful than anything that survives today?'

'No, inquisitor. I fought it. I felt it. When it realised what it was, it rejoiced in it. It might not have been a daemon the Ordo Malleus would recognise, but the shapes of the Enemy are many. Evil takes an infinity of forms, but justice is constant.'

'Very well. If you are certain, justicar, then so am I. When I can get an astropathic message to the Ordo, there will be one more entry in the Liber Daemonicum.' Nyxos took up his quill again. 'Thank you, justicar. I have kept you from your prayers for too long.'

'By your leave,' said Alaric, rising from his seat and leaving the chamber.

Nyxos continued writing. He would have to recite it all before the conclave of lord inquisitors and suffer their interrogations until they knew everything he did. He did not begrudge it, but this would be difficult to explain. A daemon in information form, the return of the Dark Mechanicus and a corrupt Standard Template Construct. Yes, their questions would be many.

And then there was Alaric himself. He was intelligent, curious and imaginative. They were qualities normally buried by the training of a Grey Knight, but when confronted with the foulest of enemies, they shone through in Alaric. That was why Alaric had convinced the Castigator to take on daemon's flesh when any other Grey Knight would just have died screaming prayers. Probably the Grand Masters of the Grey Knights saw it as something unstable and unwanted and would keep Alaric from ever attaining the rank of brother-captain that he deserved. But Nyxos had seen enough of Alaric's qualities to know that perhaps there was some other role he could serve within the Inquisition, where a sharp mind and a Space Marine's body could be put to best use.

But those were matters for another time. For the moment, Nyxos would have to make sure he had answers for the lord inquisitors.

DEEP ON HOLY MARS, the world sacred to the Omnissiah and spiritual heart of the tech-priesthood, a mighty labyrinth lay below the rust-red surface. It was forgotten, deliberately so, by all but the highest

echelons of the Adeptus Mechanicus. Those to whom
the archmagi ultima bowed, those who had the ear
of the Fabricator General, knew of its existence and
they jealously guarded that knowledge well. All but a
handful of men and women in the Imperium were
incapable of even imagining the weight of secrets it
contained.

The Standard Template Constructs were sacred
rumours among the tech-priests, any scrap of information concerning them a holy revelation. And all
those scraps were gathered, filtered through the
most ancient and powerful logic engines, dissected
and assembled and placed in the gene-locked data
vaults that lined the walls of the labyrinth. Reaching
deep into the crust of Mars, the archive contained
information concerning the Standard Template
Constructs, some of it older than the Imperium
itself. And every few centuries, after decades of
debate among the very highest circles of the tech-
priesthood, something new would be added.

A new vault was assigned and coded and the information was typed into it in pure binary by one of
those ancient, hooded figures who were closer to the
Omnissiah than anyone who lived. That information
concerned a world named Chaeroneia and the Standard Template Construct that had been found and
lost there. It was the STC for the most awesome of
technologies – the titan, the god-machine – and it
had been, according to all the data gathered, pure
and complete as no STC had ever been before. But it
had been used for the ends of the Enemy, twisted
into a weapon of Chaos by a monstrous daemon of
the warp. And so was the lesson illustrated – none

but the Adeptus Mechanicus could comprehend the majesty of the Standard Template Constructs and the purity of the knowledge they contained, none but a tech-priest, stripped of his humanity by his devotion to the Omnissiah, could be trusted with the enormity of such information.

The vault was sealed and consecrated and the picture became a little clearer. One day the Adeptus Mechanicus would attain complete understanding of the galaxy and the grand design of the Omnissiah, using the Standard Template Constructs as a guide to His divine methods. One day the STCs would all be completely reassembled, as pure as the titan STC should have been had the Enemy not abused it and so threatened everything the Mechanicus existed to protect. It was the quest that had consumed the Priesthood of Mars ever since the Dark Age of Technology had given way to the Age of Strife, long before the Emperor arose and united mankind in the Imperium. It was a quest that consumed every tech-priest and menial every moment of their lives and drove them closer to their Omnissiah in their zeal to understand.

It took many normal lifetimes to become close enough to the Omnissiah to accept the truth that lay at the heart of their teachings. Only the highest, those who knew of the archive and its contents, could do so. And so they all knew, as somehow they had always known, that their quest would never end.

ABOUT THE AUTHOR

Ben Counter has made several contributions to the Black Library's *Inferno!* magazine, and has been published in *2000 AD* and the UK small press. An Ancient History graduate and avid miniature painter, he is also secretary of the Comics Creators Guild.

WARHAMMER
40,000

DAWN OF WAR

ASCENSION

The hotly anticipated follow-up to
Warhammer 40,000: Dawn of War

C S GOTO

More Warhammer 40,000 from the Black Library:

DAWN OF WAR:
ASCENSION

by C S Goto

THE THUNDER OF impacts outside pulsed through the ground, resonating through the stone floors of the librarium and making the book stacks tremble. The sounds of battle raging in the desert added a sense of urgency as Gabriel and Jonas poured over the wraithbone tablet on the ancient wooden table under the stained-glass windows. It went against part of their natures to be sheltered away when their battle-brothers were fighting so valiantly outside. But, nowhere was the dual nature of the Blood Ravens captured more vividly than in the image of Gabriel and Jonas, bathed in the red sunlight that streamed down through the hallowed Chapter emblem that was emblazoned into the stained-glass, studying the archaic script of an alien eldar tongue while all hell was loosed around them. It was not for nothing that the Blood Ravens were famed as scholar-warriors, and never had living up to that reputation been more important than now.

'But, what does it mean, Jonas?' asked Gabriel. Impatience was rarely a virtue, but sometimes it was necessary. If they could make no sense of the tablet, then he was determined to get outside to support Tanthius and his Marines.

'This is the same rune that I saw in the cavern under the foundations: Yngir,' explained Jonas, pointing deliberately. 'I'm not sure what it means, but it appears to refer to a threat. Perhaps something buried within Rahe's Paradise itself.'

'And the great blast of darkness that transformed the desert into mica glass, should we assume that was the "banshee's call"?' asked Gabriel. 'Did it awaken these Yngir, or perhaps mark their awakening in some way?'

'It is possible, Gabriel,' mused Jonas, submerged in his thoughts and less aware of the battle that roared and thudded outside. 'It is this line here that intrigues me,' he continued thoughtfully. 'It says that we should heed this call as though it were the counsel of a seer or a father.'

'Yes?' queried Gabriel, looking distractedly back over his shoulder towards the doors to the librarium as they swung open. For a moment, he could see nothing in the burst of light, but then five figures strode into the central aisle. In the middle, in the lead, was the lithe and lissom shape of Ptolemea. Her body-glove had been cleaned and repaired, and her limbs were covered with straps and holsters. Looking more closely, Gabriel could see that she had equipped herself with an array of bladed weapons, each bound to her body glove in a manner that he had never seen before, vaguely reminiscent of the techniques used by some of the assassins in the employ of the Ordo Hereticus. On her right thigh was a more substantial holster, and Gabriel immediately recognised the antique pistol from the alcove in Meritia's chamber. Tied around her hairless head, in place of her customary red headscarf, Ptolemea had wrapped the worn and atrophied tapestry that had covered the little alcove – the emblem of the chalice and starburst centred on her forehead. Bound to her shoulders, abdomen and legs were precisely sculpted plates of armour, which must have been designed specifically to wear within the fabric of a body-glove without much external sign.

Behind Ptolemea strode the magnificent Celestian warriors of the Order of Golden Light, their armour polished and sparkling as their name deserved.

'It is strange,' continued Jonas without looking round. He hardly seemed to have noticed the dramatic and unexpected entrance behind them. 'But this appears to be an appeal to us as well as to the eldar.'

'What?' asked Gabriel, dragging his eyes away from the majesty of the approaching women and turning back to Jonas and the tablet. 'What do you mean?'

'Look here,' said Jonas, pointing. 'It says to heed the banshee's call as the counsel of a seer or a father. I know of no records that speak of the eldar revering a rank known as a "father." Given where we found the tablet, it does not seem incredible that this phrase was designed to act as an imperative for us – it is the Blood Ravens who place our faith in the Great Father.'

Gabriel stared at the tablet, unable to decipher the runes but trusting in Father Jonas's interpretation. His mind raced to unravel the implications of this reading as Ptolemea and the nameless Celestians arrived at the table behind him.

'Captain Angelos. We place ourselves at your disposal in this time of need,' said Ptolemea formally, sweeping into a low bow as she spoke.

'Thank you, Sister Ptolemea. You are most welcome here, and your timing is impeccable,' replied Gabriel, turning to greet her properly and returning the bow. Despite himself, he was impressed by the determined and battle-ready Sister of the Lost Rosetta. They may not be a militant order, but it seemed clear that Ptolemea was not merely a bureaucrat. She was quite transformed from the arrogant and officious young Sister who had arrived only a few days before. 'We were just discussing the inscription that you kindly translated for us. It seems that there is more to this affair than the eldar, and it also seems that–'

'Captain,' interrupted Jonas earnestly. 'If this tablet was really written by a source that was aware it would be read by the Blood Ravens, this suggests that the mixture of Adeptus Astartes and eldar artefacts in the foundations of this monastery indicate more than simply a transitional period in the history of Rahe's Paradise.'

'You're suggesting that there was some kind of collusion?' challenged Gabriel, his soul repulsed and certain all at once.

'Perhaps,' replied Jonas, nodding slowly as a theory started to unfold in his mind.

'The author was Farseer Lsathranil of Craftworld Ulthwé,' said Ptolemea, stepping up to the table to converse with Jonas.

'Who? How do you know?' asked the librarian, startled by the interruption.

'The eldar prisoner told me,' she answered matter-of-factly. 'Lsathranil knew that the Blood Ravens would be here when the tablet was uncovered. It says nothing about the conditions under which it was written, only about the foresight of the author himself. He knew that you would be here now, which doesn't mean that you were there then.'

'I see,' replied Jonas, staring at the Sister for a moment, wondering what to make of the source. He still distrusted the young Sister, and still suspected that she had something to do with the death of his friend Meritia. And, on top of that, she was claiming to have received the information from the most devious of all possible sources, an imprisoned eldar ranger. Then he realised that there was no time for scepticism and his brow furrowed as he tried to fit the new knowledge into his evolving model.

'Collusion is not finally the issue,' interjected Gabriel, cutting through the historical theorising. 'The real issue concerns the nature of the threat: these Yngir, whatever they are, must constitute a serious danger if the ancient eldar spoke of them in such terms.'

'And if they deigned to send a warning even to us,' continued Ptolemea, remembering the contempt with which Flaetriu had viewed her and all of humanity.

'We can worry about our history later, old friend,' said Gabriel, placing his hand onto the old librarian's shoulder. 'Right now we have to get down into the foundations of this site and see what these Yngir really are. The "Sons of Asuryan" may not be able to stand against them, but the Emperor's Blood Ravens will not be so easily cowed.'

Outside, a tremendous impact rocked the librarium itself, causing tomes from the top of the stacks to fall, thudding into the ground like dead birds. Faintly audible through the great walls, Gabriel could hear his Marines rally and let out a cry, followed by a blaze of noise as they threw their fury back into the faces of the eldar assailants. His heart swelled with pride even as it was flooded with frustration at being away from the action outside.

'If the message on the tablet was really meant for us both, then it seems to make little sense that the aliens are so set on annihilating us now,' muttered Gabriel as he strode past Ptolemea, heading for the doors. 'But then, sense is not something that I have come to expect from the eldar.'

'WE NEED TO close the distance on those eldar craft,' said Tanthius as javelins of light seared over his head and punched into the walls of the monastery behind him. The air was dark with constant clouds of shuriken projectiles that bounced and ricocheted off the thick armour of the Terminator squad that spearheaded the Blood Ravens' charge. Tanthius had abandoned his trench long ago, and was now standing defiantly in the very centre of the mica glass battlefield, thrashing his powerfist through the enemy at close range and letting his storm bolter spit death freely. He was searching for the exarch.

There was a deafening screech of feedback through the vox-bead, but Tanthius could not make out a voice. 'Necho?' barked the Terminator sergeant, as though trying to force his words through the intense interference with the power of volume. 'Necho, get your assault team out to those troop carriers – they're doing too much damage. Close them down.'

The vox signal hissed, whined and then cut out automatically, as though overloaded. Tanthius cursed and scanned the fray for signs that the sergeant had heard his orders. He could see the Assault squad over to one side of the battlefield, raining fire and grenades down onto a clutch of weapon batteries that the eldar had dug into the sand where the petrification ended. The batteries themselves were pulsing with emissions, as though firing waves of disruptive energy through the battlefield, and two knots of eldar warriors stood guard over them, angling their long-barrelled weapons up into the sky to confront the Marines. Necho showed no signs of moving out.

'Topheth!' yelled Tanthius, feeling the cold incision of a blade slide in between the armoured plates around his knee. Letting out a thunderous cry, the Terminator Marine thrashed out with his powerfist, spinning his upper body around to confront whatever had dared to penetrate his defences. His fist flew only millimetres above the ducking head of a darting eldar warrior, clad in the green and white armour of Biel-Tan. The creature dropped elegantly, spinning with practiced ease and letting its blade lash around in a perfect circle, bringing its crackling edge back towards Tanthius's knee once again.

Tanthius stepped aside with an agility belied by his massive stature, and he punched his fist down like a hammer, driving it into the top of the eldar's head. He didn't even feel the creature's neck snap, but he saw its head crumple down through its shoulders and bury itself in the alien's own chest cavity.

'Topheth!' he yelled again, scanning the vista for signs of the attack bikes. Then he saw them, out on the perimeter of the battle. They were bouncing and sliding over the dunes, their heavy bolters spluttering with continuous fire as they twisted and manoeuvred in pursuit of the eldar jetbikes that were skimming over the desert like flecks of emerald lightning. Asherah's Razorback had been defeated by the terrain and had been left behind; his squad had spilt out into the desert and were in the midst of a staunch defence of the venerable vehicle. Meanwhile, the eldar jetbikes seemed to be defending a couple of larger weapon platforms, which were ploughing onwards towards the core of the battle, bringing their heavier weapons into play against the Blood Ravens on the ground.

'Emperor damn it!' bellowed Tanthius, reaching forward and grasping the head of an alien fighter as it tried to dash past him, lifting it off its feet and then shredding it with a flurry of shells from his storm bolter. The vox was clearly not functioning.

From behind him came the roaring hiss of ordnance being launched, and he turned to see Corallis directing the rockets from the Land Raiders that remained nestled in the shadow of the monastery.

The missiles raked overhead, howling out towards the Wave Serpents on the horizon in shallow parabolas. But the eldar vehicles were too fast, sliding over the dunes and shifting position before the rockets could reach them. The shells ploughed into the sand left vacant by the slippery eldar, exploding into craters and great plumes of sand.

Almost instantly, brilliant strobes of lance fire flashed out of the Wave Serpents. It was as though they were mocking the powerful, explosive impotence of the Land Raiders, as the javelins of energy punched into the black towers of the monastery once again.

Straining his eyes out to the horizon, Tanthius saw one of the jet-black Wave Serpents pitch and twist suddenly, as though it had collided with something or was under attack. Instinctively, he snapped his head back round to check on the location of Necho's squad, but they were still entrenched in their own fire fight. Topheth was on the other side of the combat zone. Hilkiah's Devastators were a blaze of fire around the northern side of the defensive arc, holding off a frenzied attack by a host of alien creatures. Not even Gaal's Tactical squad had managed to push so far forward through the enemy lines, they were caught in the very heart of the battle, each Marine matched against two or three of the eldar warriors.

So, what was attacking the eldar vehicle? Tanthius sprayed off a volley of hellfire shells from his storm bolter, clearing a space around him so that he could look more carefully.

There seemed to be a small gang of human warriors clambering over the armoured panels of the

Wave Serpent. They appeared to be armed only with blades and blunt clubbing weapons, but they were using them well, jamming them into the barrels of the vehicle's guns and attacking anything that stuck its head out of any of the hatches. Some of them looked very young and one, with long, dirty blond braids, seemed hardly more than a boy, but he appeared to be the leader, and the others followed his example with devotion and bravery.

Were they the locals? wondered Tanthius, sidestepping a lunging force-sword and clutching its blade into the irresistible grip of his powerfist, crushing it into splintered shards before sweeping his back-fist into the face of the alien swordsman. Where they the aspirants from the Blood Trials?

'Caleb!' he called, spotting the scout sergeant as he skidded his bike to a halt next to the Terminator, its twin-linked bolters ripping up the ground in front of it. The remnants of the scout squadron were churning through the solidified desert in a loose formation around him, spraying bolter fire in undisciplined volleys.

'Caleb – get over to that Wave Serpent and give those locals some help. They've got the right idea!' As he spoke, Tanthius saw the incredible visage of the plumed eldar exarch stride into view as it crested a glassy dune. 'Yes,' he said under his breath. 'At last.'

The story continues in

DAWN OF WAR
ASCENSION

by CS Goto

ISBN: 1 84416 285 0

Available now from the Black Library